Stately homicide

Bullen Hall is the ideal English stately home, its rose-red brick, sweeping lawns and encircling moat serene under the summer sun. Detective-Inspector Ben Jurnet has no inkling of impending tragedy as he attends a party there to celebrate the retirement of the Hall's curator and the arrival of his handsome, self-assured successor.

The dreadful, mutilated corpse which is dragged from the moat next morning brutally shatters the idyllic picture and disrupts the peaceful existence of those who live and work in the lovely place. Jurnet has met them all, the murder victim included, but his task is no easier for that. Exquisite, imperious Elena Appleyard, owner of the Hall and sister of the late Lazlo Appleyard – Appleyard of Hungary, the renowned hero of the 1956 Hungarian uprising – simply wants the murder solved with the minimum of disturbance to the existing order. Steve Appleyard, the deceased hero's young son, is absorbed by his love for the beautiful Jessica. The outgoing curator, Francis Coryton, is obsessed with his discovery of some sensational letters written by Anne Boleyn to her brother George, the first owner of the Hall; whilst Ferenc Szanto, a Hungarian refugee, is concerned only to ensure that the unvarnished truth about Appleyard of Hungary should at last be published.

Patiently disentangling the intertwining threads of loves and hates, Jurnet sets to work to isolate the one vital thread which will lead to an understanding of means and motive. But dark legacies from the past overshadow the sun-drenched present, old passions destroy new loves; and further tragedy engulfs Bullen Hall before Jurnet wins through to the truth.

S. T. Haymon's new crime novel is again characterized by the wit, inventiveness and stylish writing that won her the Crime Writers' Association's Silver Dagger Award for *Ritual murder* in 1983.

Also by S. T. Haymon

Death and the pregnant virgin (1980)
Ritual murder (1982) (Silver Dagger Award
    Crimewriters' Association 1983)

S. T. Haymon

Stately homicide

Constable London

First published in Great Britain 1984
by Constable & Company Ltd
10 Orange Street London WC2H 7EG
Copyright © 1984 S. T. Haymon
ISBN 0 09 465880 3
Set in Linotron Plantin 11 pt
by Rowland Phototypesetting Ltd
Bury St Edmunds, Suffolk
Printed in Great Britain by
St Edmundsbury Press
Bury St Edmunds, Suffolk

227783

Despite the possibility that those who know Norfolk may fancy they detect some physical correspondences between Bullen Hall and one, or more, of the great country houses of that county, the Hall and its occupants are the figments of my imagination; and no reference is made to any living person.

S. T. H.

I

The scream rent the midsummer air, demanding attention. Out of the trees behind the house rooks rose in protest. On the great lawn in front, a child let go the string of its balloon and ran, crying, to its mother. The helium-filled heart wafted lazily across the rose-red frontage, surmounted the stone balustrade, and drifted away in the direction of the lake, its metallic crimson flashing signals not to be deciphered.

Detective-Inspector Benjamin Jurnet, on his way through the pleached alley that led to the Coachyard, grinned. Anywhere else, a sound like that would have had him burning up the tarmac before it had even stopped, his heart pounding as he wondered what it was this time: mugging, rape, or bloody murder.

As it was, he emerged unhurriedly from the shade of the limes into the scorching yard, and gave a commiserating nod to the peacock perched on the rim of the stone basin in the centre that had once been a fountain. As one who had just that minute abandoned as hopeless his place in the queue outside the refreshment room, the detective felt he knew exactly how the bird must be feeling. He'd be screaming like that himself if his gullet weren't as dry as a packet of soup-mix.

The peacock cocked its head to one side and regarded the detective with a red and challenging eye; then jumped down to the ground and walked away, its train drooping tiredly over the blistering cobbles. Again, Jurnet knew the feeling. The jacket he was carrying had grown steadily heavier, in direct proportion to the sun's implacable trudge up the cloudless sky. He had taken off his tie and rolled up his shirt sleeves, to no avail. The heavy stuff of his trousers rubbed his inner thighs: his Y-fronts were sticking to him as if they had designs on his virtue. What the hell had possessed him to put on a suit instead of sports shirt and slacks? If Miriam had been at home she would never have let him out of the house, in that temperature, got up like he was going to a funeral or an interview with the Chief

7

Constable. But that was just it, wasn't it? Miriam wasn't at home.

The yard, incongruously for Norfolk, had the look and feel of a Mexican pueblo at siesta time. The air trembled above the red-pantiled roofs. The flats over the converted stables had their blinds down against the glare. On the door of one of the coach houses which took up the only side of the yard where there was any shade, a notice lettered with a rather too nice regard to typography explained that the craft workshops would reopen at two-fifteen.

It was just on two o'clock.

Jurnet hesitated: momentarily contemplated rejoining the refreshment queue, then crossed to a door in the north-west corner. There, he banged on the black-painted knocker which, fashioned in the shape of a bull's head with a ring through its nose, was identical to that affixed to every other door in the yard. He had to knock several times before he heard a step on the stair within, and then a voice which he did not at first recognise: 'Stop that, blast you! You'll wake up my little boy!'

Jurnet said: 'I'm sorry, Anna. It's me – Ben.'

'Oh, God!' There was a pause. Then the voice inside said: 'You'll have to wait. I'll go and put something on.'

The detective heard the footsteps recede, and waited, wondering what was the matter with Anna March's voice, what was the matter with Anna March. That she had forgotten their arrangement was obvious – which meant, more than likely, that the earrings still weren't ready. Which, in the circumstances, wasn't the end of the world. To a man trained to detect signs of stress and distress, it hardly seemed enough to account for a voice like that.

Returning, the footsteps sounded louder. Anna must have put on shoes, or mules more likely, to judge from the heels clonking down the uncarpeted stair. Jurnet braced himself for the encounter. Anna March was not one of his favourite people.

'No need to take on about the earrings –' he began, the instant the door opened. 'Miriam's having such a fabulous time, she's decided to stay on a bit longer. The chances are she won't be back by her birthday after all.' He did not feel it necessary to add that the chances were she would not be back, ever. 'Take all the time you need.'

'I should have phoned. Bringing you all the way out here for nothing –' Anna March pushed her long, dark hair back from her forehead. She looked unwell, the purple-patterned kaftan she had put on throwing up reflections that deepened the shadows under her eyes. As Jurnet had guessed from her voice, she had been crying.

'Not to worry. Nothing else on.' Which was true enough. What else was there to do on your day off when your girl had taken herself off to some grotty island in the Aegean crawling with young fishermen with the bodies of Greek gods and the morals of alley cats? The detective put aside his own inner preoccupations and looked at the young woman with a compassion only slightly diluted with impatience. Anna had always been a bit too intense for his taste; but that was Danny's business, not his. Since it was inconceivable that Danny March could be the cause of his wife's trouble, the detective inquired cautiously, not really in the mood for doleful confidences: 'Tommy OK? I hope I didn't really wake him up.'

The woman managed a smile at that.

'I shouldn't have gone for you. Tommy'd sleep through an artillery barrage, you know that.' She pushed her fingers through her hair again, and tears, of which she seemed unaware, took their leisurely way down either side of her rather sharp nose. 'Bit on edge myself, that's all –'

'This heat! Enough to give the sun a thirst!' Jurnet paused hopefully. It did not seem the moment to ask for a drink outright. When no offer was forthcoming: 'Only sorry I bothered you.'

'I should have phoned,' she repeated. 'Look –' making a palpable effort to pull herself together – 'since you're here, why don't you give me an hour or so to see what I can do? It could save you another journey. You could go round the house while you're waiting – I'll give you a pass, if you like. Or would that be too boring? You and Miriam must have done it a million times.'

Jurnet shook his head.

'Miriam, not me. She's the culture hound. I usually opt for a snooze on the grass down by the lake. Or a drink,' he added, not expecting anything to come of it.

'But that's terrible!' Her eyes, for all her misery, widened in professional disapproval. You could tell she had once been a

9

schoolmarm, and no mistake. 'One of the most historic houses in the eastern counties and you haven't –' She broke off, then finished: 'You mean, you haven't even been into the Appleyard Room?'

'I'm not much of a one for heroes,' the detective replied truthfully. 'Still, I'll do it today, if it'll get me back into your good books. *And* I'll pay for my ticket, thank you very much for your kind offer. What time d'you want me back?'

'Give me a good hour. After that, whenever you're ready. Stay and have tea, if you've nothing better to do. Danny'll be back by then – he's gone into Angleby to pick up some wood. Tommy will be up too –'

For no reason that the detective could fathom, the tears began to fall faster.

'Look –' he proposed, genuinely concerned – 'why don't you let me take you and Danny out for a meal tonight? There's a new place in Shire Street – cheer you up if you're feeling off-colour, and with Miriam away, you'll be doing me a favour. What do you say? Can you get someone in to babysit?'

'We can't, not tonight. There's a do on here – official, sort of. Not that I've decided to go –'

Now the woman was crying unashamedly. Awkward on the doorstep, the sun burning his shoulder blades, Jurnet harboured briefly the uncharitable thought: could it be all the fuss was over a new kaftan for the occasion, a poncho, djellabah, or whatever was the right word for those ballooning draperies in which, for reasons best known to herself, Anna March chose to engulf her spare shapeliness?

Wishing he had never thought to commission the bloody things, Jurnet said soothingly: 'Forget about the earrings. Why don't you go and put your feet up for a bit? Do you the world of good.'

'Nothing will do me any good,' Anna March announced drearily.

'Don't you believe it!' *Jesus*, the other thought, *poor old Danny!* For a moment Jurnet even found it in his heart to think fondly of Miriam who, whatever other deadly weapons she kept in her arsenal, never resorted to female vapours. 'A bit of a kip and you'll be wondering what all the carry-on was about.'

'I've got to open up.' With an effort Anna March stemmed

the flow. 'Sorry about that. Conduct unbecoming. In front of a police officer too! You'll be wondering what on earth I've been up to. Come back to tea and I promise you'll find me my usual scintillating self.' The woman ended, with more intensity than the words seemed to warrant: 'Don't say anything to Danny.'

'If you say so.'

Jurnet became conscious of noises behind and about him: shutters being folded back, doors opening. Wheeling about, he discovered that whilst his back was turned the place had completely changed character, from a pueblo to a touchingly improbable version of Merrie England, well-heeled and deodorised.

Open for business, the one-time stables revealed themselves as workshops where craftsmen who appeared never to have heard of the Industrial Revolution pursued their ostentatiously labour-intensive crafts, or set out their not all that essential wares for sale. There must, thought Jurnet, be a limit to the number of corn dollies the trade would bear.

Wrought-iron trivets and weather vanes festooned one set of doorposts; clusters of baskets another where a young man in frayed jeans and T-shirt, his face shadowed beneath a hat of coarse straw, sat recaning the seat of a Victorian chair. From a third stable came the whirr of a potter's wheel. In yet another, a pallid woman, draped in what looked like recycled sacking, sat at a loom, her fingers moving hypnotically among the threads like a harpist's among the strings of her instrument. Somebody had thrown back the double doors of the great coach house, letting out the sweet smell of wood shavings.

Notwithstanding the ever-increasing number of people about in the yard, trade, Jurnet noticed, seemed to be on the slow side. Keeping the twentieth century at bay didn't come cheap. Anna's productions were distinctly pricy, as were both the potter's vases and the luminous tapestries filled with shapes ambiguous and erotic which the pallid Lady of Shalott, for all her flat-chested gentility, conjured from her consenting loom. The *Angleby Argus* had carried an article recently on the Hungarian bookbinder on the east side of the yard; and Danny March's furniture, so satisfying in its uncompromising honesty, like Danny himself, was being bought by museums –

none of which, the detective decided, could give much satisfaction to visitors eager to take home souvenir mugs and tea cloths with a picture of Bullen Hall on them. Baulked of their desire, they moved from workshop to workshop with the thrifty conscientiousness of visitors to the Zoo determined to miss none of the outlandish creatures they had paid to see; and, the chore accomplished, moved away thankfully towards the lake and the illusory coolness of the surrounding parkland.

Jurnet, who accepted the world as it was, plastic tat and all, reflected that it was lucky for the craftsmen that – as Danny had confided to him – they got their workshops and living accommodation rent-free from the trust which administered the Bullen Hall estate. He returned his attention to Anna, who had opened up her shop, and now sat at her work bench, absorbed, the wretchedness eased from her face. Because he no longer felt her to be making emotional demands on him, he prompted gently, concerned for the wife of a friend: 'Care to tell me about it?'

Instantly hag-ridden all over again, Anna March jerked her head up from her work and stared at the detective with a blank-visaged hostility.

'Tell you about what, for Christ's sake?'

2

In the great house, across the moat where giant carp moved sluggishly through the sun-warmed water, the blinds were two-thirds down to protect the precious furnishings. They excluded the worst of the heat but substituted for it a depleted atmosphere in which Jurnet, for one, found it hard to concentrate on the pictures and the furniture, the Persian carpets and the magnificent china, the carved cornices and the painted ceilings which the guide book he had purchased along with his ticket unrelentingly instructed him to admire. He felt himself seized with a monumental ennui. How on earth had the Bullens and the Appleyards, who had once owned the house, and whose dead, demanding faces stared out at him from every wall, managed to survive beneath the sheer weight of their possessions? For the first time in his life Jurnet felt that he understood why archaeologists had to dig for their booty. Century by century this tonnage of high-toned jumble must be sinking down, drawn by the inexorable pull of gravity, until not even the little gilt flags on the pepper-pot turrets outside would be showing above the enveloping turf.

And a good thing too.

'George Bullen, Viscount Rochford, the original builder of Bullen Hall,' said a voice at his side in the Library. 'Brother of Queen Anne Boleyn, of course.'

'Of course,' Jurnet agreed absently, discovering that his eyes, all unseeing, had been directed towards a dark expanse of canvas out of which a man with black hair and a long, lean face above a collar of exquisitely painted lace glowered with an air of moody disdain. 'Funny thing –' the voice went on – 'seeing you here, alongside of him. When I saw you come through the door I couldn't hardly believe my eyes. If I've told Mollie once I've told her a hundred times, that there picture of His Nibs is the spitting image of Inspector Jurnet.'

Jurnet swivelled round, his face warm with annoyance. That Tudor ponce! Why the hell couldn't he, Ben Jurnet, look like everybody else? Then: 'Good Lord! It's Percy Toller!'

The little man who had spoken jigged with pleasure at being recognised. He carefully put down the catalogue of the room's contents which he had been carrying importantly under his arm, and seized the detective's right hand in both of his.

'Mr Jurnet! It's a pleasure to see you! It really is!'

'Good to see you too, Percy,' said Jurnet, meaning it. 'But –' face darkening with sudden suspicion – 'here? What're you doing here, Percy?'

The little man laughed.

'No need to take on, Mr Jurnet. I'm retired. Done me last job I don't know when. Been drawing my pension three years an' more. You ha'nt seen me for three years, Mr Jurnet – now, have you?'

'Could be you're just getting cleverer.'

'Me?' The little man burst out laughing again. 'Never! You know me, Mr Jurnet. Could just as well have rung you up an' told you the address and where to pick the stuff up while I was about it. Saved a lot of time an' trouble. Born to be caught, that was me.'

Jurnet smiled down at the small, spruce figure with real affection.

'If it's any consolation, all of us over at Headquarters were always properly grateful. The Superintendent often said where would our figures for convictions obtained be, if it weren't for good old Perce?'

The little man's face glowed with pleasure.

'Did he say that?' With a shake of the head: 'All the same, I should 'a' listened to my Mollie. "Percy Toller," she always said, "you're as much cut out for a burglar as I am to be Miss World."'

Jurnet said: 'Never saw a Miss World yet could hold a candle to Mollie.'

Percy Toller beamed, his false teeth white and gleaming.

'Wait till I tell her what you said! She's always had a soft spot for you, Mr Jurnet, you know that. Always says you treated me a bloody sight better 'n I deserved.'

'My pleasure.' Jurnet accepted the compliment with becoming grace. 'So, if it isn't the silver you're after, what *are* you doing here at Bullen Hall?'

'Conservation, Mr Jurnet,' the other returned with dignity. 'Preserving our national heritage. We got a nice little bungalow in the village, Mollie an' me, and, I mean, they're always asking for helpers, so here I am. All the upper crust hereabouts go in for it, and I don't mind telling you we've met a very nice class of people. I'm not boasting, Mr Jurnet, when I say Mollie and me are very well thought of here in Bullensthorpe.'

'So you should be.'

'Winters, when the Hall's closed to the public, we have lectures to learn about the Bullens and the Appleyards so's we can answer questions people ask us – and as I'm doing History and English Literature for the Open University, it seemed right up my alley.'

'You're doing an Open University course! You're never!'

'In't it a scream?' The retired burglar appeared to take no offence at the other's tone of disbelief. 'Percy Toller, B.A. – that'll be the day! But Mollie says she don't see why not. You know what, Mr Jurnet?' The little man looked at the detective

14

with eyes trusting as a child's. 'A man got a wife what believes in him and gives him a belief in hisself, there's nothing he bloody can't do once he puts his mind to it.'

Reminded with a sudden pang of Miriam, Jurnet elected to change the subject.

'I can't imagine what put it into your head I look anything like that bloke up there on the wall.'

'Evidence of my own eyes, Mr Jurnet!' Percy Toller contemplated the portrait of Anne Boleyn's brother with the air of a connoisseur. 'It's the Valentino look,' he pronounced finally. 'You both got it. You know, don't you, Mr Jurnet, that's what they call you, down at the nick?'

Jurnet frowned. His dark, Mediterranean looks were a sore trial to him. Bad enough to have your mates call you, even if it was carefully behind your back, after some brilliantined gigolo of the Twenties. But to think that the clients, the villains on the other side of the counter, had cottoned on to it as well!

'How come he's Bullen and she's Boleyn?' he demanded. 'Didn't they know how to spell their own names, in those days?'

'Bloody sight more sensible than we are. Spelled a word any way that took their fancy. What's the difference, long as you could read it?' The retired burglar studied the portrait further. 'It's the nose, Mr Jurnet, and those eyes. Smouldering. Very romantic, if you don't mind me saying so. Not English.'

'Well, I am –' pushing away ancestral memories of the medieval Jew who had gone by the name of Jurnet of Angleby* – 'and so was he, wasn't he?' Jurnet jerked his head at the picture. 'Queen's brother. You can't be more English than that.'

'That's just where you're wrong, then!' Percy Toller smiled with the complacency of superior knowledge. 'Half the queens of England – intending no disrespect, of course – frogs an' dagoes, the lot of 'em. Not that this bloke was. English as roast beef, for all his looks. And Anne Boleyn, his sister, the same. She may have looked like bring on the castanets, but she weren't only English, she was Norfolk, and you can't say more English 'n that.'

'Fat lot of good it did her.'

'Lost her nob, you mean? I don't know –' The little man

* See *Death and the Pregnant Virgin*.

pondered judiciously: 'I sometimes think they must have looked at things different in the olden times. I mean, nowadays, every time we step out of doors, who's to say we won't be run over by some ruddy juggernaut? Yet it don't mean we stay in for ever, do it, on the chance it might happen. An' every time we fly to Benidorm, how are we to know there's not a bomb in the luggage compartment ready to go off an' sprinkle us over the Costa Brava like cheese on a plate of spaghetti? It's been done. But that don't stop us booking up for next year the minute we take down the mistletoe. In olden days, I reckon, the only difference was that instead of lorries and bombs, it was plagues and having your head cut off. What I mean is, there's always something. I reckon Anne Boleyn, knowing what that bugger Henry the Eighth was like, didn't have to be told what she could be letting herself in for. And I reckon, give her a second chance, and she'd 'a' done the same thing all over again. I mean, to be a queen, that's something, even if you do end up with your head tucked underneath your arm.'

Jurnet smiled at the little man, so spry in his light blue slacks, white shirt, and nautical blazer with a handkerchief folded carefully into the breast pocket. It was the first time the detective ever remembered enjoying a history lesson. He hoped the Open University appreciated what a treasure it had netted.

He looked again at the portrait of George Bullen.

'*He* didn't do badly out of it, at least, if this place is anything to go by.'

'Executed 17th May, 1536,' Percy Toller announced with unction. 'Accused of carrying on carnally with his sister, if you'll excuse the expression. His own sister – imagine! And her queen of England!'

'Anything in it?'

'Load of codswallop!' The little man spoke with the certainty of one in the know. 'Bad enough Henry give 'em both the chop, he didn't have to go blacking their characters into the bargain!' Abashed by his own vehemence: 'Sorry, Mr Jurnet. It's just that, looking as he does, so much like you, an old friend as you might say, it always churns me up to think of it.'

'Remind me to come to you for a reference next time I need one.' Jurnet lingered, reluctant to break off human contact and move on from the vast, panelled Library to more rooms, more possessions, more yawns. 'Bullen Hall been in the family ever since, then?'

'Ever since Queen Elizabeth. Now, there was a woman! Henry grabbed the estate, like he grabbed everything else he could get his paws on, but Lizzy, she had a soft spot for her ma's family, and she give it back, to a man called Ambrose Appleyard that everyone knew was George Bullen's son really, and so the queen's first cousin, even if it was on the wrong side of the blanket. And Appleyards ha' been at Bullen Hall ever since. Young Istvan Appleyard – Steve, that is, to his pals –' the ex-burglar's face became suffused with a snobbery exquisite in its unselfconscious purity – 'he's always popping in and out of our place. Says Mollie's Victoria sponge is the stuff dreams are made of. William Shakespeare, The Tempest, Act IV, Scene 1.'

'You don't say! Istvan. Funny sort of name.'

'Ah. That's account of his granny, the countess. Hungarian for Stephen. Good King Wenceslas looked out, on the feast of Istvan. That's what it ought to be, only it don't rhyme with "even". One of the Karhazy family, the old countess,' the little man went on. 'Owned half of Hungary, till the Reds took it away. You can read it all in that guidebook you got there.'

'Oh ah. Dull as ditch water. They always are. The people in charge here ought to put you on to writing a fresh one.'

'Funny you should say that.' Percy Toller's glow became positively incandescent. 'Mollie's always on at me about that very thing. Will she be chuffed to hear I ran into you! Mr Jurnet!' – the little man repossessed himself of the detective's hand – 'How about a bite of tea with us after we shut up shop here? It'd be an honour! We close at six sharp, and it don't take me ten minutes to bike home. There's a nice bit of ham – I got it myself in Bersham this morning, to be sure it's fresh in this heat, so I know there's plenty for three, an' Mollie's always got a cake in the cake tin on the off-chance someone may drop in –'

'Stuff dreams are made of, eh?' Jurnet had no difficulty in making his voice suitably regretful. Ham and Victoria sponge with the undemanding Tollers was infinitely to be preferred to the high fibre and high thinking to be expected at the Marches. For a moment he was tempted. Then: 'Only wish I could say yes. Previous engagement, I'm afraid. Like the Yanks say, can I take a rain check on it?'

'Any time, Mr Jurnet! Pippins, Bullensthorpe. Anyone 'll direct you.'

'I'll do that. Meanwhile, give Mollie my love and say how much I look forward to seeing her again soon. I must be getting on,' Jurnet finished without enthusiasm. 'I suppose if I keep going I'll end up in the Appleyard Room eventually?'

'You'll see a sign at the end of the passage.' Percy Toller shook his head in wonderment. 'Fancy you, a police officer of all people, an' never been there before!'

'There has to be a first time for everything.'

'No offence meant,' the little man responded quickly, 'and none taken, I should hope. It's on'y – I mean, a man like that, one of our great English heroes, like Nelson and Lawrence of Arabia, and him local, too –'

'I'm not much of a one for heroes,' Jurnet said, not for the first time that day.

'But he was a wonderful man! A modern Scarlet Pimpernel.'

'Give me Leslie Howard any day of the week.'

'Now I know you're joking! Just you wait till you see all the things they got there about him.'

'Drowned, wasn't he? I seem to remember something –'

'Ah, that was a tragedy, all right. Down by the old mill. You can actually see it from the Appleyard Room – well, not this time of year, but in the winter when the leaves are down. Falling to pieces even then, so they say. Bit of the old grid, or whatever it is they call it, regulates the flow of water, suddenly dropped and caught him square on the back of the neck, just as he come swimming by. Nearly took his head off, by all accounts – just like George Bullen, his ancestor.' The little man looked suitably portentous. 'History repeating itself, as you might say.'

'Not quite in the same class as going to the block for incest.'

'Beheaded, I mean. Not a common way to die nowadays, not in a civilised country. Funny thing, too – he was exactly the same age as Lord Nelson when he got killed at Trafalgar, and Lawrence of Arabia when he come off that motorbike of his. Forty-seven, all three of 'em. Makes you think, don't it?'

'If you mean, to think twice before you join the Navy or ride high-powered machines you don't know how to control, and to keep away from rotting mill sluices when taking a dip, I couldn't agree more.'

'Dying like that, Mr Jurnet!' the other persisted. 'After all the terrible dangers he'd been through without a hair of his head harmed, to go in what you might call a purely domestic way –'

'Best thing that could have happened, probably. After hitting the high spots everything that came after had to be downhill all the way. Whom the gods love die young, that's what they say, isn't it? Not that forty-seven is as young as all that.'

'Menander, Ancient Greek poet, 324–292 B.C.' Responding with due modesty to the other's admiring astonishment: 'Mollie give me a Dictionary of Quotations for my birthday. Learn a new one every day, she says, and I should get by all right. She reckons if you're a bugger with a lot of culture to catch up on, like I am, that's as good a way as any to go about it.'

'Did you say Percy Toller, B.A.? Percy Toller, Ph.D., more like it!'

'Mr Jurnet! Just wait till I tell Mollie what you said!'

3

The Appleyard Room had once been a ballroom or a conservatory, or possibly a combination of the two. Tagged on to the north side of Bullen Hall, it was mercifully invisible from the front of the house, whose lovely line betrayed no hint of the absurd glass bustle disfiguring the rear. Within, it looked like a cross between Liverpool Street Station, the Paris Opera, and Harrod's Food Hall, and, as such, may well have embodied all those elements which the Hungarian countess, whose money had paid for its building, had considered desirable in the way of architecture.

In such surroundings it was asking a lot to expect anyone to take even a hero seriously, and Jurnet did not even try, mindlessly following the prescribed route past cases filled with bric-à-brac and faded photographs to which he accorded only the most perfunctory glance. Even had he been a one for heroes, the detective felt pretty sure that the secret of what made them tick was not to be discovered in these reverently salvaged bits and bobs.

Out of the lot only two photographs stayed with him: one of a tow-headed toddler with a black-haired girl-child a couple of years older, who held the younger one's hand tightly, and regarded him with great dark eyes full of an anxious love: 'Lazlo, aged three, with Elena, his sister.' The second showed the same children older, on the verge of adolescence, the fair and the dark, mounted on their ponies. They were dressed alike, in gentrified versions of the loose blouses, baggy trousers, leather aprons and broad-brimmed hats of the horsemen of the Hungarian *puszta*: and this time, instead of one who watched and one who stood unheeding, the two had turned to each other faces full of a gleeful complicity.

Two immense blow-ups – one of a turreted country house against a background of wooded mountains, the second of a Russian tank mowing down a crowd of students in a Budapest street – next commanded Jurnet's reluctant attention. Bludgeoned by their very size, he felt compelled to read the captions beneath.

Already, he learned, long before the rising of 1956, the tow-headed toddler, grown to manhood, had made a secret journey to Kasnovar – the great estate which the countess had brought into the Appleyard family – to rescue some cousins who had survived the war only to fall foul of the new Stalinist régime. When, for a brief seven days, it looked as if Hungary had succeeded in throwing off the Soviet yoke, he was back there again – whether to celebrate the liberation of a country he loved as his own, or to investigate the possibility of salvaging some of the sequestrated family assets, was not made clear. Whichever it was, he was there in Budapest when the Russian tanks treacherously re-entered the city; when the Avo, the hated Secret Police, re-emerged from under their stones, and the price had to be paid in blood for the impertinence of preferring freedom to slavery.

A hundred and seventeen people, Jurnet read – intellectuals, workers, army officers who had thrown in their lot with the insurgents – owed their lives to Laz Appleyard; one of them Mara Forro, the daughter of Prime Minister Nagy's right-hand man, and the woman who eventually became his wife. Overtopping his actual achievements was a magnificent failure – his attempted rescue of Imre Nagy and his companions, kidnapped in a Budapest street by the Soviet MVD and carried off to imprisonment in the turreted country house, the former royal summer palace in Sinaia, Romania.

Perversely refusing to go along with the Appleyard scenario, the Prime Minister had, in the event, rejected the chance of escape; but Pal Maleter, the military leader of the rising, and Janos Farro, the father of Mara, had got away, though only to be surprised and retaken within the week, sheltering in a so-called 'safe' house near the Yugoslav border. Their deaths had followed within days. Nothing but the chance that Laz Appleyard had been away from the house at the time, reconnoitring the last few kilometres to sanctuary, had saved him from suffering a similar fate.

Better for him if he had, Jurnet decided. Nelson knew what he was about, putting on the flashy coat that made him such an easy mark at the Battle of Trafalgar. Heroes would never come back, if they knew what was good for them.

The last photograph in the display showed Laz Appleyard with a laughing youngster, tow-headed as himself, perched on his shoulders; and, at his side, a pale, exquisite young woman who did not look happy.

'It is – it is Inspector Jurnet, is it not?'

'It is,' Jurnet confirmed, wondering, who now? Someone who, despite the bumbling affability, the baggy flannels and the old safari shirt bulging with felt-tip pens, must be more than met the eye. The man had come into the Appleyard Room by the door marked WAY OUT, and, in Jurnet's experience, only members of the criminal classes and those in positions of authority possessed the nonchalance to enter through doors marked, as this one must surely be on the outside, NO ENTRY.

'You won't remember me, of course,' the other said comfortably, beaming through his thick-lensed glasses, as if to be utterly unmemorable were matter for self-congratulation. 'Francis Coryton. It must be three years at least. I came into Angleby to find out whether we ought or ought not to install burglar alarms here at Bullen.'

'In that case, it couldn't have been me, sir. You'd have seen our crime prevention officer.'

'Indeed I did! But only after your much appreciated intervention. For some reason I had a little difficulty in making clear to the young sergeant at the desk whom I wished to see and for what purpose. You happened to be standing close by and you were most kind. When I got home I particularly remember telling Jane, my wife, how very kind you'd been.'

Jurnet, who had no recollection of having rendered any such service, murmured: 'Happy to have been of assistance.'

'Most kind!' the other repeated. 'In fact, I was saying to Jane only a few days ago that I mustn't forget to let Mr Shelden know that Inspector Jurnet's the one to ask for at Angleby should the need ever arise.'

'Mr Shelden?'

'Our new curator. This is my last day in that august office. I assumed you'd seen it in the *Argus*. It was all over the front page – not my going, of course, but Mr Shelden's coming. It's a tremendous coup for the Trust to have obtained a man of his calibre. You know, of course, he got the D'Arblay prize for his biography of Rommel?' Without waiting for an answer – which, Jurnet thought, was just as well – the man continued: 'Look here – if you aren't doing anything this evening why not come along to our little party and meet him in the flesh? Any time from 8.30 on. He's a delightful chap, he is, really, and it can only be to your mutual advantage to know each other at the outset, just in case anything ever comes up. Do come! Just a drink and a nibble before I bow out gracefully.'

Jurnet looked about him, at the cases filled with Appleyard flotsam, at the giant photographs of the Russian tank and of the palace at Sinaia which looked more like one of the hotels on the front at Cromer than a backdrop for deeds of derring-do.

'You'll miss all this,' he suggested, finding it easier to change the subject than make polite excuses.

'Oh, I shall still be around.' Mr Coryton's glasses twinkled, seeming themselves to be the source of the merriment rather than a mere reflection of it. 'I shall be sitting in the Library, quiet as a mouse, working on some research of my own and thanking my lucky stars somebody else is shouldering the day-to-day burden of running Bullen Hall.'

'Interesting job just the same, I should have thought.'

'Undoubtedly, if you happen to have a talent for administration. Unfortunately, I have none.' Mr Coryton laughed, and Jurnet, who had fleetingly wondered if the outgoing curator had not been sampling the party fare ahead of time, realised, not without a pang of envy, that it was happiness, not alcohol, which was the intoxicant. 'I'm going to write a book! And not just any old book, let me tell you! I've written several before, which were excessively dull, and are mercifully out of print. But now –' the man's voice positively lilted – 'I'm going to sit down quietly and I'm going to –' He broke off. 'But come along tonight and hear all about it. Official announcement of the utmost importance! Until then, not another word! We're in the west wing – you'll see a wooden footbridge over the moat, and a door. It's the tied house, so to speak, which goes with the job. Actually, we moved to the village a couple of days ago, but we thought the flat would be a more convenient venue, and of course it's much larger and grander than our new, modest abode.'

'I don't –' Jurnet began. He was in no mood for a party, especially one where he wouldn't know a soul apart from his host, if their brief encounter could be said to constitute knowing. Then, suddenly remembering something Anna had said: 'You aren't expecting Mr and Mrs March, by any chance?'

'Danny and Anna? Of course! All the workshop people will be coming. Do you know them? Splendid! They can make sure you don't lose your way.'

What the hell! If Miriam could spend her evenings downing the ouzo with some greasy Greek in some filthy taverna, why shouldn't he, Ben Jurnet, have his own little bit of fun, even if – as seemed more than likely – it consisted of a glass of sweet plonk plus unidentifiable gobbets enrobed in salad cream and served on squares of soggy toast?

'Thanks very much, then. See you at 8.30.'

For a moment, after the inferno of the Appleyard Room, the outside seemed actually chilly. The exit from Bullen Hall, the detective discovered, had brought him out at the rear of the building, on to another lawn, not so grand as the one in front. In the distance were trees, following, Jurnet supposed, the line of the river where Appleyard of Hungary had met his untimely end.

Ah, well. A lot of water had flowed under the bridge since then, and no one should account it sacrilege if a dehydrated copper took off his shoes and socks, rolled up his trouser ends, and soaked his poor old feet in the sacred stream. Arrived under the trees, he stood still for the sheer bliss of the dappled greenness that roofed him in against the blazing sky. This, he thought, is where I stay till the sun goes down.

All the same, he did not stay, not above a minute or two. Switching his jacket from one shoulder to the other, he moved steadily among the clustering trees, only to discover that the wood was no more than a narrow strip bordering, not the river, as he had expected, but a field full of newly sheared sheep, who stood about strangely muted in their nakedness.

Some pollarded willows at the further boundary promised water at last. Nevertheless, Jurnet came to a halt in the shelter of the outermost trees. Two horses, one chestnut, the other dapple grey, tethered to the gate, were cropping the grass at the entrance to the field, their heads bent in delicate concentration.

He did not at first see their riders; and when he did, he was doubly glad he had not come crashing out of the undergrowth. Under a hedgerow oak that overshadowed the gate, a boy and a girl stood embraced. The boy's hair glinted gold in the shade; the girl's was dark, and tied back in a pony tail. The two were of a height; both tall and long-legged in their jeans and faded T-shirts. Pressed together as they were, one could easily have wondered which was the boy and which the girl, had it not been for the way they held each other; the boy masterful, the girl proffering herself with a generosity that brought a wry twist to the lips of the watching detective and, though he could hardly have said why, a lump to his throat.

Jurnet called himself sharply to order. Just because they made such a pretty picture, all that picture postcard scenery, didn't make them any different from any other two kids getting randy.

Yet the detective did not advance, approach the gate, and ask them to move their horses so he could pass through. To break in upon that circle within which the pair existed in their own time, their own place, was unthinkable. There was about them a passionate innocence that was utterly disarming. Entirely against his will, it suffused Jurnet's being with tenderness and a strange melancholy joy which he reluctantly recognised as love.

He stepped back into the wood, careful to snap no twig underfoot: retraced his path to the lawn, skirted the house and found his way round to the Coachyard to see if Miriam's earrings were ready.

4

Francis Coryton greeted them at the front door of the flat, his glasses glinting festally, his body encased in an embroidered silk shirt and pale blue slacks, the two united by a cummerbund of wine-coloured velvet.

'You brought him!' he exclaimed. 'That's wonderful! I was so afraid the Inspector was going to arrange a little murder or something, as an excuse for not coming.' He squeezed Danny March's arm with affection, and kissed Anna on the cheek. 'Anna, you look marvellous!'

Which was no more than the truth. Jurnet himself had not yet got over the transformation. No limits, it seemed, to what stone-ground wheat, organically grown, could do. Himself unable, in that temperature, to eat a thing, and, with that thirst, to do other than drink more cups of tea than he had ever drunk at one sitting, the detective had watched the wholemeal scones disappear and a new Anna emerge, a little shrill perhaps, but more human than he ever remembered her. When, after putting Tommy to bed and giving the baby-sitter her instructions, she had come back into the little living room dressed for the party, the metamorphosis was complete. She looked ravishing, clad in a shift of some shimmering white material, pleated from yoke to hem. Round her neck she wore a wide necklace of flat pieces of silver interspersed with some dark red stones the detective did not recognise, carved with what looked like hieroglyphics. From her ears hung matching earrings. Silver sandals shone on her feet, her dark hair swung straight to her shoulders, her eyes glowed dark-lashed and mysterious. At her entrance, Danny, large and awkward in his movements, had got up from his chair and knocked a bowl of nasturtiums off the table.

It had been left to Jurnet to seek out a cloth in the kitchen, mop up the water, and rescue the tumbled flowers. The two had stood facing each other, not speaking. Then Anna had put out her hand and Danny had taken it. Nothing more.

Enough.

'You ought to stand sideways on in that get-up,' said Jurnet when, a little heartsick on his own account, he deemed the silent worship had gone on long enough. 'You look like one of those paintings you see on papyrus.'

'Pa*py*rus,' the woman corrected him, and the detective concealed a smile. The same old Anna, even if tonight she did look like Nefertiti, tits and all. The pleats in the almost transparent fabric were not enough to hide that she wore no bra beneath, and precious little of anything else.

Danny, who had appeared to see nothing to object to in his wife's flimsily veiled nudity, had cried boisterously: 'My Egyptian mummy!' and the three of them had clambered down the narrow stair and gone out into the scented dusk, laughing; as if there had never been any tears, no problem requiring solution.

Tommy's aversion to bed, so long as his Uncle Ben was on hand to entertain him, had delayed them, and the three found themselves among the late arrivals at the party. The long, low room with its dark panelling and its plaster ceiling incised with Tudor roses was already crowded. People standing with glasses in their hands, or sitting with loaded plates on their knees, were hard at work being jolly.

Jurnet's heart sank. What the hell was he doing here?

Momentarily, he found himself on his own, Anna and Danny borne away on a wash of greetings. Then a woman was at his side, suggesting amiably: 'Let me get you something to eat.'

For lack of something better to do as much as anything, he followed the sturdy, middle-aged figure in its unsuitably frilly dress to a long refectory table set out with food which at one stroke restored his appetite and his faith in human nature.

'I'm Jane Coryton.' The figure turned to disclose a face

26

sweet-tempered but not gullible. 'My husband's told me all about you. Now, what are you going to have? Salmon, ham, or goulash?'

'Salmon, please.'

Mrs Coryton took a plate, and, to Jurnet's relief, began to fill it for him.

'How's that?'

'First-rate!'

Mrs Coryton endeared herself further to the detective by heaping a second plate for herself, then seating herself on a bench drawn up to the narrow end of the table, and making room for Jurnet to sit beside her.

'I hate doing a balancing act, don't you? Have I given you enough mayonnaise? And let's have some of that wine, shall we?' – indicating a bottle within Jurnet's reach. 'Mr Shelden said it was very good, and I don't think he was being polite because he's been drinking it all evening, and everyone says he's a great connoisseur.'

After a respectful silence devoted to the business of eating and drinking the woman swivelled her gaze round to her companion and studied his face thoughtfully. To his surprise, Jurnet found himself neither embarrassed nor offended by the examination.

'Francis was both right and wrong,' she pronounced at the end. 'You *are* like George Bullen, and you aren't.'

'And there was I kidding myself he remembered me for how kind I was finding the crime prevention officer for him.'

'Is that what he said? I'm sure you *were* kind,' she added, kind herself, 'but of course the likeness was the main thing. The hollows under the cheek-bones – they really are quite amazingly like. Still, it only goes to show, doesn't it, how superficial physical resemblances can be. I always feel there's a petulance, a self-pity, about George Bullen which I'm glad to say I don't see in you at all, Inspector.'

Perhaps it was because of the wine, an ambrosial amber exquisitely chilled, perhaps because he could not remember ever being with a woman with whom he felt so instantly at ease, Jurnet found himself saying: 'You're wrong there, then. Eaten up with it. My girl friend's away in Greece and I'm feeling properly sorry for myself.'

'Oh.' Mrs Coryton reconsidered. 'On holiday, you mean? Alone?' Jurnet nodded, and after a little she did the same, as if a question she had set herself had been resolved. 'Ah, then it won't be self-pity. Jealousy. Quite different. I feel quite sure, Inspector, that you can be very jealous.'

'Jealous? Who said anything about being jealous?'

The voice which disturbed their sympathetic communion was blurred, the hand that reached for the wine bottle shaking. The man to whom both belonged was grey-haired, tall and well-made, if a little run to fat. There were food stains on his canary-coloured polo sweater.

Jane Coryton rose to her feet, removed the bottle from the man's hand, and said calmly: 'Let me pour it out for you, Charles. Mr Jurnet, this is Charles Winter, who makes those wonderful pots.' Filling a glass less than half-full, she said: 'Charles, I don't think you've met Inspector Jurnet.'

'Inspector? Not police, is he? What's he doing here? Keeping an eye on that bloody pseud, our new master?'

Mrs Coryton did not answer the question directly; merely remarked with no hint of reproof in her voice: 'You've had too much to drink, Charles.'

'Quite right, Jane darling. So I have.' The man polished off the wine she had poured for him, and brought the empty glass down on the table with a thump. 'If you *will* give parties that are so bloody boring – what else is there to do, for Christ's sake?' Scowling at the assemblage: 'Hark at 'em! Monkeys screaming in the trees, parakeets squawking their silly heads off. Bullen Hall? More like the ruddy Amazon!'

'In that case,' Jane Coryton returned, the sweetness of her smile undimmed, 'you'd better go home before the piranhas get you.'

'Can't do that, love. Got to make sure Francis gets his present. Bet you didn't even know he was getting one.'

'I did have an inkling.'

'From all of us. Affection, gratitude, all that crap. Deep appreciation of all he's done for us over the years – namely, drive us up the wall with his nit-picking whenever we've wanted to do anything that might get him in bad with the Empress Elena.'

'You're very ungrateful, Charles. After all, if nothing else, it was Francis who got the Trust to give all you craftsmen your workshops and your living quarters rent-free.'

'So he did, the dear old sod. So perhaps I shouldn't grudge my 50p. Got to hang around, just the same – make sure our resident tsiganes come up with the goods, not send it back to Mother Russia as their contribution to world revolution –'

'You *are* in a bad mood,' the woman observed cheerfully. 'It'd do you good to eat something.'

'Eat?' Charles Winter knitted his bushy eyebrows in an effort of recall. 'There *was* something –' Then: 'Mike! He wanted a bit more ham. Please, Jane darling, cut Michael a beautiful slice of ham.'

Obediently, Jane Coryton got up again, carved a slice of the meat, and handed it to Winter on a plate.

'If it isn't enough, tell him to come and get some more himself.'

'Can't do that, love. He's too busy being seduced by our lovely new curator.'

'Don't be silly, Charles. He isn't one of you.'

'What do you know about it? A man of many genital parts, our new gauleiter. The poofter of Parson's Green's what they call him up in town.'

'He doesn't come from Parson's Green. His London address is somewhere near Chalk Farm.'

'Even worse than I feared!' The potter clutched at his breast with his free hand. 'Don't say you haven't been warned, ducks! Where's the bloody cutlery?'

When the man had gone, the plate of ham balanced precariously on the fingertips of one hand, the other, aloft, clicking knife and fork like castanets as he bumped his way down the room, Mrs Coryton gave a little sigh, and turned back to the detective.

'Mike is Mike Botley, our basket-maker. In case you're worried in your official capacity, he's well over the age of consent.' As Jurnet made no comment: 'I hope you aren't too shocked.'

'A copper! We meet all sorts.'

'Still,' she insisted, 'I sense your disapproval. Charles *is* a genius, you know. It does make a difference. And it isn't as if he's breaking any law.'

'Oh ah.' Those all-purpose East Anglian syllables.

'He can't help being the way he is.'

'Oh ah again.'

With no perceptible exasperation Mrs Coryton said: 'He's in love and he's jealous, my dear man, just like you.'

To that there was no answer, and Jurnet did not attempt one. Instead, with an effort, he transferred his attention to his fellow guests.

'Is everyone here – barring me – connected with the Hall?'

Mrs Coryton nodded.

'It's only when we have a get-together like this one realises how many there are. Though it's more a lot of small parties than one big one. The workshop people gang up in one corner, the maintenance men go into a huddle over clogged-up drains, and the volunteers are so overawed at actually being asked to Bullen Hall socially, you'd think Anne Boleyn herself was expected along at any moment.'

'At least it sounds as if they're all involved in what they're doing.'

'Oh, they are! You can't have to do with a place like Bullen and not get involved.' Mrs Coryton looked about her, appreciative, but not starry-eyed. 'Stately homes like this, they begin to take on a life of their own. Frightening, in a way. You're having constantly to remind yourself that, however beautiful, however historic they may be, they're still only bricks and mortar: something somebody built up and something somebody can pull down.' She regarded her assembled guests with a rueful affection. 'It'll be interesting to see what Mr Shelden makes of it all.'

'I rather expected to see the Tollers.'

'Percy and Mollie! You know them?'

'Old friends.'

'Oh, good! Francis and I absolutely adore the Tollers. Percy rang up to say Mollie had had one of her turns.' Mrs Coryton frowned. 'I've never thought of Mollie as somebody who had turns.'

'Me neither.'

'I'll pop in tomorrow and see how she is. They live a few houses along the village street from us – I may say, the only welcoming faces in Bullensthorpe so far. It's quite rum, moving from the Hall to the village – like moving from one secret society to another. It doesn't seem to count that we've been living at Bullen for years. We still have to go through all the stages of initiation.' With a smile: 'Must be something like joining the Police.'

'It is, rather. Close-knit band of brothers, and all that. Trouble is, it does tend to cut you off from the world outside.'

Jane Coryton observed, with a directness the detective was to learn was characteristic of her: 'That's probably why your girl friend's in Greece on her own.'

Jurnet answered with some bitterness: 'Don't know about that. She's Jewish. She's got her own club.'

'Oh! Quite an exclusive one, I understand.'

'You're telling me! I've been trying to get into it myself for the past three years. Easier to marry into the Royal family! *She* won't marry me unless I become a Jew, and *they* won't let me become one if the only reason I want to is to marry Miriam.'

'One can see their point of view,' Jane Coryton commented fairmindedly. 'God has to come into it somewhere, don't you think? Or don't you believe in Him?'

'It's not easy.'

'And probably mutual. I'm sure He must find it dreadfully difficult to believe in us. Being a police officer, I suppose, so moral and upright, you can't find it in you to pretend to the rabbis even a teeny bit?'

Jurnet laughed, feeling suddenly light-hearted.

'They'd see through it in a minute – just like He would.'

'Life *is* complicated.' Jane Coryton sighed, appearing in no way cast down. 'Now I really must circulate for a bit. But first, Detective-Inspector, who can I introduce you to that you'd find interesting?'

'Nobody, if you're going to call me that. That's a sure conversation-stopper, if ever there was one.'

5

In the event, Jurnet did pretty well on his own. Always having a proper respect for professionalism, in whatever field – even an expert villain earned his reluctant admiration – he attached himself first to a small knot of gardeners engrossed in the aberrant behaviour of a yew on one of the terraces that, shaped into a classical pyramid, persistently asserted its God-given right to grow square. A little further along a gathering of masons, who had done at least as much justice to the Corytons' wine as the gardeners, were deep in discussion of the condition of one of the stone bulls down by the bridge over the moat which had, it appeared, by the action of time and weather, found itself incontinently unsexed. 'An' blow me if he ha'nt put on weight already!'

Danny March came over to see how his friend was doing.

'Fine! Wined and dined like a lord! Did you know you can't cut a yew into a shape it doesn't want to go?'

'Don't talk daft,' said the cabinet maker.

'Not the wood. I mean the tree. Alive.'

'Oh ah,' said the other, losing interest.

When Mrs Coryton came back, Jurnet greeted her with the same question.

'Doesn't surprise me one bit,' was the answer. 'What does, is how any self-respecting tree could let itself be hacked about like a French poodle. At least the dogs could bite back, poor things, if only they had the *nous*. You've been chatting up the gardeners, have you?'

'I can also let you into a shameful secret concerning one of those bulls down by the moat.'

'Don't tell me!' Mrs Coryton raised her hands in mock horror. 'Bullen Hall has all the secrets it can stand, thank you! Actually, I came to conduct you to the seats of the mighty.'

'You mean the new curator? Which one *is* he?'

'There, on the settee under the minstrels' gallery, with Elena. Gorgeous, isn't he?' A slight frown appeared on Mrs Coryton's face, which made her look as vexed as it seemed possible for one of her nature to be. 'That's Mike Botley down on the floor, leaning against his legs. I do wish he'd stop it. He only does it to tease poor Charles.'

'Not the poor, seduced innocent, then?'

'Mike? Dear me, no!' For all her annoyance, Mrs Coryton spoke with an amused indulgence. 'Vicious little thug who should have been handed back to the midwife for recycling.'

Jurnet remarked: 'The lady looks even more gorgeous.'

'Oh, Elena. Elena Appleyard, sister of the great Laz. Elena's in a class by herself.' Mrs Coryton spoke quite without innuendo. 'I'd better introduce you. She's bound to have noticed you already, and wondered what you're doing here. After all, she runs the place.'

'I thought your husband –'

'So did he, poor pet! Elena's very clever about not letting the strings show.'

'But isn't there a trust –?'

'There is, indeed. The Bullen-Appleyard Trust, to give it its full title. Consisting of Elena and old Cranthorpe, the solicitor in Angleby, who's worshipped the ground she walks on ever since she was out of nappies, and treats her slightest whim as if it were a directive from on high. Of course Steve – that's Laz's boy –' Mrs Coryton moved her head vaguely, not really trying to locate him – 'comes into the estate when he's twenty-five – that's three years from now – but my guess is he'll be only too glad to leave things the way they are. It's the farm he's interested in. In the meantime, anyway, Elena rules us all with an invisible rod of iron.'

'You don't like her,' Jurnet asserted, presuming on their brief acquaintance in his surprise at discovering Mrs Coryton to be capable of such a sentiment.

'Oh, but I do – enormously!' Characteristically, she showed no resentment at the other's presumption. 'Without her, Francis couldn't have lasted a week. He's far too much in need of being taken care of himself, poor pet, to be any good at taking care of anything else. I'll never be grateful enough to Elena for the way she's always allowed him to think something that's got done was *his* idea, *his* decision. I don't understand her, of course. But that's another matter.'

33

Their way along the length of the lovely room, treading wide boards the colour of honey, was slow and circuitous, punctuated by many stops as Mrs Coryton paused to exchange pleasantries with her guests. Francis Coryton trotted towards them waving a wine bottle; only to swerve away at the last moment to fill a glass thrust forward for replenishment. Jurnet noticed the young couple he had last seen entwined under the oak tree. They were separated now, divided by a bulky, white-haired man who stood with an arm round the shoulder of each. Their faces were turned trustingly to his, and their laughter rose momentarily above the general hubbub. A pale, slight man with two sticks at his side, seated in a chair nearby, nodded approvingly at the sound, then turned his face back to the open window, to the tree-tops stirring in the night air and the starlit sky beyond.

Jurnet's progress brought with it a certain disillusion. The closer he came to Elena Appleyard, the older she grew: still gorgeous, but far from the breathtaking beauty he thought he had glimpsed from the other end of the room.

Absurd to have expected anything else. She was Appleyard of Hungary's sister, after all. She must be sixty if she was a day.

Still, in her day she must have been a smasher.

'Funny she never married,' he remarked to his companion.

'Oh, but she did. Twice – I think it was twice. It could have been three times.'

'What happened to them?'

'Ate them, I shouldn't wonder.'

Jurnet laughed.

'There you go again!' he pointed out. 'And yet you insist you like her.'

'Perhaps "like" was the wrong word.' Mrs Coryton re-examined what she had said, with a readiness to admit error Jurnet found altogether commendable. 'Elena's beyond the superficial words the rest of us use to define our mundane little relationships. You no more like or dislike her than you like or dislike a force of nature.'

'Speaking for myself, I can think of quite a few forces of nature I should dislike very much, if I happened to run into them. An earthquake, a tidal wave –'

34

'Would you really? What a waste of energy! I can't see the point of either liking or disliking something you can't do anything about. And Elena certainly comes into that category.'

Now Jurnet was close enough to the settee under the minstrels' gallery to see that he had been mistaken a second time. Elena Appleyard was both old *and* breathtakingly beautiful, one of these rare women who wear their years like a privilege conferred upon a lucky few. Take away a single line from that face – and there were more there than you might have expected from a woman in her sixties – and it would only have subtracted from her beauty. Her legs, slim and shapely as a girl's beneath the simple black dress she wore, had yet about the ankles a touch of the frailty of age; yet without that touch of frailty they would have been that much less shapely. Her arms, too thin, merely pointed up the elegance of her wrists and hands. The black hair streaked with silver which she wore in a simple chignon low down on her nape constituted the definitive statement for all time on the subject of hair.

'I was wondering when Jane was going to bring you over.' The voice was low and pleasing. Elena Appleyard held out her hand. 'How do you do, Inspector Jurnet?'

Jane Coryton said good-humouredly: 'You've had your spies out, Elena.'

'Of course! I gather the Inspector's here to reassure our new curator that he can sleep peacefully in his bed even though it *is* the wilds of East Anglia.' To Jurnet: 'I don't believe you've yet met Mr Chad Shelden, though I'm quite sure you have heard of him.'

'Biography of Rommel, wasn't it?' Jurnet's tone was suitably nonchalant.

The detective was not all that smitten with the new curator, if first impressions were anything to go by. A bit too good-looking, too arty-tarty. Still, he said, meaning it, more or less: 'Wish you luck in the new job.'

'Thanks very much!' Chad Shelden raised a hand and ran it through his tumbling curls. Jurnet noticed that the other hand remained resting lightly on Botley's shoulder. 'I'll need it. It's going to be incredibly difficult to follow Francis.'

'Tut, tut,' Jane Coryton said pleasantly. 'You'd never guess, would you, Inspector, that he's planning to turn the Old

Kitchen into a disco the minute Francis and I are out of the way?'

'What a marvellous idea!' Shelden cried boyishly. 'But seriously, Jane – Elena has been putting me in the picture and I can see that Francis has done a fantastic job.'

Elena Appleyard said: 'And is about to do an even better one – isn't that right, Jane? He's taking us all up on to the roof for cold drinks and ices.'

'Oh dear!' Jane Coryton exclaimed. 'Didn't he tell you? Mr Benby was up there this afternoon and he said, out of the question: it was much too dangerous. But we've got some marvellous ice cream down here. Caroni's sent it over from Angleby in one of those containers you plug in, so it doesn't melt. Four flavours, no less! Would you like me to tell you what they are?'

The other woman shook her head. No one in the room looked less in need of refreshment. 'I don't think so, Jane. It was just that the roof would have been –' a pause – 'nice.' As she turned towards Jurnet again, the detective noticed for the first time that, when she turned, she moved, not just her head, but her whole body. He wondered whether to take the movement as an earnest of her complete attention, or put it down to the stiff neck very probable in a person of her years. If so, she was the first woman he had met to make rheumatism sexy.

'If you step back a little, Inspector, you'll see there's a stair in the corner of the gallery that goes up to the roof. It's really glorious up there on a summer night.'

Jane Coryton said: 'Francis and I often slept up there, in this sort of weather. As a matter of fact –' to Shelden – 'we've left you the air bed, in case you ever feel like sleeping out, and have the energy to pump the thing up. The pump's there as well, just inside the door.'

'Marvellous!' the new curator exclaimed enthusiastically. 'I've only been up there in the daytime so far, but the view! I'm sure I glimpsed the sea glinting between the hills.'

'At night,' said Elena Appleyard, 'you can see to the end of the universe – or could, if only the Trust had the £200,000 it's going to take to repair the balustrades. We simply can't manage a sum like that out of the estate, and all the Government has offered us is £5,000. £5,000! But there!' She turned her cool, beautiful face and her body with it towards the new curator. 'I'm sure Mr Shelden will come up with something.'

Mike Botley, his face that of a surly cherub, looked up from the floor and said: 'I'll take the kind wi' them green nuts, ta.'

'Then you can go and get it yourself, you little horror,' Jane Coryton returned with unruffled humour. 'You must be giving Mr Shelden pins and needles as it is, only he's too kind to say so. And while you're getting it, get a plateful for Charles as well. He's over there by the window, as if you hadn't noticed, looking dreadfully hot and bothered.'

'Don' want –' the young man began. Then: 'Hey – watch it!' He scrambled to his feet with a shout as the new curator, rising abruptly from his place, caught him in the rear. Charles Winter came hurrying across the room, rendered momentarily sober by loving anxiety.

'Did he hurt you, Mike darling? What happened?'

'On'y kicked me in the balls, that's all.'

'Don't be ridiculous!' Chad Shelden said, not bothering to smile.

'Nobody hurt anybody.' Jane Coryton took charge with her usual cheerful firmness. 'Mike wants to try the pistachio ice cream.' Holding the potter and his beloved each by an arm, and pointing them in the right direction: 'It's in the metal thing that's making a humming noise like a bomb at the back of the table, and it's absolutely delicious.'

Charles Winter swayed, but did not throw off his hostess's grasp. He seemed grateful for the support.

'Why do you and Francis have to be the ones to go?' he demanded loudly, 'instead of that ringleted dolly bird? Neither of you two'd ever kick anybody in the balls.'

'I wouldn't bet on it,' Jane Coryton said. 'There's always a first time.' She regarded the potter with the amused tolerance she seemed to extend to the greater part of the human race. 'This is my party, Charles – Francis's and mine – and, dearly as I love you, I'm not going to have it spoiled by some tiresome little tyke who hasn't even been housetrained. So when you've fed him his ice cream take him home, dear man, and lock him up so he can't come back, because otherwise I might find it necessary to tip him out of the window into the moat before the

37

night's out. I used to teach P.E., you know, and I can do it.'
Without changing tone, she ended as pleasantly as she had
begun: 'Do try some of the maple walnut too, while you're
about it.'

6

Chad Shelden flung his arms wide in an extravagant gesture of
welcome.

'Anna!' he cried. 'Anna Weston! I can't believe it!'

'Anna March,' she corrected him, sounding pleased and
excited. 'I think you met Danny the day you went round the
workshops. I was away –'

'Danny – of course!' Shelden seized Danny March's hand
and wrung it with the exaggerated heartiness of a television host
greeting a guest he had never clapped eyes on until a couple of
minutes before the show. Jurnet, whilst he did not care for it,
charitably reminded himself that he was, after all, at a party;
and parties were gatherings where it was only manners to lay the
bonhomie on thick, and clap on the back people you would just
as soon kick up the arsehole.

The new curator turned sparkling-eyed to Elena.

'We knew all the same people in London. Everyone was head
over heels in love with her.'

Anna protested, with a giggle Jurnet would never have
thought her capable of: 'That's a slight exaggeration!'

'No, really! I know I was!' Shelden insisted, with that bright,
boyish looked which was indeed wonderfully attractive.

'Looking at her tonight,' said Elena Appleyard, 'I can't
imagine how you can put it in the past tense.' Studying the
younger woman with an ungrudging approval: 'You're looking
lovely, my dear.'

Chad Shelden exclaimed: 'I can see that marriage agrees with
her.'

All the while Danny, thick as two planks except when he had
a piece of wood in his hands, when he became a genius, stood
smiling, holding his wife by the hand. Jurnet glanced down at

his watch. Still half an hour to midnight. When it struck, would the naughty dress that showed everything change back to one of those dreary old kaftans, encasing the dreary old Anna with her too-sharp nose, her mysterious woes, and her maddening habit of ticking you off for not knowing the capital of Pongo Pongo?

Elena Appleyard said to Jurnet: 'I understand Danny is a friend of yours, Inspector.'

'We were at school together.'

'Having a friend is always enjoyable.' She might have been speaking about a hot bath. 'Better than the opposite, certainly. I shouldn't think Mr March would make a very good enemy.'

Jurnet stared.

'Danny? You're joking! Danny wouldn't recognise an enemy if one came at him with guns blazing!'

'Do you think so?' She returned with a detached air: a matter of small importance. 'No doubt you know your friend best.'

To cheers from the immediate bystanders, the white-haired man Jurnet had seen in conversation with the young couple crossed the floor balancing a small table upside down on his head. Behind him, carrying some tissue-wrapped objects, came the lady weaver who, in honour of the occasion, had draped a length of Chinese silk over her basic sacking.

'The moment is come!' the man announced, setting the table down in front of the settee. He spoke with a pronounced foreign accent. 'Where is the birthday boy?'

The weaving lady, busy at the table unwrapping tissue to reveal a desk set of beautifully tooled leather, objected shyly: 'It isn't a birthday, Ferenc.'

'Certainly it is a birthday! Today, Jane and Francis are born naked and squealing to a new life, am I wrong? They are out of the womb of Bullen Hall at last, and we are here like the Magi bringing gifts to celebrate their safe deliverance.'

The weaving lady, who had blushed scarlet at the word 'womb', crumpled the tissue paper with distracted fingers and then didn't know what to do with it. Jane Coryton, thoughtful as ever, took it from her unresisting hands and dropped it without fuss behind the settee.

'Delivery, not deliverance,' she corrected the white-haired man. 'Nobody's been holding us captive.' She looked in

39

admiration at the desk set. 'Jeno's done it beautifully. I hope it means he's feeling better.'

'Jeno is feeling absolutely OK! Yesterday he is in the Norfolk and Angleby and the clever doctors there say they can do nothing for him. So it stands to reason – if nothing is to be done, is no illness, right?'

'He still looks peaky. And I see he still needs those sticks.'

'That man will do anything for effect.' The Hungarian stopped playing the fool, and said with calm intensity: 'Don't worry about Jeno, you hear? Jeno is my worry. If he gets no better I will take him to London, to Harley Street, where the doctors keep a list of illnesses that in Angleby they have never heard of, and is only available to people who pay fifty guineas.'

Jane Coryton bent over the table and picked up a blotter.

'Keep your hands off, woman!' The Hungarian warned her away with a large, upraised palm. 'Is not your present! Is nobody's present till I make my speech. Ring the bell, Geraldine, my love. Let us begin.'

At his command, the lady weaver, blushing afresh at the endearment, produced a silver-plated dinner bell from among her draperies. It took some time for its genteel tinkle to gain the attention of the crowded room.

Francis Coryton came quietly to his wife's side. He had taken off his glasses and Jurnet could see for the first time that there was indeed a face behind them. Not a foolish face, either.

'Ladies and gentlemen – inmates of Bullen Hall both voluntary and certified –' the Hungarian beamed at an audience already showing its determination to be appreciative – 'I have been chosen to make this most important speech tonight because I speak so good English. Also because I am bigger than any of the others who wanted to make speech but were afraid to say so because I am bigger.' Again the man waited for the laughter to die down. 'But I think I am best chosen because, not to be modest, I am a public monument – No, I promise you –' raising a hand in rebuke – 'now I do not make jokes. Bullen Hall is public monument to George Bullen, Viscount Rochford, and I am public monument to Laz Appleyard, also of Bullen Hall, Appleyard of Hungary – a little knocked about a bit, as you say, but still good for a few more years even if my stonework, like on the roof over our heads tonight, isn't what it used to be.

'So – now you have my credentials you hear me with a proper respect, eh, when I speak of our friend Francis, who today leaves us for ever. It is true he moves only to the village and, unless we are very careful, we shall be knocking into him all the time and saying to ourselves, "Who is that old buffer? I seem to remember him from somewhere," but just the same it is an ending: and I speak for all our sorrows when I say that I am sad he goes from Bullen Hall. I fear that our new curator, who looks so kind and beautiful –' the speaker half-turned towards the settee and sketched a mock obeisance – 'will give us not nearly so much trouble, and then where shall we be for something to complain about? But there – I make jokes again. That is the worst of allowing a bloody foreigner to make a speech. They never stop trying to prove that they too have the English sense of humour. So now I will be serious. To Francis I need say no more than two words – "thank you."'

From the applause that ensued it appeared that many of his listeners thought the Hungarian had finished. He waited for the noise to die down, and continued, however.

'But this is ridiculous! Two words! I must speak more, or you will say is no speech. So I ask myself, what is this "thank you" you make such a clapping about? The man was paid. It was a job.

'But I answer myself, no: is more than a job, the way Francis has done it. So I say, for us all, thank you, Francis, for the respect you have always given equally to the best of us and the least of us; for the way you have looked after us with love and understanding: for the much you have given and the little demanded in return. And so I say – so we all say – thank you, Francis, with this little gift we give from the heart with warm wishes to you and Jane for your new life, and –' summoning a humorous ferocity which seemed designed to counterbalance his un-English display of emotion – 'with warning to Mr Shelden that he will have to be bloody good to deserve for himself half so good a present from us when comes his time to go!'

The applause this time was long and deafening. Jane Coryton

put her arms round her husband and kissed him. The retiring curator took some notes from his pocket and put his glasses back on again. The glasses twinkled with complacency at having resumed their proper position in society.

Coryton's acknowledgment of his gift was graceful, but not unduly prolonged. The ritual accomplished, he called out, his voice loud and strong: 'Can you hear me at the back? I've got something to read to you, and I want to make sure you can all hear.'

When the room had quietened to his satisfaction, he selected a piece of paper from among the sheets he had deposited on the table. 'I thought of bringing along the original, but it's a mite frail.' Again he waited. Then: 'I want to read you a letter. A letter that will alter your view of a whole period of English history.'

Certain now of every one's attention, the retiring curator went off at an apparent tangent.

'I doubt if any of you here, except for Mr Benby, looking for yet another hole in the fabric, has ever been inside that funny little tower some joker in the eighteenth century stuck on to the house in the north-west corner of the North Courtyard. I've hardly been there myself, I'm ashamed to say, except that, a couple of months ago, with the date of my retirement looming ever nearer, I decided that I really had to do something about the stuff that's stored there. I didn't want the incoming curator to write me off as a complete slut when it came to keeping my house in order. So up I went, with my duster and mop, so to speak, to do what I could in the way of tidying up.

'In justice to myself, I should say it's not quite the shambles I'm making it sound. Everything is tagged and packed away – stuff we simply can't find a place for elsewhere in the house. The Appleyards, over the centuries, though they accumulated ever more possessions, never threw anything away – which is why, as a caretaker now surplus to requirements, I'm getting out of Bullen Hall fast before I too find myself in one of those rooms under the eaves, trussed up in a dust cover and labelled "old retainer, second half of twentieth century".'

Coryton waited for the laughter to subside.

'It was the room at the top I was chiefly bothered about. It's full of chests of drawers stuffed with papers of one kind and another – rent books, old deeds, and so on. Fascinating social history – and the Bullen Hall mice love it, and, even more, the string, tape, or whatever, that's been used to tie the various bundles together. As it happened, when I'd last been in Angleby, on the Market Place, I'd come upon some balls of plastic string that tasted so revolting – the chap flogging it obligingly gave me a bit to try – I didn't think even our mice could stomach it. So I bought a whacking great ball, and what I was really in the tower for, that day, was to retie as many as I could of the bundles that needed it. If it led to Bullen Hall mice dying of malnutrition – well, that would be Mr Shelden's problem.'

This time, the glasses quelled the incipient mirth with an imperious flash.

'By now,' Francis Coryton observed, 'you'll be all agog, waiting for me to reveal the Secret of the Tower. What you're going to hear are the details of my own utter imbecility in not discovering it years ago, when I first catalogued the papers stored there. One of the chests, as I knew very well, is full of old scrap books, albums, folios of watercolours done by young ladies of the Appleyard family in Victorian times. The ribbon ties on one of these folios had been eaten through, and as I wrestled with my plastic string – it turned out to be hell to cut – out tumbled a kind of home-made wallet I had noticed several times previously – frayed silk stiffened with muslin, or something similar, and a pocket on the inside; the kind of thing some young lady of the 1880s might well have made as a Christmas present for Mama. It had an embroidered motif on the outside, and, sawing away at that blasted string – what it really needed was secateurs, not scissors – I had plenty of time to look – *really* look – at it as it lay there on the floor looking up at me. The motif, in a kind of lozenge on the faded green silk, was yellowed with age, and it took a little while for it to dawn on me that it had once been white: that it was, in fact, a white falcon.'

Elena Appleyard said: 'The white falcon of Anne Boleyn.'

'Exactly! The heraldic emblem granted her in 1532 by Henry VIII when he made her Marquess of Pembroke. So much for my Victorian doodad! I put down the string and scissors, picked up the wallet, and examined it properly for the first time – and found out that what was keeping it stiff wasn't muslin at all.

Carefully folded between the two thicknesses of silk were nineteen letters from Anne Boleyn to her brother George.' A pause. Then: 'Love letters.'

7

'My sweet lord and brother,

'Tomorrow we are away to Windsor where His Majesty hath been assured by one Thomas Bolden, a soothsayer of Dover, that I shall not fail to be brought to bed of a lusty son, whereas if I remain at Greenwich, as I am much minded to do, the child shall be a girl and mine the fault that out of woman's waywardness would not pay heed to so sage an oracle.

'In truth, brother, so that I am shortly rid of this burden I bear before me like Salome the head of John the Baptist, I care not if it be maid or mannikin, provided only that its hair be red and not black, so that I may know without peradventure whom I have to thank for this amazing discomfort of the body. Yet indeed if I might only be in Norfolk with the one to whom that body and heart are bound by ties not Hercules himself could sunder, cumbered though I be with this imp within, I would count the journey no more than from my bed to my seat in the window and so back again.

'This past week we have shown much entertainment to the embassy from France who depart hence tomorrow with gifts of worsted and kersey but nothing of what they came for. Every day, after we have eaten, His Majesty and some ladies of the court dance gavottes and galliards in the French manner in compliment to our guests, whereat the Frenchmen cry La! for wonder, never having seen the like in Paris, nor any other place, I warrant; the whiles myself sits quiet and smiling, my embroidery in my hand, remembering the night when you and I, sweet love, you and I only, danced in the Long Chamber, the moonlight coming through the window and Joris the lute player plucking his strings in the gallery. Else had he not been born with eyes that see only the black of night, such sights might he have seen, that summer eve, as would straightway have struck him blind! – or dead, had he but dared to speak of it.

'Fare you well, then, in Norfolk, sweet brother. Yet fare you not too well there, lest, being in such wise, you make no shift to come soon to the court, and to the side of one who has for you more regard than is convenient either for her safety or her salvation.

'From her that is yours wholly, though the heavens fall.'

Francis Coryton looked up from the typed copy he had been reading.

'It's signed, "Anne, sister and paramour".'

For a moment there was a hushed silence. Before the excited voices could break out, Coryton went on: 'This room, as many of you know, used to be called the Long Chamber. The windows were smaller than the ones we see today, but otherwise everything is much the same as it was then. No electricity, of course – candles perhaps, or torches dipped in pitch, stinking to high heaven. But I think, don't you, that they danced, the two of them, by the moon's light only, treading these very boards under our feet.' The man took off his glasses and raised his head. '"If a man take his sister, his father's daughter, or his mother's daughter, and see her nakedness, and she see his nakedness, it is a wicked thing; and they shall be cut off in the sight of the people." Leviticus, Chapter twenty, verse seventeen – the formulation of one of the deepest and most solemn taboos held by the human race. Today, when we read such cases in the papers, we are revolted. Disgusting! we say. Well, those two were guilty of incest, a crime that strikes at the root of everything we are pleased to call morality. And yet – and yet –' the man's face was rapt, his gaze on the past – 'picturing those two young people four hundred and fifty years ago, dancing by moonlight in this very room to a melody played by a lute player blind as Cupid himself was blind, I can't help seeing this – this squalid amour, if you like – as something poignant and beautiful. I've only read you one of the letters, choosing that particular one because it refers to the room we're occupying at this moment. But reading the whole correspondence – all on Anne's side, there are none of George Bullen's replies – there's a kind of doomed grandeur, a passionate greed –' Coryton reddened and broke off, as if he had given away too much of himself. He replaced his glasses, and retired thankfully behind them. 'So now you know,' he concluded, smiling, 'why, despite Jane's plans for me, I shall not be devoting my new-found freedom to becoming a big shot on the Bullensthorpe Parish Council, or to growing the biggest pumpkin ever seen in East Anglia. I shall be sitting in the Library at Bullen Hall, poring over the love letters of a queen, and, hopefully, writing the book that puts the record straight. I can't wait to get started!'

As soon as he had finished, the noise broke out unimpeded. The party guests looked pleased, proud to be in on a royal scandal, even if it was four and a half centuries after the event.

Jane Coryton, so kind to the living, said: 'I can't see she deserves our sympathy. She set out to catch a king, and she caught him. She knew what the stakes were. It's George I'm sorry for.'

'Oh, come!' her husband protested. 'George did all right. Until Henry tumbled to what was going on, he loaded his brother-in-law with lands and titles. You even end up sorry for the old monster.'

'They couldn't have been happy,' Jane maintained stubbornly. 'People still believed in hell in those days.' She looked down the length of the Long Chamber. 'It wasn't all dancing by the light of the moon. Underneath it all, they must have been racked by the most awful feeling of guilt. They knew they were damned to all eternity.'

Elena Appleyard exclaimed quizzically: 'My ancestors!'

Jurnet was unable to pinpoint who it was who demanded a few words from the new curator, but presently, without overmuch persuasion, Chad Shelden was on his feet, contriving to look at the same time fetchingly reluctant and managerially deft. His jacket of brown velvet was Bohemian as befitted a writer, but expensive-looking as befitted a successful one. Cuff links of gold set with sapphires glowed expensively in his white silk shirt.

'This is a farewell party for Francis,' he began with his boyish smile, 'not a hello party for me. I hope, though, our host will allow me to congratulate him not only on a well-earned retirement, but also on his marvellous discovery. The letters are a wonderful – and valuable – addition to the Bullen Hall collection, and I'm sure I speak for the Trust –' Elena Appleyard inclined her head slightly – 'when I say how grateful we are for his sharp eyes. I just want to add how marvellous it's been to meet you all this evening. Speaking for myself –' with a charming air of imparting delicious confidences – 'I can truly say it's love at first sight. I can only hope that, when you know me better, and discover my sterling qualities – and find out what an intelligent, lovable, and above all, modest, chap I am – you will feel the same for me.'

The laughter that greeted this extravagance was loud but a whit uneasy. As if recognising that sentiments which went down well in NW3 were perhaps a little lush for the Norfolk outback, Sheldon modulated smoothly to another key.

'You're wondering about me,' he asserted, with a forthrightness which went down better than the gush. 'Very naturally. You want to know, am I hard to get on with? Shall I be making any changes? As to whether we'll get on together only time will show, but –' with a practised and pretty twinkle – 'let me say I'm hopeful. As to whether I plan to make any changes,' Shelden continued, the tone still light, but underpinned with a hint of steel, 'the answer, as I'm sure you'd expect, is yes, of course I do. Francis has set me a marvellous example, but I know he won't take offence if I say that a new man coming in is bound to have a fresh perspective –'

Jurnet thought: he's had this speech planned all along. Ever since he came down to Bullen and cased the joint.

Ever since he'd had a talk with Elena Appleyard.

'As you all know, we simply have to get in more money. The stonework is only one priority. And that means somehow, by hook or by crook, we've got to attract a lot more people to Bullen than we've managed to do up to now.' The new curator paused, and regarded his audience with a shrewd blend of amusement and sympathy. 'Do I see an apprehensive look in your eyes? Of course I do! You love the Hall the way it is – its tranquillity, its exquisite orderliness which you labour so hard to preserve. And so do I. What I don't like –' and now the challenge was out in the open, all part of an adroit, if rough, wooing – 'is that it's completely unreal. A fairy tale. Is it

47

possible that all the time you've been lovingly polishing the silver and dusting the pictures, you yourselves can't see that dust on the sideboards thick enough to write your names in would be infinitely preferable to the spurious air of refinement which has somehow crept into every corner? How have you lovely people with the best intentions in the world managed to drain off the very life-blood of Bullen Hall, leaving it a wan and anaemic shadow of what it once was, and must become again? Do you honestly think that if Laz Appleyard were alive today he'd feel at home in what is basically – if you'll allow me to be brutally frank – a boring old house full of boring old furniture that people only come to see when they're bored out of their minds, and can't think of anywhere else to go?'

Chad Shelden paused. He settled his jacket on his shoulders in a quick, agreeable way, and surveyed his hearers with an expression so open-faced and quaintly mischievous as to make it implausible to believe that anything but high spirits and a wonderfully life-giving energy informed his every word.

Sober as a judge, Jurnet decided, despite all the wine. And very, very clever.

Chad Shelden said: 'When I said Francis had done a fantastic job I meant every word of it. But times change, and every so often one has to readjust the focus –'

'Bullen Hall bullshit!'

Suddenly Charles Winter was there, swaying, so close to Shelden that the canary-coloured sweater – whose front, Jurnet noticed, had gathered several additional stains since he had seen it last – brushed the sleeve of the brown velvet jacket. Mike Botley came to a halt a few paces behind, looking well pleased with himself.

Jane Coryton stepped forward and took the potter's arm.

'Now, Charles,' she reminded him, 'you know I told you to go home. It's long past your bedtime.'

'So it is, and so you did – except that I'm allowed to stay up late on special occasions. I'm a big boy now, ducky, and God knows somebody's needed to tell this Little Lord Fauntleroy where he gets off.' The man looked at the expectant faces that filled the room. 'In case you haven't managed to work out what all that pretentious twaddle you've just had to listen to was in aid of, I'll translate. It means we're in for Bingo in the Banqueting Hall, camel rides for the kiddie-wids on the front lawn, only £6.50 for an inflatable Laz Appleyard to take home and enjoy in –'

'What a marvellous idea!' Chad Shelden interposed, the smile still brilliant, the eyes unamused. 'You really must get together with a chap we've got coming in – used to work at Longleat – simply bursting with ideas. I know he'd love to hear your views.'

'How to muck up a stately home in three easy lessons.' Charles Winter thrust his face close to the new curator's. The latter – to his credit, Jurnet thought – did not flinch. 'You're a curator, now, laddie – *curare*, Latin for to take care – not the manager of an amusement arcade on Yarmouth front.' The man backed away, thick grey eyebrows drawn together, seeking someone.

'Ah, there you are, Maigret!' Jurnet's opinion of the new curator's strength of will rose abruptly as he found himself gripped by the lapels, the distillation of a vile pistachioed ferment diffusing over his face and up his nose. Unlike the other, the detective made no bones about flinching. He jerked his head away sharply.

'Pay attention, Sherlock!' Winter admonished. 'I'm speaking to you as a member of the public with reason to believe a serious crime is about to be committed, if steps aren't taken to prevent it. If that bloke's a curator, I'm the Queen Mum. He's here for what he can pick up – and there's plenty. Snuff boxes, Fabergé Easter eggs, Nicholas Hilliard miniatures – lovely loot you can stick in your pocket when no one's looking. Don't say I didn't warn you, Poirot!'

'He's absolutely right!' Shelden admitted with a chuckle. 'The trustees and I *have* been going over the inventory to see what can be turned into much-needed cash without any gaps showing. But we shall see –' the new curator's expression as he smiled directly into Charles Winter's bloodshot eyes had become one of tender concern – 'just as we shall have to re-evaluate the position as regards the rent-free accommodation in the Coachyard –' Turning back to the assemblage at large: 'I'm going to let you into a secret. Mr Winter's not the only one to know some Latin! Just in case there are some of you who feel, like him, that I'm planning to lower the tone of Bullen Hall – to

49

make it, shall we say , a bit *vulgar* – if there are any who think that, let me say at once that you're absolutely right! Because – watch for it, here comes the classical bit – *vulgus* in Latin means the crowd, the multitude – in other words, all the people who ought to be flocking to Bullen Hall and, instead, are staying away in their thousands. A little judicious vulgarity, so far from spoiling Bullen, will be like opening a window in a stuffy room, and letting in some much-needed fresh air. There!' Shelden pushed a wayward lock from his forehead. 'I've said it while I still have enough of that gorgeous wine in me to give me courage. Nothing's going to happen in a hurry, I promise you that. There'll be no one breathing down your necks. Most of the time, you'll be glad to hear, you won't even know I exist. Wearing my other hat, as you may or may not know, I'm a writer. Francis isn't the only one at Bullen with literary plans, whatever comes of them. Miss Appleyard has done me the enormous honour of commissioning me to write a biography of Appleyard of Hungary, the first, full-length portrait, warts and all, of one of the heroes of our time. The tremendously exciting thing is that Miss Appleyard has turned over to me, with unfettered discretion to make what use of them I will, all the family papers, private and personal, relating to her brother. It's the kind of opportunity any biographer would give his eye-teeth for, and all I can say is that I hope most fervently that the finished work will justify the great trust she has placed in me.'

There was quite a lot of clapping when it was clear that the speech was really over, though exactly what people were applauding was less clear. His pretty blue eyes, as likely as not, thought Jurnet, who had long ago tumbled to the fact that speeches which went on for more than two minutes, so far from imparting information, actually sucked it out of the atmosphere like some linguistic vacuum cleaner, leaving its listeners, if anything, more ignorant than before.

Francis Coryton, in a puzzled kind of way, inquired of the room at large: 'What did he mean, "Whatever comes of them"?'

8

Chad Shelden returned to the settee to find that the Hungarian, Ferenc Szanto, had taken his place, and was deep in conversation with Elena Appleyard.

The latter greeted the new curator's return with: 'I've been telling Ferenc that he's to be your translator, when it comes to anything in Magyar.'

'But that's marvellous! I'll try not to be too much of a nuisance. Though, of course, Mr Szanto, quite apart from that, I'll be pumping you for your own personal memories of Laz Appleyard.'

'Ah!' returned the Hungarian, who appeared fairly impervious to the new curator's charms. 'Memories, is it, you want? I thought, from what you said just now about warts and all, that what you wanted was the truth.'

Shelden, looking startled but wary, protested: 'But of course! Your memories of what really happened.'

The Hungarian shook his head in a parody of astonishment.

'This from a writer of biography? To equate what happened with the memory of what happened? Elena, you sure you hired the right guy?'

Still smiling, if with a little less than his usual eagerness to please, Chad Shelden said: 'I think you can take it I've had enough experience to make a proper allowance for the fact that any description of a person or an event is inevitably filtered through the mind and personality of the observer. Besides, I warn you –' back to the playfulness which normally served him so well – 'I never accept anything as fact until I've checked it out against every available alternative source.'

'Until, you mean, you've checked it against the memories of other men who also have their own personal vision of what is and what is not reality?' The big man chuckled, and wedged his broad shoulders deeper into the cushions at his back. He regarded the new curator with a kindlier eye. 'You mustn't mind me. I'm an old tease. Elena will tell you. The truth is –

there, you see! I myself use that foolish word as if it actually meant something – that I am jealous of you, Mr Shelden, of your youth and your sublime cheek. Only the young believe it possible to find out the truth about anything or anybody. It takes the passing years to reconcile yourself to the fact that the best one can hope to do is select the most plausible lie.'

Elena Appleyard observed mildly: 'It's very naughty of you, Ferenc, to try and put Mr Shelden off before he's even begun. He'll do his best, I'm quite sure.'

Chad Shelden declared robustly: 'It won't be for want of trying.'

People were beginning to leave. In ones and twos they came up to the Corytons to say thank you, and to receive thanks in return. Several of the guests glanced at the new curator as if uncertain what was called for; but only a few summoned up the courage to go and say a few words.

Charles Winter shambled over to the settee and bent over Elena Appleyard.

'Did you hear what the bugger said about charging us rent? Or was it your idea all along?'

'Move further off, Charles,' Miss Appleyard commanded, neither flinching nor stoical. 'You smell horrid.' When, without contesting the order, he retreated a little, she said equably, but with precision: 'You know quite well that I've never interfered in any way with Francis. Equally, I've no intention of interfering with Mr Shelden. If you've anything to discuss, you must deal with him direct.'

'Any time!' Chad Shelden interrupted in his enthusiastic way. 'Let me say I only mentioned the Coachyard rents as one option among several –'

'Go and screw yourself,' Charles Winter said dismissively; and to Elena: 'Where'd you find a shit like that? He'll send the place to the dogs. You'll see.'

Jane Coryton disengaged herself from the embraces of two elderly ladies, and came over.

'Charles, this isn't doing your blood pressure a bit of good. Please! Let Mike take you home.'

'Mike doesn't want to go home – do you, Mike?' – wheeling

round to confront the young man who stood staring at Shelden. 'Mike would much rather shack down here for the night – wouldn't you, Mike?'

'Can't have everything we want in life, can we?' With an impudent swagger of hip the youth went up to the new curator, so close that, for an appalled moment, Jurnet thought he was going to kiss the man on the lips. 'G'night, Mr Shelden. Lovely to meet you.'

'Goodnight to you both,' returned Chad Shelden, pushing his hair back from his forehead.

'Do it for Jane,' Winter announced suddenly. 'Go home for Jane. Only friend in the world and I spoilt her party. Did I spoil your party, Jane darling?'

'On the contrary,' said Jane Coryton. 'You made everyone's evening. Given them something to talk about for the next six months. But now –' she finished good-humouredly – 'for God's sake go before I forget I'm a lady and land you one on the hooter.'

When the two had gone at last, she turned, calm and smiling, to Jurnet. 'When your girl friend gets your letter about the Bullen Hall party she'll be kicking herself, wondering what she's doing, frittering her time away in boring old Greece.'

'I think I'll tell her, hurry back for the next round. If Mr Sheldon means all he says, I reckon it's only the beginning of the fight.'

'Oh, he means it all right. That's what he's been hired for.'

'Your husband seems to be taking it very well.'

'Francis?' Mrs Coryton's eyes crinkled at the corners. 'But it was his idea in the first place. It really wasn't very grateful of Mr Shelden to make him out such a fossil. Francis wrote a report to the trustees over a year ago, saying that, awful as it was, and though he himself wasn't the one to do it, he couldn't see any other way of keeping the place going. These days, it's only the National Trust that can get by without gimmicks.'

'Was it Mr Coryton who chose Mr Shelden, then?'

The other smiled.

'Mr Shelden chose himself, baiting the trap with the biography. Seems Appleyard of Hungary was his childhood hero.

Good thing, too!' she added quickly. 'I'm sure he's right for the job. Under that romantic exterior there's a tough cookie who'll be able to get the necessary changes through with a minimum of aggro. And he *is* a first-rate writer.' After a moment, with reluctance but an apparent relief at actually articulating her misgivings: 'I only wish I could say the same for Francis.'

The boy and girl Jurnet had noticed with such sentimental approval came over to say goodnight. They were a remarkably handsome pair whose beguiling youth moved the detective to modify his usual mental strictures upon good looks in the male. Close to, the young man's resemblance to the young Laz Appleyard was startling, though there was a softness which Jurnet did not remember from the photographs in the Appleyard Room. The great man's son hardly seemed the type to snatch prime ministers from the jaws of ravening Reds. But then, Jurnet could not recall ever hearing that heroism ran in families.

'I don't think you've met Steve and Jessica,' Mrs Coryton said. 'Steve, this is Detective-Inspector Jurnet, who's been hanging about on the chance that the ghosts of Anne Boleyn and George Bullen will show up at the party, and then he can run them in for unnatural vice.'

The young man laughed.

'What a family, eh! Whatever must people think of us?'

Jurnet grinned. 'You've got a nice little pad here.'

'Not my pigeon, thank goodness. I'm at agricultural college. With luck, in the fullness of time, I'll be able to take over the management of the farm and the rest of the estate.' Adding with a likeable modesty: 'Not that I can ever see even that happening. Driving a tractor's about my mark.'

Jane Coryton said with unusual warmth: 'You ought to take more interest in the house, Steve.'

'I'll wait till Mr Shelden's finally dragged Bullen screaming into the twentieth century. Then I can run the Dodgems while Jessica looks after the shooting gallery. How about it, Jess?' The girl blushed, but said nothing, pressed closer to the boy. 'Anyway, Aunt Elena is going to live for ever, so my services, such as they are, won't be needed. Excuse us – we've got to go over and say hail and farewell to her. Oh – and Uncle Ferenc!'

At the summons the big Hungarian looked round with a face full of love. 'Jeno wants to go home. I told him to stay and wait for you. I didn't want him walking more than he had to. He *is* going to be OK, isn't he?'

'Jeno is already OK. Soon he will be OK plus. I will make him give me a piggy-back, back to the Coachyard, so you can see for yourself how OK he is.'

The man lumbered away like an amiable bear. The others watched as he came to the chair where his compatriot was sitting, his hands gripped tightly on the two canes, his face shadowed with melancholy or fatigue. At his friend's approach he pressed down on the sticks and stood up, swaying. There followed some kind of argument.

Jane exclaimed: 'I bet he's insisting on not going without taking formal leave. These Continentals are such ones for doing the correct thing! I'd better go and let him kiss my hand or he'll be here all night.'

She hurried away. After a moment of silence, Steve Appleyard said: 'We ought to be getting along too.'

Jurnet said: 'Nice to have met you. And you, Miss –'

'Oh – Chalgrove. Jessica. Everybody calls me Jessica.' Suddenly the girl looked apprehensive. Jurnet knew without asking that she was dreading the imminent encounter with Elena Appleyard.

Yet, when the two went over to her, the older woman could not have been more gracious, kissing first the boy and then the girl; a mere touch on the forehead, but performed with apparent tenderness.

'How are you, my dears? Though I'm not speaking to Steve, miserable boy! Now that he's moved away, he never comes to see me.'

The boy at least was perfectly at ease, the bright blue eyes slightly aslant in the tanned face. The Magyar inheritance, Jurnet supposed.

'You make it sound as if I'd gone to the moon,' the boy objected, 'instead of only across to the stables.'

'Since you never come to see me, it could just as well be the moon.' Elena Appleyard turned to the girl. 'If he won't come, then you must.'

'I – I'd love to –' the girl managed.

55

Steve Appleyard said: 'I've got to run Jessica home, Aunt Elena.'

'Goodbye, then, you thoughtless boy.' The woman leaned forward and kissed the girl again. 'Don't forget your promise, now. And please remember me to your father. He never comes to see me either.'

'Yes, I will.' The girl spoke happily, the ordeal over. The two young people went towards the door, holding hands tightly.

When Jane Coryton came back, Jurnet said: 'Time I was pushing off, too. Thank you for having me.'

'Thank you for coming. But don't go just yet, do you mind? It's even possible you may be needed in your professional capacity. Francis and Mr Shelden are having a little difference of opinion, and it sounds as if it could be physical.'

Francis Coryton, however, was looking more bemused than aggressive.

'I don't understand!' he was saying, as his wife and the detective came up. He gave the impression they were words which he had repeated several times already. 'It isn't as if there's any copyright in them.'

'That's true!' The new curator turned his most engaging smile on the new arrivals. 'Francis and I were chatting about those marvellous letters.'

Coryton's glasses were off. He said to his wife: 'You speak to him, Jane. I can't seem to get through.'

'Speak to him about what?'

'You know I handed over the key ring this afternoon? Well – the key to the study drawer was there with all the others. All I have to do is ask for it when I want it, I thought. Well, silly me! I thought wrong.' Coryton swung back to Shelden. Anger had firmed the flaccid contours of cheeks and jaw, giving them definition. 'If I'd taken copies, there's not a damn thing you could have done about it.'

'You're absolutely right!' Shelden made the words sound like praise. 'I don't mind saying, I'm amazed you didn't. In your place, it's the first thing I'd have done.'

'In my place,' Francis Coryton said with a bitter deliberation, 'you'd have known what a twister you had to deal with. As it was, I was waiting for Harbury in the Records Room at Angleby to get back from his holiday. The letters are so fragile I wanted to be sure there was no danger of damaging them on the copying machine. If I'd had even the slightest idea – !'

'Please don't think I don't understand!' Chad Shelden's face was wreathed in commiseration. 'But you do see, Francis – or I'm sure you will, after you've had time to think – that the Trust has no alternative but to take steps to protect itself.'

'Protect itself from what, for heaven's sake? In what possible way can I be a danger to the Trust?'

'Oh dear!' Shelden rumpled his curls, and looked at Jurnet with a pleading air. 'I'm sure the Inspector understands my predicament. He must often find himself obliged to do something he absolutely hates, but still he has to do it, because it's his duty. Well, I have a duty to make sure the Anne Boleyn letters are used in the Trust's best interests. We mustn't –' with a winsome smile – 'go charging in like a Bullen in a china shop. First, they have to be officially authenticated –'

'You'll find all that in the drawer, along with the letters. The B.M.'s been over them with a fine-tooth comb, and the Record Office. I've been to Windsor and Cambridge, and God knows where else. D'you think I'd ever have let out so much as a peep without first making sure I knew what I was talking about?'

'So you've done the groundwork for us – that's marvellous! Don't think for a moment that we're trying to take any of the credit away from you. You'll get full and complete acknowledgment, I promise you.'

'A mention among the thank-yous! Thank you for nothing!'

Jane Coryton put a restraining hand on her husband's arm.

'What exactly *are* you trying to do, Mr Shelden?'

'Do call me Chad!' the new curator begged. Then, with a fetching little wriggle: 'I'm sure I'm hating this, Francis, even more than you. But – I have to be frank – those dreadful books you turned out, back in the sixties . . . My dear chap, how can you in conscience expect the trustees, with the best will in the world, to entrust the writing of such a sensationally important book to someone who – God, how I hate saying this, I do really! – simply isn't up to it?'

Francis Coryton was shouting now.

'As I suppose you are!'

Chad Shelden spread out his hands in elaborate disclaimer.

'My dear fellow, you've got me completely wrong! I've more than enough on my plate with Laz Appleyard, I do assure you. No – my concern is to get one of the really big names interested. Delamine, perhaps, or Singleton. We've got something marvellous to offer and – even you, Francis, must see it, once you've got over your understandable disappointment – we've got to put it into the hands of somebody we're completely sure can make a proper job of it.'

Jurnet interposed: 'Does Miss Appleyard know about this?'

'She knows,' Jane Coryton said positively. '*Chad* here wouldn't dare to take a decision like that off his own bat – not on his first day, anyway. Francis –' she put her arms round her husband, her face against his face. The man stood stiff and unresponsive. 'It isn't the most important thing, is it? It's important, but not the most important.'

Francis Coryton shrugged himself free.

'Yes, it is,' he said. 'The most important.'

9

Downstairs, on the walls of the crowded little hall, were more pictures of Anne Boleyn and her brother; crude in execution and, Jurnet guessed, not rated worthy of a place in the rooms open to the public. Knowing what he now knew about the late Viscount Rochford's private life, the detective resolutely refused to see any resemblance between himself and the first owner of Bullen Hall. Over the heads of the people moving towards the outer door he peered at the long, dark face with undisguised repugnance. It struck him that while there were words and to spare for every other kind of sexual sinner – adulterer, sodomite, lesbian, rapist – there was no one word to describe people who committed incest. It was as if, faced with such monsters of iniquity, language itself had recoiled from providing the label which would confirm the fact of their existence.

The departing guests spilled gaily out on to the strip of grass which divided the house from the moat. Mrs Coryton, Jurnet thought, had been magnificent; despite all, bringing the party to an untroubled close. Even Francis, with the help of his glasses, had managed pretty well. Mr Benby, the estate surveyor, who had brought his camera, had taken several pictures of the old and new curators together, one of which showed the two standing smiling with arms linked.

When the caterers came to pack up the remains of the feast, Jane gave orders that Chad Shelden's fridge should be stocked with a selection of the residual goodies – 'to keep you going till you've discovered where the village shop is.'

'It's enormously good of you.'

'You're doing us a favour. We don't want to still be eating salmon, ham and goulash come Michaelmas. Mrs Barwell will be in, in the morning, to do the room. Francis, will you bring the desk set? Well –' with a final, comprehending glance in which there was more relief than regret – 'that's it. Elena, can we walk you home?'

Miss Appleyard rose from the settee and wrapped a shawl about her thin shoulders.

'Thank you, but I don't think I'll risk the night air. I shall go through the house. Maudie is waiting up for me.'

'All that switching on and off of lights –'

Miss Appleyard opened a handbag of gold mesh and produced a serviceable torch.

'None at all. I've come prepared, you see.'

'Francis will go with you just the same.'

'Francis,' said Miss Appleyard, 'will do no such thing. I was running about these passages before he was born. If I felt I needed an escort, I should ask our visiting policeman. That's what policemen are for – isn't it, Inspector? – To protect the weak.'

Jurnet said: 'Happy to oblige.' *Weak?* he thought. *You!*

'I'm sure you are. But, as I've said – this is my home. You could blindfold me and put me down anywhere in Bullen Hall, I'd know where I was straight away. Goodnight, Inspector.' Miss Appleyard held out a hand which trembled a little in the detective's. 'I hope you won't wait until Mr Shelden has *his* farewell party before coming to see us again.'

59

Danny March at Jurnet's elbow said: 'Anna says to tell you the couch opens out to a full-length put-u-up, in case you'd care to sleep over at ours.'

'Ta all the same, but no,' Jurnet replied. 'I'm on duty first thing in the morning. If I don't get myself a change of socks and a clean shirt they're liable to drum me out of the Force.'

He did not add that he didn't fancy a night listening through the bedroom wall to the sound of jouncing bed springs. 'I'll be back in Angleby in no time.'

The partygoers' cars were, by special dispensation, parked in the front drive. Jurnet made his solitary way towards the car park in the old orchard. Behind him the Hall, floodlit against the night sky, looked like a cardboard cutout out of a child's picture book. Then, just as the detective turned round for a last look, the lights went out. For a moment, there was a terrifying emptiness; then, eyes making the necessary readjustment, a new, moonlit Bullen Hall sprang into being, lovelier by far, floating on a moat full of diamond stars.

There was ample light between the bands of shadow striping the grass to see the way to the car park, and to see that the only vehicle left there beside his own was a jeep parked, hood up, with its back to him. Jurnet unlocked his car, got in, put on his seat belt, and put the key in the ignition. Why he did not immediately turn it, switch on the lights and drive away to the dismal flat he laughingly called home, he could not have said. Instead, he sat on mindlessly, perhaps even dozed a little; and awoke dismayed to remind himself that he had drunk only one glass of wine.

The jeep door slamming was what brought him out of his reverie. Himself unseen in the darkened car, Jurnet watched as two tall, slender young figures, hand in hand – though the girl, or so it seemed to the detective, hung back a little – threaded the intricate traceries which were the shadows of the old apple trees, and disappeared behind a bank of shrubbery. In another minute a bright rectangle of window spilled its light out into the night, striking reflections from the dark-polished rhodo-dendrons and touching the tender new growth with a frosting of silver. Somewhere, as if disturbed by the light, or, perhaps, by

60

the sound of footsteps overhead, a horse snuffled and moved its hooves on a hard floor.

The light over the stable went out. Down below, to judge by the sound of large teeth champing, the horse was having a midnight snack.

'You and me both,' Jurnet said aloud, feeling along the shelf under the dashboard for the bar of chocolate he kept there against emergencies.

He located it at last, a gluey mess which clung to his fingers as he tried to unwrap it. When finally he got a piece into his mouth he seemed to be eating more silver paper than chocolate.

He started up the car and drove out of the car park, out on to the road. A tenderness possessed him which even the melted chocolate on the steering wheel scarcely diminished. He felt sure that the youngsters up in the stable flat were making love for the first time, and he wished them well. Winding along the ribbon of road, he tried to remember how it had been with himself first time round, and could only remember that it hadn't been very good. Not surprising, really. Hate, fear, joy – every other feeling you could name – came instinctively. Love you had to learn to make, like a cake; and not one that came ready-mixed, either. Only beginner's luck if you got it right first time.

Jurnet wound down the car window. The night air on his face was cool and fresh. Even in the Angleby suburbs the wind was still scented with summer.

The detective drove quickly across the city to the further, the unfashionable side, weaving through the ancient streets with a skill born of long acquaintance. He loved his native city and found it hard to understand that anyone would actually choose to leave it, even for twenty-one glorious days of sun, sex and gastro-enteritis. When Miriam was there to share it, he could even find something good to say about his flat in the run-down block where the stairs smelled of slow-simmered underwear except on the days Miss Whistler, the late-blooming spinster on the first floor, burned joss sticks, when they smelled of yashmaks, or, possibly, yaks.

Jurnet parked his car on the forecourt, next to the black plastic bags put out for the dustman. Overhead, the sky, so spacious above Bullen Hall, had contracted to a niggardly strip above the street lights. Cutting me down to size, the detective thought, and quite right too.

Getting out his key, he unlocked the street door and entered into his very own stately home.

10

Mrs Barwell rode magisterially up the front drive of Bullen Hall. She was a large woman, who rode her ancient bike with the dignity of the Queen her horse at the Trooping of the Colour, even managing somehow to give the impression that, like Her Majesty, she rode side-saddle.

Refreshed by the morning dew, the vast lawn in front of the house sparkled in the sun. Mrs Barwell, as she processed along, favoured it with more attention than she normally accorded grass. Camel rides for the kiddies would be fine, she decided, at the end of her examination, so long as they didn't come with Arabs, which, it was her understanding, in the general way of things they did. Bingo in the Banqueting Hall, on the other hand – that would be a real step forward. She looked at the front elevation of the house, still sombre in shadow, with a critical eye. When Mr Shelden had said it could do with a bit of brightening up he never spoke a truer word. Even those who last night had made a song and dance about how shocked they were at the very suggestion – just wait till the Bingo got going and they'd be there, Mrs Barwell would take a bet on it, getting their eyes down along of everyone else.

Mrs Barwell was in no hurry. There wasn't all that much to do in the curator's flat; and Mr Shelden would soon find out she wasn't one to make work where there wasn't any. Last night, in the big room, she'd noticed one of the catering women going round with a dustpan and brush. More of a lick and a promise, as you'd expect from those fly-by-nights, but at least it would have skimmed off the top layer.

Altogether, Mrs Barwell was quite looking forward to the hours ahead. Working for a bachelor had to be more congenial than having a housewife, however biddable, looking over your

62

shoulder to see what you were doing, and telling you to do it differently.

She had brought along her new flowered overall for her first day under the new dispensation. It lay neatly folded in the wicker basket attached to the bicycle's handlebars, along with several freshly laundered dust cloths and the bread for the carp. Begin as you mean to go on was her motto.

Arrived at the ornate stone structure with which some nineteenth century Appleyard had replaced the drawbridge and portcullis which once had guarded Bullen Hall against all comers, Mrs Barwell made a stately descent from her conveyance and propped it against one of the stone bulls which stood on either side of the narrow way. She took the bag of stale bread from her basket and went on to the bridge.

There were some, Mrs Barwell knew, who said fish had no more brains than a bloater; but Mrs Barwell knew different. The carp in Bullen Hall moat knew her, and she them. Indeed, sometimes, as she watched them moving through the water, dark and secretive, it seemed to her that there wasn't much about Bullen Hall and its occupants they didn't know, if they could only talk and had a mind to it.

She was a widow with an only daughter married and living in Tasmania, on the other side of the world, and the carp had become a solace for her loneliness, pets of whose intelligence she was given to loving boasts. You could, she asserted, set your clock by them, and probably your calendar as well. 9.15 every weekday morning and there they were, waiting for their breakfast with their tongues hanging out, so to speak. But try turning up on a Saturday or a Sunday when Mrs Barwell was off work, and you'd be lucky to see hide or hair of them anywhere in the moat; an occasional stirring up of the bottom, or a sudden eruption of bubbles the only giveaway they were there at all.

It was Thursday and there were no carp.

More upset than she cared to admit, Mrs Barwell peered over the bridge, first one side, then the other, scanning the sludgy waters which heartlessly gave back only reflections of rose-coloured walls, bright morning sky and her own worried countenance. She opened the bag and took out a few bits of bread which she threw experimentally into the water. They jiggled on the surface for a little, ignored by the swallows hawking for flies; then, saturated, sank slowly out of sight.

Mrs Barwell replaced the bag in the basket, and wheeled her bicycle along the gravelled path which followed the moat round the house. She walked slowly, her eyes on the water. It occurred to her that the caterers, mucky lot, might have emptied their waste into the moat before taking their departure; and the carp, in consequence replete, had accordingly been in no mood to eat again after so short an interval. The explanation did not satisfy. *Her* carp would have come to the bridge irrespective.

She was nearly abreast of the footbridge when, with a lift of the heart, she came upon the fish at last, hanging in the water and browsing in a somewhat agitated way on some greyish fragments difficult to identify. They took no notice of Mrs Barwell's arrival, and, although she was by nature a rather phlegmatic person, tears came into her eyes at their desertion.

She leaned the bicycle against a garden seat at the side of the path, took out a tissue and blew her nose strongly; then bent over the edge of the grassy bank which at that point sloped steeply down to the water. She was determined to clear up what it was that had lured the fish from their allegiance.

As she did so, the surface of the moat, a few yards further along, shattered in a sudden convulsion. The mirrored house and sky broke up in a turbulence in which all that could be distinguished with any certainty were momentary glimpses of serpentine bodies of a yellowish-grey looping above the surface and then dropping back to the depths.

Mystified, Mrs Barwell hurried along the bank to a point directly opposite the area of greatest disturbance. With a certain amount of effort she lowered herself on to her hands and knees, the better to see what was happening. As she did so, a segment of smooth, silvery body arched itself in the air before submerging again; and slowly, very slowly, just below the surface, like a barrel rolled over by the pull of ropes fastened round its middle, something in the water turned over.

For a moment, Mrs Barwell's eyes failed to make sense of what they saw.

For a moment.

Then she began to scream.

I

The Superintendent settled back in his chair and said: 'If I
hadn't been sure you'd stop off for a beer I'd have had the
scotch out. From what Colton told me on the blower I guessed
some restorative might be called for.'

'Two beers, actually.' Jurnet evinced no appreciation of his
superior officer's kind thought. Condescending bastard!

Choking back his annoyance as, earlier that morning, he had
choked back his nausea, the detective asked: 'Dr Colton have
anything to say yet?'

'Give the man a chance! He's hardly got the body on to the
lab. Tremendously chuffed, though. Says he's never seen
anything like it.'

Detective-Sergeant Jack Ellers, whose chubby face,
bleached of its normal high colour, looked like something
which had been laundered on the wrong programme, raised his
eyes to the ceiling and vowed: 'Strike me dead if I ever touch
another dish of 'em, not if I live to be a hundred!'

'Funny things, eels,' the Superintendent remarked conver-
sationally. 'Used to go bobbing for them myself, down on the
Bure, when I was a kid. All you need is a ball of your Mum's old
knitting wool, a few hooks, and forty or fifty worms. Thread the
worms on to the wool, weight it, and tie it on to a short line.
Then you take your boat out – coming up to dusk's the best time
– and so long as you know the right places to look, you can get
five- or six-pounders. The eels bite at the worms, d'you see, and
get their teeth tangled up in the wool. All you have to do is jerk
the line out of the water smartish, before they can saw themselves free.'

'Thanks for the natural history lesson,' Jurnet said, risking
the impertinence and not giving a damn anyway. 'We know all
about eels, Jack and I.'

When, in response to a call, the two had arrived at Bullen Hall,
it had not been immediately obvious which was the casualty. A

5

large woman, her dress rucked up to disclose formidable bloomers, lay on the gravel path, mewing. A short distance away, young Steve Appleyard sprawled white-faced on the grass, Jessica Chalgrove kneeling by his side. On the grass above the moat, two men – one of them Mr Benby, the estate surveyor; the other, judging by his apron bulging with tools, a carpenter or handyman – stood guard over a sheet of black polythene, from beneath which a pair of feet protruded.

The feet were what attracted Jurnet's first attention. There was something decidedly odd about the feet. Tatters of brown stuff that could conceivably once have been socks adhered to them, and tatters of skin and bone that could conceivably once have been toes.

The handyman, whose name was Bert Archer, said shakily: 'Wait till you see his bloomin' face.' Mr Benby stumbled away without saying anything, and sat down clumsily on a nearby seat, dislodging an antique bicycle propped there. The bicycle clattered to the ground where it lay like an additional victim of the prevailing calamity. A wheel revolved frenetically for a few seconds, then stilled: dead like whatever was under the black polythene.

It would have been hard enough, even without the heaving stomach, to have recognised in those ravaged remains the debonair new curator of Bullen Hall, the well-known author, the romantic young man with the tumbling curls. Sergeant Ellers, who had turned back the polythene a little way, did not see fit to turn it back further.

Jurnet lent a hand to drag the sheeting back into place.

'Get back to the car, Jack, and get things moving.' To the handyman: 'Anyone done something about getting medical aid for the lady?'

'She'll be all right.' Bert Archer did not sound notably sympathetic. He crossed over to the woman and stood looking down at her. 'Police is here, Mabel, and you showing your what's-it. Ought to know better at your age!'

The woman did not stop mewing, but a large hand moved like a questing lobster and tugged unavailingly at the skirt of her dress. The large bottom levered itself off the path to release the bunched-up material.

'Tha's more like it,' the handyman said encouragingly, 'though you sound a right old fool, Mabel, belling away like a randy heifer. When I tell 'em back in the village —'

'That'll do, Bert Archer!' Mrs Barwell sat up abruptly. 'Stop your gabbing and gi' me a hand.'

Jurnet murmured softly to Ellers, who had remained standing where he was, looking green and shaken: 'What are you waiting for, boyo? Get on with it while I find out what ails the young gentleman.' He watched as the little Welshman disappeared at a sudden run round the corner of the house. Hope he makes it to the shrubbery, he thought, forcing back the vomit he felt rising anew in his own throat.

On the narrow strip between moat and house some stones of varying sizes lay strewn about the grass. Raising his eyes to the roof, Jurnet saw that the line of the balustrade was interrupted by a gap perhaps two feet wide, whence several pieces of masonry seemed to have fallen away.

From the garden bench Mr Benby moaned: 'If I told him once not to go near that edge, I told him a dozen times. Never mind it looks solid as a rock, don't trust it, I told him.'

'Not your fault,' Jurnet returned soothingly. 'No call to take on.'

So: fell off the roof at the end of the peninsula which housed the curator's flat and the floors below, and landed in the moat. Only, what in heaven's name did they keep there? Man-eating crocodiles?

Jessica Chalgrove stood at his side and said: 'You don't have to be worried about Steve. It's just that he's never seen a dead body before.'

The detective looked at the girl curiously. She looked pale, the dark eyes enormous in the heart-shaped face. Yet there was something – the way she held herself, the small breasts thrusting against her T-shirt; a sense of power and elation at being in control. For the first time Jurnet saw her as a person in her own right, not as one half – the compliant half at that – of a pair.

'What about you?'

'Oh, I haven't either. But I'm fine,' the girl answered, as if irked by the question. 'Steve and I were the first ones here. We heard Mrs Barwell screaming, and we came running. At first we couldn't imagine – we thought she'd gone bonkers or something. Then she pointed to the moat and we saw them.'

Her eyes, if possible, grew even larger.

'Them?'

'The eels. Great, enormous things, like the sea serpents that came out of the sea at Troy and killed Laocoon and his sons –'

Jurnet, who did not recognise the allusion, nodded nevertheless.

'They were tumbling about in the water. Some of them were coiled round Mr Shelden's body. They kept rolling him over and over, almost as if they were playing with a beach ball. Only all the time they were biting and tearing –' For a moment the girl's voice trembled. Quickly recovering: 'I didn't have to think who it was because he was still wearing his velvet jacket. Steve said last night he'd like to get himself a jacket like that. Mrs Barwell was lying on the ground having hysterics, and Steve nearly passed out, but I –' now there was no mistaking her pride in her own self-mastery – 'first I went and phoned the police. I particularly asked if they could send you. I hope you don't mind –'

'What we're here for,' Jurnet answered stolidly, concealing his gratification.

'– And then, when I came back, there was a spring rake one of the gardeners had left out on the grass, and I went and got it, and tried to beat the beastly things off. I would have, too, if Mr Benby and Bert Archer hadn't come to see what was the matter.' She sounded aggrieved. 'Bert lay down at the edge and got hold of Mr Shelden's jacket, and the two of them dragged him out on to the grass.' Jessica Chalgrove broke off and flushed a deep red which made her look more like the girl the detective had seen the day before. 'I wouldn't want you to think badly of Steve –'

'Never occurred to me,' Jurnet replied truthfully. 'All I could do not to throw up myself, and I've seen more bodies than you've had hot breakfasts.'

'He's awfully sensitive, that's what it is. Things affect him more than they do some people. But being Laz Appleyard's son –'

'Feels he has to be a toughie, eh?' Jurnet smiled. 'Want to

68

know what my colleague, Detective-Sergeant Ellers, is doing at this moment? Bringing up his eggs and bacon somewhere we can't see him. Tell that to your boy friend when he's feeling ready to listen. It may help him feel better.'

'I will!' she exclaimed. Soberly she persisted: 'It's because Mr Appleyard died the same way – drowned, I mean – and Steve's probably wondering if there aren't eels like that over at the mill.'

'Sounds very unlikely to me.' Knowing about the deceased hero's near-decapitation enabled the detective to speak with conviction. 'Anyway, as yet, we don't even know how Mr Shelden died – whether by drowning, or a fall from the roof, or something else altogether. Could have had a coronary, for all we know to the contrary, as of this moment. Take the young fellow home and make him a good, strong cup of coffee. He'll feel better in no time!'

By the time Sergeant Ellers came back, looking pale, Mrs Barwell had gone, angrily rejecting the offer of a lift home. Steve Appleyard and Jessica Chalgrove had gone, too, the girl doing the leading this time, but already with enough sense to conceal her new-found awareness of her power. Bert Archer and Mr Benby stood about uncertainly, hoping for their dismissal, but not liking to ask for it.

'All laid on,' the little Welshman reported. His eyes turned, unwillingly compelled, towards the square of black polythene. His whole body stiffened.

'Ben! He's moving!'

Jurnet began: 'Don't talk so daft –' when Bert Archer shouted: 'Oh, my God!' Mr Benby collapsed on to the seat again.

Unbelievable as it seemed, the polythene was moving, in light-catching undulations which gave it a life of its own. Then, out of the end of pyjama leg which showed above a macerated foot, a yellowish head with small eyes appeared, weaving from side to side; a heavily muscled jaw, and teeth like executioners. Mesmerised, the men on the lawn watched as the great eel, a good four feet long and thick in proportion, with a grace that was more baleful than all its ugliness, slid from its hiding place and slithered towards the moat.

It had almost reached the water when, with an inarticulate cry, the handyman sprang forward, a knife in his hand. Jurnet closed his eyes involuntarily. When he opened them again, the creature's head lay almost severed from a body which rippled a moment longer, then was still.

'The bloody bugger!'

Rage shook the handyman; but the hand with the knife held steady. When the head was off, and lay gleaming on the grass, the man turned his attention to the body, planting a foot squarely on the severed end, and taking a firm grip on the tail. The knife flashed, too fast for Jurnet to follow: a sharp pull and an odd rasping sound, and the eel's skin peeled off like one of those long white gloves debutantes used to wear halfway up their arms when they went to Buckingham Palace to curtsey to the King and Queen.

For a moment longer the denuded corpse, unexpectedly frail without its protective sheath, lay on the grass, a monster made piteous. Then the man kicked out and sent it sliding down the slope into the moat. He looked down at the skin in his hand as if surprised to see it there, and threw it after the body. The head lay forgotten, a bluebottle already buzzing at an unregarding eye.

A sound of splashing came from the moat. The eels had returned for another funeral wake.

'Not fair on the eel, of course,' the Superintendent remarked. 'Only doing what it was put on earth for – to eat whatever fate sends it, so that it can grow big and strong enough to fulfil its own particular destiny. Just as it's ours to discover exactly what happened to poor Shelden.'

'Yes, sir,' Jurnet said. 'After the boys took the body away, Jack and I went over the bit of lawn in front of the flat door. It's a kind of recess, with the building sticking out on either side, like a letter E, only without the middle bit, if you follow me. There were several bits of stone that appeared to have fallen from the parapet. What we also found was a small stained area that could have been blood – Forensic 'll be letting you know – and the top joint of a little finger.'

The Superintendent's head came up with a jerk.

'On the grass? At the edge of the moat, d'you mean?'

'A good bit further back than that. You tend to think of it as a little bit of grass because the scale of the house is so great it dwarfs it. If it was your back garden you'd think it quite a fair size. I reckon Mr Shelden must 've landed there, and not in the moat at all; and – not knowing what he was doing, most likely – started to crawl across the grass, and rolled down the slope into the water.'

'Poor devil!'

'Yes, sir. We had a look at the roof as well. Acres of it. It's like another world. Shelden must have shot the bolts on his front door last thing, after the party. We had to get up there the long way round, through the main house.'

'Party?' the Superintendent inquired sharply. 'Are you suggesting Shelden may have been the worse for drink?'

'I wouldn't have said so. He certainly drank a lot of wine, and I suppose it could have made him forget it wasn't safe to lean on the parapet, but it didn't seem to affect him –' Jurnet added with calculation – 'that I could see.'

'You mean you were there? I didn't know you were friends with the Appleyards of Bullen Hall.'

'No more I am.' Jurnet had no heart to prolong the tease. 'Never set eyes on 'em till last night. I just happened to be over there to see some friends of mine who live in the Coachyard, and Mr Coryton, the retiring curator, asked me along.'

'Oh.' Coldly: 'Enjoy yourself?'

'Very interesting, thank you, sir. In the course of the evening Mrs Coryton happened to mention that she and Mr Coryton, when they'd occupied the curator's flat themselves, often used to sleep out on the tiles on summer nights. She said she'd left behind an air bed for Mr Shelden, in case he ever fancied doing the same. And, sure enough, we found the bed on the roof, pumped up, with a blanket and a pyjama top on it. So I reckon Shelden went over to the balustrade to admire the night view before turning in; leaned against it without thinking, and had the whole caboodle give way under him.'

'Hm. Sounds probable. Soon as we hear what Colton's proposing to tell the Coroner we'll get out a statement for the Press. Well-known literary figure, the media 'll be down in droves. Didn't I read somewhere he was going to do a life of Appleyard of Hungary?'

That was a funny thing. They had come, he and Ellers, down from the roof by the stair which led to the minstrels' gallery and so into the room where Anne Boleyn and her brother had once danced in passionate partnership; and from there across the little landing into the flat proper. In a room plainly intended as a study they had found Ferenc Szanto, the Hungarian, in the act of loading a number of files and cardboard boxes on to a metal trolley.

The man had shown no dismay at the detectives' sudden appearance; greeted Jurnet as an old friend, and acknowledged his introduction to Detective-Sergeant Ellers with a handclasp that made the little Welshman wince.

'Good to see you again, Inspector!' Then, rearranging his broad features into an expression of appropriate gravity: 'Though for such cause as I guess it must be – dreadful, dreadful! Last night so full of life, so full of plans, and this morning –!' The man threw out his hands in a gesture more Asiatic than European. 'We are indeed the playthings of fate, alas!'

'Alas it is and no mistake,' Jurnet agreed. 'May I ask how you came to know about Mr Shelden?'

'Elena told me, is how. Is why else am I here?' The Hungarian looked at the detective with a childlike confidence that nothing he said would be taken amiss. 'Elena says to me the police are bound to come and poke about, and they are so clumsy they will mess up all the papers she has put into proper order with so much trouble. So I am to go quick and bring them all back to her before the police arrive, and she will put them away until she finds another writer to write the life of Appleyard of Hungary.' He finished: 'Myself, I think she will have to wait for a long time.'

'I should have thought people would be falling over themselves applying for the job.'

'Elena does not want just people. She looks for somebody special who may not be there to be found.' The Hungarian lifted a box off the desk which was the principal piece of furniture in the pleasant, oak-panelled room. 'You permit me to remove, as Elena wishes? They have, after all, been here for one day only. They cannot, as you say, be evidence.'

Perversely, because well as he understood Miss Appleyard's

strictures on the police he could not, for that very reason, let her off scot-free, Jurnet said, in his best TV cop manner: 'Nothing must be taken away, sir, till we've completed our inquiries. In the circumstances, I won't ask you to unload that trolley. Just stick it over there, in the corner. Leave everything else exactly as it is. And tell Miss Appleyard we shan't poke about a minute longer than we can help.' The detective looked appraisingly at the large, lumbering figure in front of him. 'About that life of Appleyard. Aren't you the one should be doing it by rights? You were with him in Hungary. Coming from you it'd be first-hand.'

'Words!' Ferenc Szanto exclaimed, as if the other had just demanded of him something utterly preposterous. 'I am a blacksmith. If I have bad iron I throw it away, but who throws away bad words? I am afraid of words that tell falsehood and deceit.'

'Words don't have to be lies. They can be truth as well.'

'Then I am even more afraid.'

'I wonder who they'll get instead,' the Superintendent ruminated aloud. 'The book should be a sure-fire bestseller, judging by some of the stories about Appleyard of Hungary one still hears going the rounds. What they say about him in Budapest I've no idea; but here in Norfolk, if a quarter of the tales they tell are true, King Solomon and Don Juan put together weren't in the same league. Some of the women must still be alive, though. So it probably couldn't be published, anyway.'

'Miss Appleyard, his sister, seemed to think Mr Shelden's was to have been the definitive biography.'

'She may not have had a clue as to what her brother was up to.'

'Shouldn't have thought, myself, there was much escaped Miss Appleyard.'

'Ah,' said the Superintendent sourly. 'I'd forgotten you'd met the lady.'

The phone rang, and the Superintendent, taking it off the hook, listened a moment; and then signalled to the other two, who were moving unobtrusively towards the door, to stay.

'Yes,' he said quietly into the mouthpiece, and occasionally: 'I see.' As the one-sided conversation prolonged itself, he printed the words GRASS and then BLOOD in capitals on his desk blotter, embellishing them with scrolls and curlicues. 'Fracture dislocation at level C 5–6. Right –' He wrote that on the blotter, too. When, after a final 'Yes', he hung up, he sat for a little in silence, looking down at his handiwork.

At last he said: 'Colton says Shelden died from drowning – but only just. If he hadn't drowned, he'd have given up the ghost within minutes from the multiple fractures and internal injuries – the details of which I'll spare you for the moment – which, until you turned up with that fingertip and Forensic confirmed that it was Shelden's blood on the grass, Colton assumed to be the result of falling from a considerable height into a body of water nowhere deeper than four feet six.'

He paused, positively inviting Jurnet's inevitable question: 'What were Dr Colton's second thoughts?'

'Submersion in the moat for some hours – Colton estimates the time of death to be between 2 a.m. and 4 a.m. – coupled with the voracious and undiscriminating appetite of the eels, have between them, as the good doctor was at pains to stress, not made his task any easier –' The Superintendent broke off again; added some extra decoration to the word BLOOD.

Jack Ellers offered: 'With Dr Colton there's always something.'

'Agreed. But today, I'd say, wouldn't you, that he had a point. He says the man's spinal cord was fractured. If I follow him correctly, cervicle 6 had been slipped completely across cervicle 5, which, in layman's English, as Dr Colton was at pains to translate, means that Shelden must have been completely paralysed by the fall.' The Superintendent waited to let the full consequences sink in; then, in a voice carefully devoid of nuance, spelled them out nevertheless. 'It would have been absolutely out of the question for Shelden, in the condition he was in as a result of that fall, to get himself across that stretch of grass and into the moat.'

'Then –'

'Quite right,' the Superintendent pronounced encouragingly. 'Then somebody must have done it for him, mustn't he?'

I've just had an idea,' Sergeant Ellers announced, as he turned the Rover out of the road, through the magnificent entrance gates of Bullen Hall, and slowed down to a walking pace to accommodate the sightseers, bedecked with cameras or encumbered with small children, who surged backwards and forwards across the gravelled driveway. 'What say we go to the National Trust and make them an offer? They lay on the stately home, and for 20% of the increased takings we provide the corpse. What do you think?'

Jurnet in the passenger seat looked about without committing himself. Whatever else you could say about murder, it was certainly good for business. Good for fish, too, judging by the family groups hanging perilously over the moat, hoping to tempt the eels from their lairs with offerings of everything from half-eaten sandwiches to worms dangled on a string. Good for newspaper men enjoying a day out in the country; and for telly reporters posed fetchingly against ancient walls and speaking to camera in the slightly breathless voices they affected when they had nothing to report except the fact that there was nothing to report.

Good for everybody, except the poor bugger lying in the morgue. Jurnet frowned. If truth were told, he hadn't taken much of a shine to Chad Shelden, alive. Dead was another matter. Someone had to protect the dead man's interests. He certainly wasn't in any position to do it himself.

'Why the hell did that blasted handyman and the cleaning lady have to let on about the eels? The papers have had a field day.'

'Only human nature. Keep something like that bottled up inside you, you'll end up in the loony-bin. You have to let it all come out. Very cathartic. Like Syrup of Figs.'

'Thank you, Dr Freud!' Jurnet gave his colleague an ironic pat on the knee, released his seat belt, and got out of the car. A little girl holding a completed daisy chain looked up at him and asked: 'Can you lift me up, please? I want to put it on the cow.'

Jurnet obediently picked up the child and held her while she carefully worked the floral necklace over the head of one of the pair of bulls guarding the bridge over the moat.

'There! Doesn't she look pretty?'

'Beautiful!' The detective lowered the child to the ground. 'Are you going to make a chain for the other one, as well?'

'I haven't time.' The little girl smoothed down her smocked dress, and made sure the ribbon in her hair was in place. 'As soon as Daddy comes back with the lollies we're going to look at the eels which ate a man up.' She bent her brows in charming thought. 'I wonder what he tasted like.' She ran off, calling back in childish glee: 'I bet he tasted horrible!'

Elena Appleyard said: 'I really am put out about my papers.'

'You'll have them back,' Jurnet assured her, 'the minute our people have finished. They're quite safe, I promise you.'

'So I keep telling myself,' the woman came back, her calm presence contradicting the agitation to which she laid claim. 'Yet I feel very uneasy not to have them in my hands, now that the flat's unoccupied. It isn't as if there are any copies.'

'Your Hungarian friend was a bit glum we turned up when we did.'

'Ferenc?' She uttered the name in a tone which made plain both her dissatisfaction with the man and with the status the detective had accorded him. 'It was all his doing they were there in the first place. I had intended to give Mr Shelden a few days to settle in, before unloading them on to him, but Ferenc persuaded me –'

She crossed her long, elegant legs, and uncrossed them again. With the midday sun full on her face, Elena Appleyard looked older than she had the night before. Older and more beautiful: every line a positive statement to the effect that, however it might be with others, she was imperishable.

A lesser mortal, thought Jurnet, a woman especially, would have chosen a chair out of the light. Elena Appleyard sat in its full glare, as if to show that she had no vanity.

Unless it were a subtle form of vanity, to make such a point of having none.

76

The conviction that he would never understand this extra-ordinary woman made the detective feel clumsy and ill at ease; and the room in which she received him completed his disorientation. Shown in by an elderly maid encased in a dress of some shiny black material which highlighted every whalebone and suspender of her old-fashioned corset, he had expected to find himself among the chintzes and little tables loaded with photographs in silver frames which, over the years, he had come to associate with country-house living. Miss Appleyard's sitting room at first shocked, and then pleased, by its almost complete emptiness. It was, one might say, furnished with space, as fastidious as its owner. Such pieces as there were – and there were few enough of those – were modern Scandinavian. A number of seats, resembling up-market deckchairs, were propped, folded, against a wall.

One such had been placed ready for the detective. That, to his surprise, he found it superbly comfortable, in no way allayed his feeling of being far from home.

As if she sensed his discomfort, Miss Appleyard said smilingly: 'It isn't really so out of keeping. The Appleyards who first used these rooms, like everybody else four hundred years ago, went in for very little furniture. A bed, a trestle table, a few stools . . . How very sensible!'

Jurnet who, alone in his flat, quite often had fantasies in which three-piece suites covered in dralon figured prominently, and Miriam naked on a bed with built-in telly and Teasmade and fifty-two weeks to pay, agreed cravenly: 'Very!'

'Besides, there's so much past enshrined in the rest of Bullen Hall, I decided to dedicate my own tiny corner of it to the present – or even the future. So long as life remains there are always possibilities, are there not?' The woman looked at the detective, but not as if she expected an answer. 'That's really why I've been so anxious to get Laz's biography over and done with. Propitiate the ghosts once and for all. Then one can go on to the next thing.'

Jurnet said, with intent: 'I can see how annoying it must be for you to have all your plans knocked out of kilter –'

The other smiled, understanding perfectly.

'You think it unfeeling of me to give priority to my private concerns, instead of expressing distress at Mr Shelden's untimely – not to say, inconvenient – death.' Making condolence sound unutterably non-U: 'Consider the formal words spoken, if it makes you feel any better: but, apart from his literary gifts, which are a great, and possibly irreparable, loss, you mustn't expect me to mourn unduly the passing of a really rather bumptious young man. It was simply that, in his person, as it seemed to me, two things came together very conveniently. Bullen Hall needed a new curator; and I couldn't stand the thought of any more of those *Boys' Own Paper* effusions about Appleyard of Hungary.'

'It can't be easy to find somebody else who can undertake both jobs.'

'One of them, at least, has been taken care of. Fortunately, Francis has agreed to come back *pro tem*. When I telephoned him and told him what had happened, he offered at once to fill the gap. Not to go back to the flat, but to come in from the village for as many hours a day as may prove necessary.

'And that reminds me –' Miss Appleyard produced a handbag of soft white leather and took out a bunch of keys. Selecting one, she removed it from the ring, and held it out on the flat of her palm. 'Will you please take charge of this? It seems to me a quite unnecessarily theatrical gesture, but Francis insists. He wants to be sure you have the key actually in your possession before he sets foot again in Bullen Hall.'

Jurnet got up from his chair and stood looking down at the thin, fine-boned hand.

'I was under the impression Mr Coryton had already given Shelden all the keys. What are these you've got – duplicates?'

'I do have a duplicate set, which I keep in the safe. These, however, are the ones Ferenc brought back with him, after he'd seen you.'

Jurnet exclaimed angrily: 'I told him nothing was to be moved!'

'So he said,' Miss Appleyard responded serenely. 'But he told me he'd already put the keys in his pocket before you arrived, and it quite slipped his memory until after you'd gone. He asked me whether he should return them to the flat, but I said no. I felt sure you wouldn't want the Bullen keys left lying about any more than I would. Please take this one, Inspector, or I shall be left without a curator all over again.'

78

Jurnet took the key with some reluctance.

'Opens the drawer with the famous letters, I take it?'

'Exactly.' The woman smiled. 'You are now the custodian of state secrets, Inspector. Guard them well.'

'Evidence of unlawful carnal knowledge, is how I'd put it. By two people old enough to know better.'

'Have it your own way, Inspector.' There was no denting that lacquered composure. 'I feel myself under no obligation to justify either the sins or the virtues of my forebears. Francis, however, is at great pains to impress upon the police that he has no wish to take advantage of Mr Shelden's sudden demise to gain access to the letters – that's so you shouldn't think he killed poor Mr Shelden in order to get hold of them. He told me, in fact, that, in bed after the party, Jane had already persuaded him that he was not, after all, the right person to undertake the task of editing them.'

'Remarkable woman, Mrs Coryton.'

'A very good soul.' Miss Appleyard might have been speaking of an upper servant. After a brief silence, she inquired politely: 'Have you arrested anyone yet?'

'Give us time!' Jurnet exclaimed, startled. 'We've barely been introduced to the corpse. We weren't even looking for anyone, at first. We thought it was an accident.'

'Exactly what I thought myself –' Elena Appleyard inclined her head slightly – 'when I found him lying there on the grass, and the stones from the balustrade lying all about.'

'When you *what*?'

Jurnet, who had sat down again, sprang from his seat. His hostess, her unruffled calm in pointed contrast to the other's vehemence, regarded him with mildly disapproving eyes.

'When I found him lying on the grass,' she repeated. 'I'm a poor sleeper at the best of times, and after all the stimulation of the party I knew going to bed would be hopeless. The night was so warm and so bright. So after I'd read for a while I went for a little walk in the grounds, as I often do, when I have difficulty sleeping. It must have been about 3 o'clock, or a little after.'

'But why, in heaven's name, if you found the man lying hurt, didn't you get help? It might have saved his life.'

Miss Appleyard shook her head.

'Quite impossible. As you may or may not be aware, I was a

79

nurse during the war. I know whereof I speak. It was obviously hopeless. Mr Shelden was deeply unconscious, haemorrhaging from nose and mouth. There was barely a pulse. I could see no point in getting police and ambulance men out of bed in the dead of night, knowing he was bound to be dead long before they could arrive.'

'Just the same,' Jurnet insisted obstinately, 'it seems – not to put too fine a point on it – pretty callous to leave a badly injured man lying, knowing he was still alive.'

Miss Appleyard's self-possession was a little jarred by that.

'Nothing of the kind! I stayed until he stopped breathing.'

The detective shook his head.

'The post-mortem showed that Shelden was still alive when he went into the moat. Either you were mistaken about his condition – in which case, nurse or no nurse, you could have been equally mistaken when you decided there was no point in seeking help, or –' the detective broke off.

'Or,' Miss Appleyard finished for him, 'it was I who pushed him in. In which case, Inspector, why should I ever have mentioned my nocturnal stroll? I'm quite sure I left no tell-tale clues.'

'You have a point there,' the other admitted, readily enough.

'Of course, in the morning, as soon as I telephoned Steve – actually, it was Jessica who answered and told me what had happened – I knew it must be murder: that, irrespective of whether Mr Shelden had fallen off the roof or been pushed, somebody must have come along later and put him in the moat. I can only think that I must have chanced along while the murderer was on his way down from the roof himself – unless he was there all the time, hiding in the shadows.' The woman sounded quite untroubled. 'I suppose, if we'd come face to face, he'd have had to kill me too!'

The detective observed soberly: 'You may have had a lucky escape.' More soberly still: 'What I still don't get, though, is why, once you realised Mr Shelden had been murdered, you still didn't get in touch with us.'

'It was very wrong of me,' she agreed submissively. 'I see that now. At the time, having spoken to Jessica, I merely thought, good, the police are here, they'll take care of everything. If and when they come to see me, I'll tell them what I know. I'm afraid

I'm rather a passive person. I tend to let things happen to me, rather than make them happen. On the other hand –' smiling – 'you must admit, Inspector, if we at Bullen Hall have been remiss in one respect, we've been most cooperative in another.'

'How do you mean?'

'The party, to which you came as a guest. There can't be many cases, surely, where the police are introduced to the prospective victim and the suspects, and provided with a full set of motives, before the murder is even committed.'

'It helps. It also confuses.'

'Oh dear! And I thought we'd made it so easy for you – especially as Mr Shelden was only at Bullen Hall for a few hours all told.'

'Time enough for somebody to fancy him – dead.'

13

Jack Ellers was waiting for him by the car, his chubby features rubicund in the sun, his mouth rimmed with brown from an elaborate confection of ice cream, nuts and chocolate flake, topped by a couple of improbable cherries.

Jurnet, whose taste ran to savouries, eyed the rapidly disintegrating structure with distaste.

'What's that on top, for Christ's sake?'

'Crown jewels, I shouldn't wonder, considering what they stung me for it.' The Sergeant dug in his plastic spoon with gusto. 'Whatever you do, don't tell Rosie. She'll kill me, all these calories – and in this heat I couldn't stand another murder, not even my own.'

'You still don't have to stuff yourself with that muck.'

'Peckish, are we?' The little Welshman eyed his superior officer shrewdly. 'Her ladyship didn't bring out the caviare and champers, then?'

'Only information.' And aggravation, Jurnet might have added. It hurt his professional pride not to call the shots. 'What d'you think of her? – says she actually found Shelden on the grass in the early hours, and, thinking him dead, did sweet Fanny Adams. Left him lying there, can you credit it, like he was an old crisp bag, for the serfs to sweep up in the morning, and put out for the dustman along with the rest of the rubbish. Charmingly apologetic, of course. But the question is: suppose Colton hadn't put us on to it, would she have stayed mum and let them bury Chad Shelden as the victim of a tragic accident? In other words, is she covering up for someone?'

'Such as who, for instance?'

'You tell me. Could be herself. She's the only one could get into the curator's flat without even going outside. *And* she's got a duplicate set of keys.'

'Fragile ageing lady pushes vigorous young stud off the top of the house?' Ellers looked doubtful. 'She's not going to get her brother's life written up that way. Maybe all she wanted was a quiet life. The bloke was dead. Let dead curators lie.'

'You may be right.' Jurnet looked thoroughly discontented with himself.

Jack Ellers, recognising the signs, busied himself with his ice cream. The Detective-Inspector, as he well knew, always reacted to violent death with anger: – anger at the act itself, anger at his own thick-headedness in not being able instantly to put his finger on the perpetrator of the deed. Anger which could even include the corpse, lying there knowing all the answers and maddeningly saying nowt.

The Sergeant waited until he had successfully negotiated the last of his sweet goo, wiped his hands and face on his handkerchief, and disposed of the plastic spoon and container in a nearby litter basket. Then he began briskly, without prior introduction: 'While you were gone I had a good look round the Coachyard, like you said. Everything pretty much as usual, far as I could tell. One place in the corner had a card on it: "Back in 20 minutes".'

'That'll be Anna, giving Tommy his lunch.'

'Oh ah. Foreign-looking chap came in, hobbling on two sticks. Something to do with leather.'

'Bookbinder. He was at the party. Got something the matter with his legs.'

'Turn 'm in for a new pair 'd be my advice. Don't know if you've already met the geezer does the basketwork. Even if you have, doesn't mean you'll necessarily recognise him when you see him next.'

'What's that supposed to mean?'

'Come and see for yourself.'

The Coachyard was crowded, bright with people in summer clothes actually buying things, so anxious were they to take home a souvenir of the murder. On the stone basin in the centre of the cobbled space the peacock, enraptured by the presence of an audience, pivoted slowly on its axis, displaying its magnificent plumage at one moment, its ridiculous rump the next.

Oblivious of the sightseers at his elbows, Danny March, the detective noted, was having intimate relations with a piece of oak, moving his plane over the surface with a caress that was at once a wooing and a consummation. Geraldine, the lady weaver, stood at the entrance to her workshop waving a number of five-pound notes in a bemused way, as if paper money were something outside her experience. After a moment, she fumbled among the hessian at her neck, and stuck the notes into what, for lack of any better word, Jurnet charitably took to be her bosom.

On the east side of the yard, Jeno Matyas, his dark head with its bald spot making him look like a medieval monk, bent in silent concentration over a morocco binding. Opposite, in full sunlight, Mike Botley sat on a low stool outside his shop, making a basket.

'Christ!'

The young man's face was bruised and swollen. One eye was completely shut, the other an inflamed slit through which a watery pupil gazed out at the world without charity. His upper lip was split and encrusted with scab. A blood-flecked bandage covered his head and ears.

'What happened to you, mate? Walked into a door?'

The young man looked up at the detective, tall on the cobblestones; found the effort too painful and went back to soaking a length of cane in a bucket of water at his side.

'Care to tell me how you caught that packet?'

'Up yours.'

'Face like that, you could lay a complaint, if you wanted to.'

'Go and screw yourself.'

83

'Look,' Jurnet said reasonably. 'I'm sure you know a bloke's been bumped off here at Bullen Hall. I'm not suggesting you or your face had anything to do with it; but in the circumstances I'm sure you understand we have to take notice of anything out of the ordinary run of things. And that definitely includes your kisser.'

'What makes you think there's anything out of the ordinary about it?'

The voice came from behind the police officer. Jurnet swung round and found himself facing Charles Winter. The potter pushed past, leaving a smear of grey on the detective's shoulder; bent over the young man and lifted his chin with a clay-encrusted forefinger. 'Is it the fourth or the fifth time this year, Mike darling?'

Botley jerked his head away, but made no other acknowledgement of the other's presence.

'He's always a bit surly for a day or two after,' Winter confided. 'He's not one of those who get a kick out of it, otherwise I'd have to think up some other way, wouldn't I, of getting it through his thick head that you can't go through life behaving like a cat out on the tiles without suffering the consequences.' Winter rubbed his eyes with the back of his hand. He wore an apron of filthy canvas over the stained yellow sweater Jurnet remembered from the party, the sleeves now rolled up above the elbows, tiny beads of clay threading the hairs of his powerful forearms; clay in the crevices of the haggard, hung-over face. 'Believe me, Inspector, it hurt me more than it hurt him.'

At that Mike Botley got up from his stool, picked up the bucket and flung the contents at the potter. A passer-by who got splashed reacted with an angry 'What d'you think you're doing!' Charles Winter, soaked from chest to foot, rocked slightly on his feet and murmured softly: 'Mike darling!'

Jurnet, his face tight with disapproval, turned to go.

'Poor, unhappy peeler –' Charles Winter's voice was vibrant with mock-pity – 'Never to have known the pangs of love.'

'Not your kind, that's for sure.'

'The same kind as yours, friend.' No mockery now. 'The same kind as everybody's. The one unique thing.' A deep breath: 'Except perhaps – and I say it without boasting – my kind's the purest. Not corrupted by the desire for children, nor by the fear of begetting them. No sheaths, loops, pills, none of that revolting paraphernalia which turns the act of love into a branch of your neighbourhood chemist's. No bloody menstruation –'

'Bloody nose instead,' Jurnet interrupted. 'Some improvement!'

Charles Winter faltered. He bent over the young man again, fingertips gently touching the bruised flesh as if in benediction.

'Mike knows I was pissed – don't you, Mike darling? He doesn't hold it against me.'

'Thank me lucky stars.' Botley inclined his head so as to bring the detective into the purview of the one functioning eye. 'Gimme an alibi, don't it? Too busy being beaten up, weren't I, to go ringing Mr Shelden's bell. An' after Charlie got through I weren't exactly love's young dream any more.'

Jurnet said: 'Could be you went and rang that bell after all, and caught that lot from your pal when you came back.'

The young man pondered.

'It's a thought,' he agreed at last. 'So what you think? I knocked off Mr Chad Shelden defending my virtue? Charlie, now –' Botley favoured the potter with a glance of pure venom – 'if it's suspicious characters you're looking for, he's another kettle of eels. There's me for starters, an' the rent he's going to have to pay, an' turning Bullen into a fun fair – you heard him blasting off yourself, didn't you? Well – knocked me out cold, he did. So who knows what Charlie boy was up to while I was lying there on the floor, dead to the world?'

14

At the flat over the jewellery workshop there was no shortage of weak tea, as well as buns that – or so it seemed to Jurnet – would have been just the thing for making good the clapped-out masonry on the Bullen Hall roof. Sergeant Ellers, whose wife, Rosie, cooked like a fallen angel, so irresistible were the temptations she devised for the inner man, asked for the recipe, demanding shamelessly: 'Why can't my wife turn out cakes like these?'

Anna March, kaftaned and dogmatic on the subject of stoneground flour, was, to Jurnet's relief – people should stay the way they were: otherwise how could you ever tell who you were yourself? – back to her old self.

He began: 'We'll be sending a bloke up to London; but I thought you wouldn't mind having a word, seeing you're the only one at Bullen Hall knew Shelden before he came here.'

'If you hadn't turned up I was going to phone you. Danny and I talked it over, and we decided you'd have to know sooner or later, and it might as well be sooner.'

'Have to know what?'

Anna March looked across the table at the two police officers.

'That Chad Shelden was Tommy's father.'

'What!' Jurnet made no attempt to hide his surprise, even as, in a flash of recognition, he saw the dead man's face in the little boy's. 'At the party you both acted as if – I mean, you could have been casual acquaintances.'

'That's exactly what we were.' Anna's tone was one of wry detachment. 'He was part of the student crowd I tagged along with, just like he said. What he didn't say was that he was at the heart of it, the centre of gravity round which everyone else revolved, and I was way out on the perimeter – a plain, gawky kid from the provinces who couldn't even understand their language, let alone summon up the courage to say something off her own bat. Every now and again somebody would take pity on me and fling a few words in my direction, like some scraps to a dog. Why I kept on, hanging on to the fringes, I'll never know – except that my mother had been dead against my coming up to London to Art School in the first place, and if there was one thing I was sure of, it was that I wasn't going to crawl back to Horncastle and a secretarial course, saying: "You were right all the time, Mum!"'

Jurnet protested, out of the goodness of his heart: 'I'll not believe that bit about being plain. Shelden singled you out, after all.'

Anna March shook her head.

'Not even that. We'd all been to a disco, and he was one of the few who had a car – oh, even in those days, it was obvious he was going to go far.' She stammered a little at that, taken unaware by the contrast between all that golden promise and the actuality, a moat writhing with eels. Tears came into her eyes: genuine, thought Jurnet, watching and listening, but not without a modicum of complacency. At last *she* could patronise *him*. 'As usual, I spent the evening propping up the wall, numbed by the noise and the lights, and when we got outside at last, into the dark and the cold air, I nearly passed out. Next thing I knew, someone had pushed me into the back of Chad's car and told him to run me home. He wasn't best pleased, I can tell you. I had a room out in Neasden, light-years away from trendy Islington, where he hung out in those days. But he took me, I'll say that for him. And when we got to my place, he helped me out of the car, fished my key out of my bag for me, unlocked the front door, came up the stairs and went to bed with me.'

Anna March caught sight of the detective's face, and actually burst out laughing.

'Oh, you mustn't think he was taking advantage of a poor half-conscious girl! I'd wound the window down on the drive, and the air on my face had brought me back practically to normal, for what that was worth.'

'You mean, it was what you wanted? Were you in love with him?'

The woman pondered both questions as if she had never before given them consideration.

'I don't think so, on both counts. I thought he was groovy, of course, the way we all did. But love? I know it'll tell you what an unbelievable ninny I was, but chiefly, I think, I let him come up to my room because, as usual, I felt tongue-tied. I simply couldn't get out the words to say no.'

'Occupational hazard of being young.' Jurnet's voice was warm with understanding. 'So that was the start of the affair?'

'What affair? It was the beginning and the end. I'd never been to bed with a man before, and despite all the school biology classes I hadn't a clue what to do. And Chad, for all the airs of worldly sophistication he always put on, wasn't much better. But there you are. It was enough to make me pregnant.'

'What did he say when you told him?'

'I never did. Next time I saw him, among all the crowd, and

every time after, we both acted as if it had never happened. Perhaps he wasn't proud of his own performance, or, for all I know, he really did forget – it was so completely unmemorable. I'd have forgotten myself, except that, a couple of months later, I found out it wasn't going to be as easy as all that.'

'You could have got an abortion.'

'I suppose I could, if I could have got over my shyness and gone to a doctor. But I kept putting it off until it was too late, and by then –' Anna broke off. When she spoke again, it was as much to herself as to the two police officers.

'My father was killed in a car crash when I was six. Mum never cared for me. She was – is – a great one for the Mothers' Union; but I think now, every time my father wanted to go to bed with her, she thought it was assault and battery, if not actually rape. And I was the tangible evidence, the perpetual reminder, of all she had had to suffer, up there in their darkened bedroom. The chief thing I remember about my father dying was the day after the funeral, my mother getting rid of the big double bed. She couldn't wait to get it out of the house.' A brief silence, then: 'You'd have thought, when I got my place at St Martin's, she couldn't have seen me off to London fast enough. But no. Somebody had to pay for all she'd gone through, and for that she needed to have me under her hand.'

Anna March got up, her draperies billowing: went to the window and looked out.

'I thought I heard Tommy. Mary's taken him down to the village shop. I said he could have some Smarties for being such a good boy.' She turned, and if her face was wet with tears, her voice remained steady.

'After I'd gone three months without a period, it suddenly came to me that, at last, I could have somebody of my very own to love; somebody who, if I played my cards right, might even love me back. That day, two things happened. I went to see the doctor, and I stopped being shy. I even –' with a strangely girlish giggle – 'began to be quite good-looking. I stopped going round with the crowd, though funnily enough, once my belly began to get big, they went out of their way to seek *me* out. But by then I couldn't be bothered.'

'Shelden must have put two and two together when he saw your condition.'

'He never did. He wasn't actually at St Martin's. He just hung out with that crowd.'

'Someone must have been bound to mention it to him.'

'I doubt if he'd have thought twice about it. You've got to get it into your head that our going to bed was a complete non-event. And that was the way I wanted it. I didn't want to share my baby with anybody. That is, not till I met Danny.'

Anna said: 'That's the reason you found me in such a state when you came about the earrings. It isn't easy, lying to someone like Danny. He's so straight himself, it makes you feel even more guilty. Without actually saying it in so many words, I'd given the impression that Tommy was the result of a passionate affair which had burnt itself out of its own heat. I was just too ashamed to let him know the stupid, unthinking way he'd been conceived. It wasn't so much that I was afraid he'd think worse of me for it – I'd have deserved that, and couldn't complain – but that it might somehow make him think worse of Tommy.'

'You know Danny better than that.'

'Of course I do, really; but on that one subject, I suppose, I couldn't think straight. Then, on top of everything, Chad came down to Bullen for a preliminary look round. I pretended I had to go into Angleby, but actually I hid myself up here, peeping out from behind the curtains as he went round the Coachyard. And I was appalled. I'd put him out of my life so completely I hadn't realised that Tommy was the spitting image of his Dad –' the final word pronounced with a pained twist of the mouth which had Jurnet wishing, for his friend's sake, that he liked the woman better.

'So what?' he demanded, with what he hoped was a salutary getting back to basics. 'You didn't expect Danny to think it was a virgin birth, did you? It had to be someone.'

'But not someone we were going to have to rub shoulders with, every day of the week! Never mind Danny: what if – no, not if: when – Chad noticed the resemblance, what then? He was bound to see Tommy sooner or later. And then again, didn't Tommy have the right to know who his real father was? Didn't Chad, even, have the moral right to know he'd fathered a son?'

Jurnet, who had lived long enough to know that people

seldom got their moral rights, and, when they did, were seldom grateful for the gift, commented: 'You're too high-minded, that's your trouble. All you had to do was talk things over with Danny. He'd have put you right.'

'That's exactly what he did.' The woman smiled, an inward-regarding smile that sent the detective's thoughts winging painfully to Miriam, offering herself to the sun and God knew who else on a Greek beach. 'When he came in for his tea and saw the state of my face, I couldn't keep the truth from him any longer. All he said, in that simple way of his that isn't simple at all, once you know him, was: "Tommy's your boy and mine – get that into your thick head." And then we went to bed.' She spoke without embarrassment. 'He kissed every inch of my body – every inch of it – and he made me beautiful. He told me to dress myself up so that everyone could see how beautiful his wife, Tommy's mother, was. And he told me to treat Chad Shelden for what he was – a casual acquaintance from the old days. Nobody who mattered.'

Jealousy made Jurnet heartless.

'From which I'm to gather that you didn't go back to Shelden's flat after the party was over, and spill the beans about Tommy?'

Anna March gathered the folds of her kaftan about her and regarded the detective with chill disapproval. It came to the latter, with no notable regret, that she cared for him no more than he cared for her.

'That's the kind of remark,' she said at the end of the examination, 'reminds me you're not only Ben Jurnet, Danny's friend and Tommy's godfather – you're also a bloody police-man.'

'That's me,' Jurnet agreed. 'So you'd better answer my question.'

'A rerun of the good old days in Neasden, is that what you think? Only, this time, with me the one asking to be let up the stairs. And this time, because I'm looking smashing, he's really keen.'

'Your scenario, not mine.'

'What happens next? Do I come to my senses, resist his lewd advances, and push him off the roof accidentally while defend-ing my honour? Or do we settle down for a right old screw –

after which, my revenge accomplished, I deliberately pitch him into the moat?'

'In either case,' Jurnet answered, 'I hope you didn't leave your glass slipper behind.'

15

'Not bad!' said the Superintendent.

Keeping a prudent distance from the balustrade, he looked out at the landscape. A warm breeze ruffled the trees. It ran rippling through the barley ripening from gold to bronze. On the lake a solitary swan rocked on its puckered reflection.

'D'you know,' the Superintendent exclaimed, eyes narrowed, 'I do believe – yes, over there, Ben, do you see? – You can actually see the sea!'

'Yes, sir.'

With the sensation of looking through the eyes of a dead man, Jurnet looked as directed, and located the small vee of metallic blue filling in a narrow gap between the hills like an old-fashioned modesty vest. He blinked hard and thankfully lost it; though the knowledge that it was there regardless seemed suddenly to sharpen the air with a tang of salt.

'Ah, well.' With a small exhalation of breath, not enough to count as a sigh, the Superintendent turned his attention to the foreground view. Upon either side the roof receded round turrets and clustering chimneypots that numbered the rooms beneath. 'They certainly knew how to live in those days!'

Jurnet scowled and said nothing.

'Brings out the Bolshie in you, does it?' The Superintendent smiled sunnily, well aware of the true cause of his subordinate's ill humour. 'Never learn, do you? You're at it again, Ben, however many times I warn you. Getting involved.'

But the detective, his eyes on the stretch of parapet from which several pieces of the coping were missing, was in no mood for the ritual sparring with which the two regularly cemented their bonds of brotherhood and cock-eyed affection.

'It's the damnedest thing!' he exploded. 'Here's the one time

I actually get to meet a murder victim in person, alive and kicking, and, for all the good it does me, I could just as well have seen him first time on a tray in the morgue. I don't *know* him, and I need to.' Kicking moodily at the marl which covered the roof: 'Oh, a pretty boy, I saw that. Maybe AC – DC, and maybe not. No fool, though he sometimes made himself out one – in fact, bloody clever, and enough cheek deliberately to risk putting a lot of backs up at Bullen first time he opens his mouth. A first-class writer, so everyone tells me. But what does it all amount to?'

'I'd say it amounted to something.'

The other shook his head.

'Not a row of pins. The bloke had just that moment arrived. There wasn't time for anyone to build up a sufficient head of steam. Enough, that is, to kill.'

'There's that young woman, of course. The mother of the boy.'

'Yes.' Going a shade too quickly on to the next thing: 'Unless the target was the office, not the man; and any other curator would have filled the bill equally well.'

'Only a curator, surely, with plans to write a life of Appleyard of Hungary? No one seems to have attempted the assassination of the retiring incumbent, who appears to have had no such ambitions.' The Superintendent considered the implications of what he had just said. 'Mr Coryton, now – what, say, if he's been helping himself to a choice objet d'art or two when no one was looking? He wouldn't be too welcoming to a new man, nosing around and checking that all was present and correct. Have you questioned Coryton yet?'

'Not yet. I'm letting him stew in his own juice for a bit. I've been on to the accountants, though, and the solicitors for the Trust, for a copy of the inventory.'

'We've been thinking along the same lines,' the Superintendent conceded. 'Place this size, take you six months to check it – but who's pushing you?' Coming to the point at last, as Jurnet knew he was bound to – it was one of the classic moves of the game they played: 'You know, don't you, Ben, you're going to need some help.'

'I've got Sergeant Ellers, sir.' The classic response.

'Ha ha. *And* Sergeant Bowles, so I hear, to man your incident room. Makes the best cup of tea in the Force. You must ask me over some time.' The Superintendent regarded Jurnet with a mixture of exasperation, fondness and conspiratorial glee. 'Know what, Ben? I get run over by a bus and you'll be out on your ear before you know what hit you. I hope and trust that every night, before you get into bed, you go down on your knees and thank that Jewish God of yours you've got me for a boss instead of a lot of others I could name.'

'Not on my knees, sir!' Jurnet's heart lifted at the oblique intimation that he was to be left to go his own way, even though he had as yet only the haziest notion where it might lead.

'Just the same, we have to go through the motions. Shelden came from Hampstead – so I'm sending Dave Batterby up to town, to investigate the London angle, if any.' The Superintendent's eyes twinkled as he pronounced the name of the most ambitious officer on the Angleby strength. 'If he does nothing more than stand on the pavement outside the Yard, surveying the scene of his future triumphs, at least I'll be able to go to the Chief with my hand on my heart and set his mind at rest that, for once, Detective-Inspector Jurnet is not being left to his own devices.'

Immaculate in his light grey summer suit, the Superintendent made his way briskly across the roof, making for the narrow door which led down to the minstrels' gallery. Jurnet, following more slowly, paused by the air bed where Chad Shelden had intended to sleep under the stars. The bed, covered with a black groundsheet save for a corner which disclosed a triangle of orange canvas, had a bump in the middle which the detective diagnosed as the foot-pump dumped there by the scene-of-crime team which had swarmed over the place like worker ants, penetrating every nook and cranny, examining every stair and skylight with the dedication of astronomers seeking a new star.

Jurnet nudged the exposed part of the bed with the toe of his shoe. It was still reasonably pneumatic, still harbouring air pumped in by one who, in his present situation, could have done with a bit of it himself.

He found the Superintendent looking over the wooden rail of the gallery, down at the room below. After the radiant outdoors the Long Chamber looked dim, slatternly with crumpled paper napkins and dishes that had once held ice cream. It was only too evident that Mrs Barwell had preferred not to return to her duties.

The Superintendent leaned over the rail and observed with a romantic lilt to his voice: 'So this was where they danced to the sound of the lute –'

Jurnet countered tartly: 'Funny how an offence suddenly becomes OK so long as it was committed hundreds of years ago, preferably by royals –'

'What a puritan you are, Ben! Can you honestly say –' the Superintendent demanded – 'that the story doesn't touch you? Two doomed young people snatching a fugitive happiness before time runs out?'

'Case turned up on our patch,' the other maintained stubbornly, 'I doubt you'd be going on about fugitive happiness and all that.'

'Right as usual!' the Superintendent capitulated gracefully. 'Well – since it's a bit late to bring the Boleyns to book, let's see who we can put the finger on instead, shall we? Is the chance to edit some sizzling letters of a long-dead queen sufficient motive for murder? Though, if Coryton did do it, I don't suppose it'd be the first time a man killed for the sake of that black-haired witch. Did you know, Ben, that she had a rudimentary sixth finger on one hand with which, so her enemies asserted, she gave suck to the devil?'

The Superintendent descended the stair and began to walk slowly along the length of the room, keeping to the same board, like a child trying not to step on a line.   'Where exactly have you pitched your tent?'

'We've taken over the dining room, sir. I'd have preferred the study, only it's chockful with Laz Appleyard's papers. On the other hand –' demurely – 'the dining room's next to the kitchen. Very handy for Sergeant Bowles.'

Sergeant Bowles, a large, comfortable man not far from his pension, and a widower who often had to be reminded to go home at the end of a duty, had already turned the dining room of the curator's flat into a home from home. The table, thoughtfully covered with a length of green baize, was set out with paper and pens, clipboard and paper fasteners. An earthenware jug full of marigolds stood on top of a grey painted filing cabinet; an electric typewriter rested on a thick pad. The geraniums on the wide, white-painted window sill looked newly refreshed. Through the open window came the croo-crooing of woodpigeons and the muted scream of a passing jet, a white trail feathering slowly across the high blue sky.

There was also a girl.

Jessica Chalgrove put down her cup and saucer and got up from her chair blushing prettily.

'I do hope it's all right –'

'Please!' The Superintendent held up a hand, smiling. 'We interrupted you. Miss Chalgrove, isn't it? I'm glad to see Sergeant Bowles has been looking after you.'

Sergeant Bowles said: 'Young lady's come to work on those papers next door, if you and Mr Jurnet have no objection, sir.'

The Superintendent exclaimed: 'Don't tell me *you're* going to write the life of Appleyard of Hungary!'

'Goodness, no!' The girl blushed even more deeply. 'Elena – Miss Appleyard – has given me a job. I told her I was looking for one. Mucking out horses or something, was what I thought, actually: but she said she'd been meaning for ages to get somebody in to make an index of the Appleyard papers, and she didn't see why I shouldn't be able to do it as well as anybody. She explained exactly how you went about it, and it didn't sound all that difficult – at least, I hope it won't be, but Elena's so clever she makes everything sound easy. Anyway, she rang up Herrold's in Angleby there and then, and ordered a lot of cards and some little metal boxes to keep them in. But the thing is –' she ended, suddenly nervous, and tucking the bottom of her T-shirt into her jeans – 'it all depends, really, on whether you'll let me stay.'

Jurnet said: 'I understood from Miss Appleyard she wanted to get the papers returned to her part of the house at the earliest possible moment.'

'She told me about that. But then she said, since they were over here already, in a good place for working in, it might be better if I went through them here first, box by box, and every time I finished one, I could take it over to her flat, and she'd know that was one done, anyway.' With a touching lack of self-importance: 'I rather think, once she thought about it, she

95

decided it'd be better not to have me under her feet all the time, bothering her with silly questions.' An endearing anxiety surfacing: 'I only hope she didn't invent that bit about wanting an index simply because I'd told her I needed a job.'

The Superintendent declared nobly: 'Any archive requires to be indexed before it can be of use. Otherwise, it's simply a hodge-podge of miscellaneous information nobody can make head or tail of. Make a good job of it, young lady, and the new biographer, whoever he may be, will call down blessings on your head. You'll have cut his labours by half, and I only hope he has the decency to make you a handsome acknowledgment in his preface.'

'That would be marvellous!' The girl glowed. Addressing herself to the Superintendent as to the obvious fount of power: 'Does that mean it's OK for me to stay?'

'That's a matter for Detective-Inspector Jurnet,' the Superintendent returned with a familiar touch of mischief.

'With respect, sir,' Jurnet demurred, 'the fact that Miss Appleyard's given us the use of this one room doesn't entitle us to make conditions as to what she does with the rest of the space.'

Jessica Chalgrove cried: 'That means it's all right, then? Oh, goody!' as the detective nodded smilingly. 'Ferenc promised to pick up the cards this afternoon, so I'll be able to start tomorrow first thing. And you needn't worry, Mr Jurnet. I'll be so quiet, you won't know I'm here.' The girl's delight was charming to see. 'The most you'll hear is a faint moan whenever I make a particularly awful bish of something, which I reckon will be once every five minutes, roughly. After the first hour or two, you shouldn't even notice it. And now,' she finished, making another attempt as she spoke to tuck in the T-shirt, which had come out of the waistband once again, revealing a circlet of tanned young flesh, 'I mustn't interrupt your work any longer, or you'll never catch your murderer.' The light faded, the girl's eyes darkened with memory. 'Who could possibly hate anybody enough to kill him?'

'You've got it wrong, my dear.' The Superintendent's voice was gentle. 'Wars are about hate. Murders are about love.'

'Oh, no!'

'Oh, yes!' the other insisted. 'If you were a cynic you might even say they are the purest expression of it. Love – for a man or a woman, for money, revenge, religion, or even for love of oneself. One way or another, all murders are crimes of passion.'

'But that's horrible!'

'What else would you expect murder to be? Which is why what we have to do – haven't we, Inspector Jurnet? – is figure out what on earth it was that made Mr Chad Shelden so lovable.'

When the Superintendent and the girl had gone, departing together like old friends, Sergeant Bowles brought Jurnet a cup of tea with two biscuits in the saucer.

'Miss Jessica had the Lincoln Creams. I kept back the Bourbons for you, sir.'

'You spoil me.' The detective took one of the biscuits and bit into it, savouring the chocolate taste: savouring, above all, the peace of being his own man again. So, he fancied, Moses must have felt in the wilderness, in between those inescapable visitations when the Lord God of Hosts called by to find out what the hell was going on.

He surveyed his new domain with a satisfied air.

'Those marigolds certainly brighten the place up,' he remarked, to the good Sergeant's manifest gratification. He twisted round in his seat, sipping his tea the while. 'We're going to need a lock for that door. Once that cabinet starts filling up –'

'I already rang Headquarters. They're sending a man out.'

'Might have known you'd have thought of it already.'

'Thank you, sir.' Sergeant Bowles hesitated, then said carefully: 'All the same, I'd be willing to sleep over, if you think it's a good idea.'

'Hardly seems necessary, when we're not twenty minutes out of Angleby.'

'That's true. I'll take your cup, sir, if you've finished.'

'Ta. First-rate cuppa.' Into Jurnet's mind came the comfortless picture of his own flat. No Miriam: but at least the hope, or maybe the delusion, that one day she would be back; the two of them back in bed together, possessing and possessed. He could not bear to imagine how it must feel to know, as Sergeant Bowles must know, that there was no hope, ever.

'Sleeping here might not be such a bad idea at that, if you're quite sure –'

'Not every day I get put up in a stately home.' Sergeant Bowles perked up considerably.

'There's a four-poster in the bedroom. *And* the ghosts of Anne Boleyn and George Bullen to keep you company.'

'I'll make sure they don't get at the Bourbons! Mattress 'd suit me fine. There's one up on the roof I could bring down –'

'Air bed. I'll give you a hand down with it. Easier than letting the air out and having to pump it up again. I've been thinking it ought to come in, anyway. The cover was blowing about, and it has to rain sometime.'

Back on the roof, Jurnet did not look for the sea, and would not have found it had he tried. The breeze had dropped, a heat mist blurred the outline of trees and fields. From somewhere over to the west, thunder rumbled like a remembered bellyache.

Jurnet remarked: 'With a bit of luck we'll get the edge of it. Anything that cools the air off –'

Sergeant Bowles, who had grown up in a village the other side of Bersham, observed with reproof in his voice: 'Won't do the barley a lot of good.'

Revealed, the air bed in its orange cover looked bright and bawdy.

Jurnet said: 'Better give it a turn over before we take it down. The Bullen-Appleyard Trust won't thank us for infesting their curator's flat with creepy-crawlies.'

Gingerly, the bed curving as they up-ended it, the two laid bare the space beneath. No woodlice, no earwigs nor spiders: a skeletal leaf, a few twiggy bits that Sergeant Bowles leaned over and brushed away.

Jurnet's first thought, upon perceiving what else lay where the air bed had lain, was what to tell the Superintendent – or rather, what not to tell him. He'd not be the one to let it be known the lads had missed something they had no business to have missed.

Sergeant Bowles, who knew exactly what was going through the detective's mind, observed realistically: 'Can't hardly say it fell out o' the beak of a passing eagle.'

'S'pose not.'

Only when he had put that first problem out of his mind as

insoluble did Jurnet turn to the second, the greater, one. He squatted down on his haunches and examined the small, glittering object with an attention which he knew to be a mere postponement of action. From one trouser pocket he produced a small bag, and from another a scrap of facial tissue – one more tattered relic of Miriam, who thought handkerchiefs unhygienic. He teased open the edges of the little bag, took the tissue between thumb and forefinger, and, with infinite care, holding it delicately by the edges, picked up the earring and dropped it into the bag.

Picked up the beautiful earring, silver and strange red stone carved with hieroglyphics; one of the pair Anna March had worn at the party.

16

They brought the air bed down to the Long Chamber and left it there, out of the way. Jurnet, who could see that the sight of the party debris was more than Sergeant Bowles's nerves could stand, left him happily going round with a waste paper basket, whilst he himself made for the dining room.

In the little hall, a sound of shuffled papers decided a change of direction. The detective passed the dining room by, moved further along the Bokhara runner, past the bedroom and the bathroom, and stuck his head round the study door.

Ferenc Szanto sat at the desk, in front of him one of the boxes containing the Appleyard papers. The lid was off and Jurnet could see the man's hands, sausage-fingered as they were, moving through the contents with precision and economy.

Looking for what?

Jurnet said: 'Good morning. Anything I can do for you?'

There was no start of surprise. A frozen moment, though, before the man swung round in his chair, the thick, white hair flying, the broad, comical face a moon of smiles.

'The detective-inspector in person, and hot on the scent!' The Hungarian rose, approached Jurnet with hand outstretched. The latter, at a loss how to avoid it, suffered his hand

99

to be shaken. 'And are you close on the heels of the murderer of poor Mr Shelden?'

'Pretty close.' Jurnet's voice was firm with a confidence he did not feel. He directed his gaze pointedly at the open box. 'Don't tell me you're at it again!'

'Suspicious, eh?' The man's broad chest heaved with suppressed laughter. 'Next thing I know, eh, if I'm not careful enough, I shall find myself down at the police station, as they say in the papers, helping the police with their inquiries!'

'I hope you're always ready to help the police without having to be carted down to Headquarters to do it.'

'Headquarters! Then I *must* be important!' The Hungarian looked intently at the detective, thrusting his big head forward. Apparently satisfied with what he saw, and with an abrupt end to raillery, he stated calmly: 'I am here, as a matter of fact, not only to take away, but also to bring: to make sure that the papers are not Laz Appleyard, authorised version, nor yet Laz Appleyard, revised version, but Laz Appleyard the complete omnibus edition, unexpurgated and unabridged.'

The man took a step or two about the room, moving with an indecision that seemed foreign to his nature. He came to a stop with his back to the window, a position that bothered Jurnet who preferred the people he was interviewing to place themselves where the light fell full on their faces.

The detective said: 'So long as it isn't Laz Appleyard, the plausible lie.'

'Ha!' the other exclaimed, throwing up his hands in a gesture Jurnet classified as foreign. 'You remember my own words against me, eh, when all I wanted, at the party, seeing the poor young man so cocksure he could clap my old friend Laz between hard covers like a bluebottle you only have to stay very still till it is inside, then *bang!* you have squashed it dead on the page, was to prick his conceit, if that were possible; sow a seed of becoming doubt. St George of England, Lawrence of Arabia, Appleyard of Hungary – all three, I think equally fairy stories: legends, useful like a double Scotch for stiffening the spirits in times of national emergency. But Laz Appleyard the man, not the hero –' into Ferenc Szanto's voice had come a note of deepest melancholy – 'the devil, not the man – that is another story altogether.'

'I think,' said Ferenc Szanto, 'you wonder if I have not killed Mr Shelden in fear he might put into his book something I do not want written there.' With a palm upraised to stop Jurnet, who was on the point of making an interjection: 'Unless, perhaps, with your renowned British justice, you are prepared to give me the benefit of the doubt until Mr Biographer Two, and Three, and Four are also found dead at the bottom of the ramparts. You see how absurd it is. So, though it is partly for my own protection, it is chiefly to bring you closer to the person you seek that I tell you now that other story – the story of the real Laz Appleyard. At the end of it, if you believe me, there will be one less name on your list.'

'You called him devil.'

'Ah! I am glad I have caught your attention!' The Hungarian resumed his seat, now in full light; the shallowness of shadow accentuating the Asiatic cast of his broad features. 'What strange things you discover in this beautiful place, eh? – so peaceful in the English way, so well-bred about keeping its secrets in the family. First you learn that Queen Anne Boleyn slept with her brother like any feeble-minded peasant. Now you hear that Appleyard of Hungary –' The man broke off and sat for a moment motionless, looking down at his hands splayed on the desk top. Jurnet, the man trained to listen, said nothing. Waited.

At last Ferenc Szanto raised his head. Looked past the detective, out of the window.

'It was magic, those childhood days at Kasnovar, the estate the old countess brought to the Appleyards as her marriage portion. Magic not just because I was a boy and the world seemed an apple that was mine for the picking; but because Laz Appleyard was my friend. That I was only the son of the Kasnovar blacksmith and he the heir to land and riches I knew very well, but, to a child, what do such things matter? Together we galloped the half-wild horses of the *puszta*, climbed trees, swam naked in the lakes and rivers, rode on top of the great hay-waggons, half-drugged by the scent of the hay.' The man regarded the detective with a quizzical smile. 'A pastoral idyll, eh?' Shaking his head: 'Not so. Because, young as I was, I knew even then that there were things wrong with my friend – a cruelty, a love of destruction for its own sake which both repelled and intrigued me. Once he climbed a tree that was as skinny as a pole – not a single branch from the ground to its sprouting head, you would have said not even a monkey could climb such a tree – but up he went, up and up, until he had climbed to a great, untidy nest a stork had made at the very top. The nest was full of baby birds a few days old, and I watched from below as Laz reached in, and picked them up, and threw them down, one after the other. Their little bones were so frail they splintered to nothing on the hard ground. Then the mother bird came back to the nest, and she went for Laz with her great beak, squawking like a demon. But he had a knife in his belt, a beautiful curving dagger one of his ancestors had taken from the Turks, and in another minute the great bird was lying dead at the foot of the tree along with what remained of her chicks.

'Shall I tell you something?' The Hungarian shook his head in a kind of awed disbelief. 'I knew he had done something unforgivable, yet it only bound me to him more closely than ever. We were friends. Whatever he did, I was part of it. The blood of the stork and her brood was on my head also. I was captivated by his terrible audacity, joined to him by dark forces I could not understand.' A sigh. 'And still do not understand after all these years.'

With a shake of the head Ferenc Szanto set the insoluble problem aside, and returned to his narrative.

'Well, Inspector Jurnet, as you may have heard, the war came and childhood ended. I hardly know which was the greater tragedy. For you in England the war, eh, was to beat Hitler, and, when you had beaten him, the war was over. So simple! For Hungarians, nothing is ever simple. Some people – like the English, I think – have learnt to control their own history, to canalise it, build locks and weirs which regulate its flow. For Hungarians, history is a devouring flood which sweeps everything before it, good and bad alike. The most an individual can hope to do is find a convenient rooftop to straddle, or a piece of wreckage to cling to, while the waters rage past.'

'Laz Appleyard,' Jurnet reminded him.

'My friend Laz,' said Ferenc Szanto. Again there was a moment of quiet before the man began to speak again. 'Some of it is true,' he said. 'Some of that stuff they have put in the

Appleyard Room for visitors to see. During the uprising, he got more than a hundred people out of the country.'

'That must have taken some doing.'

'A great deal of doing.'

'Including his wife, I understand.'

'Mara.' The man pronounced the name like a benediction. 'Mara Forro, the daughter of my employer and benefactor, Janos Forro, who was himself the righthand man of Imre Nagy, our Prime Minister. Except that Mara wasn't Laz's wife in those days. She was going to marry me.'

'I see.'

'You see nothing,' said Ferenc Szanto, without animus. 'No Englishman makes a fool of himself for love unless he is a fool already; and you, Inspector, are no fool. So: suddenly my friend Laz comes back to Hungary. How happy I am to meet him again! At once we are so close, we could have been children again. Except that he has grown tall and beautiful, a fairy prince, and I – even though, thanks to Janos Forro, I too have got on in the world – I still looked like what I was, the son of the Kasnovar blacksmith. The surprise would have been if my Mara had *not* fallen in love with the young god who had appeared out of the blue to help Hungary in its fight for freedom.'

'You must still have been surprised to see him.'

'Surprised?' The man repeated, as if the point had never before been put to him. 'I do not think so. It was a time when nothing could have surprised us, when everything that happened was strange and wonderful, as in a dream. Until the day the Russian tanks rolled back into Budapest, and we woke up.'

Jurnet remarked inadequately: 'We heard all about it on the radio.'

'I hope you found us sufficiently entertaining.' The Hungarian's lips twisted with uncharacteristic bitterness. 'We screamed *help!* to the world, and the world answered with a deafening silence. The Russians trapped our General, Pal Maleter: they tricked Prime Minister Nagy and Janos Forro into leaving the Yugoslav Embassy where they had taken refuge, and they took all three to Romania and imprisoned them in the palace at Sinaia. I had Laz to thank they hadn't caught me along with the other lesser fry. Already, at his urging, we had gone underground. Mara was safe in England, Hungary was back under Red tyranny, and I was a child again, playing cops and robbers with my friend. Except that, this time, the cops and the robbers were on the same side – the Avos and the Red soldiers who were going about the city stripping it of everything of value that wasn't actually bolted to the floor. And I was so happy!' 'The man's eyes, aslant in his head, widened at the absurdity of it all. 'Can you believe it? My country in ruins, I had lost the woman who, to me, was the joy of life, and I was happy, playing games with my friend – only this time, games in which men got killed nastily and silently, none of your English nicety for the Queensberry Rules. But I tell you, I lived life, in that time as a hunted and a hunting animal, as I have never lived it since. And when my friend said one day, why not get Imre Nagy and Pal Maleter and Janos Forro out of that Romanian palace where they are locked up, I answered light-heartedly, why not? If my friend Laz says it can be done, it can be done.'

Jurnet said: 'I saw what it said about the escape in the Appleyard Room. You almost pulled it off.'

'You think? We were seven kilometres from the Yugoslav border, in a forester's hut deep in the hills. Laz had gone to spy out the little river that was the frontier crossing. Pal and Janos were playing cards with a pack they had picked up somewhere on our travels. The courage of those two men! They could have been on a picnic. I was the uneasy one. So near to safety, yet so far! I am country born and bred, and in spring a countryman expects the country to be noisy with birdsong and the many small noises animals make as they find their livings after the winter cold. But not a sound.' The Hungarian looked bleakly at the detective. 'As a countryman, then, I was not really surprised when, all of a sudden, the hills were full of soldiers, Russian voices shouting commands; grenades, guns firing. We had settled among ourselves that if the Reds came we would each go our own way, as offering the best chance of escape; and I found for myself a pond in which I crouched below the surface, breathing through a hollow reed until the noises died away, and at last the birds began to sing. When I dared to come out from my hiding place I was so cold from the water I could not walk. Somehow I crawled back to the hut. Empty: but blood on the cards. I have them still. I would not exchange them for the riches of all the Rothschilds.'

This time the silence was so prolonged that Jurnet asked at last: 'And that's the end of the story?'

'The end and also the beginning.' The man's face was sombre. 'Laz came back and found me, and for two weeks he nursed me night and day, or I would have surely died. When I was well enough to walk a little, he got me across the border to Yugoslavia, carrying me for most of the way on his back. And from there we came to England, to Bullen Hall where he was the English milor and Mara was already waiting for him.'

'They married.'

The other nodded agreement.

'They married, my loved one and my friend. In Bullensthorpe Church the bells rang out. But alas they did not, those two, as should happen with fairy princes and princesses, live happily ever after. No one woman was ever enough for Laz Appleyard. Once possessed – finished! He was on to the next one, and the next one, and the one after that. I watched Mara's beauty fade away, and after Istvan – Steve – was born, her bodily strength also. The child that could have been a consolation was only an additional torment. I do not know if Laz truly loved him, or if he only acted love to bind the boy to him and hurt the mother further; but bind him he did, with bands of steel. The boy lived for his father. My poor, pale Mara had no place in his world.' In an even tone, carefully colourless, Ferenc Szanto said: 'I did not think I could ever be glad that Mara should be dead. But when she died, when Steve was six years of age, I, who had never believed in Him until that day, thanked God for it.'

Jurnet commented: 'I wonder you stayed on.'

'I have not yet told you the worst thing. Eighteen months after Laz and I came back from Hungary, the news came for certain that Imre Nagy and Pal Maleter and Janos Forro had been executed. Six months after that, information came to me from sources which are quite unimpeachable that Laz Appleyard, for money paid into a Swiss bank account, had sold Pal and Janos to the Reds. That charade in the forester's hut had all been prearranged.'

'I wonder even more that you stayed on. Surely you had it out with Appleyard? Why didn't you expose him for what he was?'

'Questions! Questions! I said nothing, did nothing. Does that surprise you? Then this will surprise you more – that, despite everything, Mara still loved her husband with all the love of a passionate woman. I could not add to her griefs by letting her know that this devil, her husband, had sent her own father to his death and taken money for it, like Judas Iscariot. And after she was dead, how could I tell Steve the true nature of the hero-father he worshipped like a god? Especially as I gradually came to see, with the passing years, that justice does not exclusively fall to be administered in courts of law. Much as Steve looked like his father all over again, that was the whole of the resemblance. Everything that mattered – his loving nature, his inability to hurt any living creature – was all from Mara. So, I stayed on at Bullen to be a shield to Mara's son. And when his father was killed, I stayed on to take the dead man's place, so far as I could, and to undo such harm as might have been done to him.'

Ferenc Szanto fell silent. Jurnet, having pondered what he had heard, said: 'Quite a story. Except that I still don't see it adding up to you wanting it written up in a book for all the world to read – above all, for young Steve to read. You said yourself you've kept it dark so far to protect him from the truth. So what's changed?'

'Time is what's changed, my friend. Steve is no longer a boy. It is time to grow up.' The Hungarian smiled, a smile of great sweetness. 'Don't think I have any illusions about him. He is a decent, ordinary young man, only moderately clever, who, providing he is allowed to, will lead a decent, ordinary life. That is what he must be given the chance to do – to stand on his own feet without forever measuring himself against that heroic father figure who never existed. I give you an instance –' The man jumped up and began to pace the room again. 'I hear from Jessica that when Steve saw Mr Shelden's body in the water with the eels, he was sick, he nearly fainted. What is wrong with that, such a horrible thing? It is only natural in a person of sensitivity. But no: the boy is ashamed. It is not the way the son of Appleyard of Hungary should behave. You see? For more than two years now I know it is time to destroy this pernicious

myth if Steve is to have a proper life. This I do not tell Elena –
only that it is high time a definitive biography should be
written. And at last, when it is Mr Coryton's time to go, she
makes arrangement with Mr Shelden.'

'You're not telling me Miss Appleyard actually wants to have
all the dirt about her brother spread around? Or doesn't she
know all you've told me?'

'Unless she has information not told to me, the betrayal in
Hungary she does not know. All the documents relating to it are
in Hungarian which she – unlike Laz – could never be bothered
to learn. And the reason I am here today is to remove these
documents before Jessica notices anything out of place, and
translate them into English, so that they will be ready and
waiting when Mr Shelden's successor comes to Bullen.'

'Miss Appleyard will never allow them to be used!'

'Is possible,' the Hungarian readily admitted. 'But I think
yes, she will allow. Elena is a very remarkable lady, and I think
she too is tired of this Appleyard of Hungary who is the real
ghost of Bullen Hall. When she was a child, at Kasnovar, she
was very close to her brother. I was the one she did not like,
because Laz would rather be with me, doing boys' things. But
after they grew up, it was different. Elena is also a very correct
lady, with much pride of family; and although she did not, I
think, regard Mara as a grand enough match for an Appleyard,
neither did she like the womanising and the wild parties, the
drinking and gambling – oh, I haven't told you the half of it!
Only enough, I trust, to convince you that I did not push Mr
Shelden off the roof, nor shall I any future biographer who may
be so reckless as to come to Bullen.'

Jurnet digested what he had been told. Plainly not satisfied,
he demanded: 'What I don't get is – why hang about waiting? If
Steve's the one it's all in aid of, who says it has to be in book
form? What's stopping you from taking him aside, man to man,
show him your proofs, tell him the story as you've told me?'

'Don't think I haven't thought about it. But I am a coward. I
admit it.' The Hungarian sighed deeply, rubbed a hand over his
face. 'I cannot bear the thought of Steve's face when he learns
the truth about his so wonderful father. Ah yes, in later years he
may bless me, but how will that pay for losing his love now?
And who could blame him? So –' with a fatalistic shrug – 'only

at second hand, the printed page. Black and white doing my dirty work for me. In spite of all, I cannot forget that I owe Laz Appleyard my life. Even though I know it was all a play-acting, the hiding in the hills, the stealing out at night to get food, even the carrying me over the border. He could have handed me over to the Reds and been rid of me. True, I was no Maleter or Forro, but still I was someone the Reds would have been happy to get their hands on. They might even have paid money for me. Yet he chose to save me. He threw the baby storks to the ground from the sheer pleasure of killing, yet he chose to save me, his friend.' The Hungarian sighed once more. 'He is not the only Judas.'

17

They parted at the entrance to the lime alley, Jurnet politely declining an invitation to inspect the smithy, hidden away behind shrubbery in what had once been a gardener's bothy.

'On such a day I cannot blame you. But if you come at once I will not yet have made my fire.'

'I have to have a word with your compatriot, Mr Matyas.'

'Jeno?' A note of concern sounded in Ferenc Szanto's voice. 'Be gentle with him, if you please. He is not a well man. Besides, what can Jeno know about Mr Shelden and his murderer?'

'That,' Jurnet returned reasonably, 'is what I propose to find out. Who knows? Perhaps he too has a story to tell me.' A sudden thought disturbing him: 'I take it he speaks English?'

'Jeno?' Szanto's laugh was warm with affection. 'Too well, the simpleton. He has not my sense, never to speak it except like a comic turn in the music hall. Nothing in England, I tell him, more arouses suspicion than a foreigner presuming to speak English like an Englishman. But he doesn't listen.'

'He certainly doesn't look very English.'

'Neither, my good sir, do you,' the Hungarian pointed out, his face crinkled with mischief. 'But I know you to be so because you are too good-mannered to knock me down for my impertinence. I cannot sufficiently tell you, Inspector, what it means to a Hungarian not to be afraid to be cheeky to a policeman!'

'Don't push your luck,' Jurnet advised with a grin. Then: 'This Jeno – did you and Appleyard bring him over to England with you?'

'Certainly not! Jeno was only a child in the rising. You must not go by his ill looks. Even so, he played his part. His father was a printer and bookbinder, and every morning, before light, Jeno was out pasting up the posters his father had printed during the night. After it was over, his father went on printing books and articles it was not permitted to print, and one day the Avos came and took him away. A week later Jeno's mother was called to the police station where they gave her her husband's clothes wrapped in brown paper, and a note from the police doctor to say he had died choking on a chicken bone.' The man's face twisted into its clownish semblance. 'Oh, he was a comedian, that one! Chicken served in an Avo cell! A wonder he did not tell Mrs Matyas what was on the wine list for that day.'

'What happened to Jeno?'

'That was a boy! Young as he was, he took over the business, and he was cleverer than his father. The books and articles were still printed, but with wiliness and organisation, so that he was not found out. I think he would still be in Buda today except that his mother died and he wanted to see the English birds.'

'English birds? Girls, you mean?'

'No, Inspector –' with a flapping of arms by way of explanation – 'English birds that fly in the sky and sing songs in the English language. Ever since a boy, Jeno is a bird lover, and from somewhere he had a book about the birds of the Norfolk coast of England. So it happens that one afternoon in summer I am drowsing on the beach at Holkham, when suddenly somebody on a sandhill above me trips and drops his binoculars, and says something very naughty in Hungarian.' The Hungarian chuckled. 'So long it is since I have heard such words, for a moment I wonder if it is not Norfolk dialect! But it is Jeno.'

'You were the one, then, who brought him to Bullen Hall?'

'It was providential! Somebody was needed to take care of the books in the Library, and repair the bindings. It was a very good day when I find him – good for the books, good for all of us here at Bullen. Jeno is a good man.'

There were not all that many people about in the Coachyard, the threat of wandering storms enough to keep attendances down. The peacock moved about dispiritedly, pecking at the cobbles as if it expected little to come of it.

Mike Botley was outside as usual, doing something to an outsize laundry hamper. He had his old straw hat on, perched high on his bandaged head, and Jurnet, on the opposite side of the yard, could not make out his face. No whirr of potter's wheel: Anna's shop was still shuttered. In Danny March's coach house, by the sound of it, somebody was using a lathe. The detective felt in his pocket for the little bag that contained Anna March's earring, and wondered what the hell he was going to say to his friend's wife.

'Melanchthon,' said Jeno Matyas, the needle, held between thumb and wiry forefinger, finding its way with practised ease along the backs of the yellowed pages, dragging its thread after it. '*Initia doctrina physica*. Shocking condition.'

'Oh ah,' said Jurnet.

'Very popular textbook in the sixteenth century and for two hundred years after. Well used. Just the same –' the bookbinder negotiated a tricky bit, the needle probing for a safe anchorage – 'you'd think they'd have had too much respect for books in general, wouldn't you, to let it get into this state.'

It really was amazing, and the detective lost no time in saying so.

'You speak English like a native.'

'Too well, you mean, ever to be taken for one. Still, it's kind of you to say so. There's no merit in it. I merely happen to be blessed with an acute ear and a halfway decent memory.' Matyas settled the book carefully on the worktable, section upon section, the needle on top. 'I hope you'll forgive me for not getting up. Legs playing me up a bit.'

'Sorry to hear it, sir. I shan't keep you for long.'

'As long as you like. It isn't every day I have the pleasure of entertaining a real live police officer.'

'You know who I am, then?' Jurnet reached belatedly for his warrant card.

'Please! No proof required. I saw you at the party. Your presence was much commented on.'

Jurnet made a face.

'Does it stick out that much?'

'That you're a policeman? By no means. I myself was greatly surprised to hear it.' With a brisk dismissiveness that was in no way offensive: 'That you possess a face and figure which command attention must be sufficiently well known to you by now to require no further explanation for our curiosity. Please clear those books off that chair, Inspector,' the man went on pleasantly, 'and make yourself as comfortable as you can in the circumstances. I keep on meaning to get a proper chair for visitors, but somehow I never seem to get round to it.'

A somewhat abashed Jurnet, having made a place for himself as requested, observed: 'No worse than you provide for yourself.'

Jeno Matyas settled himself against the slatted back of his chair.

'Ah, but then I make a cult of austerity. It is – or so I'm vain enough to delude myself – my only vanity.'

The room was indeed bare – monastic, save for a number of superb colour photographs of birds pinned haphazardly to a cork bulletin board hung to catch the best of the light. The walls were white, rough-plastered, the floor the original brick, pitted with age and usage, its multifarious cavities occupied by crumbles of rosy dust. Apart from the two wooden chairs and the worktable – scrubbed deal fitted with a clamp and a rack for tools – there was no other furniture. An arched opening that added to the impression of cloistered calm afforded a glimpse of an old-fashioned printing press, shelves piled with boxes, jars and plastic containers; a hide of rich brown colour stretched out on a bench as if awaiting the sacrificial knife. A smell of leather infused the air.

The tranquillity of the place complemented that of its master. Awaiting the detective's questions, the man sat unmoving, vigilant. The bird watcher, thought Jurnet, crouching quiet in his hide, alert for the soft twitter of dunlin, perhaps, skittering along the shore; or lapwing exploding off the winter furrows like a rocket full of stars.

In the event, the Hungarian was the first to speak.

'In case you were going to ask me, Inspector, I did not kill Mr Shelden. But I think, perhaps, I may be able to help you discover who did.'

'If you've some information –' Jurnet began, leaning forward.

'It's difficult.' Jeno Matyas sighed. 'That's why I've waited for you to come to me, instead of seeking you out, as no doubt you'll think I should have done. Nobody wants to get friends into trouble –' He closed his eyes briefly, then opened them. 'But murder is another matter.'

'Yes.'

'I have to tell you what I saw. I have no alternative. Even though –' turning on Jurnet a warm regard – 'here in England, heaven be praised, you won't beat me with rubber hoses or keep me awake all night if I elect to withhold my evidence. In fact, of course, it is your very faith in my integrity which makes it impossible to stay silent.'

'You saw something.'

The man said slowly: 'I think so. I'm not sure. That is, I saw something – but what did I see?'

'What do you think you saw?'

'The ghost of Anne Boleyn.'

Jeno Matyas said: 'You may well think three o'clock in the morning altogether too early to go birdwatching for anything except owls, and I was on my way to Hoope – strictly sea birds and waders who get up with the sun. I'm afraid it all sounds very suspicious – and even more suspicious that I have so many reasons, all of them excellent, for leaving Bullen at that ungodly hour.' The bookbinder looked at Jurnet with an expression which combined friendliness with an endearing, impish glee. 'Having too many reasons, don't you think, is almost as bad as having too few?'

'Try me.'

'All right! First, then, there are these ridiculous legs of mine. At Hoope it's a good three-quarters of a mile from the car park to what I like to call my hide – though, of course, it belongs equally to whoever pays his money to the warden. So, crawling like a snail, the way I do these days, I have to make an early start if I hope to get there by dawn. Second, I'm a very poor sleeper. I won't take sleeping pills, but if the Department of Health would only package a tablet of sea air mixed with the sound of waves breaking on the shore I'd become an addict overnight.

112

Sometimes, to be truthful, I don't even go birdwatching. I drive down to Cromer, park on the cliffs, get in the back, and have my first sound sleep for days. Reason three is the dawn – no, not the dawn, but the time a little before. Still pitch black but you sense something . . . sometimes I almost think you hear it. Something left over from an earlier stage of man's development – perhaps even earlier than that. An apprehension of life beginning –'

'Know what you mean,' said Jurnet, who, in his day, had seen out more night duties than he cared to remember. The detective kept to himself his own overriding recollection of that premonition of day: only one more hour to a hot cuppa.

He asked: 'So it was 3 a.m. when you left Bullen Hall?'

'I couldn't swear to the minute. Even getting from here to the drive in my present condition takes more time than I care to take note of. Nowadays Elena kindly lets me park my car in front of the house. I only hope my frequent early departures don't disturb her, but if so, she's made no complaint so far.'

The man hesitated, as if unsure how to continue. Then: 'I had just got myself into the car, which was parked facing the Hall, and fastened my seat belt – and incidentally, may I assure you, in case, as a police officer, you're wondering if anyone with legs like mine should be driving at all, that I have automatic transmission, have presented myself for retesting, and been passed fit to drive. So – there I was, about to turn on the ignition and switch on the lights, when I happened to glance up at the house front.'

'What did you see?'

'It was a very bright night,' the man replied, 'as no doubt you remember. But by that time, as often happens, a mist was rising from the moat, so that the house no longer seemed rooted in the ground, but to hang in the air a little above it, like an enchanted castle in a children's story. Once you switch on your headlights you dispel the illusion; and so, for a moment, I stayed still, admiring. And, as I waited, a woman came round the corner of the house, from the west wing.'

'Your ghost,' commented Jurnet, articulating his disbelief. 'Can you describe her?'

'Not easy, because she was moving along the grass edge of the moat, and the mist blurred every outline. I can't even say with certainty whether she was young or old, only that there was something about her which made me feel sure she was beautiful. She wore a dress with long wide sleeves, and she had dark hair which hung down to her shoulders and perhaps further. Of the darkness I'm quite sure, because the starlight caught it: gave it a bloom, like a raven's wing.'

'Couldn't you see her face? Miss Appleyard was out for a walk in the grounds, she says, about 3.30.'

'Elena? Well, well!' Matyas looked taken aback. Then: 'No –' he said decisively – 'it was definitely earlier than 3.30, and whilst I can't say who it was, I can be quite sure it wasn't her. The reason I can't be more explicit as to what the woman looked like is that she held her hands to her face, both hands. She moved along, weeping. I don't think Elena is a woman to weep.'

'You mean, you actually heard her crying?'

'No, no! Only that her posture was grief personified.' Jeno Matyas fell silent, absorbed in contemplation of the image he had resurrected. 'Even as I tell you about it, its poignancy touches me all over again.'

Jurnet demanded: 'What did you do?'

'I can see,' remarked the Hungarian, with a gentleness that was itself a rebuke, 'that I haven't made myself clear. What I saw was something very private. I didn't feel I had any right to intrude, even if it was upon a grief more than four hundred years old. What comfort had I to offer? I sat quiet, watching, as the woman crossed the entire front of the Hall, from west to east.'

'And then –?'

'I only wish I could tell you.' The man's brows knitted in concentration. 'As you can imagine, I've thought about it a great deal since. Useless! One moment she was there: the next – vanished!'

'What else would you expect of Anne Boleyn?' Jurnet's voice was now openly mocking. 'If you'd waited a bit longer, maybe you'd have seen George Bullen coming after her.' Rearranging his voice and his manner into something more befitting a paid-up member of Angleby CID: 'You don't really mean to tell me, Mr Matyas, you believe in ghosts?'

With an urbanity to which it was hard to take exception, the man answered: 'Forgive me, Inspector, if, from the very vehemence with which you deny it, I say I think that you do, too, in your heart. Do you really think, in a house like Bullen Hall, four hundred years of history leave no more trace than rising damp in the basement and beetle in the rafters?' The pale face was at once friendly and remote. 'The dead cast long shadows.'

'Not half as long as the living, at any rate at three o'clock in the morning! I have to believe,' Jurnet insisted obstinately, 'that what you saw was a real live woman with dark hair.'

The Hungarian clasped his thin white hands together.

'Have it your own way, Inspector.'

Jurnet's hand, in his pocket, fingered the little bag containing the earring. What the hell was he going to tell Danny?

He parted from the bookbinder with the minimum of courtesies; sneaked out like a felon himself, for fear of running into the cabinet maker, and made his way back to the curator's flat. Back to Sergeant Bowles, who took one look at the Inspector and vanished into the kitchen, shortly to reappear with a plateful of sandwiches and some tea strong enough to stand a spoon in.

'Sardine,' said the good man, with infinite tact. 'Heard somewhere you'd gone off ham.'

18

'Bloody hell!' growled Sergeant Ellers, as the Post Office van came round the bend and whizzed past with a cheery toot. The briars and brambles in the hedge reached out thorny fingers towards the shining coachwork of the police Rover. 'Must 've planned this road as a tight fit for a couple of cavemen dragging their birds home to the bridal suite. What they're going to say back at the garage I don't care to think!' The little Welshman loosened his tie, took out his handkerchief and mopped his face. 'Hate to think what 'd happen if they had a fire in Bullensthorpe, and the fire engine had to get through.'

'Not to worry,' Jurnet returned comfortably, glad to be

away, if only temporarily, from the stateliness of stately homes. 'Doubt if the natives have learnt yet how to rub two sticks together.'

The village, the detective was pleased to note when at last, having negotiated a hump-backed bridge over a stream whose banks were bright with kingcups, they drew up by a small green, was pretty, but not demandingly so: a pleasant medley of houses, from Tudor brick to plastic clapboard, none of them beautiful enough or ugly enough to upset the sensible balance of the place. Even the church, made of flints off which the sun struck sharp lights, veiled its bulk behind several ancient yews, comfortably unkempt like old women who had let themselves go and if you didn't like it you could lump it.

All that was wrong was the watchful quiet that, in villages, Jurnet always found so disquieting. Birds twittered, trees rustled, aeroplanes passed overhead – all the sounds of nature that, in his book, added up to silence. Of inhabitants there was no sign. The fact that the detective was quite certain they were present and aware, somewhere behind the potted plants which filled every window, only deepened his sense of unease.

Jack Ellers got out of the car and stood, hands on plump hips, surveying the scene.

'Buzzing little hive of activity,' he observed. 'Which one's the Tollers?'

'Mr Jurnet!'

Mollie Toller, plump and birdlike with her high bosom and perky way of moving, opened the front door of 'Pippins', to which the chimes in the hall had summoned her with the first four notes of 'D'ye ken John Peel'. Was it, Jurnet wondered, his overactive imagination, or had there been an instant of hesitation before the warm, generous voice proclaimed its surprised pleasure?

'And Sergeant Ellers! This *is* nice!'

'Beautiful as ever, Mollie,' declared the little Welshman, taking the woman's hand in both of his, and looking her soulfully in the eye. 'You and me both!'

'Still full of your jokes!' Mrs Toller was all blushes and smiles. 'I'm sure I don't know what the Inspector 'll think.'

'Same as Jack here,' Jurnet assured her gallantly. 'While the rest of us have been growing old and grey, you've found the secret of eternal youth. Especially,' he added with elaborate concern, 'as you've just had one of your turns.'

'One of my –' Mrs Toller stopped abruptly: then said, in a voice that was a little too emphatic, 'Oh, I'm quite over that, thank you.'

She led the way through the hall into a bright room where flowers rampaged over carpet, curtains and wallpaper; swarmed across cushions and upholstery, crammed into vases, bloomed in pots. 'Make yourselves comfortable while I tell Perce you're here. You'll have a cup of tea? Soon as I've told him I'll put the kettle on.' She waited a second before adding, as if in anticipation of a question she had already deciphered in the police officers' eyes: 'My auntie left me the bungalow, Mr Jurnet. Principal of Rackworth Primary. Never married. *And* a nice little bit of money to go with it.'

'Why haven't I got an auntie like that?' the detective demanded. Then: 'No need to tell me, Mollie. As if I didn't know that on Percy's ill-gotten gains you'd be lucky to be living in the hut at the bottom of the garden.'

The woman's gratitude and relief were lovely to see.

'Then it *is* just a social call! Percy told me he'd asked you over, but I said you'd never come, just like that. Not socially.'

'He didn't tell you what he told me about your Victoria sponge.' Jurnet skilfully dodged the question. 'Matter of fact, I've been hoping to run into Percy at the Hall again, but no luck.'

'You can thank me for that.' Instantly on her guard again, Mollie Toller declared: 'There were some jobs to do about the house, couldn't be put off any longer.'

Summoned from his grove of Academe, Percy Toller came in vociferous with welcome, and – while Mollie busied herself in the kitchen – showed his two visitors over the bungalow, expatiating on the beauties of fitted carpets and low-flush loos – 'Two of 'em, Mr Jurnet, think of that!' – and the unparalleled convenience of fitted cupboards, every one of which he flung wide for inspection.

Detective-Inspector Benjamin Jurnet addressed himself to the question of why Percy Toller should think it advisable thus to lay bare the intimacies of his household arrangements. Charitably, he was ready to accept that so might any retired villain behave, eager to demonstrate that he no longer had anything to hide. Except that every sentence begun and left dangling, every embarrassed silence, made it only too apparent that Percy Toller had something to hide.

Only in his study, a small room furnished with a desk and chair and bookshelves of which only a shelf or two was occupied, did the ex-burglar relax, touching his books and papers with little pats at once comical and touching.

'Mr Jurnet,' he declared, with the air of imparting great news, 'you can't imagine how much there is to learn in the world! Have you ever thought about it, Mr Jurnet?'

'Can't say I have, Percy. Leave it to university students like you.'

The little man beamed.

'There's no end of it! Even s'posing you could manage to learn it all, which you couldn't possibly, next day there'd be a whole new lot, and the next, and the day after that –' He broke off, awed by the tremendous prospect. 'Makes you think, Mr Jurnet, don't it?'

'Just so long as you mug up enough for that doctorate –'

'Mr Jurnet!' squirming with pleasure. Then, serious: 'What you have to do, see, is specialise. I –' Percy announced proudly – 'am doing Humanities.'

'Oh ah. You'll have to translate for us ignoramuses.'

'Culture, Mr Jurnet! All the things that make us civilised –'

'Don't tell me Perce is off on his hobby horse again!' Mrs Toller poked her head into the little room to announce that tea was ready. 'That man!' she asserted fondly, leading the way back to the sitting room. 'Sometimes I think, if he stuffs his head with one more fact he'll burst like a ripe melon.'

Seated with Ellers on the couch, Jurnet drank several cups of good, strong tea, and pronounced the Victoria sponge all and more than Perce had promised. Mollie dimpled and protested at the praise. But it still wasn't a party. There was a wariness in the air, a nervous apprehension of what was to come.

So that when, leaning back against the flowery cushions, Jurnet wiped his mouth on the floral paper napkin with a sigh of contentment, and remarked: 'Beats anything at the Corytons' party,' it was almost as much a relief as a fear realised. 'And *they* had it professionally catered!'

'Can't beat home-made,' Sergeant Ellers offered jovially. Percy Toller stayed silent. Mrs Toller said, in a hurt way, as if an unfair advantage had been taken: 'I didn't know you were there, Mr Jurnet.'

'Quite by chance. Ran into the curator – the retiring one, I mean – and he asked me. Half the reason I said yes was the thought of seeing you the belle of the ball.' As there was no response to this, the detective tried a new tack. 'Terrible thing about Mr Shelden.'

Percy Toller said: 'It don't hardly seem possible.'

'It was that all right! You should 've seen him when we fished him out of the moat after those bloody eels – oh, pardon! No need to upset you with the gory details.' Getting down to the nub: 'What I want to know from you, Percy, is why you and Mollie weren't at the party after all. From what you told me, you're tickled pink to be part of the Bullen crowd – so why stay home from the big do of the season?' Ending, after a moment, with: 'If staying home's what you did.'

The little man spilled some of his tea into the saucer.

'I told you! Mollie had one of her turns.'

'Seen a doctor, has she?' The other shook his head. 'Know something, Percy? I don't believe you ever intended to go to that party. Would you have asked me back to tea if you had, with Mollie needing time to put on her glad rags and the war paint? It stands to reason. Can't expect me not to find it all a bit fishy.'

With a feeble attempt at his old self, Toller contradicted: 'Fishy? It was ham.'

'So it was,' the other agreed unsmilingly. 'Ham which, in this heat, you said, you always bought fresh to eat on the same day. You'd never be having a ham tea, knowing you were going on straight after to a big blow-out, with the eats laid on – now, would you?'

Percy Toller seemed to have regained something of his humour.

'I must say,' he exclaimed, 'it's the first time I've been grilled by the dicks about *not* being at the scene of the crime!'

'Who's talking about crime? No crime was committed at the

party, unless you mean the speeches. A good time was had by all. Just can't understand why you decided to give it the go-by. Of course –' as if the thought had just that moment occurred to him – 'there *was* a break-in over at Itteringham that same night. Some very nice antique silver, so they tell me. From all I hear, a very clever job.'

'Not mine then, that's for sure! Think I've become a Raffles in my old age?' The little man added, in an editorial undertone: '*The Amateur Cracksman*, author, Ernest William Hornung, 1866–1921.'

'I don't know.' Jurnet kept a straight face. 'You've been studying. No saying what they teach you at university these days. Open University – how to open a safe, for all I know.'

'Humanities!' The little man shouted. 'Culture and civilisation!' He banged a hand down on the tea table, and the cups and saucers with their full-blown roses jumped as if they might shed a petal. 'How many times I got to say I'm retired before you believe me?' Percy Toller drew himself up with a bruised dignity that made Jurnet feel a little ashamed of himself. 'You hurt me, Mr Jurnet. You really do. I honestly believe I'd rather you thought I bumped off Mr Shelden than that I'm still thieving.'

'I could, just as well. Anyone tells a lie, like you have, only has himself to blame if the police come along asking questions. To our way of thinking, a bloke who isn't straight with us over one thing, who's to say he's straight with us over anything?'

Percy Toller repeated, on a rising note of despairing obstinacy: 'I told you. Mollie had one of her turns.'

19

The road through the village ended, a little past the church, at a five-barred gate with the name 'Bullen Hall' painted on it in black.

Jurnet leaned on the top bar, taking in the leafy parkland beyond, the rutted track curving off into the distance.

'Must be the back entrance. Wonder how far it is to the house, this way.'

Sergeant Ellers stared.

'You're not suggesting our pocket-size Perce could 've tossed a big boy like Chad Shelden over the battlements?'

'He's not the only one connected with the Hall who lives in the village. The Corytons hang out here as well, somewhere. And, incidentally, don't underestimate Percy. He's a Karate black belt.'

'He's never!'

'It's the truth. Once told me he took it up to be sure of getting away from any rozzer who tried to arrest him. Only thing was, whenever it actually came to the point, he never could bring himself to, in case he hurt us. Knew us all too well for the lovely bunch of buggers we are.'

'Hardly sounds like your cold-blooded murderer.'

'No such animal. Murders are done in hot blood, not cold.'

'If you say so.' But the chubby Welshman still looked unconvinced. 'I still can't see old Percy as an angel of death.'

'Maybe we should suspend judgement till we find out the real reason why he stayed away from the party.' Turning back to the prospect before him: 'Tell you what. While I'm rustling up the Corytons, if they're home, why don't you take yourself back to the Hall by the tradesmen's entrance. Let me know where the path comes out in relation to the house. Time how long it takes you. Keep your eyes skinned for anything that may be there to be seen.'

Jack Ellers frowned.

'Need a ruddy tractor to clear that hump. Take the Rover down there, we'll be lucky to finish up with a back axle to call our own.'

'Who said anything about the car? I meant, walk it.'

'In this heat!'

'Good for your waistline.' The detective straightened his lean length and moved away from the gate. 'See you back at the house, then.'

The little Welshman called after him: 'Tell Rosie my last thoughts were for that leg of lamb with rosemary she's got laid on for dinner.'

121

'Better than that,' the other returned heartlessly. 'I'll eat a few slices myself in your memory. Rosemary for remembrance. What's for afters?'

Passing by the church, Jurnet noticed with a mixture of annoyance and professional concern that the oak door with its iron latch was slightly ajar. Concern, because he had already taken in the announcement on the notice board to the effect that the building was open for services only one Sunday in four: annoyance because, ever since his Baptist boyhood, with its bleak little chapel where the spirit of God descended without the aid of stained-glass windows and angels spreadeagled against the roof, churches had always made him feel uncomfortable. Since, in addition, setting in train the apparently interminable process of becoming a Jew, he liked them even less: accusatory reminders that, the way some people did their sums, God came out, not one, but three.

Probably some old bag giving the brasses a rub up.

Just the same, concern won out, as it was bound to. The detective pushed open the wooden gate splotched with lichen, went up the path and into the church.

It was deliciously cool after the inferno outside, but with the damp coolness of a cellar, smelling of fermentation. Its small, high windows were embedded deep in the plastered walls like arrow slits, the sturdy pillars of the nave marching towards an oak table where a brass cross was set between bowls of roses that had seen better days. There was a stone font carved with a frieze of headless figures, a Victorian pulpit heavy with the weight of sermons, and rows of pews with seat-pads of a faded red and carved poppyheads at the ends.

In one of the pews Jane Coryton was down on her knees.

At sight of her, Jurnet came to an abrupt halt, grateful for his noiseless shoes. Before he could beat a retreat, the woman raised her head and inquired pleasantly, her voice resonating between the high, narrow walls: 'How on earth did you guess I was here?'

She rose unhurriedly, sat back on the pew bench, smoothing her striped cotton skirt.

'Do sit down,' she invited, as one making comfortable a guest in her own sitting room. 'I've been wondering when you'd get round to us.'

'I'm sorry if I interrupted your praying.'

'You didn't,' she answered smilingly. 'I don't. Pray, that is. I believe in God.' Observing the detective's look of bewilderment, she added kindly, but in the slightly impatient way of one explaining the obvious: 'Believing in Him, naturally I believe He knows best. To plead for something He hasn't seen fit to bestow unasked would be a kind of blasphemy.'

'But – forgive me – you were down on your knees –'

'So I was.' The smile broadened. 'Women do tend to make a habit of it, don't they? If they're not scrubbing the floor, they're looking for the needle they dropped on the carpet, or even assuming one of the less dignified positions for performing the act of love. What I was doing just now, if you want to know, was thinking about Chad Shelden. I suppose you still haven't found out who killed him?'

'Early days.'

'Not really.' The woman shook her head, her eyes troubled. 'Early for you, perhaps. Late for us, the Bullen people, looking each other up and down and wondering which of us has it in him – or her – to end a human life.' Then: 'Elena did give you the key?'

'The one to the fateful drawer with the Anne Boleyn letters?' Jurnet nodded. 'I don't mind admitting I took a look. Put me properly in my place. Could just as well have been Chinese for all the sense I could make of them.'

'You have to get your eye in to read Tudor handwriting. After that, it's easier than most of the scrawls that go by the name of letters nowadays.' Jane Coryton hesitated, then went on, a little tentatively: 'Did Elena also let you know that Francis has quite genuinely come to the conclusion he isn't the right person to do the book?'

'She said you'd persuaded your husband in bed that same night it wasn't for him.'

Mrs Coryton laughed.

'I did it in the car on the way home. Otherwise it would have had to wait till morning. All that excitement, I couldn't wait to get upstairs and get my head down. I was out like a light the minute it touched the pillow.'

'And Mr Coryton the same, I don't doubt.'

'We were both flaked out. It was all he could do to take the dog out before turning in.'

'And were you awake when he came back?'

Jane Coryton stood up.

'This really won't do,' she said crisply. 'You're trying to get me to incriminate my husband.'

Jurnet protested: 'All I did was ask a straightforward question which could be answered yes or no.'

'So you did.' The woman's habitual good humour returned, only modulated to a minor key. She put a hand across her eyes, and rubbed them, as if they troubled her. 'You need to know all about us, don't you? Which is difficult, because we don't begin to know ourselves.'

She showed Jurnet over the church, much as Percy Toller had shown him over the bungalow, with as much pride, but less hyperbole. She explained that she was a churchwarden, which also explained her presence in the place. They had to keep the church locked for fear of vandals, but she had a key and could come and go as she pleased. She took him into a side chapel he had not noticed, crowded with tombs of bygone Appleyards.

'Luckily for the village, they buried George Bullen in the Tower, under the altar of St Peter-ad-Vincula. Three days later they prised up the stones again, and shoved Anne Boleyn down beside him. Did you know there's a story that Henry was so wild with the two of them he had them crammed into an old arrow chest, body to body and the two heads pressed together in a kiss? Sick, wasn't it, if it was true – but I don't find it horrible, do you? Just very sad.' Mrs Coryton considered for a moment, then resumed brightly: 'Well! Can you imagine, if they'd brought them back here! The coaches ploughing up the lane, the litter on the green –'

Jurnet asked: 'What about Appleyard of Hungary? Isn't he in here with this lot?'

'In his will, bless him, he left instructions that he was to be cremated and the ashes strewn from the roof of Bullen Hall. All that's here is a plaque Elena had put up. Not enough, thank heaven, to be worth going out of your way for.'

The tablet, gold letters on black marble, stated merely:

To the undying memory of Lazlo Appleyard
Appleyard of Hungary
A Hero of our Time
1926–1973

Jane Coryton said: 'Francis and I hadn't come to Bullen then, of course, but, from all I've heard, the funeral rites were quite hairy. Elena went up on the roof to scatter the ashes, and, being her, I don't suppose she'd ever noticed that the wind sometimes blows from one direction, sometimes from another. Anyway, she opened the box containing the ashes facing the way the wind was blowing from. Instead of drifting away over the grounds, which was the whole idea, they blew back against her, plastering her from head to foot. Mr Benby, who was there, says she screamed. Elena screaming – can you imagine! He says he scraped as much of the ash off her clothes as he could, back into the box, and tipped it over the balustrade, but he didn't like to touch her face, of course, and she just stood there screaming, her face, her lips and eyelashes, grey with ash.'

'It must have been a harrowing experience.' Jurnet stood looking at the memorial plaque. 'I wonder who she'll get to write his life now.'

'The time she took to fix on Mr Shelden, Francis doesn't think it'll ever get done in her lifetime, even if she lives to be a hundred.'

'So that if Shelden was killed to stop it being written, the murderer's pulled it off.'

'For all he knew, she could have gone out the very next day and brought home a new writer to do the job. How could he ever be sure?'

Jurnet pointed out without drama: 'Mr Coryton appears to have been, for one.'

'There you go again!' Mrs Coryton protested angrily. 'Laz Appleyard had been dead for nearly two years before we came to Bullen. How can it possibly matter to us whether somebody does or doesn't write his life story? Francis must be right when he says the reason he hasn't heard from you yet is, you're doing it to make him sweat.'

'We're all of us sweating, this weather. Not to say touchy. All I'm saying, with respect, is, your husband's so certain Miss

Appleyard's not going to make up her mind in a hurry, other interested parties could be equally certain. On the other hand, if they're wrong, and she does come up with a substitute for Shelden, who's to say the new boy won't end up in the moat like him?'

Mrs Coryton asserted calmly: 'You'll never know till you try it out, will you? What you ought to do is get Elena to hire someone – anyone – and then stake him out on the Hall roof like a goat to catch a tiger.'

The detective laughed.

'Not a bad idea, except I doubt we'd find a goat willing to cooperate. From what I hear of them, writers are a nervous lot.'

'More heads off,' Jane Coryton said, in front of the font. 'It must be something in the Norfolk air.'

'What are they – saints?' Jurnet asked, taking in the mutilated figures with a certain feeling of commiseration for a God who couldn't even cope with dilapidations on his own premises.

'They're supposed to represent the Seven Sacraments – baptism, confirmation, the Eucharist, matrimony, extreme unction – that's five, isn't it? I can't think of the other two.' Mrs Coryton bent over the wide rim of the empty basin and dabbled both hands inside, an invisible swishing of holy water. 'As if a child – or anybody else brought for the first time into the fellowship of Our Lord, needs any other sacrament than the sacrament of love.'

Jurnet said with careful calculation: 'I reckon Mr Winter's one to go along with that.' The detective was not unprepared for the head uplifted in sudden alarm. The tears momentarily brightening the bright eyes were more of a surprise. 'Except, when it comes to love, some might say he's got a funny way of showing it.'

'You can't possibly think Charles had anything to do with –' Mrs Coryton broke off and began afresh, with more attention to her own words. 'I don't have to tell you he drinks too much – you saw that for yourself – and he's a terrible tease. But underneath he's a gentle, loving person who just happens to find life more than he bargained for.'

'Don't we all? At least he's lucky to have a pal like you to give him a reference.'

'He's a genius.'

'Is that why you make yourself so responsible for him?'

'It's part of it.' The woman looked at the detective in her forthright way; with appraisal, and finally – or so it seemed – a deliberate decision to trust. 'You're a bit of a tease yourself, Inspector, if it comes to that. I think you know quite well what I feel about Charles Winter.'

'Not really,' Jurnet answered, with truth. 'After all, the man's a queer.'

'Isn't it lucky for me? No temptation, no danger. Fifty-two, and still feeling the fire in the belly! Isn't it ridiculous?' The light half-mockery did not quite cancel out a tremor in the voice. 'Not that I wouldn't elope with him tomorrow, if only I had the chance, and anyone eloped any more. Though, having said that, who knows? If the impossible happened, and Charles started chasing me instead of the other way round, I might equally run away, screaming blue murder.'

'Run, perhaps. Not scream.'

The other nodded gratefully.

'Not scream. Not even if they cremated him and the ashes blew all over my face. D'you know what I'd do if that happened? I'd put out my tongue and lick them off. Eat him the way I partake of Christ's body at the Communion table. Does that disgust you? It oughtn't to – I saw your face when you spoke to me about your girl in Greece. You know what love is.'

Jurnet said: 'I got the impression you and Mr Coryton had a good marriage.'

'Oh, we do! We have what I believe people today call a caring relationship. But love's a many-sided thing, Inspector Jurnet. Loving Charles doesn't imply unfaithfulness to Francis. In a way, it isn't even sexual.' Jane Coryton put her hand out to the font; touched with a delicate sympathy one of the maimed sculptures at the point where the neck had been broken off. 'Charles is not only the lover I've never had. He's the child I've never borne, and never will.'

'A cruel, vicious child.'

'What do you mean?' The woman's eyes flashed an angry denial. 'You don't know what you're saying. Charles wouldn't hurt a fly.'

127

'He's certainly hurt young Botley.'

'Charles! You're joking!'

'I can see you haven't paid a visit to the Coachyard these past few days.'

'What do you mean?'

'Because, if you had, you'd have seen young Botley with two black eyes, a split lip, his head in bandages – and that's only reporting on what's visible to the naked eye. If Botley had been prepared to make a complaint I'd have had your gentle genius down at the station before he knew what hit him. And it wasn't the first time, either.'

Jane Coryton countered fiercely: 'Now I know you're joking!'

'He admitted as much to me himself. Not to put too fine a point on it, Mr Winter's a ruddy sadist.'

'If you only knew how ridiculous you sound! Next, I suppose, you'll be telling me he killed Chad Shelden.'

'No. Only that he could have. If you feel the need to check up on what I've said, I'm going back to the Hall. I could give you a lift.'

'No, thank you!'

For a moment, face flushed, breasts heaving, the woman confronted the detective. She didn't look fifty-two, thought Jurnet, who wouldn't have minded seeing Miriam get as angry on his behalf. As he watched, she took a deep breath, regained control of herself.

'I'm sorry. I know you're only doing your job. It's not your fault you have to come out with such nonsense.'

'Do you want that lift?'

'I don't think so, thank you.'

'Ah. Take the back way, do you?'

'No.' Surprised. 'It's terribly overgrown. Nobody uses it any more except the woodcutters, and riders going to the forge, or cutting through to the bridle path.' With a sudden tilt of the head she challenged: 'Was that another of your trap questions?'

'There aren't any such things. Questions don't trap. Only lying answers.' When she made no further observation he said: 'I'll be getting along, then.'

She moved away, without speaking; down the centre aisle

and into one of the pews. Jurnet was almost at the door when she called to him; and turned to find her regarding him almost with affection across the intervening space.

'Would you like me to tell you what I was thinking just now, down on my knees, when you came in?'

'If it's relevant.'

'Oh, it's that!' She clasped her hands together as if each took comfort from the other. 'I was thinking that at the very moment of death – even a violent death like Mr Shelden's, full of fear and terror – there must be a sudden piercing of joy, a sense of being on the point of regaining something one has been looking for ever since the moment one came unconsulted into the world.'

Jurnet commented, but not as if he would have bet any money on it: 'Let's hope you're right.'

With what sounded like pity in her voice, the woman said: 'I don't think you're a religious man, Inspector.'

'That's right,' he answered, feeling vaguely affronted.

20

Sergeant Ellers sat on a bench in front of the house, examining the big toe of his right foot with a tender concentration. When he saw the police car turn into the driveway he drew on his sock, levered the foot painfully into its shoe, and hobbled across to greet his superior officer.

'What happened to you?' Jurnet asked unfeelingly. The detective released his seat belt, slid out of the car and locked the door. 'Somebody tread on your toe?'

The little Welshman looked hurt.

'Next time you send me out unarmed into darkest Norfolk, remind me to make my will first, will you? What with being dive-bombed by mosquitoes, mugged by stinging nettles, and bogged down in cowpats the size of manhole covers, I'm lucky to be here to tell the tale.'

'Glad to hear you had a pleasant stroll. How far, d'you reckon? Mile? Mile and a half?'

'Somewhere between the two. Felt more like twenty. Tell you one thing, though. Nobody's going round by that way for choice, long as there's a road.'

'Unless he wants to make sure nobody sees him.'

'Never get up it in a car, that's for sure. Even a tractor'd think twice. About two-thirds of the way along, on the left, there's a track that goes off through the woods. That's the one bit that looks navigable. The main highway – if you can call it that, which you can't – ends in a paved yard and a lot of outbuildings, and there's that foreign fellow – the one with the eyebrows – shoeing a horse. If he hadn't bared his ruddy great teeth at me – the horse, I mean, not the eyebrows – I'd have asked him to do the same for me.'

'Hm.' With his eyes on the house, Jurnet digested what he had just heard – or rather, allowed it to seep without conscious thought into that makeshift reservoir where random droplets of information accumulated like water draining off a roof into a cistern. One day, with luck, there'd be enough of the stuff to be useful.

In the brilliant light of late afternoon it seemed to the detective that he could count every single brick of the great south front of Bullen Hall, had he a mind to. The stone mullions round the windows shone white, the glass reflected patterns of cloud polished to as high a shine as the goblets set out on the sideboards within. Thistledown drifted down the air, and motes of dust that might, or might not, be all that was left of Appleyard of Hungary. Beyond the stone bridge that crossed the moat the shadowy courtyard hinted at mysteries.

A plaything, an outsize toy. Come time for bed, every one of those bricks must be put back in their box ready for another day's play. How Nanny would carry on if she found some of them still strewing the nursery floor after lights out!

Jurnet came out of his reverie and started across the gravel. Behind him, Sergeant Ellers was still limping. Contrite, Jurnet waited.

'First Aid box in the car, Sergeant.'

The little Welshman grinned.

'Only doing it to make you feel bad.'

In perfect amity the two moved towards the west wing of Bullen Hall.

Jack Ellers asked: 'What's next on the list?'
'We're going to ask Rapunzel to let down her hair.'

The elderly maid with the crustacean corset was not pleased to see them, and took no trouble to disguise it.

'Madam is engaged.'

'We'll wait,' Jurnet returned. 'Please let Madam know we're here.'

'Can't do that. And I'm sure I can't say how long she'll be.'

'Then we'll just have to wait and find out, won't we?'

She showed them into a small room off the hall, and went away with an ill-tempered flounce of sateen, and a long, meaningful look round, as if making a mental note of the whereabouts of anything which might be worth pinching. Since the room was as bare of ornament as the rest of Elena Appleyard's apartment, it was a symbolic gesture merely.

Jurnet sauntered over to the window, pushed the casement open, and stood looking down at the moat immediately below. In shadow, the water looked impenetrable, black with a glaze of grey-green, like mould on old jam.

The detective made a face.

'You'd never get me living in a house with a moat.'

'Not to worry,' Ellers returned reassuringly. 'Who ever heard of a moated semi?' He joined the other at the window. 'I suppose, in the old days, they needed them for protection.'

'Pongs a bit.' Jurnet wrinkled his nose and shut the window. 'Now they've got us instead, eh? Police force, the modern moat. Not much cop at stopping you getting yourself pushed off the roof, but smells a whole lot sweeter.' He padded about the room a little, then demanded of nobody in particular: 'Who's she got in there, for Christ's sake, she can't be disturbed?'

They were soon to know. At the end of the corridor a door burst open. A man's voice shouted: 'Might have known I'd be wasting my time!' Angry steps stumped along the oak floor. Then the same voice again, nearer. 'All I'll say is, you've had your chance. From now on I'll deal with this my own way, and to hell with the lot of you!'

Jurnet opened the door of their anteroom, just in time to find himself face to face with a square, tweed-suited man with an ancient tweed hat rammed down over grizzled hair, a nicotine-stained moustache, and a complexion whose probably natural floridness appeared enhanced well beyond danger point.

The man raised the heavy blackthorn stick he was carrying, and pointed it menacingly at the detective.

'And who the hell are you?' he demanded.

Without waiting for a reply or slackening his pace, he pushed past to the front door: wrenched it open, and would doubtless have banged it shut after him, had not the maid, corset creaking, materialised from somewhere and gained command of the big brass knob without apparent effort.

She said, in the neutral voice of the well-trained domestic: 'Good afternoon, sir.'

Whence, then, did Jurnet get the strong impression that the woman's voice was full of a triumphant, derisive mirth?

'And to hell with you too!' cried the visitor, disappearing from view as the door shut behind him.

The woman came back into the room, so dour, so poker-faced, that it was unthinkable she could ever have been anything else.

'Miss Appleyard will see you now.'

'Well, Inspector –'

There was no heightening of Miss Appleyard's colour. The explosive departure of her recent caller appeared not to have disturbed one whit of that sequestered calm which was itself the most disturbing thing about her. As always – or so it seemed to Jurnet – an invisible sheet of glass interposed itself between her and the rest of the world.

The detective introduced Sergeant Ellers, who bent over her proffered hand in a way that would have had the boys back at Headquarters falling about, except that they would have done exactly the same themselves, given the chance.

'Ah,' she remarked, when, her two visitors accommodated in the strange deckchair-like seats which were so seductively comfortable, she saw the little Welshman take out his note-book, 'my words are to be taken down and may be used in evidence, is that it?'

'Nothing like that,' Jurnet assured her. 'It's purely a matter of getting one or two things straight so that we can go on from there.'

'I can't say I'm conscious of having anything useful to add to what I've already told you; but naturally, if there *is* anything –' She broke off and regarded the detective with a cool, yet somehow secret, amusement. 'Aren't you both bursting with curiosity to know the meaning of Mr Chalgrove's extraordinary behaviour just now?'

'That wasn't Miss Jessica's father?'

'It was. Richard – though, judging from what you've just witnessed, you may find it hard to believe – is an old and dear friend of the family. When he and my brother were boys together, they were quite inseparable.'

Jurnet suggested: 'An English version of Mr Szanto.'

'Ferenc has been talking to you about Kasnovar.' Miss Appleyard considered this intelligence before appearing to decide there was no harm in it. 'I suppose he was – taking into account, of course, the difference in social background. Even in those childhood days my brother was a natural leader. Wherever he happened to be – Bullen or Hungary – there were always children to follow him about like the pied piper – into mischief, more often than not, I'm bound to say.' She touched her hair in a gesture that, in any other woman, Jurnet would have called coquettish. 'Poor Richard. He's so behind the times. He's furious with me because I've given Jessica a job. He thinks it – demeaning. He can't forget his ancestors came over with the Conqueror.'

'Poor Jessica, I should have thought.'

'Would you really?' The woman's wide-spaced eyes examined the detective's face unhurriedly. To his chagrin he reddened under the inspection. 'Jessica loves and is loved by a young man who is good-natured, handsome, moderately intelligent, and will, one day, be comparatively well-to-do. I can't honestly feel her to be in need of pity.'

'I meant, as regards her father's attitude to her working. The anger – threats, you might say – it all sounded a bit excessive in the context.'

'It must have – to an outsider who doesn't know what the context is. Whenever Richard sees me – which is seldom enough these days – he never seems able to restrain his anger for long. The fact is – it's too foolish, almost, to speak about – he's an old suitor who has never forgiven me for turning him down.

Jessica is merely one more excuse for punishing me for the blow to his self-esteem. Quite absurd! After all, until comparatively recently, he hardly ever saw the child. Her mother, as you may not know, died giving birth to her, and Richard handed her over to his sister in Gloucestershire, an appalling woman.'

'Did Mr Chalgrove never remarry, then?'

'Richard? Oh no, never!' The idea appeared to amuse Miss Appleyard. Her youthful laughter tinkled dismayingly. 'After Carla died his old nanny came back to look after him. He's always been her Master Dickie who can do no wrong. It's only because she's grown too frail to cope that he's finally brought Jessica back to live at the Manor, to carry on where Nanny left off. So, Inspector –' Elena Appleyard crossed her lovely legs with that hint of effort Jurnet found so poignant, and looked at the detective with calm anticipation – 'now I've reassured you that Mr Chalgrove's childish tantrums are nothing to do with the death of Mr Shelden, perhaps we can get on to those "one or two things" which still appear to be troubling you.'

'Right!' Jurnet marshalled his thoughts with some difficulty, wondering if Elena Appleyard had the same effect on other people she had on him. 'About Mr Shelden – could you tell me this? If he *had* lived to write his biography of your brother, and, when you read the manuscript through, you found out it said some very nasty things about Appleyard of Hungary, would you have made him take them out?'

Miss Appleyard responded frostily: 'That would be a very vulgar thing to do. Believe me, Inspector, I'm as well aware of my late brother's weaknesses as of his virtues; and I know which outweighs the other. My arrangement with Mr Shelden was for a biography which would portray Laz Appleyard as he was. As to what that was, I'm quite content to let history decide.'

A little overawed by her majestic certainty, Jurnet nevertheless persisted.

'But suppose you came upon something for the first time, something you'd never even dreamed of? Something which might alter the whole picture you yourself have formed of the man? What then?'

Miss Appleyard thought for a moment, her gaze intent on her elegant sandals, bands of navy and white leather that complemented her simple dress of navy linen with a touch of white braid at the neckline. Her face, when she looked up, was young and mischievous, divested of the years.

Jurnet thought, *the woman's a witch!*

Elena Appleyard decided: 'It has to be something that happened in Hungary – something written in Hungarian, and never translated. I've been through all the papers in English. I know the best – and the worst – about my brother. Or so I've thought. Ferenc has been talking to you,' she said again. 'Whatever could Laz have been up to?'

'You could always ask Mr Szanto.'

'So I could!' The window between herself and the world came down again, a little of the mischief trapped on Jurnet's side of the glass. 'I've often suspected the Hungarian material might well contain what the newspapers' – a delicate curl of the lip – 'like to call revelations. But it must surely have occurred to you, Inspector, that if I *had* been concerned to doctor the record, it would have been far less trouble to remove and destroy the tell-tale evidence than to remove and destroy Mr Shelden.'

'I couldn't agree more,' Jurnet said. 'Here's another of those little things. As I recall, you told me you took your little walk in the grounds at about 3.30 a.m.'

'I did.'

'Are you quite sure of the time? Could it possibly have been half an hour earlier – say three o'clock?'

'It could not. The clock in the hall chimed for 3.30 as I unbolted the door, and it is an exceptionally reliable timepiece.'

'Right. Next question. Were you still wearing the dress you wore at the party?'

'No.' The woman expressed no surprise at being asked. 'I had undressed and put on a housecoat.'

'Could you please describe it?'

At that, she rose with the stiff grace which was her unique characteristic, crossed the room to the marble fireplace and pulled a bell-pull at the side. When the maid appeared, pointedly ignoring the presence of the two police officers, her mistress ordered: 'Maudie, my housecoat – the Liberty's one. These gentlemen wish to look at it.'

From the time it took to fetch, Jurnet reflected, it might have been stored in some closet three courtyards away instead of, presumably, in Miss Appleyard's wardrobe, somewhere close at hand. When it finally arrived, it was worth waiting for. Even Maudie, the iron maiden, handled the cloth with something approaching tenderness, spreading the garment out on a chair where it lay in lovely folds of peacock and plum touched with light. The billowing sleeves and the square, low-cut neck could have come straight out of one of the Tudor portraits on Bullen Hall walls.

'Was your hair up or down?'

This time Elena Appleyard commented lightly: 'What a very odd thing to ask! My hair was down.' She raised her arms to the back of her neck, plucked out a pin or two, and her hair, heavy and lustrous, fell about her shoulders. 'Like this.'

'Thank you,' Jurnet said, shaken. The woman's beauty was almost beyond bearing. 'The reason I ask is that we've had some reports of a woman with long hair seen crossing in front of the Hall at about 3 a.m.'

'Oh,' she returned comfortably, 'is that what all this is in aid of? That would have been Anne Boleyn.'

'You don't really believe that.'

'Don't I?' Elena Appleyard considered. 'She does it most nights when there's a moon, so why should she leave out that particular one?'

'I meant, a person of your intelligence. You can't possibly believe in ghosts.'

'Of course I don't!' she agreed, with more animation than was usual with her. 'Anne Boleyn, I said. In the flesh: not some ridiculous apparition.'

Jurnet exclaimed: 'Anne Boleyn's been dead for four hundred years!'

'Time –' Elena Appleyard enunciated the word with a certain weariness, as though the detective had dropped a clanger to be expected of the lower orders. 'Do you really believe the past arranges itself for our convenience into those paltry little squares they print on calendars?'

At risk of confirming her poor opinion of him, Jurnet maintained robustly: 'All I know is, if Anne Boleyn's still around, she's getting on a bit.'

The other shook her head pityingly.

'Neither older nor younger than the words you've just spoken about her. Can you bring *them* back again, any more than you

136

can her? Of course you can't. They're gone, Inspector, like everything else, into that great, timeless catch-all we call the past, and which is the only reality. The future, after all, is only a dream, the present no more than a punctuation point. Which is why –' the woman tilted her head to one side, pulling a lock of her hair over her shoulder and stroking it in long, sensuous strokes as if it were a cat, a Persian or Siamese, expensive, of ancient pedigree. 'I think it could quite likely have been Anne Boleyn herself who was seen crossing the grass.'

Jurnet said acidly: 'We're going to have our work cut out getting *her* to make a statement!'

'Quite likely, I said. But on the whole, on that particular night, at that particular time, probably not.' Miss Appleyard went to the escritoire which was the only sizeable piece of furniture in the room, opened a drawer, and took something out. 'I can hardly think Anne Boleyn would have been wearing this.'

She came back and opened her hand. On her palm lay an earring, chastely beautiful, vaguely Egyptian, wholly Anna March. Twin to the one Jurnet already carried in his pocket.

'Where did you find this?'

'Chad Shelden was holding it in his hand.'

'Why are you only just telling me?'

'You could call it womanly solidarity.' Miss Appleyard's tone was lightly mocking.

'Then why are you telling me now?'

The mockery deepened.

'You have me worried, Inspector.'

21

The grass outside the west wing door was white with index cards in place of the usual daisies. PC Bly, down on his knees with a half-filled metal box at his side, sat back on his heels and wiped his hot face. Down by the moat, PC Hinchley was using a spring rake to manoeuvre to shore a number of cards which had landed in the water beyond arm's reach. As the two detectives drew near, as yet unperceived by the card gatherers, the flat door opened and Sergeant Bowles appeared, a portly figure bearing a handsome silver tray which he set down on the ground.

'Spread the wet ones out on this,' he said to PC Hinchley. 'I've put a good pad of blotting paper under.'

'What's this, Jeeves?' Jurnet demanded, as he crossed the little footbridge, Sergeant Ellers close behind. 'No gin and tonic?' Looking about him: 'I take it you've had a visit from Daddy.'

'Know about him, do you, sir? Her own father! Can you credit it? Bellowing like a bull and telling her to stop what she's doing, they're going home. Calls her a few choice names along of it, I can tell you! And when she tells him – upset, but cool as a cucumber, you couldn't help admiring her – that she won't go with him, then or ever, what does he do but grab all those cards she's been writing out so careful, and chuck the lot out of the window.'

'Wonder you let him in, in the first place.'

Sergeant Bowles looked hurt.

'Said he was her father – what else could I do? Spoke quite civil; and when I took him through into the study, Miss Jessica looked up and said "Oh, hello, Father," quite normal. So I went back to the other room, not wanting to intrude. I only came back when I heard the shouting, and by then the damage was done. He pushed past me and down the stairs like a blind man, couldn't see where he was going. Blinded by rage.' The good man looked at Jurnet in some distress. 'Hit her too, the bastard. Jessica says he never, but she's got a whopping red mark on her cheek, weren't there five minutes before. Why she'd want to protect him after some of the things he called her is more 'n I can make out. But there! I always say there's nothing so peculiar as families.'

The study was very quiet when Jurnet came through the door in his quiet shoes: filled with the ripeness of the westering sun. Jessica Chalgrove sat at her desk, her head bent over a card which she was filling in with a childlike care for the formation of every letter. Her ponytail hung down over one shoulder, leaving the long nape of her neck exposed.

The detective repressed an impulse to bend over and kiss the knobs of vertebrae poking up the thin skin. Not a sexual act: more a loving acknowledgement of the girl's youth and vulnerability.

And not all that vulnerable either. Suddenly aware that she was no longer alone, Jessica swung round in her chair; and the detective saw that, along with the evident signs of distress, the girl still managed to look triumphant. She wore the bruise on her cheek as if it were a military decoration.

'I did try to love him,' she began at once, with a directness that delighted Jurnet, who was only too wearisomely accustomed, as part of his job, to having to ask questions to which he already knew the answers. 'I kept on telling myself how awful it must have been, losing his wife when I was born. I thought that perhaps he blamed me for her death – I've read that does happen – but then I thought, if that's the case, he really ought to blame himself even more, shouldn't he, for getting her pregnant in the first place.' She paused, inviting some confirmation of her thesis. When none was forthcoming, she added, with a touch of defiance: 'I just don't think it's possible, that's all, to love someone who doesn't love you.'

Jurnet said: 'It's possible.'

She was quick. She said: 'Oh, I don't mean that kind of loving. I mean fathers and mothers and children. Sometimes I tell myself that my mother would have loved me very much if she'd lived. But I don't know, really.'

Jurnet said: 'She'd have loved you.'

Jessica Chalgrove burst out laughing.

'How nice you are! And Sergeant Bowles, and those constables outside picking up all those wretched cards. Nobody ever told me how nice policemen were! But you don't have to say things like that to make me feel better, because I feel absolutely fine, I really do. In a funny sort of way –' the vivid young face went rosy with satisfaction – 'I'm even glad. No more pretending – not to other people, not to myself. My father's a hateful man. There! I've said it, and it's such a relief, you've no idea! All that fuss about my working! You'd think we were still living in the Dark Ages. And even there, it was one thing one day, something else the next. Only this spring he was all for my taking a secretarial course in London; and when I said I'd never be clever enough to be a secretary, he sent away for some bumph about cordon bleu cookery in Eastbourne. Yet here he is, creating over what's only a temporary job anyway. Sometimes –' her mood quieting – 'I wonder how my mother could ever have loved him. But perhaps he was different when he was young. And anyway, people do sometimes fall in love with people who aren't worth it, don't they?'

'Yes.'

After a moment Jurnet added, disingenuously: 'If you meant what you said about not going back to your father's place, you'll have to find somewhere to live.'

'I *have* somewhere to live. I shall move in with Steve over the stable.' The girl looked a little anxiously to see how the detective would take this. 'Are you shocked?'

'Take a bit more than that to shock a copper. Will you be getting married?'

'One day, I expect.' Jessica Chalgrove dismissed the subject as of small importance. 'Oh, I suppose if I got pregnant –'

'You realise that you'll be making your father even angrier than he is already? Or is that the idea?'

'A little, perhaps.' The girl dimpled. 'No, not really. I couldn't care less what he thinks.' She jumped up from her chair and moved about the room in an impromptu dance, her skirt of flowered cotton swirling about her long legs, her arms hugging her ribs in a way that seemed special to her, at once a homage and a gesture of loving protectiveness to her splendid young body. It was the first time Jurnet had seen her in something other than jeans and a T-shirt. She looked like a child pretending to be a woman. A passionate child.

She came to a stop, and exclaimed: 'I'm so happy. Isn't it awful? – I mean, after what's just happened, and Mr Shelden getting murdered, and all the bad things there are, going on in the world. But really, it just takes over. It could just as well be mumps or chicken pox for all the say you have about it.' She whirled away across the room, singing out in a voice of excruciating refinement: 'So sorry I can't come to tea today, Mrs Fortescue-Fortescue. I have happiness. It may be catching.' She danced a little jig and desisted once more to inquire: 'Do you like dancing?' Kindly: 'You're still young enough. Steve dances like a herd of elephants trampling down the jungle. Last

140

summer, when we had the pageant, I was one of Anne Boleyn's ladies in a gown of crimson velvet, and Steve was a courtier in doublet and hose and a cap with some of the peacock's feathers stuck in it. We danced a stately pavane – like this –' the young body swayed in a grave and noble curve – 'that is, until Steve tripped over my dress and fell flat on his face.' The girl whirled away again, her eyes shining. 'We brought the house down.'

Jurnet said: 'I can imagine. I didn't know about the pageant. Who –' he asked offhandedly – 'took the part of Anne Boleyn?'

'Mrs Coryton. She's a marvellous actress. Didn't you know?'

22

'Eels,' announced the Superintendent, leaning back in his chair and elongating the vowel sound so that the word became fish. 'The Chief's not at all pleased about the eels.'

On the other side of the wide desk, the three detectives looked at each other; Jurnet and Ellers with incomprehension, Dave Batterby – newly returned from London in a suit that must have set him back a bit – with an air of weary sophistication.

After a little, the Welshman, the court jester, ventured: 'We only found them in the moat, sir. We didn't actually put them there.'

'The Chief is well aware of that, Sergeant.' The use of the title was ominous, the Superintendent's crisp elegance at the end of a hot, wilting day somehow even more of a threat. 'Where you *did* put them, in the Chief's book, was all over the front page.' The Superintendent stretched out a hand and with a well-manicured fingernail tapped first one, then the other, of the two files which lay on the desk in front of him. One, the thicker of the two, contained Dr Colton's report: the second, a number of photographs of as much of Chad Shelden Deceased as the eels had left to pose for the police photographer. 'Unnecessary sensationalism, the Chief says. Pandering to the morbid interests of a public that ought to know better. Shelden died from the combined effects of a fall and drowning. The eels, the Chief says, are a complete irrelevance. To let them out to the media was unpardonable.'

'Only postponing the day, sir!' Jack Ellers protested. 'Bound to come out in court.'

'Where it couldn't be laid at your door, could it?' The Superintendent shook his head. 'You and Ben won't be supplying the medical evidence. That's Colton's business, and you know what he's like in the box. Dry as dust. By the time he gets through with a corpse it's a job to convince the court it wasn't a dummy out of a shop window to start with. No unhealthy titillation. No emotive reaction that's going to make it all the more difficult for the accused – assuming you lot eventually succeed in capturing one of that vanishing species – to get a fair trial.' The Superintendent looked directly at Jurnet. 'Has Detective-Inspector Jurnet nothing to contribute to the conversation?'

Jurnet answered mildly: 'Only, firstly, that the Chief Constable's got it wrong. It wasn't us, it was Mrs Barwell, the cleaning lady, who let the eels out of the bag. And that's to say nothing of Benby, the estate surveyor, and Bert Archer, the handyman, the two who dragged Shelden out of the water. Secondly –' and into the detective's voice had come an inflection which only the Superintendent – and perhaps Jack Ellers – would recognise: an acknowledgement that the two of them were at it again, one more skirmish in that war which was also, in a way Jurnet did not profess to understand, a declaration of love – 'I can't help noticing, sir, that you keep quoting the Chief Constable. May I ask if you hold the same views yourself?'

For a moment the room was silent; Ellers waiting quietly confident of the outcome: Batterby, the ambitious cop, not quite hiding his hope that at last Detective-Inspector Benjamin Jurnet had gone too far.

Then the Superintendent smiled, without irony or equivocation, almost.

'No, Ben, you may not ask. You know that I hold the Chief in the highest esteem.' The smile faded, the friendliness endured. 'But you can give Mrs Barwell my compliments when you next run into that lady, and tell her to keep up the good work. In my book, violent death is the ultimate insult, and, like justice, when it's done it has to be seen to be done, in all its unmitigated ghastliness, if that's the way it happened. If a few weirdoes get a kick out of reading all about it, too bad. If tender susceptibilities are hurt in the process, or if it frightens the kiddies, so much the better. That's the way the world is. I hold that it's never too early to learn that a human being foully down to death is more than a gambit in a guessing game.' The Superintendent got up from his chair and went towards a small table where a little pile of chastely jacketed books awaited his attention. '*Rommel.*' He picked them up, one after the other. '*Jan Smuts. Cecil Rhodes. Bernadotte.* Significant, d'you think, the way he went for strong men?'

Dave Batterby said, too happy to be able to put his superior officer right to consider the risk inherent in doing so: 'Not *his* choice. Every one of them commissioned by the publishers. It's all in my report.'

'And a very remarkable report it is, too,' the Superintendent asserted, with a warmth that only a Jurnet might think suspect. 'I'm looking forward to Ben seeing it. Give him some very useful ideas, I don't doubt. According to Dave, Ben, there was more to Shelden than met the eye. Seems the greenery-yallery, Grosvenor gallery bit was all a front, merely putting on the persona expected of a writer, while privately he beavered away at his job like it might have been a grocer's assistant or a plumber.'

'Civil servant or stockbroker, more like it.' Batterby was clearly enjoying his position of man in the know. 'Nothing arty about his flat, even if it was in Hampstead. Word processor, micro computer, notes filed away in cabinets, bank statements and bills dealt with up to date. He had quite a portfolio of shares there –'

'Who gets his money?' Jurnet broke in. 'Do you know?'

'Neither his solicitor nor his bank know anything about a will. Young chap – probably never got round to making one. Unmarried. Mum and Dad killed in an air crash five years ago. No brothers or sisters or near relations. As of now, looks like the Treasury's in for a nice little windfall –'

'Girl friend?'

'Nothing much on, male or female, far as I can make out. In the time available, that's to say.' Adjusting his best sleuthing face, eager yet attentive, Batterby leaned forward in his seat and addressed the Superintendent. 'I take it, sir, you'll be wanting me to return to London to continue with my inquiries?'

'What do you think, Ben?' No mistaking the glint in the Superintendent's eye. 'Could the key to Shelden's death lie in London after all?'

Jurnet replied with all due gravity: 'Anything's possible, sir.'

'It is indeed. So, yes, Dave – we'll be sending you off on your travels again.' Surveying the detective with a benevolence so marked as to be positively alarming to one with eyes to see: 'Besides, how else are you going to find yourself a shirt to go with that suit?'

Jurnet put his hand into his pocket and brought out the earrings. He put them down on the desk, where they lay, the silver gleaming, the strange red stones cool and ambiguous.

'You'll be wanting to know about these,' he said.

Anna March had held her hand out for the earrings with a little cry of pleasure.

'Oh, good! You found them! Had they slipped down the back somewhere, then?'

Jurnet did not yield up the earrings. His fingers closed over them, pressing the red stones into his palm.

'Slipped down where?'

'In the bedroom, of course. It was so hot and they began to feel like a ton of coal. One ear even began to bleed a little. If I ever use that design again it'll have to be lighter altogether. Honestly, I thought, if I don't take them off, by the end of the evening I'm going to have lobes like those African women, hanging down to my navel.'

'So you took them off. What did you do with them?'

'Put them in my bag – that little evening bag of Chinese silk I –' The woman stopped abruptly. Her nose seemed to have become even sharper. 'What is this? Why are you asking me all these questions? You're interrogating me, Ben Jurnet. Are the earrings anything to do with Chad?' She stared at the detective's folded fingers as if they concealed a lethal weapon. 'You're not by any chance suggesting –'

Jurnet said: 'I'm simply trying to find out what happened.'

'I told you! I took them off in the bedroom when I went to powder my nose, and I put them into my evening bag.'

'Which you then carried about with you for the rest of the evening?'

'No. I left it in the bedroom, on the bed, among the coats and scarves. All I had in it besides was a comb and lipstick and a bit of change. There seemed no point in carrying it around. When I came back to fetch it, just before we left, I found the bag open and the earrings gone.'

'You never said anything.'

'What was I supposed to say, for Christ's sake? First off, I told myself I couldn't have shut it properly. The earrings must have fallen out, and they were on the bed somewhere. I looked as best I could, moving the coats and scrabbling under the bed in case they'd fallen to the floor. But nothing: and the trouble was that people were coming in and out all the time, so I couldn't take a really thorough look.'

'I'm sure if you'd told them you were missing your earrings they'd have been happy to help you look for them.'

Anna March's body jerked in exasperation.

'God, you're thick, Ben Jurnet! If I'd done that, and the earrings still hadn't turned up, don't you see what it would mean? That someone at the party had stolen them. Somebody who's part of this community where we all have to get along together, even if it kills us, otherwise it'd be bloody hell. What would you have me do? Run and tell you, so you could lock the door and not let anyone leave till you'd searched their bodily orifices?'

'You're a bloody cow, Anna,' Jurnet said, and felt better for it. '*And* dirty-minded. *And* unconvincing. I reckon there were at least six people from the caterers, maybe more. Outsiders. Nobody for whose feelings you needed to have such exquisite consideration.'

'I *did* think of them, if you want to know. But then I thought, you can't go flinging about accusations you can't prove. *You'd* have had something to say, wouldn't you, if I'd come to you and said it was one of the waitresses – just like that, with nothing to back it up. But, most of all –' and now, fleetingly, Jurnet caught a glimpse of the beauty which had possessed her on the night of the party – 'the way I felt that night, I thought, what's a pair of earrings when suddenly everything's come right for you as you never expected it to, even in your wildest dreams?' Anna March looked at the detective challengingly. 'Pity you didn't happen to come round when Danny was home. He'd have punched you in the nose, copper or no copper.'

'Maybe. Maybe not, once he heard that one of your earrings was found in Shelden's mattress, and the other was in his hand as he lay dying on the grass.'

The woman looked at him wide-eyed with horror, but also – Jurnet realised with a surge of aversion, the greater for having been so long repressed – with a certain odious self-satisfaction. 'You mean, it was Chad himself who took them?'

'As a souvenir of your one night of love?' Jurnet demanded coarsely. 'From what you've told me, it wasn't anything to write home about.'

Anna March said nothing for a moment. Then: 'Know something, Ben? When this is over, you and I aren't going to be friends any longer.'

'Who says we ever were? Only pretended, or maybe kidded ourselves, for Danny's sake.'

'You're just jealous because I married him.'

'Now I know you're crazy.'

The Superintendent asked: 'Do you believe Mrs March's story?'

'For the moment,' Jurnet answered carefully, 'I neither believe nor disbelieve. I just take note. I certainly don't set much store by her suggestion that Shelden himself might have taken the earrings. Bit of women's magazine sentimentality.'

'Keep it on the cards just the same. No use being high-minded. Sentimentality's what makes the world go round.' The Superintendent looked down at the earrings with an evident pleasure. 'The woman knows her job, I'll give her that. I take it the lab's had a go at them?'

'Yes, sir. Unfortunately, the one Miss Appleyard says she found, she left it on her dressing table when she came back from her stroll, where her old battleaxe of a maid found it in the morning before Madam woke up. Seeing it was dirty, she took it back to the kitchen and gave it a good rub up. That's her story, anyway. Either way, the lab didn't find a thing except silver polish.'

'What kind of dirty? Did she say?'

'Merely that it looked dull, and the little bit which goes through the ear was stained brown. She thought it might have been blood, but couldn't say for sure. That would fit in with what Mrs March says about one of them making her lobe bleed. The other earring had one of Shelden's prints, plus another, the lab says, too blurred to be any use. As you can see, being pressed under the mattress, it got coated with some of that marl they've got up there on the roof, which doesn't make things easier.'

The Superintendent observed tetchily: 'If things were easy, there'd be no need of coppers.' And to Batterby: 'Well, Dave – it's back to London at first light, then.' He opened a drawer, took out the detective's report with a care that brought a glow of pride to the cheek of its compiler, and handed the folder over to Jurnet as if it were something precious. The two exchanged looks, for once, of perfect complicity.

'Take this with you, Ben, and give it the attention it deserves.'

Trading was long over for the day when Jurnet and Ellers emerged from Police Headquarters on to the Market Place: the litter cleared, the wide plain a skeletal grid of empty stalls. Hard to believe that tomorrow the pyramids of oranges and apples would rise again, the cauliflowers stare moon-faced out of their green ruffs: T-shirts swinging in the breeze, budgerigars hopping from perch to perch, toasters and cassettes, Japanese watches and second-hand ginger beer bottles, all at once in a lifetime prices; and a rich mix of voices – Norfolk, Cockney, Brum, with cadenzas of the mysterious East – that spoke of buying and selling, hello and goodbye, but mostly of belonging, to that time, to that place.

As always, when he had occasion to cross Angleby Market Place, even in the melancholy of evening, Jurnet felt a great surge of love for his native city. It mingled with his love for Miriam, and intensified his loneliness and longing. Tomorrow, the market would be back, in all its aromatic variety.

He would still be alone.

'Rosie,' said Sergeant Ellers, as if he had guessed what the other was thinking, 'said I wasn't to come home unless I brought you back with me. She said I was to tell you it was

Chicken Marengo, your favourite, and if you say no she doesn't want to see neither of us ever again.'

'Give her my love and tell her I know she doesn't mean it.' Jurnet smiled at his colleague with affection and understanding. Rosie Ellers, plump, pretty and devoted, and the best cook in Angleby, was a woman in a million. 'You, I can understand. But how can she bear to cut me out of her life for ever?'

'That'll do, Valentino! Cost her a quid, anyway,' the little Welshman announced with satisfaction. 'Had a bet on it. I said you'd never accept, not with Miriam away *and* this bloody murder. One or the other, I said, but not both, not even if the menu was apple pie with sultanas – real live ones hot from the harem – coming out of the pastry doing the belly dance.' Voice charged with a concern that was comically paternal: 'You're not going to bed without anything?'

Without anyone's what you mean, thought Jurnet. Aloud, he said: 'Don't talk daft! Miriam filled up the fridge before she left, enough for an army.'

Too softhearted to nail the patent lie for what it was, Sergeant Ellers said nothing more until the two reached the roadside where they had parked their cars. There, he made one last try.

'Rosie 'll kill me.'

'That's OK with me, so long as she waits till we've finished over at Bullen Hall. One corpse at a time's as much as I can manage at my time of life.'

For lack of anything better to do he went to bed early; drew the curtains and lay in the dark outfacing the convulsive tic of the digital clock which Miriam, in the name of progress, had substituted for the dear old wind-up alarm he had been given as a twelfth birthday present. If this was the best modern technology could do, he didn't think much of it.

What was it Elena Appleyard had said? The future a dream, the present no more than a punctuation point: only the past was real. Anne Boleyn and George Bullen, Appleyard of Hungary and Chad Shelden – all dead by violence; past, and, according to that strange woman's strange way of reckoning, timeless, and therefore contemporary. Between waking and sleep, the clock winking at him with unremitting ferocity, Jurnet grew uncertain of where, who he was. It seemed to him that he had seen more than Chad Shelden chewed by eels: been present on

Tower Green when the Frenchman specially fetched from France had sliced off Anne Boleyn's head with his sword as neat and nice as a turnip, and when a more journeyman executioner had done for George Bullen with an axe. Surely he had watched Laz Appleyard diving through that opening in the sluice gate, and cried out a warning, too late, as the centre board fell on his neck.

Nearer to sleep, a great sadness overcame him – not for the past remembered, but for all the happy times he had forgotten. Nearer still, something else that had slipped his memory struggled upward towards the light, and sank back into unconsciousness.

Something about Shelden?

His life? His death? His –

Jurnet slept.

23

Francis Coryton exclaimed: 'At last!'

'Exactly what I was feeling myself,' Jurnet responded, deliberately misunderstanding. 'I knew the house was large – but not such a maze! Even the ghosts must get lost. One more wrong turn and you'd have had to send out the St Bernards.'

'Bad as that?' inquired Coryton, looking pleased. 'I used to have a little room off the front hall. Dreadful! Every little problem landed on my desk. So I decided to make myself scarce back here – and peace descended like the sweet dew from heaven. People find it such a fag to seek me out whenever something has to be done that they seldom bother. Which means, in practice, that I'm blessedly spared all those boring decisions which they are perfectly capable of taking for themselves, and I can sit here full of honour and mystery, doing absolutely nothing.'

'But now that there's no Mr Shelden to take over, you're going to have to take a few decisions, aren't you? All those things in that report you prepared for the trustees.'

Coryton sighed.

'Camel rides for the kiddies, etcetera?' He regarded the detective with a thoughtful amiability which seemed more an expression pasted on to his face than an intrinsic part of it. 'That all depends on you, doesn't it?'

'On me?'

'On whether or not you arrest me for Shelden's murder, of course.'

'Why should I be doing that?'

'Oh, come now, Inspector! Don't tell me my fifty-odd years of devouring whodunnits have been wasted. You saw with your own eyes, heard with your own ears, how the new and late and indifferently lamented curator of Bullen Hall snatched from my trembling hands my last chance of fame and fortune. Probably too, trained as you are to see what one can manage to hide from lesser mortals, you sensed the black hatred that flooded into my heart when he refused to make the Anne Boleyn correspondence available to me, its discoverer. I'm sure men have killed for less.'

Jurnet said mildly: 'On the other hand, Mrs Coryton assured me you'd got over your disappointment before you'd even got back home. She said you'd agreed with her – and Mr Shelden – that, all in all, it was a work of scholarship you weren't really up to.'

'Did Jane say that? Then no doubt she also told you that I took the dog out while she was getting herself to bed; and that she hadn't a clue what time I got back. Jane's enthusiasm for the truth knows no bounds.'

'Do I detect a note of sarcasm?'

'Perish the thought! Apprehension, perhaps. The truth should never be published without a health warning. But my dear wife was absolutely right. I *had* calmed down. I *had* come to realise how ludicrously unqualified I was for the task which, in a moment of hubris, I had thought myself capable of bringing to a successful conclusion. Where she was absolutely wrong was in assuming that recognising the truth made me *ipso facto* willing to accept it. On the contrary! The more I accepted my undoubted shortcomings the more I hated the man who had, so to speak, rubbed my nose in them. I took Lulu – that's our dog's name, by the way: spaniel with a dash of this, that, and the other – partly because she asked to go, and because, even if it's your

150

intention to hurry off and clobber somebody to death, it doesn't mean you necessarily want to come home afterwards to a pool of dog piss on the hall rug. But chiefly, it was to give myself an alibi. Who could imagine anything more innocent than an Englishman taking his dog for walkies?'

'So you did go back to the Hall?'

'Actually, no.' Francis Coryton's tone was apologetic. 'I recognise how annoying this must be for you, Inspector: having such a promising lead fizzle out – but there it is. Man proposes, dog disposes, even though I set out with the murder weapon actually in my hand. I must digress to tell you that Jane and I and Lulu have been looking recently at a television series about how to train your dog. I'm bound to say Lulu didn't seem to think much of it, but Jane and I thought it was terrific; and high time, as now at last seemed possible, to turn Lulu into a civilised member of society. So, as the programme advised, I bought a choke chain – only, unfortunately, Lulu took against it. Either we didn't follow the TV instructions properly, or Lulu didn't appreciate that being half-asphyxiated whenever she did something wrong was really for her own good. After a number of differences of opinion on the subject I'd given up even trying to get the damn thing on – but, as it turned out, the outlay on that chain wasn't all loss, because even though it didn't work on a dog, I thought it might work quite well on a human being. Even before the night of the party I'd often thought – in a purely hypothetical way, you understand – of using it on the bloody woman who did the television programmes.'

Francis Coryton broke off. The glasses became disconcertingly blank. Jurnet waited, making no comment.

Then the curator said, in a quite different voice: 'I am, Inspector, as you've no doubt perceived, a frivolous man. I tend to talk lightly of serious things. But now, I assure you, I speak seriously. I had genuinely forgotten about Jane's key to the curator's flat when I handed over the rest. Now, I had it in my pocket, the dog chain in my hand, and murder in my heart. Lulu ran ahead, snuffling in the hedge bottoms as the fancy took her. It was, as you will remember, a lovely night. I felt extraordinarily peaceful. It isn't often that I know unequivocally what I have to do, and the unaccustomed absence of doubt made me feel serene and purposeful. In the moonlight every leaf, every blade of grass, was astonishingly beautiful. The beech trees in that tongue of woodland which comes down to the lane about halfway along were powdered with a green iridescence. There were none of the usual night noises. It seemed to me that nature itself was holding itself in abeyance so as not to disturb my concentration on the task in hand. Even Lulu seemed to sense the unearthly enchantment – until, that is, we actually came abreast of the wood. Then, with a sudden outburst of hysterical barking that made even the moon wince, she made for the trees, disappearing from sight.'

Coryton shifted in his chair, clasped his strong, stubby fingers, and sat looking down at them.

'I could have left her,' he continued presently. 'Gone on with my murder. There was nothing to stop me. You notice the possessive "my"? Yes, in the brief interval since I had decided upon it, it had become very dear to me. It filled all my imaginings. Lulu would have come home sooner or later. Perhaps she had scented a rabbit or a badger – I don't know what set her off – only that the hideous noise advertised that she too had murder in her heart, and that if I continued on to Bullen Hall I should be no better than a stupid tyke who couldn't even learn manners from the television.'

The man took off his glasses, as if it had become important that the Detective-Inspector should see his eyes. In the event, they were grey and rather bulbous, revealing nothing of interest.

'Lulu came back presently. I don't think she'd caught anything. How could she hope to, the silly bitch, making all that noise? Anyway, there was no blood on her muzzle. She seemed suddenly tired and depressed, disoriented – just like myself. I got the choke chain on her without any difficulty and we went back home together.'

The curator picked up his glasses and hooked them over his ears.

'I opened the front door, let the dog in, came in myself, and turned to lock up. And what do you think? When I turned round again, there, in the middle of the hall rug, was a great big puddle, and Lulu looking up at me as if to say, hang it all, old cock, there have to be some compensations.' The glasses glinted with a sardonic glee. 'As for me, being house-trained, I went to the loo and pulled the chain.'

Jurnet said: 'There must be a lot of valuable stuff at Bullen Hall.'

Francis Coryton beamed his admiration of this new move.

'So I still haven't convinced you of my innocence! Ah well! It doesn't do, does it, to assume all policemen are, by definition, thick behind the ears?'

'Not for me to say.'

'Modest as well! I should have known you'd never overlook *that* line of country. Been helping myself over the years – is that the way your thoughts are running? An ivory here, a medieval enamel there, nothing big enough to be missed among all that *embarras de richesse*, but, added up, worth a king's ransom: – and suddenly, with the imminent arrival of a new curator, the day of reckoning is at hand! The inventory will be gone over, the discrepancies noted. I shall stammer and prevaricate, guilt written all over my face. Mr Shelden will have no alternative. The police must be called in – you yourself, Inspector, for all I know, arriving hotfoot with the manacles. How much simpler for all concerned, how much more economical of effort and public money, to push the new man off the roof and continue as if nothing had ever happened – at least until the next nosy parker shows up, by which time I shall either have arranged a credible fire in which the inventory will be destroyed – not so easy, that, with the accountants and the trustees each having copies, to say nothing of the volunteers, each with a list of what's on show in his or her particular territory; or else have successfully transferred my ill-gotten gains to some South American country which has no extradition treaty with the UK, where Jane and I can live out our twilight years indulging all the vices we've never been able to afford in our years as pillars of the Norfolk cultural establishment.'

Coryton opened a cupboard and brought out a number of loose-leaf books, bound in sumptuous red morocco.

'Jeno did us proud, didn't he? There's one of these for the furniture, one for paintings, one for silver, another for china, and so on. Christie's did them originally, when the Trust was set up, and we've been updating them ever since. There has to be a record and, of course, a valuation we can use as a basis for calculating insurance cover.' Smiling: 'Not that the Trust'll get back a penny if you find that I really have been making away with its property. We're only covered for fire. We couldn't possibly afford the premiums to cover theft. The best we've been able to do was fit the alarms your Crime Prevention Officer recommended, and hope for the best. And even those are only in the state rooms, not the wings.'

'And even those in the state rooms,' the detective pointed out with some grimness, 'were switched off on the night of the party.'

'But that,' the other protested, 'was on Elena's account! I knew she'd be wanting to come and go through the house, not go round outside. The police wouldn't have thanked me any more than she – you know how she hates fuss – if the alarms had gone off accidentally, and brought your cohorts at the gallop, all to no purpose.'

'Bad enough to have left them turned off while the party was on. You could at least have remembered to switch them back on after it was over.'

'I didn't forget. I had fully intended to tell Shelden the system should be turned back on, last thing, and show him where the master switch was. But after what happened I thought; "You're curator now. Look after your own bloody burglars!"'

'I see.' Jurnet thought for a moment. Then: 'Were there any plans for checking the inventory to coincide with the change of management?'

'Indeed there were. In Shelden's interest as well as my own. Not exactly coincide, mind you. Bullen isn't a holiday let where the incoming tenant can check with the landlord as soon as he arrives how many sheets and egg cups he's made himself responsible for. Took us best part of two weeks, one way and another. Elena, in her high-handed way, thought it all a waste of time, but old Cranthorpe, the other trustee, sent down a couple of his clerks, and we all mucked in. Oh, you don't have to worry –' chuckling at the detective's changed expression – 'the clerks did the actual checking. They were instructed to satisfy themselves that the item listed was actually in front of their eyes before making that all-important tick.' Ending with pride: 'The only thing unaccounted for was a brass weight off an Edwardian postal scale.'

'Not bad.'

'So we thought. A tribute, not just to ourselves, but to the type of person who comes to look round Bullen Hall.' Coryton continued: 'If you're going to say somebody could still have stolen something after the inventory was checked, you're quite right, of course. The possibility of theft is always present. But equally, if something *was* taken after the checking was over, it doesn't begin to fit in with murder. A thief would be particularly careful that nothing should disturb the even tenor of our ways. Without a murder to gum up the works, and provided he chose his loot with care, it could be years before anyone noticed anything was missing. With it – or even if Shelden's death was accepted as an accident – there was bound to be yet another check when yet another replacement curator arrived on the premises.'

Jurnet observed: 'You've been giving this a lot of thought.'

The glasses twinkled with some show of agitation as Coryton inquired, the note of anxiety in his voice not entirely humorous: 'I haven't gone and overdone it, have I? Given myself such a clean bill of health as to make it positively suspicious?' When no answer was forthcoming, he said, hesitating a little over the words: 'As we're on the subject of theft, there is perhaps one other thing I ought to mention. One of our volunteers at Bullen is – was – a thief. When he applied to become a helper he came to me and told me quite frankly that he had had a number of convictions, but that was all behind him: only he felt in justice to the Trust he ought to mention it. I liked him enormously. I still do, and I've no reason to fear that my trust in him was misplaced.'

'If you mean Percy Toller, Percy and I are old friends. Matter of fact, I had a few words with him in the Library on my way here. He was the one said I'd never find you without a guide – only, of course, he couldn't leave his post to show me the way.'

Percy Toller had, in fact, been standing in the Library, head to one side, studying the portrait of George Bullen, Lord Rochford. His absorption was such that he started in alarm when Jurnet's voice sounded at his back.

'Just to let you know you'll have to alter that guide book of yours. If you'd been at the party you'd have heard all about it. Stop press news: Georgie boy and his sister *did* have it off together. Ask Mr Coryton: he'll confirm. Proved beyond a shadow of doubt. What d'you think of that?' The detective re-examined the portrait in his turn, discovering to his annoyance – it must, he decided, be a trick of light, the time of day – that the first owner of Bullen Hall had indeed been the very double of one Ben Jurnet of the Angleby CID. The painted face scowled back, seeming no better pleased with the resemblance than did the one of flesh and bone contemplating it. 'If they hadn't got him for that,' Jurnet continued, 'I'd have run him in myself for passing himself off as a police officer.'

'Didn't I say so?' the little man demanded absent-mindedly. He did not seem quite his usual, cheery self. 'Anne Boleyn. A queen! Who'd 'a' thought it?'

'Henry VIII, for one. Not as bad as mother and son, father and daughter, I'll give you that. But all the same, a crime against nature.'

'Who'd 'a' thought it?' Percy Toller repeated. He looked and sounded disconsolate. Then, with a shake of the head: 'It's no use, Mr Jurnet. I know he did very wrong, but I just can't get het up about it. Not after all this time standing face to face – your face, Mr Jurnet! It'd be like turning your back on an old friend. There must've been some extenuating circumstances.'

'Like what?'

'Like love,' the little man said, with a simplicity that cut Jurnet to the core. 'If Mollie'd been my sister I wouldn't 've let a little thing like that stop me.'

'If Mollie'd been your sister you'd never have thought to fall in love with her in the first place. Mind you,' Jurnet finished, smiling, 'if she *had* been your sister and turned out teas like the one she laid on for us at a moment's notice, that *would* have been extenuating circumstances!'

'Mollie can do that with her eyes closed and one arm tied behind her back.' The retired burglar cheered up a little. 'Know what she said after you left, Mr Jurnet? That you were as smashing as ever to look at, but a sight too skinny. What you

156

needed was a wife to fatten you up a bit. Hope you don't think I'm speaking out of turn, Mr Jurnet.'

Jurnet said: 'You tell Mollie the reason I'm not married, I'm still looking for a girl like her.'

'I'll tell her! I'll tell her soon as she gets back.' In response to the detective's questioning look: 'Her nephew in North Walsham – he come over for her yesterday. They all turn to Mollie when anything needs doing! His wife's due home from hospital today with the new baby, and could Auntie come over to help get them settled in comfortable? He's bringing her back tonight. I always kid her she fancies you, Mr Jurnet, and if I get run over by a bus I know who'll be standing in my shoes if she has any say in it. And you know what she says? If she was twenty years younger and she thought she had a chance, she'd 'a' pushed me under one years ago!'

'Great little kidder, Mollie. Don't forget to learn your daily quotation while she's away. What's it today, Percy?'

The little man hesitated a moment, cleared his throat. Then he recited: '"Rob me, but bind me not, and let me go." John Donne, 1571–1631.'

'That all there is of it?'

'Tha's all they give you. I just open the book anywhere, first thing after breakfast; and it's whatever happens to catch my eye.'

'Must've reminded you of the bad old days. Not that I recollect you ever tying anyone up in the course of a job.'

Percy Toller looked horrified.

'Frightening people out of their wits! You know I'd never do anything like that. Never went into a house without first making sure there was nobody at home.' Shoulders drooping: 'I hate Mollie not to be home, and that's a fact. Even for a day. Especially when I –' The little man stopped, seemed to fumble with his words, and began again. 'It's my night for my tutor, over in Angleby. I've got an essay to hand in, and Mollie always goes over it for spelling and grammar.' There was another pause before he finished: '"From *Pamela* to *Sense and Sensibility* – the Emergence of the English Novel, 1740–1811" – that's the title of it.'

'Very interesting.' Jurnet, who had received a strong impression that this was not what Toller had originally intended to say, pounced, though still in a tone of dulcet concern: 'To say nothing of the way you must worry when she's out somewhere, in case she comes down with another of her turns –'

'That's right,' the other agreed, avoiding the detective's eye.

Jurnet regarded the retired burglar with a friendliness judiciously seasoned with a hint of threat.

'Come off it, Percy! Don't you think it's time you let me into the secret of what you were really up to, the night of the party?'

'No secret,' Percy Toller insisted doggedly. 'I was home with Mollie, like I told you.' The little man moved his head, his whole body, in an ungovernable spasm of exasperation, surprising because it was so out of character. 'How long does a bloke have to keep out of trouble before you coppers stop treating him like he was still a thief?'

Jurnet said: 'It's not thieving we're talking about, Percy. The subject's murder.'

'So I know all about Percy Toller,' Jurnet assured the glasses. 'He's tremendously proud of being accepted as a Bullen Hall helper, and I'm sure you can rest assured, Mr Coryton, it wasn't him took the weight off your postal scale. Beside which,' the detective pointed out, for the second time that day, 'we're not actually talking about thieving, are we? The subject's murder.'

'That's what's so incredible!' the curator exclaimed. 'I simply cannot imagine any of us here at Bullen Hall, myself included, when you come down to it, in the role of murderer.' Brightening up: 'There's Ferenc and Jeno, of course. Splendid fellows, both of them – but after all, foreigners –'

Jurnet made it clear he was in no mood for further jokes.

'I'm surprised, after what happened the other night, you didn't think to mention Mr Winter.'

Coryton stopped fooling and said: 'In case you haven't found it out for yourself, Inspector, I want you to know that Charles Winter is the gentlest of souls. I suspect all potters are the same – that you can't spend a lifetime handling something as brittle as clay without developing a special feeling for the frangibility of flesh and bone.'

'Oh ah,' Jurnet returned deflatingly. 'Mr Winter also appears to have had a special feeling for the – frangibility, was it? – of Mr

Mike Botley. Have you taken a look at that young man's face lately?'

'I've been in the Coachyard.' Francis Coryton took off his glasses, as if, with them, he could remove the pained image trapped behind his eyes. 'I can't understand it! It's so completely out of character. You saw for yourself that Charles had had too much to drink. But even so –' The nondescript face looked crumpled and upset. 'Especially as you can take it from me, Inspector, that what happened at the party was nothing to some of the humiliations Charles has put up with from that depraved little punk. There've been times, I don't mind admitting, when I myself could have cheerfully strangled him, to shut him up once and for all. But Charles – he just stands there, his face grey like his clay, but still – the only way I can describe it – transfigured by love. Jane always says it's an example to us all of what love's really about.'

'Letting someone tread all over you like a doormat?' Tormented by a sudden vision of Miriam, wanton on her Greek island, Jurnet's voice held disbelief and comprehension in equal parts.

The curator put his glasses on again.

'Anyone who treads on your doormat,' he pointed out, 'at least has come through your door.'

24

Jurnet came up the stairs to the curator's flat, purposely seeking out the squeaks in the uncarpeted treads. The old oak obligingly cooperated, and the detective's features, dark and dissatisfied, relaxed into an expression that was almost paternal as, above, the clatter of teacups, the animated rattle of conversation ceased abruptly. A girlish giggle cut itself off in mid-hilarity. Footsteps lighter than those of a policeman receded down the hallway.

By the time, taking each stair with deliberation, he achieved the landing, the incident room was a hive of quiet industry, PC Hinchley busy at the filing cabinet, PC Bly on the phone to the Lord knew who, Sergeant Ellers at a typewriter which he attacked with one-fingered ferocity. Only the smallest noise of crockery came from the adjoining kitchen, whence Sergeant Bowles issued benign and unruffled to announce that, by a happy coincidence, he had just that second put the kettle on.

Jack Ellers declared an armistice with the typewriter, and came over to let his superior officer know that Mrs Coryton had been on the blower several times, asking for him.

'Didn't you get out of her what it was about?'

'All she said was, you'd know if I told you she was phoning from Mr Winter's, in the Coachyard.'

'Ah! She's been gazing into young Mike Botley's beautiful black and blue eyes.'

'She said she was there, and would stay there till you came. When I said I'd get you to call her back when you came in, she said it wasn't anything she could discuss on the phone. It was something you had to hear, and see, for yourself.'

Jurnet said: 'We'd better get on down there, hadn't we?'

Even as he spoke, Sergeant Bowles, that kindly man, appeared, bearing tea and biscuits. Jurnet gulped down the scalding liquid, and took the Bourbons along 'for afters'. A minute later, crossing the little footbridge over the moat, he broke the two biscuits into several pieces, and dropped them into the water. They floated on the surface for a little, before descending leisurely into the murk.

If the eels were waiting, they did not let on.

In the pottery, the dust hung heavy. It revolved sluggishly in the shaft of sunlight that sloped through the open half-door, kept aloft – or so it seemed – by nothing more affirmative than a listless disinclination to obey the laws of gravity. In the gloom that bounded the sunlight upon either side, the dust was something to sense rather than see; a weighing upon the spirits that had bowed the broad shoulders of Charles Winter and twisted Mike Botley's face into an expression of rigid petulance. The young man, arms flopped between his legs, sat slouched on a low stool. Between the first and second fingers of his right hand a lighted cigarette slowly reduced itself to ash and a wisp of ascending smoke.

As the two detectives came in, the potter, hollow-eyed and unshaven, ejaculated 'Oh, Christ!' in a voice naked with suffering. He stood at his wheel, wearing the same canvas apron, slacks and dirty yellow sweater in which Jurnet had seen him earlier; his large hands resting on a damp cloth which covered a small mound of clay. Into Jurnet's mind came some half-remembered story about giants who renewed their strength by contact with the earth. He looked closely at the man, who returned his look with something between aversion and despair.

Even Jane Coryton, in her white cotton dress, seemed diminished by the prevailing greyness. Just the same, the voice with which she greeted the police officers' arrival held an undeniable note of triumph.

'Oh, good!' she exclaimed. 'You've brought somebody with you to take notes.' Wheeling round to where Mike Botley sat contemplating his cigarette as if mesmerised: 'All right, then! Tell them! Tell them what really happened!'

The young man raised his head momentarily: long enough for Jurnet to note that his face, though plentifully scabbed, was halfway back to its normal coarse prettiness. The head and ears were still bandaged, but more lightly than before, and with a clean bandage.

'Get stuffed!'

'Charles!' Mrs Coryton appealed to the tall, anguished figure at the potter's wheel. '*You* tell them, if he won't.'

'Darling Jane,' said the potter, in a gentle tone more piercing than swords, 'this is *your* party. You laid it on. You invited the guests. So why don't *you* do the honours?'

'But I can't do that!' the woman cried. The two detectives, waiting, watching, listening, said nothing. 'It would only be at second hand.' Appealing to Jurnet: 'That won't do, will it?'

Jurnet said: 'It's quite true that if either, or both, of these gentlemen have anything to say as a matter of evidence, they must say it for themselves.'

'Mike!'

Jane Coryton planted herself in front of Botley. The young man's face, behind the spiralling cigarette smoke, held a deliberate vacuity that was as much of an insult as a smack in the face. Mrs Coryton waited a moment longer. Then: 'Well, don't say you didn't ask for it!'

With a characteristically efficient gesture that brought the overlapping windings of gauze away as one entity, still retaining the shape of the skull they had moulded, she whipped the bandage off the young man's head. The cigarette dropped to the floor and lay smoking in the dust.

'Ow!' Botley jumped to his feet, knocking the stool over. 'You lousy scrubber!' He raised a tenderly exploring hand to a wound on the left side of his forehead, just below the hairline. 'If you've started it bleeding again I'll bleeding sue you!'

It was indeed a nasty gash; Jurnet could see that. It should have been stitched, especially for a young man whose face was his fortune. Judging by the look of the livid split, the skin on either side ridged and iridescent, Angleby CID could count itself lucky not to have ended up with another case of murder on its hands.

Just the same, Jurnet's gaze was concentrated elsewhere; upon the torn, swollen ear lobes, from each of which, it was only too evident, a vicious hand had wrenched an earring with none of the finesse required to disengage it without harm. From one of them, black with dried blood, a thin thread of flesh dangled as if it were itself some barbaric ornament.

Mike Botley demanded mockingly: 'If women *will* leave their handbags about, what can they expect?'

'You saw how we had to leave early on account of he was pissed to the eyebrows.' Mike Botley looked at the potter with a lively malice. The hurt incised deeply into Charles Winter's face seemed positively to stimulate the other to garrulity. 'Well, no sooner are we out on the landing than his lordship wants to throw up.' Turning to Jane, strong young teeth bared in a caricature of a smile: 'You got me to thank, Jane, for getting him to the lav on time. Sick all over yer carpets would 'a' been nice, wouldn't it?'

Jane Coryton pointed out: 'Not my carpets any more.'

'Her Imperial Majesty Elena's, then. She'd 'a' done her nut.'

Jurnet interposed, on a note of cold inquiry: 'The earrings.'

'Hanging about waiting for the old cack-arse, had to do something, di'n't I? Thought he must've fallen down the hole, but no such luck. Anyway, I wandered into the bedroom where the women had put their coats an' things. Combed my hair in front of the glass, poked about a bit −'

Jane Coryton said succinctly: 'All the drawers had been cleared out days before.'

'You got a suspicious mind, ducky! All I did, someone had dumped a Spanish shawl on the bed. I draped it round me shoulders, took a flower out of a vase and did a bit of olé in front of the mirror, just for laughs. Christ, was I fed to the teeth with Charlie boy!'

'The earrings,' Jurnet said again.

'The earrings!' the other echoed mockingly. 'There was this one bag someone had left behind. Well, it had to be Anna March's, di'n't it? Ethnic. A pair of earrings and 47 bloody p! I bet she doles out 10p to Danny for a sherbet sucker if he behaves himself and don't answer back.'

Jurnet said, in the same even tone: 'You stole them.'

'47p? I wouldn't demean myself. I borrowed the earrings, that's all. Anna weren't using them, was she? We're all mates here in the Coachyard – right? – so what's wrong with borrowing a pair of earrings from a pal just for the fun of it?'

'You were on your way home. Planning to wear them in bed?'

'Just an idea I had,' the young man said airily. His tone changed, he jerked a shoulder irritably in the direction of Winter. 'Then *he* came blundering out of the lav, stinking like a drain, an' I was the one had to get him home. *And* going on like a nagging wife about what did I mean by making eyes at Mr Shelden. I don't mind telling you, if he'd fallen off that bridge into the moat – and he could have, easy, if I hadn't seen him over like he was a baby – I'd've left the bloody eels to get on with it and good luck to 'em! Go on? I thought he'd never give over!'

Jurnet observed: 'If he was that drunk, he must have gone out like a light once you got him back home.'

Botley surveyed the detective with a fresh, almost childlike, interest.

'Know what, rozzer? You're bright. But then, I suppose you're trained to it. Got his shoes off, that's all, and there he was, sprawled out on the bed snoring fit to blow the roof off.'

'Leaving you free, for the rest of the night at least, to put on Anna's earrings and go your own sweet way.'

The young man giggled. Jurnet, despite himself, felt his face stiffen with distaste.

'Not just the earrings, Inspector! You *are* a one! I had a dress

163

I'd been keeping for a special occasion. Crimson velvet with lovely sleeves –'

'One of the dresses from the pageant. Where are they kept stored?'

'There you go again!' declared the other. 'You'll cut yourself, you're so sharp. They're kept in one of the empty coach houses –'

'Something else you borrowed –'

'Saved from certain death, more like. They got rats in there.'

'Never mind that. You put on the dress, and the earrings –'

'And my wig. That's my own property. Charlie give it me for Christmas – didn't you, Charlie boy?'

The man said, out of the depths of some private hell: 'I was only pretending to be asleep. I waited until he'd changed into that dress and was tiptoeing towards the door, and then I got up. I'd guessed all along he'd made some private arrangement with Shelden, to go to him after the party was over. That's why I dragged the earrings out of his ears, why I beat him up. He never got through the door.'

Mrs Coryton sprang forward, ready to protest, when Mike Botley forestalled her with a weary contempt beneath which the potter bowed his head silently.

'You don't want to pay no heed to him! Won't be happy till he's sacrificed his good name to save me from a murder rap. He'd been Jesus, he couldn't wait to be crucified. Pity I didn't leave those earrings alone, though. Didn't even care for 'em, particularly. Not my style. You'd have never found out, otherwise.'

'We'd have found out.' Jurnet spoke with a conviction he did not entirely feel. 'Had you, in fact, made a date with Shelden?'

'Not in so many words. But I knew, he knew – what more do you want?'

'More of a code, is it, then – like the Masons? What made you so sure he was gay?'

Botley's fists clenched. His face darkened.

'I knew. I knew all right!'

'OK. You knew. Calm down and tell us what happened.'

'I rang the bell and he opened the door so fast I think he must've been waiting on the other side of it. Either that, or he come down the stairs four at a time. I don't think he recognised me at first – you'd be surprised, that black wig makes me look a different person altogether – and then I said, "I've come to read the meter." Laugh? You could've heard him all the way to Angleby, if you'd been listening.'

Mike Botley looked at Jurnet, and said with a confiding air in which there seemed no artifice: 'I don't mind telling you I really fell for him in a big way. He was so lively, so full of get up and go – not like Old Constipation here, brooding over his clay and counting his senna pods. I felt like I was coming alive again after being left in suspended animation like those blokes in *2001*. We went up the stairs laughing, his arm round my waist, and it was laughs all the way from then on. He took me into the kitchen and I made some sandwiches out of the leftovers while he put the kettle on and made us some coffee; and then we took it into a nice room with a desk in it, and we sat on the edge of the desk, eating and drinking, and chatting away as if we'd known each other all our lives. It was really great!' The young man's face brightened at the recollection. 'No sex, believe it or not. Just friendliness. It wasn't till we were doing the washing up together that he suddenly made a grab for me and kissed me – put his tongue in like he was looking for my tonsils. By the time he whispered in me shell-like ear, "Let's take the mattress out on to the roof, what do you say?" I was as hot as he was.

'I don't mind admitting, I was real gone on him. I waited while he went and slipped into something comfortable. He said it like Mae West, wriggling his hips – and laugh! I thought I'd die. At last I managed to get out, "We'll never be able to do it, if you don't take it a bit more serious." And do you know what he did then?' Botley's face had become white and intent, the damaged area round the eyes standing out purple by comparison. 'He took my face between his two hands, very gentle, and he said, "You silly little goose, this *is* serious. This is for life."'

'Not all that long, as it turned out.' Jurnet had to find some way of venting his discomfort.

'Too long by half!' The bitterness, the brutal change, was all the more shocking. 'When he came back – gold pyjamas he had on, and his velvet jacket – we went into the party room, and then up the stairs to the roof. The mattress was propped up against the wall, just inside the door. It was one of those inflatable ones, partly blown up, but not as far as it would go. There was a foot pump to pump it up higher, and once we got outside Chad started pumping away as if his life depended on it. Me, I thought it was OK the way it was. I mean, when you're boiling for a screw you don't usually stop to check how many pounds pressure there is in the blooming bedding.'

Mike Botley paused, and considered a moment. Then he said, quite softly, possessed of a rancour that imploded within, devastation invisible to the naked eye: 'I told you he was gay, di'n't I? I told you the way he kissed me. On'y thing I didn't tell you, because I had to find it out for myself the hard way, it turned out Mr fucking Shelden didn't really feel it right to be natural an' enjoy the nature the good Lord seen fit to give him. Felt he ought by rights to be laying some flabby cow, all breasts and buttocks you could bounce off like a trampoline. Not that he didn't still want me – he was looking like he'd got a prize marrow stuffed down his pyjamas – only all of a sudden lover boy has what I understand are called qualms. Bloody fool! Not that I made a scene, or anything, you understand. Disappointed, but then, that's nothing new, living with good old Charlie. Only –' and now the young man's voice took on a note of harsh complaint – 'why the hell I got to be the one to suffer, all on account some bloody weirdo's got problems of identity?' He petered out to a sulky silence.

'What happened next?'

'Here's what happened next! Here and here and here and here –' Mike Botley pointed to his face, his gashed head, his mutilated ear lobes. 'All of a sudden the geezer went berserk – goes for me like a raving lunatic, punching, kicking, I don't know what. When he wrenched the earrings out of my ears –' the young man shuddered – 'I think I passed out –'

Jurnet asked with scant sympathy: 'You didn't think to fight back?'

'You could've soon fought back an earthquake. I did the only thing I could – rolled myself up like a Swiss roll, an' waited for the earthquake to stop.'

'You didn't by any chance leap up, lock your strong young arms round your attacker and heave him over the parapet?' While Botley stared at him in silent contempt, the detective added: 'It could have been self-defence.'

'You ain't been listening. There *weren't* no defence. Shelden beat me up like he'd been saving it up to take out on someone ever since he got potty-trained. Just my luck, that someone had to be me.'

Jurnet pursed his lips reflectively.

'If he was acting as crazy as you make out, how come he knew enough to turn it in before he did for you for good?'

'You'll have to ask him, won't you? All I know is, suddenly he stopped hitting, put his hands up to his face, and screams at me to get the hell out. I didn't have to be asked twice! An' you know what?' The damaged face twisted in a grimace. 'Rushing down all them stairs in that bloody dress, what do I do but trip and fall all the way down the last flight! Oh, it was my night all right!'

'What time was it when you left the flat?'

'How the hell should I know? I weren't charging by the hour, you know!'

Charles Winter came to life again, and said, in a voice as grey as the clay that caked him: 'He got home just after three.'

'With respect, sir,' said Jurnet, in a voice that indicated that he felt no respect, 'you were in no condition to know what time he got in.'

'You're wrong, Inspector' – and now it was as if the blood had begun to circulate again, the voice growing deep and vigorous: 'Mike and I are on the same wavelength. Even in my drunken sleep it got through to me that he was in danger. The knowledge woke me up. I switched on the bedside light, and saw it was five minutes to three. I called "Mike!" and when he didn't answer, and I could see he wasn't anywhere in the place, I put on my shoes to go out and look for him.' The potter passed the back of his hand across his forehead, leaving a further smear of clay. 'I knew where to look for him, of course – except that it didn't matter any more; only that my darling was hurt. He needed me. I'd just opened the flat door when he came stumbling up the stairs.' The man closed his eyes, then opened them. 'If you had only seen him! The pity of it!' In a voice vibrant with emotion: 'If Chad Shelden had put in an appearance at that moment I'd have torn him limb from limb!'

Jane Coryton cried: 'Not you, Charles! Never!'

Jurnet had a suggestion to make.

'Quite sure, having got yourself dressed, you didn't go over to the curator's flat to do just that very thing?'

The other brushed aside the question impatiently.

'I had more important things to do. I bathed Mike's wounds. I bandaged them. I comforted him –'

'Da-da-*da*, did-da-da-*da* –' Botley broke into a phrase from *Hearts and Flowers*. 'You'll have the Inspector weeping into his pinny. All you did, you silly old sod, was slosh disinfectant around like I was a bunged-up S-trap. It's a miracle I got any skin left.' The young man spoke with a calculated cruelty which plainly afforded him enjoyment. 'Your bloody bandages either came undone in five minutes, or else they nearly strangled me –'

The potter bowed his head, moved his hands gently over the mound of clay.

'We'll take a trip, darling. Anywhere you say. That Club Méditerranée brochure you showed me –'

'Mr Botley won't be travelling anywhere yet awhile,' Jurnet cut in. 'Not for pleasure, at least.' To the young man: 'I must ask you to accompany Detective-Sergeant Ellers here to our incident room in the west wing, so that you can make a full statement, which will be typed, which you can read through, and which you can then sign, once you are satisfied it's a faithful transcript of what you have just told us. There are a good many other questions which have to be asked, and Sergeant Ellers will then drive you to Headquarters at Angleby. You will, of course, be cautioned that anything you say will be taken down and may be used in evidence.'

'You mean, you're charging me?'

'I mean exactly what I say,' Jurnet returned smoothly. 'Call it helping the police with their inquiries. The duty of every citizen.'

Charles Winter put in anxiously: 'Will you be keeping him there overnight?'

'It's conceivable.'

'I'll pack a few things.' The potter rubbed his hand against his slacks, trying, not very successfully, to dislodge the clay. He moved away from the wheel, towards Mike Botley, and put a loving arm round the young man's shoulders. 'Your tooth brush. Socks. A shirt. There's that slab of chocolate in the fridge –'

'Stick it up your what's-it.' Botley reached up and pushed away the hand resting on his right shoulder. With an irritated gesture he brushed some clay from his T-shirt. 'Stick the toothbrush and the socks and the shirt there as well, while you're about it. They can't hold me. I done nothing. All I was, was the victim of an unprovoked attack. They'll be lucky if I don't go for them for Criminal Injuries, the way that louse roughed me up.'

'I'll find out who's the best solicitor –'

'Don't bother yourself. Let them lay one on. They want to play games with me, let them bleeding well pay for it.'

'Phone me,' Charles Winter implored, 'and I'll drive in to fetch you right away.'

Mike Botley said: 'You must be joking! If you think I'm coming back to this stately dump, you need your head examined.'

'Mike!'

The two detectives watched silently as the young man, tight-jeaned, flaxen-haired, his face the face of an angel who had somehow got himself involved in a pub brawl, derisively sur-veyed his clay-encrusted lover. Jane Coryton, too, watched; waited, her lips a little apart, her eyes bright with hope.

'*Darling* Mike, don't you mean?' Botley inquired, parodying the other's agony. 'Don't forget the darling! Well, let me tell you, darling, just in case you haven't guessed, darling, that darling Mike's been ready to move on for a good six months now. You bore me, darling Charlie. You disgust me. You never wash, you never want to stir out of this pigsty, all you're good for in bed is to get crumbs of clay on the sheets. Know what? The Inspector's done me a favour. From what I hear, there's some dishy guys in the nick. Never know where I may end up! I'll let you know where to send my things.' To Jurnet, with an expression of depraved innocence: 'OK if I take my drag?'

After Sergeant Ellers had left with the young basket maker there was a long silence in the pottery. The dust motes in the shaft of sunlight, agitated by their departure, bumped about in the air for a little, before settling once more into their former, slow, down-drifting indolence.

Charles Winter, watched by Jane Coryton with an intensity

of love Jurnet had never before seen on a woman's face, removed the cover from the lump of clay reposing on the potter's wheel, carefully folding the tattered cloth and placing it to one side. With his long, strong fingers he first prodded the clay, then kneaded it like dough, the hands caressing even as they pummelled. Jurnet, albeit with a certain native cynicism, awaited with interest the moment when the wheel would be set in motion, the hands at present so domestically engaged come into their own as instruments of creation; wheel whirring, hands shaping a masterpiece born out of the struggle of one man's hands against the centrifugal forces of the universe.

Instead, with a sudden deft movement, Winter scooped the clay off the board, hefted it in his right hand, and threw it out of the door into the Coachyard.

A cry sounded from without; and a large pugnacious face thrust itself in at the door.

'What the hell d'you think you're playing at?'

'I'm so terribly sorry!' Mrs Coryton hurried forward, radiating middle-class charm. 'I'm a learner, you know. I can't think how it possibly happened. Do forgive me! Have I ruined your lovely shirt?'

'Nothing that a visit to the laundrette won't put to rights,' declared the face, mollified.

'You *are* kind to take it so well! I shall have to leave potting to Mr Winter here in future, shan't I? Have you seen the display of his work in the house? Don't miss it, whatever you do – quite ravishing! It's the room on the left at the end of the entrance hall –'

To murmurings of mutual good will, the face withdrew. Jane Coryton laughed, pleased with herself. She moved back, away from the door and the sunlight, into the gloom where Charles Winter stood, face blank, arms hanging limp at his sides. She touched his left arm, on the bare skin, beneath the rolled-up sleeve; and when he made no response, ventured softly, in a voice full of tenderness: 'Charles?'

At that he raised his right arm and hit her brutally across the face.

25

Jurnet parked his car on the forecourt of his block of flats.
Nothing had changed, except that the black plastic bags left out
for the dustman had begotten young. Next to them someone
had put out an oddly shaped carton that looked as though it
might have contained a coffin. Jurnet locked his car and, being a
copper, went over to reassure himself that the carton really was
empty. As he lifted the flap a bony cat, black as the plastic bags
but a good deal less well filled, streaked out with an imprecatory
hiss and vanished over the low wall into the street.

'Welcome home!' Jurnet said aloud.

He climbed the stairs, holding his breath until he was safely
behind his own front door. To no avail. The assorted stalenesses
of the building had foregathered there, awaiting him. In a kind
of dispirited rage he hurried from room to room, flinging open
windows; only to discover that the outside air – and who could
blame it? – hung back reluctant to accept his invitation to enter.

There was no letter from Miriam.

Never mind. He had enjoyed his own little bit of Greece that
evening, courtesy of the Acropolis Taverna in Petergate: – if,
indeed, enjoyed was the right word. Taramasalata and all that
muck. For the fact that, even at that moment, his guts were still
engaged in a fretful dialogue as to the best way to deal with the
foreign bodies forced upon them without notice, he had only
the Superintendent to thank. Driving home from Bullensthorpe in the tender light of evening, there had been no
problem. Open a can of beans, and then, if he felt like it, pop
out to the late-night delicatessen for a block of ice cream. Maybe
even go mad and treat himself to a packet of wafers to go with it.

The sight of the Superintendent, beautiful in dinner jacket,
preparatory to attending a dinner of his lodge, had put paid to
that. Here, obviously, was a man privy not only to the childish
secrets of freemasonry, but to those far more mysterious ones
which taught you how to arrange the business of living so that it
became, like entryphones and central heating, a provided

service included in the rent, instead of an H.P. agreement on which you could never quite keep up the payments. As always, in the man's presence, Jurnet felt at once enhanced and diminished; as proud of the piercingly white shirt and the impeccably tied bow tie as if they were his own, yet reminded with additional force of his own end-of-the-day dishevelment.

The Superintendent said: 'Didn't want to shove off till I'd had a word.' Then, with a look of concern which warmed the other's heart, even though, as ever, he could not feel absolutely convinced of its sincerity: 'You're looking fagged, Ben. I know only too well how you are when you've got a case on your mind – forgetting to take on fuel until you've got it sewn up. Where are you eating tonight?'

'I thought of going to the Acropolis, in Petergate,' Jurnet had answered unblushingly. It was the first name that had occurred to him. Miriam had taken him there one night, shortly before she left, 'to get the feel of Greek food'. On that occasion he had sat transfixed by the sight of the octopus on his plate; and even more by the way Miriam had tucked into her portion of the rubbery horror with every appearance of enjoyment.

'They're very good.' The Superintendent had looked surprised. 'Glad to hear you're broadening your gastronomic horizons. Nobody in Angleby does octopus like they do.'

'That's right!' his subordinate agreed wholeheartedly.

'I'll be thinking of you tonight with my mouth watering,' said the Superintendent, 'when I'm working my way through my boring old beef and two veg. Now, what about our young Mr Botley? I had a look in on him, and Jack brought in his statement as he'd signed it. Have we or have we not got our man?'

Jurnet said: 'It must've been him the Hungarian chap saw crossing the lawn crying, with her – his – hands up to his face. Naturally he thought it was a woman, got up like that.'

'Not the ghost of Anne Boleyn after all, eh? What a disappointment!'

'Must have been her night off. Matyas says it was just after three, and Winter confirms three, or just after, as the time Botley arrived back home.'

'So?'

'So I had a word with Dr Colton. And what he says is that if

Shelden was in fact pushed off the roof at around three, there's no way he could possibly have survived until three-thirty, when Miss Appleyard came upon him, in extremis but still alive. Ten minutes, he says, would be an over-generous allowance, taking his injuries into account.'

The Superintendent sighed.

'It also doesn't explain how Shelden ended up in the moat, does it? Unless, when he got home, Botley blurted out what he'd done, and Winter went running to cover up the traces as best he might.'

'Or unless Winter took one look at Botley's face, and went out gunning for Shelden for roughing up lover boy.'

'Hm. In which case we're holding the wrong man.'

'Oh, we're going to have to let him go, in any event. I know that. What I'm still banking on, if it *was* Winter, now that the two have broken up, Botley may, out of sheer malice, give us a lead.'

'Just as likely, from what I saw of him, to concoct a tissue of lies.'

'So long as it's a tissue, not a blanket. Something you can see through, to the truth behind.'

The truth, Jurnet thought later, standing under the shower, considerably lighter in weight as in wallet, was that English stomachs weren't made for Greek food. If Miriam could keep the stuff down it must be because she was Jewish, member of a race which could never have made it down to the present day if, in their wanderings, they hadn't persevered with the local nosh. Or had he got it wrong, and they'd defended their digestive systems against anything they didn't like the look of simply by branding it *tref*, forbidden? The water trickling pleasurably down his chest and between his shoulder blades, he wondered desultorily if octopuses were kosher. He doubted it. They certainly hadn't cloven hooves, and he thought it unlikely that they chewed the cud, the only tests of acceptability he could remember from his course of instruction with Rabbi Schnellman.

To become a Jew, the Rabbi constantly warned him, if you weren't privileged to be born one, was to set out on a long, lonesome road to a distant goal only to be achieved by study, determination, and a disinterested love of the One God, blessed be He. Perhaps, Jurnet thought, his spirits also lighter now that his body had rid itself of alien infiltrators, his stomach had cottoned on to the idea ahead of the rest of him, and from far down that long, lonesome road was beckoning to his heart and mind to get a move on, for Christ's sake.

The phone rang as he turned off the taps, and he ran to the bedside table dripping, on the chance it was Miriam reversing the charges.

It was Mrs Coryton. Knowing her to be a woman of energy and resource, Jurnet did not enquire from whom she had contrived to obtain his ex-Directory number.

'Francis is out walking the dog,' she began, her voice unwontedly subdued, 'and it occurred to me, in case you should happen to run into him at the Hall, that I ought to let you know I told him I'd tripped over the crazy paving, and that's how I hurt my face.'

'Crazy paving's as good an alibi as any, I suppose.' Jurnet spoke coldly, putting a slight but significant stress on the 'crazy'.

'That,' she explained, recovering some of her accustomed humour, 'is what is called taking the war to the enemy. Francis put the crazy paving down before we moved in here, and made a terrible hash of it. Bits of it keep jumping up and clipping you on the shins. While I was being a liar I thought I might as well go the whole hog and be a bitch as well. I've made him feel horribly guilty, poor man, and now he can't wait for daylight, to start all over again, and lay it properly this time.'

Jurnet made no comment. At the other end, Jane Coryton waited a little, and then she said: 'You *do* understand why I'm phoning, don't you? To ask you – to beg you –' the voice sounded less supplicatory than surprised at what it was saying: not the voice of one practised in the shoddy arts of domestic deception – 'not to let on to Francis that it was Charles.'

'Ah, yes,' answered Jurnet, his resentment rising to the surface, naked as his wet body: the chagrin of a police officer who has seen an arrestable offence committed in front of his eyes and been unable to do a bloody thing about it. 'Mr Winter. The gentle one who couldn't hurt a fly.'

'No need for sarcasm, Inspector. It was all my fault. What I

174

did was unpardonable. I was so eager to prove Charles couldn't possibly have beaten Mike up that I didn't stop to think –' She broke off abruptly. When she resumed, her voice was under careful control; arid, sexless. 'Well, it's done now. No use crying over spilt milk, except that I don't think I could face losing *both* props of my life at one fell swoop. If you think about it, Inspector, you're the only one to come out of this in the black. I've cleared up one at least of your squalid little mystifications, haven't I? So I see nothing wrong in asking for a quid pro quo. Will you promise not to tell Francis?'

'I'm a police officer, Mrs Coryton. I can make no such promise. Mr Winter's behaviour has been duly noted: also that you refused to press any charge against him. If it should ever prove necessary to bring the fact of his assault upon you to the notice of a court of law, it will be so brought, together with any other relevant evidence. Meantime, however, I may say that I have no plans to go out of my way to inform your husband of what happened in the pottery. But if he asks me a direct question, I am not prepared to say that, so far as I know, it was the crazy paving.'

'Ah, well. I suppose that's as much as I've any right to expect. More than, after what I did. By rights, Inspector, I'm the one should be locked up in your prison cell. In irons, if you have any handy. Whoever murdered Mr Shelden killed a body. I murdered a soul. Bless you!' Jane Coryton said harshly, and rang off.

26

Anna March hadn't blessed him – far from it – when he had emerged, fuming and frustrated, into the Coachyard, leaving Winter and Mrs Coryton – the one ashy-grey, the other banded with purple across nose and cheek, staring at each other as though each were seeing a new species. Afterwards, the detective decided that she must have been looking out for him, the door to her workshop ready locked, the security shutter in place. At the time, watching her bearing down on him, sibylline in her draperies, his only thought had been: 'Christ – not now!'

'Hi, there!' he greeted her, overcompensating.

There was no returning smile.

'I really do think,' she began, in that hectoring tone he had, upon no evidence whatever come to associate with low church and high fibre, 'that you might at least have had the decency to come yourself and let me know about Mike Botley having taken my earrings, instead of leaving it to Jane Coryton to tell me.'

'Give us a chance!' Jurnet protested. 'I've just this minute found out myself.'

'Oh –' the woman looked taken aback, but only for an instant. That she should be put into the position of needing to apologise appeared to be only additional cause for dissatisfaction. 'Our wonderful police force! I must say it seems funny you had to get Jane to do your work for you.'

Jurnet swallowed hard. He said easily: 'All complaints to be addressed to the Chief Constable.' Adding, and, for Danny's sake, even managing a grin: 'First time anyone's complained because an Inspector *hasn't* called!'

'I wish you wouldn't make a joke out of everything. Danny's very upset with you. He can't bear to see me unhappy, and what was I to think when it was as plain as pikestaff you didn't believe a word I told you about the earrings, and about Chad – oh, and everything! My work's suffered, I haven't been able to settle to anything. Even Tommy's sensed something's wrong and has gone right off his food –'

Tommy as well! Jurnet thought. She wants it all, the greedy cow, she grudges every last crumb. Wishing with all his heart that he could imagine Miriam so ferociously possessive, he said, still making himself sound amicable: 'Well, now you're off the hook you must all be feeling fine again. All three of you.' He did not feel it necessary to add that, in his book, nobody who had become, however, peripherally, caught up in a murder investigation was ever off the hook until the culprit was delivered up to justice.

'Danny's gone in to Angleby. I haven't had the chance to tell him yet.' Spoken as if this too were the detective's fault.

'Never mind. Pleasure in store.'

Anna March said angrily: 'I know you think he's dim. Believe me, Ben Jurnet, he can see through *you*!'

'I should hope so,' the other returned simply. 'I've never pulled any blinds down, where Danny is concerned.'

Behind him, perched on the defunct fountain in the centre of the yard, the peacock let out a despairing cry.

The detective wheeled about in the baking glare.

'Doesn't anyone ever think to give that blinking bird a drink of water?'

He had earlier noticed a standpipe in one corner of the yard, with a bucket hung over the tap. Now, thankful for the excuse to cut short the conversation, he went over and filled the bucket; brought it back to the centre of the yard and tipped the water into the basin. The peacock, perched on the rim, supervised the operation with what seemed to the detective sardonic amusement.

No wonder. As fast as he poured, the water found its way through the cracked stone, and spread itself out on the cobbles. Jurnet could feel it soaking into his socks.

Anna March was laughing, the sharp-nosed cow.

Jurnet waved to her cheerily.

'Now you know why I never joined the Scouts! Give Tommy my love!'

On the drive in front of the house, parked next to his own car, and in front of the stone bulls guarding the bridge over the moat, Jurnet had come upon the two Hungarians, Ferenc Szanto and Jeno Matyas, unloading their gear from the latter's small Renault. Which was to say, Szanto was doing the unloading, watched by his friend propped on his sticks, shoulders hunched, his face shaded by a straw hat whose underbrim had been lined with some green material which imparted to the pale skin something of the faint, unearthly glow Jurnet had sometimes noticed in corpses on the point of putrescence.

'The Detective-Inspector!' Szanto had hailed him jauntily. 'Just the man I wanted to see! I have made a discovery of the greatest interest!' He put down a canvas holdall in order to clasp the detective's hand and shake it warmly. 'Tell me – do the police know that madness is catching? Because – can you believe it? – thanks to this lunatic here, I, a man hitherto sound in all my faculties, have just spent hours, starting from before daybreak, bent double in a wooden box, horseflies biting, my spine fractured with the weight of binoculars, one cup of instant coffee, and a sandwich filled with sand – for what? To peep at young girls dancing naked on the beach, perhaps? In that would be sense. No, Inspector – to look at birds! Birds! Flap, flap, they fly. Flap, flap, they sit down again. I tell Jeno the excitement is killing me. Especially since, for most of the time, I do not even see this miraculous flap, flap, which sends him into ecstasies. Perhaps you do not know that there is on binoculars a little wheel you must turn: – too much one way is all fuzzy one way, too much the other way is all fuzzy the other way. In between is all fuzzy also. I tell you, Inspector, only a madman can see through binoculars, and not until the afternoon – by which time I am become as mad as Jeno – do I see without fuzzy. And then, what do I see? Flap, flap, sit!'

Jeno Matyas looked at his friend with affection.

'He comes because he doesn't want me to carry things, and because he's afraid I may be taken ill out there alone on the marshes, with no one to help me.'

'Nonsense!' the other protested. 'I come because I cannot believe that, mad or sane, he goes all the way to Hoope just for flap, flap. I want to know who is the beautiful lady he goes to meet. Is she a mermaid, perhaps, or a foreign spy who comes ashore from a waiting submarine? All I know, Inspector – and you, as a policeman, will understand my feelings – it is very suspicious!'

The bookbinder said: 'In a little while the terns will be leaving. We think it's hot, still high summer, but they know better. One of these mornings they'll be off – a few at first, the over-anxious or the impatient ones – then more and more until it is hard to remember they were ever there.' In a voice devoid of all self-pity, he concluded: 'We know, of course, that next year they'll be back again, so why make a song and dance about it? What we can't be sure of is that we'll be here to welcome them.'

Jurnet, a little at a loss, turned to Ferenc Szanto.

'Want me to give you a hand with that stuff?'

'You hear that, Jeno?' the big Hungarian demanded. 'What a country it is, this England, where, without loss of face, a

Detective-Inspector can offer himself as a baggage boy! I'm honoured beyond words, my dear sir, but I'll not hear of it. Give me the keys, Jeno. I'll see you home first, then come back for all this. I'll be needing the car keys for tonight, anyway.'

The other handed over the car keys as requested, but announced stiffly: 'I don't need any help, thank you.' With a brief nod in Jurnet's direction, he moved slowly away.

'A porcupine has not more prickles,' Ferenc Szanto remarked, watching the painful shuffle. 'I tell him, you fill in a form and there is a special card you can get to put in the car window, lets you park in special places only for the disabled. But he says no, he will not – there is on the card a picture of a cripple in a wheelchair, and he is not a cripple.' With a shake of the head: 'A young man, still. It is a tragedy.'

'Is there any prospect of a cure?'

The other shrugged his shoulders, and went back to the task of removing binoculars, cameras and tripods from the car.

'He, as you say, bites my head off when I try to ask. So I don't ask.'

Jurnet asked: 'Why do you need the car tonight, if you don't mind my asking?'

'Aha!' The big man straightened up, twinkling. 'So you have not found your murderer while we were gone.'

''Fraid not.'

'You still think you will find him?'

'I know we shall.'

'Bravo! And yet –' the Hungarian swung round and stared at Bullen Hall as if he had never seen it before – 'one more little murder in all the long perspective of history – Is it truly worth all your effort?'

Jurnet said: 'I'm not much of a one on perspective. I reckon we only live – or die – one minute at a time.'

'How typically English! And how strange when you, Inspector, if you will allow me once again to say so, look yourself so un-English. But perhaps that is the essence of Englishness – disguises, always disguises.' Eyes still on the house: 'How typically English, eh, the old bricks, the little turrets, the lawns and trees, the lake with waterfowl. And how typically English the worm in the apple, the violence which lies concealed within the so peaceful exterior! The Queen Anne and her brother, my black-hearted friend Laz, poor Mr Shelden – and that is to speak only of what we know –'

'Enough to be going on with.' Jurnet refused to be deflected. 'The car, sir. You were saying –'

'I see you are not to be put off. I shall have to confess, Inspector, and hope you will let me off lightly. As an antidote to a day of lunacy I propose to spend my evening in the company of the sanest people who ever lived – the Marx Brothers. You know them? Fantastic! They are on tonight at the Classic in Angleby.'

'Something the matter with your own car, is there?'

'I have no car. I share with Steve the jeep, bought from the American air base – very strong, but with the steering wheel on the wrong side. Or perhaps it is your English roads which are on the wrong side, I am not sure which. All I know, when your police constables see me in the distance they sharpen their pencils and turn over a clean page in their notebooks. They have even learnt, with practice, to spell my name! So, when he is not using it, I borrow Jeno's car, which is made with the wheel, and the roads, in the right place.' With a broad grin: 'OK?'

'OK!'

It had begun to rain; a noisy, intemperate storm as overdone as the heat it displaced. Jurnet went round the flat hauling in the drenched curtains, shutting the windows he had earlier thrown wide. As he reached for the bar which anchored the small casement in the bathroom, the cat he had seen on the forecourt scrambled over his bare forearm and plopped down softly on to the vinyl floor.

The detective finished fastening the window, and went into the kitchen; filled a bowl with milk and called 'Puss, puss!' feeling pretty sure, however, that his uninvited guest was not the kind of cat to come when called. Sure enough, no animal materialised, then or later. Jurnet looked under the bed, the gas cooker, everywhere. No cat. Had he not borne the proof of two long scratches on his right arm he would have thought he had imagined it.

Feeling rejected by the world, human and animal alike, he went and lay down on the bed, counting the interval between lightning and thunder as he had always done, ever since he was old enough to count. One, two, three, four miles away. The familiar ritual soothed him and, for all the racket and flash outside, he fell asleep, a descent into a limbo empty alike of dreams and vague half-thoughts that floated tantalisingly just out of reach. When he awoke, the rain had quietened to a muted strumming, and the telephone was ringing. The bedside clock showed 3.47.

His caller was Mollie Toller. No need to ask how Mollie came to know his home number. She had begged it from him back in the days when Percy had stumbled from disaster to disaster. Now, as always in the past, she began with an apology for bothering him outside working hours; a set piece, her voice soft, the accent posh: and, as always, Jurnet waited, not interrupting, until the thin shell which encased her mounting hysteria cracked, and an anguished wail came over the wire.

'He hasn't come home, Mr Jurnet! Perce hasn't come home!'

27

At Headquarters he picked up WPC Frampton, a sensible girl not given to small talk. The duty sergeant who had taken the detective's earlier call and put the necessary wheels in motion was able to pass on the news that there was no news – no accident involving anyone answering to Percy Toller's description, no one of that name in custody anywhere in the region; no break-in bearing the unmistakable marks of the little man's genius for making an almighty botch of it.

On the rain-slashed drive out to Bullensthorpe Jurnet tried to convey to the quiet girl at his side something of his feeling for the ex-burglar: only to shut up in mid-sentence when he suddenly realised he was speaking in the past tense.

Every light in 'Pippins' was on, flooding out to the garden. Mollie Toller had the door open before the two police officers had got the garden gate off the latch; and they ran through the downpour and into the little hall like children rushing in from school.

'If it's all the same to you,' said Mollie Toller, 'I'll have your coats. No point in getting the upholstery damp.'

Her voice was level, her hair combed, her flowered housecoat buttoned from throat to hem. No trace of the distraught woman on the telephone. There was even a hint of a smile upon discovering that the Detective-Inspector had thought fit to bring along a chaperone. This appearance of normality struck ice into the detective's heart. It could only mean that Mollie had given up her husband for dead, and was already concentrating on hiding her grief from the impertinence of official commiseration.

She said: 'Lionel brought me home. He's my nephew, just become a father for the first time. A lovely little girl. They've asked me and Percy to be godparents. But now –' she paused, as if contemplating with composure an unavoidable change of plan. 'Half-nine, it must have been,' she went on, 'or a little before. Lionel 'd remember, probably, though he's so cock-a-hoop about the baby he hardly knows what day of the week it is, let alone the time. Dark, anyway: darker than you'd expect because the storm clouds were already piling up, and the first drops began to fall just as I came through the door. I knew it was Percy's night for his tutorial, so of course I didn't think anything of it till half-past ten, when I thought, well, he's late tonight and no mistake. Though, even then, I wasn't too surprised because I knew he was to take his finished essay in for sending off to Milton Keynes, and he's always full of himself when he's just got a bit of his work signed, sealed and delivered. He and Miss Grant – that's his tutor's name – always go at it hammer and tongs, in the nicest possible way, of course. "I don't know about the others," I always used to say to him, 'but she earns her money with you."'

'He'll be a Ph.D. yet!'

The woman did not deign to comment.

'By then, too, it was coming down cats and dogs, and I thought, he's taken shelter somewhere that hasn't got a phone, and that's why he hasn't let me know.' Mrs Toller took a deep breath. 'At eleven on the dot I phoned Miss Grant. Got her out of bed, but she was ever so nice about it once she knew who I was. She told me Percy hadn't turned up for his tutorial at all, something that had never happened before. She also said what a pleasure it was to coach him, and how one student like him made her whole job worth while. Wasn't that nice?'

'Very nice,' Jurnet agreed. He noticed that Mollie had begun to tremble slightly, as if with cold. WPC Frampton, who had noticed it ahead of him and left the room, came back with a blanket which she draped round the plump little shoulders. The detective said: 'You should have got in touch with me earlier.'

'If he'd had an accident, I thought, the hospital would have been in touch. He always carried his Bullen Hall card in his pocket, the one they give out to the volunteers, so anyone who found him would know who he was.' After a pause: 'If, on the other hand, he's out on a job, I thought, I can't help him.'

'You know he's finished with all that!' Jurnet found himself coming heatedly to the absent Percy's defence. 'Besides, I told you. Nothing's come up of any break-in with his signature on it.'

'It was when I thought about the break-ins that might not have come up that I got on the phone to you.' The woman looked at Jurnet stonily. 'Since we came here to "Pippins",' she said, 'Percy's become very handy with Do-it-yourself. Plumbing, rewiring the electricity – saved us I don't know how much.' After allowing time for the implications of this last to sink in: 'I think after all these years he's learnt at last how to disconnect a burglar alarm without having the whole police force come down on him like he'd rung for the butler.'

'You're only guessing.'

'That's right.' Mrs Toller inclined her head in agreement. The trembling had become more pronounced. 'Guessing that I see him lying with a broken neck under a skylight, or fallen down some cellar stairs, and nobody knowing a thing till they come to work in the morning. He may have learnt about electricity, but he was still the same old Perce, never put a foot right when you can put two wrong.'

Jurnet went over to the trembling little woman, and took her cold hands between his own.

'What a carry-on!' he chided gently. 'Look, Mollie, you know me. Whenever I caught Percy up to his tricks I ran him in – right? And much as I like him personally, if I were to catch him at them again I'd run him in again without thinking twice

183

about it. But the way I've heard him talking lately – so respected, so proud to be at the Hall; studying for the Open University and all that – he'd never throw away all you've built up here for a few watches, a bit of silver he can't get tuppence for. Give the man the benefit of the doubt, for Christ's sake.'

Mollie Toller went on dully: 'You know that clapped-out old van he used to run about in? When it fell apart and I came into my Auntie's money, he wanted us to get a car, something with a hatchback, but I said no: what do we need a car for? Actually, I'd have loved it, living out here, a mile and a quarter to the bus. But what I'd really decided was, you need a car to be a villain. You can't pull off a job and then ride off on your bike with the pickings clanking away on the carrier. I didn't want to put temptation in his way.' She considered what she had just said, and then amended it with a painful honesty. 'What I really mean – don't I? – is, I didn't trust him.' Bleakly: 'If you're right and all that's happened is he's fallen off his bike and hurt himself, it'll be my fault for not letting him buy that Volkswagen he'd set his heart on.'

'Don't talk daft!' Jurnet's tone was warmly jocular. He was sorry to have to follow it up with: 'But there *was* something, wasn't there, Mollie, not quite kosher, or you wouldn't even be thinking along those lines. I noticed it the day you gave us tea, and again this afternoon – yesterday afternoon now – when I ran into Percy at the Hall. I've never known him out of temper before. He didn't seem to want to look me straight in the eye.'

Mollie Toller heaved a tired sigh and said: 'I suppose you still want to know why we didn't turn up at that party.'

'Yes. I still want to know.'

'It's simple, really. Perce mentioned he'd heard that the alarms in the state rooms were going to be switched off for the night.'

'So?'

'I didn't dare for us to go. I knew in all that jam of people I'd never be able to keep my eye on him every minute. The only way I could be certain was for the two of us to stay home in front of the telly till it was time to go to bed.'

'You aren't telling me he was planning to steal from Bullen Hall!' The detective did not hide his disbelief. 'Every item catalogued and photographed a dozen times over!'

184

'It depends what you mean by stealing.' Mrs Toller was crying a little now, the detective noted with relief. WPC Frampton unobtrusively produced some tissues and pressed them into the woman's hand. Mrs Toller blew her nose into one of them, regained a precarious equilibrium, and lamented: 'And I had to put the Open University into his head!'

'How's that again?'

'Books, Mr Jurnet. Once he signed on and started in on the foundation course all I heard was books. Especially old ones, antiquarian. You'd think they'd just been invented. It was like a madness. "A book's the words inside," I used to tell him, "not the year it was printed." But he'd say no: to hold an old book in your hand was to hold history and literature at one go. Perce wasn't lying to you when he said he'd given up the kind of thieving you used to pick him up for. Anyone try to knock off a postage stamp at the Hall, he'd have been on to them like a tiger. But books were different. I think he'd have whipped out every book in the Bullen Hall Library if he'd thought he could get away with it. Not to sell. To keep. He said it was shameful the way they were kept there, nobody doing anything but read the titles on the spines, caged up behind bars like wild animals, unable to live the life they were meant for.'

'And you were afraid that, if you went to the party, he might seize the opportunity to slip away and liberate a few?'

'He said it'd be an act of charity. He said, even when they came to take the inventory, they didn't let them out of their cases. One of the clerks just read off the title, and the other ticked it off his list. And he said they were packed so close together nobody would notice if he took one or two.'

Jurnet demanded: 'Why the hell didn't you tell me when I asked before?'

'He wanted you to think he was an honest man.'

Daybreak took him by surprise. 'D'ye ken John Peel' sounded on the door chimes, and there on the step was a young police constable, rosy as the light inching minute by minute into the eastern sky. The rain had stopped, the battered annuals along the path were picking themselves up and getting their act together again. High above the trees, a scrap of blue promised felicities.

Jurnet was sure he had not slept, even though he had no recollection of how he had passed the unaccounted-for hours. Mollie still sat upright on the chrysanthemum-covered sofa, her hair-do impeccable, WPC Frampton in her facing chair bent forward in unflagging vigilance.

The young policeman's name was Ledbetter, and his mother was the Bullensthorpe postmistress.

He had a message for Mollie.

'I told Ma about Mr Toller. She says, if there's anything she can do –' The plump little figure on the couch made no acknowledgement. Red with earnestness, the young PC promised: 'We'll find him, Mrs Toller! Don't you fret yourself.'

To Jurnet, in the hall, out of earshot of the silent woman, he was less sanguine.

'What a night, eh, sir? What a blooming night!'

'I've known better.'

'I'd look out at the bridge, sir, if I was you. The water's almost up to the top of the arch, and it's well over the carriage-way either side. That Rover of yours is a bit low on the ground.'

'Thanks for the warning. I'll take care. Tell your Ma there *is* something. Anyone she can get to come in and stay with Mrs Toller? Someone she knows and likes?'

'I'll pop in and tell her. She'll know. She'd come herself, if she didn't have to open up the shop.'

Jurnet accompanied the PC as far as the garden path, and stood there for a little after he had gone, breathing the sweet, cleansed air. Leaving the door open, he went back in, into the bathroom; found Percy Toller's shaver, and thankfully took off the dark stubble which, every morning, to his unfailing disgruntlement, did its best to distort the unremarkable image to which he aspired.

He switched off the shaver and became aware of a louder noise coming from the road; and, pushing open the opaque glass window, was in time to see Steve Appleyard drive past in the jeep. The young man looked bronzed, muscular, smiling.

When the happy young man, his clothes soaked, his boots leaking mud over the floral carpet, came bursting through the front door of 'Pippins' not many minutes after, the smile had gone. Even the tan seemed to have paled.

'I saw your car outside when I came past just now,' he began breathlessly. 'I thought you must be here. There's a big branch caught up under the bridge. It was holding back the water, so I thought I'd better have a go at getting it free.' He slowed down, made a determined effort to regain his composure, and achieved, even, a travesty of a grin. 'I seem – don't I? to be developing quite a gift for finding drowned bodies. It must be like dowsing. Only this time, at least –' a shudder of remembrance and relief shook the taut young form – 'there aren't any eels.'

28

Colton, in the suspicious way he had with the spoken word, distrusting any which was not written down and, for preference, enclosed in triplicate in an official folder, said: 'You'll have to wait for my report to the coroner. I'll let you have a copy. The most I'm prepared to say is that at the moment – at the moment, mark you – I can see nothing inconsistent with a verdict of accidental death. That damn bank –' the police doctor leaned over the parapet of the little bridge and scowled at the drop down to the river – 'slippery as glass. That PC, the local one, says, what with the oil and the hot weather, the road surface lately hasn't been much better. I'd have been in the water myself if he hadn't grabbed hold of me. Someone ought to have a word with the Highway Authority. Extremely dangerous, the way that opening falls away directly down to the river, without so much as a strand of wire to stop a vehicle that's come off the road.'

'I understand the village kids use it all the time to go fishing for tiddlers.'

'Oh, do they? In that case, it's only a matter of time before one of *them* breaks his neck.'

'Is that what happened to Percy?'

'Have to wait till we get him on the table, won't we? His neck certainly is broken, along with both legs and one arm, but any or all of those injuries could well have been caused after death by being caught up in that branch, and banging about against the arch all night long. My guess – and, mind you, that's all it is – is that a blow on the left temple was what did for him – or at least rendered him unconscious, so that he couldn't pick himself up and scramble out of the water.'

'All nine inches of it. Ledbetter says that's all it could have been when Percy came along. It didn't start raining till after nine.'

'More than enough to drown in, if you've just knocked yourself out – maybe on a stone, maybe on your own handlebars – and have the bad luck to land face downwards.'

'Yes.'

On the further side of the bridge, men were stripping off rubber suits and overalls, and packing them into polythene bags. They had already parcelled what remained of Percy Toller's bicycle, and put it into the back of their van. Jurnet himself had retrieved the dead man's briefcase, a bit of pseudo-executive nonsense in which, the detective guessed, Percy must have taken great pride. It had contained a sodden notepad, a plastic mac still neatly folded, and a small bundle of pencils, freshly sharpened, only one or two points broken.

While the detective and the doctor watched, the mortuary van, which had been parked on the grass verge, reversed, making a turn in the road which took it perilously close to the gap which had been Percy Toller's undoing. As it mounted the hump of the bridge, the two men pressed themselves against the old brickwork to allow it room to pass, the driver saluting cheekily.

In a minute or two more they were all gone, Colton included, leaving Jurnet still staring down at the water. He raised his head, and found to his surprise that Steve Appleyard had joined him.

'Yes?' he enquired abruptly. Then with more kindness, seeing the young man falter: 'What can I do for you?'

Steve Appleyard said: 'I heard Jim Ledbetter talking about oil on the road, and I wanted you to know . . . What I mean is –' making a fresh start – 'the jeep's been leaking – not much, but a bit – so I wanted to say this is the first morning I've brought it round this way. I've been working in the Hundred Field up the road, and always taken the track that goes through the wood. The back drive's in such a state you take your life in your hands.

It's only because, after last night's rain, the wood's a bog, that I came along here at all.'

'No need to answer an accusation that hasn't been made. Enough cars use this lane without your contribution.'

The young man looked relieved nevertheless.

'Percy knew how it was, that's the funny thing. People never take their own advice, do they? Couple of days ago, when I'd stopped by the gate for a bit, he came by, pushing his bike. I asked if he'd got a puncture, but he said no: only that the lane was a blooming death trap, and he didn't fancy breaking his neck.'

It was as an act of homage to the retired burglar that, arrived back at the Hall, Jurnet, for all his preoccupations, did not make straight for the west wing and the continuing saga of finding out who had done for Chad Shelden. Instead, he passed over the bridge between the rampant bulls, crossed the courtyard, and entered the house, which had just that moment opened for business. The elderly woman busy replenishing the picture postcards in the revolving stand turned towards him moist-eyed: 'Terrible about Mr Toller, isn't it?'

Well aware that, in the country, news – especially bad news – travelled faster than the speed of light, the detective knew better than to ask how she had come by the information with so little delay. He inclined his head slightly as he passed by, and murmured, as was expected of him, 'Terrible!'

Yet strangely, once in the Library which had been Percy Toller's bailiwick, it did not seem as terrible as all that. Some echo of the little man's artless enthusiasm seemed to hang in the air, another ghost to add to the many who already populated the place.

What a naive delight the ex-burglar must take at finding himself one of such exalted company! Jurnet glanced up at the portrait over the fireplace, and fancied that even that dour and dyspeptic face looked a little happier. Could it be, at that very moment, in some dark cranny between space and time, a spectral Perce was eagerly exclaiming to George Bullen, Viscount Rochford, that he was the spitting image of a chap he used to know, a certain Detective-Inspector of the Angleby CID?

Setting such fancies aside, the detective moved slowly along the ranks of books, peering through the gilded grilles and scanning each tier with an attention which plainly aroused doubts in the volunteer – a thin man, with a military manner – called in as an emergency replacement. The man crossed the room to where Jurnet, stretching his neck, was trying to check that there were no books missing from a top shelf; coughed to get the other's attention, and then delivered himself of the fairly dispensable remark: 'Books.'

Jurnet agreed. The books were packed close together, all present and correct. Mollie could have that much consolation, at least.

'A lot of them,' the man said.

'Yes. A lot.'

From the Library, the detective found his way to the Appleyard Room; and this time, despite the heat already beating down through the glass roof, found himself – now that he knew it was all a load of old cobblers – actually enjoying the reverential display. Though the handsome blonde giant whose shrine it was was even less to his taste as a scoundrel who traded in men's lives than as the hero of a fairy story, at least he had stepped out of the photographs into three dimensions. A real villain, a real man.

By contrast, the photographs of Elena Appleyard as a child produced an exactly contrary impression. The child clasping her brother's hand, the young girl seated on her pony, glowed with a flame the years had long since extinguished. The pallid woman who had been Laz Appleyard's wife and Ferenc Szanto's lost love stared out at the room with eyes which saw nothing but the wasteland of her own life. On his father's shoulders, with perfect confidence in the arms clasped round his chubby knees, Istvan Appleyard – young Steve – frolicked gleefully.

As on his earlier visit, the detective left the great glass bubble by the exit on the north side of the house, and made his way round to the west wing. Away to the right, as before, a solitary swan balanced on its reflection in the water.

A fake, Jurnet decided: the whole landscape a stage set. Everything in its place, preprogrammed, waiting for the curtain up. Cast assembled in the wings, even the murderer awaiting his cue.

If only Benjamin bloody Jurnet could remember what it was.

Something, someone, was not going according to the script. As Jurnet made his way along the west front, divided from him by the darkly gleaming line of the moat, a slender figure ran across the little bridge that led from the curator's flat: Jessica Chalgrove, her ponytail flying, her blouse and skirt billowing with the speed of her going. Solitary, she ran as if pursued. Halfway across the lawn, one of her white sandals came off. To the detective's surprise, she did not stop and pick it up; instead, kicked off its fellow and ran on. Even when she came to the end of the grass there was no slowing as the soles of her bare feet met the gravel underfoot. On she ran and vanished among the rhododendrons.

Thoughtfully, Jurnet diverged from his route, crossed the lawn to where the shoes lay, and picked them up, still warm from the girl's feet. In the flat he found Sergeant Ellers standing on the landing. The little Welshman looked puzzled.

'What's got into young Jessica?' Jurnet demanded. 'Just saw her streaking across the grass like the bloodhounds were after her.'

'Exactly what I was wondering myself. She barged into me as I came out of the door. Never so much as said she was sorry, let alone offer to kiss it better.' He finished, with all the assurance of a married man: 'Reckon she just remembered she forgot to turn the light off under lover boy's dinner.'

Jurnet set the sandals down side by side on the old oak chest in the hall. He made his way into the incident room, his subordinate following.

'I suppose you've heard about Percy?'

'Everybody back in Angleby's feeling real cut up, even the Super. He particularly said to tell you how sorry he was.'

'Oh ah.' The detective fiddled with some papers on the table. He said: 'I want you to go and see Mollie. Ask if there's anything we can do. Find out where her nephew Lionel lives and get him over, if somebody hasn't fetched him already. Tell her,' he finished, ashamed of his own cowardliness in putting off the encounter, 'I'll be along soon as I can.'

'Want me to go right away?'

'If you've nothing further to report on Mike Botley.'

'Depends what you want to know. Last time I had word he was threatening to complain to the European Commission on

Human Rights. Otherwise, he sticks to his story that Shelden, after slobbering him with love and kisses, suddenly goes off into a blinding rage, and beats him up like a three-egg omelette.' The little Welshman eyed his superior officer. 'Think he's telling the truth?'

'Let's say I don't disbelieve. Botley's a devious little bugger, but I don't believe he's clever enough to invent a balled-up character who first gives in to the homosexual side of his nature, but then draws back at the brink, because the other half – maybe it was more than half – wants to be straight.' Jurnet was silent. Then he said: 'I could begin to feel sorry for Mr Chad Shelden, and not just because he ended up in Bullen Hall moat.' Voice hardening: 'But then he has to go and take it out of that noisome little punk when it's himself he's angry at, really.'

Ellers commented cheekily: 'Thereby forfeiting your good opinion of him, once and for all!'

'That'll be enough of that, Sergeant!' Jurnet laughed, and felt better. Even the Mike Botleys of the world had their uses. At last he was getting upon terms with his current corpse. 'Did Botley have anything else to say?'

'Only what time did the next train leave for London, and would I please ask Mr sodding Winter to put together a small pack with his necessaries.'

'Nerve!'

'No sweat delivering that particular message, anyhow. The poor prick's been hanging round the duty desk like a lost soul ever since we took Botley in.'

Love! thought Jurnet, with a sudden pang that could just as well have been the last knell of that bloody octopus.

At one o'clock, Sergeant Bowles, who had been into Bersham to stock up the larder, came into the incident room with some tongue sandwiches and a cup of tea. He looked worried.

'Seen Miss Jessica, sir?'

Jurnet, looking up from the file he had been working on, saw no reason to add to the good man's anxieties.

'Just a glimpse. Why? Doesn't she always go home, these days, to fix a midday meal for young Steve?'

'It's the way she left her room.' Leading the way down the

hallway, rightly confident the detective would follow. 'It's not like her to leave a room like that.'

Jurnet took in the papers strewn about the floor.

'Not as bad as it looks,' he pronounced, disguising the fact that he had caught some of the other's foreboding. Why had the girl gone haring off in that way? 'It's only one box. She could easily have knocked it off the desk as she got up to go, and not even noticed what had happened.'

Sergeant Bowles visibly brightened. He said indulgently: 'She's always got her eye on the clock these days.'

Jurnet again omitted to report that it had been not much past eleven that he had seen Jessica Chalgrove running from the house. The Sergeant bent over and began to scoop up the papers. Jurnet said: 'I'd leave them where they are. It's none of our business, and she knows where everything belongs.'

'Right, sir.' The other straightened up unwillingly. Below them, the outer door opened and shut with a clang that reverberated through the ancient structure.

'PC Bly's back early,' the Sergeant remarked with disapproval. 'He'll have that door off its hinges. If I've told him once, I've told him a dozen –'

But the footsteps on the stairs did not sound like a constabulary tread. Jurnet came out into the hall, in time to collide with a wild-eyed boy who shouted: 'Jessica! Is she here?'

Steve Appleyard pushed past the detective into the study. His eyes took in the papers on the floor, the overturned box, and the neat stacks waiting along the wall. At the sight of the empty room he burst into sobs that were painful to hear; not because it was a man crying, but because it wasn't. They were the sobs of a frightened child.

'Jessica! Oh my God!'

Sergeant Bowles, because he could think of nothing better, hurried off to get a nice hot cup of tea. Jurnet, arm round Steve Appleyard's shoulders, half-pushed, half-dragged the distraught boy to a chair.

'Turn it in!' the detective commanded, in a voice that contrived to combine authority with concern. 'What's all this in aid of?' He cupped a hand under the young man's chin, forced the fair-lashed blue eyes to look into his own. 'What's happened?'

The eyes shut. Tears trickled down the suntanned face. The mouth, soft and defenceless, opened and closed again.

Jurnet said softly: 'Take your time.'

The young man shuddered. He stuffed a hand into a jeans pocket and brought out a paper – two papers – which he thrust at the detective. The action seemed to use up the last of his strength. He slumped back into the chair, and put his head in his hands.

Jurnet smoothed out the crumpled sheets, which consisted of a letter handwritten on blue paper and, stapled to the back of it, a strip of lined paper torn roughly out of an exercise book. The printed letterhead said Chalgrove Manor, the date was in 1966.

'Laz, you wretch,' the detective read,

'No, I will *not* get rid of it! Keep your dirty little addresses for the next gullible goose you get into trouble. *I* don't want them.

'And yes, you were quite right – I *did* get myself in the family way deliberately. If that mooncalf Mara can bear your child, so can I! I want you to know that I am wildly happy and that there is absolutely nothing for you to worry about. Even if it turns out to be the image of its pa (which is what I hope) the most people can do is gossip. Let them! As for Richard, who cares what *he* thinks? One thing's certain. Even if it turns out to have two heads, *he* won't talk.

'Don't *worry*! Nothing, I promise you, is going to interfere with your lovely, lecherous life style. Everything will go on the way it always has, except for the couple of months when I shall be, so to speak, *hors de combat* – and I know you too well not to know you'll soon find someone to stand in – or do I mean lie down – for me, until I'm once more ready for the fray. You see how I'm a woman after your own heart – how I don't make a perpetual hoo-ha about being faithful, like some I could name. I love you for what you are, you gorgeous bastard – which is why, however many women you may make use of in the course of your misspent life, I'll always be the one you'll come back to.

'Your Carla.'

On the strip of paper was scrawled in a different hand: 'I've been to see my "father" and it's true. Goodbye, Steve. I love you.' The apostrophes enclosing the word 'father' were heavily impressed.

The boy raised his head and saw that Jurnet had finished reading. In an exhausted voice, he demanded, less of the detective than of the world at large: 'If you don't feel like you're brother and sister, how can it matter if you are or if you aren't?'

'It seems to matter to Jessica.'

'Only because she's heard that policemen like you put people in prison for incest. What's incest? A word. She ought to be glad to know the same blood's running through our veins, the same people going before us, shaping the way we are.'

'If Jessica felt like that, she'd never have taken herself off.'

'Just because she's hiding herself away somewhere, doesn't mean she's gone.' The blue eyes were brimming again. 'She can't go. Now that she knows Laz Appleyard's her father too she's as much bound to Bullen as I am. Besides –' a look of artful triumph came into the stricken young face – 'if she'd left, she'd have taken her things, wouldn't she? And they're all there, back at the flat. Everything her father – I mean, Mr Chalgrove – had sent over from the Manor. Even her bag's on the dressing table, exactly as she left it this morning, with her money in it, and all her bits and pieces. Girls never go anywhere without their handbags.' The young man thrust his face close to the detective's. 'You'll find her for me, won't you, even if incest *is* something you're against? It's the police's job to find people –'

'Girls usually have more than one handbag.' Even though it felt like whipping a puppy, Jurnet said what had to be said. 'I'm sorry, Steve, but if Jessica – for what, I'm bound to say, on the basis of this letter, seems to me ample reason – decides to call it a day, that's strictly between the two of you. It's not a police matter, and you ought to be glad she's not prepared to stay on and risk letting it become one.' He put a hand on the other's arm, despising his facile consolations even as he uttered them. How would *he* feel if he suddenly discovered that Miriam was within the forbidden degrees? 'When you've calmed down and had time to think, you'll understand she's done the only thing possible in the circumstances. One day you'll thank that girl for having sense enough for both of you.'

Steve Appleyard pushed the hand away.

'What's sense got to do with it? We're two halves of a whole. Can't you get that into your head? You can't cut yourself in half because of a word.' He darted past Jurnet to the window; stuck his head out, and shouted: 'Jess! Jess darling, where are you?'

Rooks rose squawking out of the beeches. Jurnet crossed the room and, again, put an arm round the young, bony shoulders. The boy twisted himself free.

'Let me go! If you won't do anything, I'll find her myself!'

He ran from the room, down the hallway, past Sergeant Bowles and PC Bly standing uncertain in the doorway of the incident room.

Jurnet called out: 'Let him go!' Below, the door clanged to and shook the building. 'Not a bloody thing we can do.'

Sergeant Bowles stood looking down the stairs.

'Those lovely kids.'

He shook his head, and went slowly into the kitchen to pour himself out a cup.

29

Elena Appleyard said, with delicately raised eyebrows: 'Not *more* questions! I begin to understand why they gave Socrates the hemlock.' She looked at Jurnet imperturbably, and settled a square of patterned chiffon about her shoulders.

Jurnet, who had already refused a seat, stood, grim, in front of the fireplace.

'No more, I promise you, so long as you'll give me the answers without my asking.' He held out Carla Chalgrove's letter, and watched closely as the woman took it with polite incuriosity. 'Read that –' after a perceptible pause – 'if you haven't already.'

'I haven't read it,' she replied equably, 'but I hardly think I need to. The handwriting is very distinctive – a little vulgar, wouldn't you say? – like Carla herself.' With a humorous pursing of the lips: 'And that absurd name! Laz always said her mother must have been frightened by a performance of

"The Gipsy Baron" by the Angleby Operatic Society.' Miss Appleyard put the letter down on a small table at the side of her chair without further examination. 'Perhaps *I* should be the one asking questions. My first would be to inquire how a confidential family matter going back the best part of twenty years could possibly have anything to do with the death of Mr Shelden.'

'The answer to that –' Jurnet spoke carefully, holding down the anger he felt rising within him – 'is, firstly, that a letter which you had already handed over for incorporation in what would almost certainly have been a best-selling biography, can hardly, by any stretch of the imagination, any longer be described as confidential; and secondly, that *any* information which enables us to know more about the occupants of Bullen Hall than we did before is germane to our inquiries. Thirdly, even if this were not the case – for God's sake!' – the detective's sudden explosion was not entirely without guile – 'how, knowing what you must have known, could you positively encourage those two children to fall in love with each other?'

'There – you see!' the woman exclaimed, with a childish glee that the detective found at once ravishing and deeply disturbing. 'You couldn't keep away from questions! And what an idiotic one, if you'll forgive my saying so. As if those two needed any encouragement!'

'I'll put it another way. Why didn't you do everything you could to discourage it?'

'But I did exactly that! I knew nothing for certain, you understand, but I knew that somewhere among Laz's personal papers which, let me make it quite clear, I have not gone through in any detail – it seemed an invasion of privacy only excusable in a total stranger – there could well be something about his affair with Carla. I gave Jessica the indexing job fully aware of what she might come upon – indeed, half hoping she would.' With superb effrontery: 'It hardly seemed fair to saddle the poor girl with a Richard Chalgrove for a father when she might possibly have the pride of discovering herself an Appleyard. Ferenc wanted me to vet the correspondence first, and take out anything which gave the game away. Whatever he may have said to you, that's what he was trying to do when you came upon him in the curator's study soon after the murder.

The silly man, he keeps saying he wants Steve to know his father whole, as he puts it – but then, when it actually comes to the point, he's always wanting to make exceptions – remove anything that might hurt Steve too much. It wasn't my idea at all. What I said was, let's leave it in the lap of the gods.' Pleased with her analogy: 'It was, you might say, a very Greek situation.' Adding kindly, at the look of incomprehension on the detective's face: 'Ancient Greek. Oedipus and Jocasta. Theseus arriving back in Attica with a black sail hoisted, when it should have been a white –'

'You had another alternative –' Jurnet persisted, refusing to be diverted along unfamiliar paths. 'You could have told both of them the truth before it even started, and nipped the whole thing in the bud.'

Miss Appleyard sighed.

'My dear man! They set each other alight the moment they set eyes on each other. Do you think, without concrete evidence, they'd have taken notice of anything I said, when every atom of their beings urged them irresistibly into each other's arms?'

'Mr Chalgrove would have borne you out –'

'Richard! He'd have called me an evil mischief-maker. He's already offered me money to keep the entire Carla thing out of the biography. On other days, when he's had enough to drink, he threatens me with libel proceedings. He can't bear to have it known that Laz hung the horns on him.'

'His best friend, I understand.'

'How moral we are!' she mocked. 'Let me tell you, my brother, for all his womanising, was a great deal more moral than that poor, cuckolded nincompoop, to whom nothing matters more than salvaging his own vanity. Richard was so frightened that people might put two and two together if he fell out with Laz that, despite, everything, he went on being his "best friend" to the day Laz got killed. And after,' she ended, her eyes bright with amusement, 'he was chairman of the appeal fund for Hungarian refugees started in Laz's memory. Which was really such a joke –' her young laughter bubbled up from that unquenchable source deep within her – 'because if there's one thing Richard can't stand, it's foreigners.'

Jurnet reflected aloud: 'The Chalgroves couldn't have been

sleeping together during the time Jessica was conceived, or Mr Chalgrove could never have been so sure it wasn't his child.'

More laughter.

'Oh, he could have been sure! Richard's impotent.' The dismissive contempt in her voice, Jurnet felt quite sure, advertised knowledge that was more than second-hand. *You've tried a toss with him yourself, you bitch, you witch.* Elena Appleyard went on: 'So far from doing him wrong, Laz did Richard an enormous favour – established him in the eyes of the world as the one thing he wanted to be taken for above everything else – a virile man.'

Miss Appleyard got up from her chair with that suspicion of infirmity which, even through his outrage at what he saw as the woman's criminal irresponsibility, made the detective eager to assist her, though he knew better than to try. She stood austerely in the empty spaces of the room, furnishing it with her beauty. She said: 'I'm sorry to hear that Jessica took it so badly.'

'I thought she took it very well, all things considered. A clean break. Hard, but the best thing, in the long run.'

The other shook her head, light catching the silver among the black hair strained away from the worn, lovely face.

'Disappointing. One wouldn't have expected Appleyard of Hungary's daughter to take the easy way out.'

'The only possible way out.' Jurnet made no attempt to hide his disapproval. 'But then – those of us who aren't lucky enough to boast an Anne Boleyn in the family can't be expected to take your indulgent view of incest.'

Elena Appleyard smiled, unoffended.

'What a snob you are, Inspector!' She stood quietly a moment, then said, without challenge, a simple statement of position: 'Let me say that if the purpose of your visit is to make me feel either guilty or repentant, you're wasting your time. All love walks a thin edge between dangers. When I think of the suffering that girl's desertion is bound to cause Steve, I can only deplore her provincial narrow-mindedness in allowing an outworn taboo to come between her and happiness.'

Outside in the hall a telephone rang. The teetering footsteps of Maudie the maid sounded on the oak floor.

'If there's nothing else, Inspector –' Miss Appleyard had

begun when the maid entered without knocking. She spoke to her mistress, ignoring the detective completely.

'There's someone asking for the policeman.'

'Thank you, Maudie. And you can bring in the tea now.'

'For two?'

'For one.'

The maid's heavy features lit up with a rare smile. She left the room, her stays creaking. Jurnet was about to follow her out when Elena Appleyard said: 'You may use the phone in here, if it isn't private.'

'Thanks.'

Jurnet picked up the receiver, and listened to what Sergeant Bowles had to tell him; then answered carefully, no giveaway in his voice. 'You've been on to Headquarters, of course. Get Jack back from Bullensthorpe. Tell Hinchley and Bly to cordon off . . . yes . . . that's OK . . . I know the place –'

The detective returned the receiver to its cradle.

'I'll put the one in the hall back on as I go out.'

The very lack of inflection seemed to trouble Miss Appleyard a little; or, perhaps, arouse her curiosity.

'Nothing wrong, I hope.'

'Not a thing,' said Jurnet, 'except that somebody just fell off the thin edge.'

30

Jessica Chalgrove hung naked from the oak tree where Jurnet had caught his first glimpse of her, leaning back against the trunk with Steve Appleyard's body pressed against hers until, in the green shade, the two had melted into an image of love delightful in its innocent abandonment. Now, naked and dead, she hung with a perfect modesty, her long-thighed, small-breasted body a pleasure to the eye; the face, head tilted to one side, not unsightly. On the grass, with a stone on top to prevent them blowing away, the small pile of her clothes lay folded, as if ready to be put away in her chest of drawers: and she had managed her death with similar neatness.

A hangman, Jurnet thought, could have been proud of the noose the girl had fashioned for herself, the length of drop nicely calculated, the neck that must have broken quickly and easily, no slow asphyxiation to turn death into an obscenity. Only some purple striations, showing where twigs and rough bark had reached out for her young flesh as, naked, she had climbed upward to her doom, marred the utter restfulness of the sight which greeted the detective as he arrived back at the gate to which, a short time and an eternity ago, the lovers had hitched their horses.

The girl hung naked from the tree. The boy clung to the girl, his hands clutching her buttocks, his face buried deep in the gulf between her legs, eyes shut in ecstasy.

It should have been disgusting. It was, thought Jurnet, breathless from more than the haste of his coming, sublime. Sacred. Here there was grief, certainly, even agony: but, beyond it and yet part of it, a terrible joy. To have loved like that, Jurnet thought humbly, shaken for once out of his self-pity, was something to give thanks for.

The boy dropped to his knees, setting the body swinging gently. He bowed his head to the ground, making no sound. The girl's feet brushed against his hair two or three times, and then were still again.

Jurnet let him stay as long as he could. Flies on iridescent wings had already begun to assemble. Their mounting buzz of excitement only intensified the silence. By the time the team arrived from Angleby, cars and vans bumping over the grass, the transcendent moment had long passed. Steve Appleyard lifted his head, saw the approaching caravan, and sprang to his feet. Ran off without a further glance at the carrion hanging from the tree in a mist of flies.

Sergeant Ellers began: 'I sent PC Hinchley over to Chalgrove Manor to tell her father –'

'Except that he isn't, poor sod. Still –'

'Sod's about right. Bob Hinchley came back boiling. Seems the gentleman wanted to make a bargain. He'd go along to the mortuary so long as he got an undertaking nothing would be said at the inquest to bring his paternity into question. Otherwise, so far as he was concerned, the police could find somebody else to say it was or it wasn't the ungrateful little trollop he'd been misguided enough to give his ancient name to.'

'Did he agree, finally?'

'Oh, he agreed – soon as Bob mentioned the newspapers. Just the word, casual-like. Could have been something to wrap his skate and chips in, but it did the trick.' The Sergeant looked at his superior officer a little uncertainly. 'Madam in the east wing wasn't all that better. Gave me a look when I was shown in like I was selling brushes and she didn't want any. Then, when she'd heard what I had to tell her, said "How very unfortunate!" in that frost-bitten voice of hers, and had the maid show me out without another word. Know something?' Jack Ellers finished. 'Somebody ought to give that one a bit of padding for Christmas – inside as well as out. Foam rubber'd be better than nothing.'

'Can't all be like your Rosie.' Jurnet sat back on the seat overlooking the lake, where the two had seated themselves. He lifted his face to the sun. With eyes shut you could still think Bullen Hall a place of loveliness. The smell of green things growing. Children laughing in the distance. Lambs bleating, and a buzz of insects.

A buzz of insects. The detective stood up abruptly.

'Time to get on.'

At his side Sergeant Ellers offered: 'Accident and suicide in one day! All go at Bullensthorpe. Only thing – can't see how it gets us any further on with who killed Chad Shelden.'

'Look on the bright side, boyo! Number of suspects reduced by two. If they only continue to drop off at the present rate of progress, the crime'll solve itself with no sweat from us whatever.'

The two walked a little way in silence, making for the door in the west wing, until the little Welshman said, sounding troubled: 'I suppose it was OK to let that kid Steve go shooting off like that?'

'You think he should have stayed and watched our lads doing their stuff?'

'Not that. I only meant –'

'The boy's at home, among friends, family. We're police officers, Sergeant, not universal aunts, for Christ's sake.'

'Shouldn't think there's all that much comfort to be found on Aunt Elena's bony bosom –'

202

'There's always the Hungarians –' Jack Ellers hid a smile as the Inspector's next words made it clear that he was by no means as unconcerned about young Steve Appleyard's well-being as he had pretended. 'You might as well pop over to the smithy, Jack, and put Mr Ferenc What's-his-name in the picture. The boy may even be there already.'

'Will do.' The little Welshman turned to go.

'Wait a minute, though. What's that?' Jurnet stared at the west wing, at that protruding H of brickwork which housed the curator's flat and the Long Chamber: then broke into a long-legged stride which left his chubby companion far in the rear.

'Come on!'

The smoke curled out of the open window, a single ringlet spiralling upward into the summer sky. A tongue of flame peeped over the sill, and coyly withdrew. Suddenly, with a sound like a rifle crack, one of the diamond-shaped panes of glass exploded, to be followed by another, and another. By the time the two detectives reached the footbridge an alarm bell was ringing distantly in the main part of the house, and billows of smoke, orange-tinted at the base, were shrouding the parapets.

Sergeant Bowles, scorched and smoke-blackened, leaned against the bridge handrail, striving to regain his breath and the dignity proper to his calling. On the grass, somewhat the worse for its precipitate descent down the staircase, lay the steel filing cabinet from the incident room.

'Got the records out all right, sir,' he gasped, as Jurnet ran up. 'Called the Brigade. Phoned Mr Coryton to clear the house.' Coughing: 'If Jack could just drag that file a bit further away –'

'Don't worry. He'll see to it. Did the boy get out all right?'

'Boy?' The Sergeant shook his head dazedly. 'Weren't no boy –'

'How did this get started?' Urgently: 'You're sure there's nobody up there – nobody's been up there, in the study?'

Sergeant Bowles passed a hand over his red-rimmed eyes and, with an effort, came to attention.

'Nobody but me up there. The bloke what found Jessica said he had to go and tell his wife, she'd be wondering where he'd got to – Boy!' On a mounting note of alarm: 'You don't mean young Appleyard?'

'That fire didn't start itself. It's the Appleyard archives that are burning.'

'Nick Bly had a fag in there before he went on duty, and I thought –' Sergeant Bowles started shakily across the grass. 'Young Steve!'

'You've done your bit!' Ellers, unbidden, caught the portly police officer by the arm, and guided him away from the house. Jurnet took off his jacket, dipped it quickly in the moat, then draped it, dripping, over his head and shoulders.

'Let's hope to God you're right, and there isn't anyone.'

The stairs were hot, but the air breathable, just about. A Persian rug smouldered on the landing. The smoke was thinner than Jurnet had anticipated, a curtain which did not so much conceal what was there as teasingly distort it into shapes which, as soon as the eye had painfully deciphered them, dissolved and re-formed into others, equally deceptive.

The heat was horrific, illuminated by flames which, except that they had the power to singe and scorch and burn, seemed equally an illusion, so inconstant were they – at one moment reduced to the merest pinpoints, at the next, reaching for the ceiling. Crouching and weaving, relying more on his knowledge of the layout of the flat than on what he could actually see, Jurnet found himself at last in the study. Ablaze, the Chippendale desk was still unmistakable.

'Steve!' he called, startled at the harsh croak that came out of his mouth. 'Steve!'

No reply. The fire in the cardboard boxes had died down a little. Scraps of the raw material for the definitive life of Appleyard of Hungary floated about the room like moths, the ghosts of moths. One of the oak floorboards hissed a spray of sparks and settled down to a stolid burning, nothing fancy or extravagant. By its steady glow, the detective at last caught sight of what he was seeking, and hoping against hope not to find.

Huddled in an angle of the wall, his chin on his knees, Steve Appleyard sat and watched the fire with blank, blackened face. His clothes hung in shreds. What showed between the tatters seemed themselves patches, bearing little resemblance to skin. When Jurnet, by a supreme effort, at last reached his goal and put his hand on this odd, violated body, the boy screamed in sudden, surprised agony.

After that, it was easy. The boy had fainted, and suddenly become as light as thistledown. Jurnet, astonished, could not make it out – but by then he could scarcely make anything else out either. It was not the impossibility of breathing which surprised him, but rather that to stop breathing had become a positive pleasure. All that huffing and puffing, day in and day out – when you came down to it, what was the point of it all?

Had he possessed breath enough to say it, he would have made some such observation to the dark presence he felt to be looming over him, and whom – to his even greater surprise, not being what you would call a religious man, he took to be God. It was not until some hours later, when Sergeant Ellers and the Superintendent were at last allowed to see him in the Norfolk and Angleby, that he discovered his saviour to have been the Hungarian, Ferenc Szanto.

31

Sergeant Ellers said: 'I'd not have believed it, if I hadn't seen it with my own eyes. He came down the stairs and out of the door with the two of you slung over his shoulders like a couple of bags of wet wash –'

'The kid!' Jurnet sat up in the narrow bed, swung his legs over the edge. Back to the huffing and puffing, he thought, not sure whether to be glad or sorry. 'Is young Steve OK?'

'They think so.' This from the Superintendent. 'He won't look quite so pretty, but otherwise they think he'll do.' He looked down at his subordinate's blistered legs, bedecked in bits of gauze soaked in something yellow and strong-smelling. 'And where do you think you're going?'

'Out of here. They'll be wanting the bed for someone who needs it. I feel fine.' The detective stood up, immediately feeling anything but. 'Fine!' he croaked, daring contradiction.

'Thinking about yourself, as usual! Here's Dave Batterby back from London, burning for a chance to prove he can succeed where the great Jurnet has failed – and you say you're fine! Don't tell me you'd deny the poor chap his big chance?'

In no mood for their usual joustings, Jurnet demanded: 'Is it OK, sir, for Sergeant Ellers to go and ask where they've hidden my clothes?'

'In the dustbin's my guess,' the little Welshman put in cheerily. 'Walk out of here the way you came in, boyo, I'd be obliged to run you in for indecent exposure.' Relenting: 'Not to worry! I rescued your keys, went back to your place, and picked up some replacements that look marginally better. You'll have to wheedle them out of Sister, though.'

'Are you sure you feel up to it, Ben?' For once there was no residual irony in the Superintendent's voice: a generous admiration. 'I'm hanged if I'd've rushed into a blazing house to rescue an idiot boy from the consequences of his own folly.' Oh yes you would, Jurnet thought; *and* emerged without a trouser crease out of place. 'I shall, of course, be placing a full report before the Chief. Won't do any harm on your record.'

'Can't see why, sir. I had to be rescued myself.'

'Szanto says he could never have located the boy in time if you hadn't found him first. The ceiling came down a second or two after he'd got the two of you out of the room.'

'Is there much damage?'

'The Fire Brigade managed to confine it to the curator's flat – though that splendid Long Chamber's going to need a lot of restoring. Did you know that Coryton was in the flat too?'

'Coryton!' The detective digested this surprising information. Then: 'After the Anne Boleyn letters, I suppose.'

'So he was,' said the Superintendent. 'And now he's here, down the corridor, with his hands in a fairly nasty mess, and his temper to match.'

'Why? Didn't he find 'em?'

'He did, in a manner of speaking.' Sergeant Ellers took up the story. 'He'd got into the flat from the main house, so nobody even knew he was there until he came stumbling out, waving a large envelope and grinning like he'd just won the pools. He tore the envelope open and took out a lot of yellowed old papers – the famous letters, I presume, though I can't say for sure because, for a second or two, they held their shape, and then the whole shoot collapsed, disintegrated before our very eyes. They must have been baked to a biscuit – over-baked – only, being yellow anyhow, I reckon, it didn't show up immediately. One minute they were sheets of paper, or parchment, or whatever – the next, little scraps blowing about like so much confetti. Mr Coryton carried on something dreadful, chasing after the bits like a butterfly catcher gone round the bend. Some of them blew into the moat, and he'd have followed, if Szanto hadn't caught hold of him by the scruff of the neck, and made him give over.'

Discovering it was uncomfortable to be indebted to someone for saving one's life, and doubly uncomfortable when that someone was somebody you might conceivably, one day, in the line of duty, have to arrest on a capital charge, Jurnet inquired ungratefully: 'How did Szanto come to get into the act?'

'He arrived back in his jeep from somewhere, with his pal, the lame one, just as people were streaming out of the main entrance after the alarm went off. PC Bly told him he weren't to go any further, but he took blow-all notice, sounded his horn and kept on going, round the corner of the house and right up to the footbridge. And when he heard that young Appleyard might be inside, he just let out a roar and went charging through the flat door. Crazy!'

'Lucky for me.' Reluctantly.

'You can say that again. Somebody must love you. Even the lame one wanted to have a go – ran a couple of steps like he was going to follow his mate – and, of course, fell flat on his face. When I went to help him up, he pushed me away and sat there, screaming something – in Hungarian, I suppose. I couldn't make head nor tail of it. I tell you, what with him and a raving lunatic chasing bits of old letters wafting in the breeze –'

'Was it really a breeze?' the Superintendent inquired whimsically. 'Or was it Anne Boleyn and George Bullen making quite sure their passion remained private, not something for prurient academics to stick their noses into, in the name of history?' Putting fancies aside: 'Makes you wonder, though – eh, Ben? If a man's willing to risk his own life for a bundle of letters, might he not be at least equally prepared to sacrifice someone else's, to get his hands on them?'

'It's a thought.' Jurnet nodded agreement. 'That handing over of the key – that's always got up my nose. A bit too pat, too contrived. You couldn't help suspecting he had a duplicate stashed away somewhere, and one day – when we were finally off the premises and the coast was clear – he'd spirit the letters away, get them Xeroxed and returned to the desk drawer with nobody the wiser till he was ready to spring them on the world. Just to be on the safe side, on the off chance he couldn't bring himself to wait for us to go, Jack here made it his business to keep tabs on them. The uses of a bit of thread! We checked those letters daily, and they were never touched.'

'Stands to reason,' the little Welshman pointed out. 'If Coryton *had* managed to get them copied, there'd have been no cause to risk getting himself barbecued to get his hands on them.'

Jurnet demurred: 'Don't know about that. Would the experts accept photostats without having the originals to compare them with? I wouldn't know.'

'Give it some thought, anyhow,' said the Superintendent kindly, but with that familiar undertone of threat which made Jurnet feel instantly better. 'What shall I tell Dave Batterby?'

Whatever else he had done, the curator of Bullen Hall had at last succeeded in making himself look memorable.

'You should have seen me twenty-four hours ago,' he declared boastfully, his eyes, deep in a still swollen face, bright and watchful. 'Out like a football. Really something to see. Besides, then you would have had to be nice to me, wouldn't you? Can't kick a football when it's down. Could hardly have asked me, as I'm sure you intend to ask me today, with all the sinister overtones that implies, how I could have risked my life to rescue those bloody letters.'

Jurnet said, without beating about the bush: 'Consider it asked.'

Francis Coryton looked down at his hands, inert on the bed. They were encased in clear plastic bags containing small quantities of some pink solution, and they seemed, almost, separated creatures: goldfish awaiting transport to the home aquarium.

'The answer, Inspector, is that I did no such thing. Risk presupposes a conscious selection between choices. I simply didn't stop to think – just as I didn't stop to think what, given its exposure to heat and flame, would be the almost certain consequences of extracting the correspondence from its envelope

208

instead of handing it over unopened to the conservation john-nies at the BM.' Francis Coryton chuckled, a curious rumble of sound from between rubber lips. 'Just as I didn't stop to think that my unpremeditated action would undoubtedly restore me to the Number One spot in your list of suspects – assuming, that is, that I haven't stayed there all along.'

Jurnet said: 'I make a point of treating all my suspects the same. No favourites. No top of the pops.'

'I hardly know whether to be relieved or affronted. On the whole, I think, flattered. Such a macho thing, murder. Nobody before has ever thought me capable of it.'

Jurnet said deprecatingly: 'Crippen was a mingy little man. You don't have to be anything special to kill someone. All you need's a defective moral sense and an overblown idea of your own importance.'

'How deflating!' Coryton looked at his hands again. Then: 'Ever heard of the Judgement of God, Inspector?'

'The Judgement of –?'

'Trial by ordeal, if you prefer. In the Middle Ages, when they had someone up on a serious charge, they had two very effective ways of determining the truth, or otherwise, of the accusation. The accused person either was required to pick up a stone lying at the bottom of a cauldron of boiling water, or else was ordered, barehanded, to carry a lump of red-hot metal over a specified distance. The scalded or the burned flesh, as the case might be, was bound up and left for a few days, and then the bandages were taken off and the wounds examined. Though you, as a modern police officer, might not think so, they were reasonable beings, the people who devised such tests. They knew from bitter experience that the Judgement of God, like God himself, could be mystifying and equivocal. So they didn't expect miracles – only that the hands should be well on their way to healing.' Coryton raises his own, bagged, hands and held them out to the detective as if proffering a gift. The pink liquid swirled about his wrists. 'Come back in a little while, Inspector, and see how mine are getting on. Maybe they'll convince you.'

'Of your guilt or your innocence?'

'That will be for you to say.'

32

It was a very nice funeral, as funerals went; the weather good, and Bullensthorpe churchyard as good a place as any for a kip pending the dawn of the last day. The whole countryside, of high and low degree, seemed to have turned out to wish Percy Toller happy dreams.

Jurnet, arriving late, noted with some surprise that even Miss Appleyard had come along. She sat in a front pew clasping a prayer book bound in ivory. In the row behind, Anna March, making an elaborate pretence of not seeing him, had engaged Mrs Coryton in an intense conversation, to which the curator's wife was responding with her customary good humour, but a little absent-mindedly, fingertips gently touching the area of abraded skin above her left cheekbone. No sign of Danny, who had made Percy's coffin – a farewell gift, if ever there was one.

No Charles Winter either, which was no surprise. According to the detective's information, the potter spent his days hanging about outside the derelict warehouse where Mike Botley had found sanctuary with a squat of like-minded companions.

Jurnet found himself a seat in the side chapel off the chancel, out of sight of the bulk of the congregation, and out of earshot of most of what the officiating cleric had to say in praise of the dear departed. The detective, who thought it unlikely the panegyric included any mention of Percy's career in crime, felt saddened by the omission, for the little man had been a burglar in a million. Angleby CID would not soon see his like again. And where fitter than in church to celebrate his special talents? How did that bit go – about there being more joy in heaven over one repentant sinner than for ninety-nine law-abiding citizens? The reverend gentleman, beseeching God's mercy on the soul of Percy Toller, clearly hadn't a clue that even as he pumped out his pious platitudes the trumpets in honour of the dear old ex-villain must be sounding fortissimo on the other side.

Jurnet joined in a couple of hymns, careful to shut off the sound whenever he came to a 'Christ' or a 'Jesus' or a 'Saviour';

names which, as a Jew in the making, it now embarrassed him to let pass his lips other than as an expletive, which somehow didn't count. A sudden sharp longing for Miriam transfixed him: an odd place to feel randy, and for an odd reason. He fixed his eyes intently on the black marble tablet on the facing wall.

To The Undying Memory Of Laz Appleyard
Appleyard of Hungary
A Hero Of Our Time
1926–1973

It was, on the whole, a jolly get-together. Even Mollie, her plump prettiness sadly diminished, shone with a pride in which there was more rejoicing than grief. Outside in the churchyard, the grass, the trees, the women's summery dresses, made it seem more a village garden fête than a funeral, the flowery box moving slowly on the shoulders of the dark-clad bearers an outsize cake of which you were invited to guess the weight.

Back at 'Pippins' the ham was as succulent and moist as if the little man himself had cycled into Bersham to get it fresh that morning. Jurnet helped himself to a slice without thinking; found it delicious and himself, to his immense gratification, devoid of guilt feelings. A milestone. To have reached the point where you could sin comfortably in a new religion must be progress.

Miss Appleyard, Jurnet noted, had not stayed to partake of the funeral baked meats, but both the Hungarians were there, a circumstance which embarrassed the detective considerably, since it meant he could not in decency postpone any longer thanking Ferenc Szanto for saving his life.

He waited until the blacksmith had settled his friend into an armchair, the sticks placed carefully to one side, and then joined him at the dining table where, with no genteel holding back, the big man was loading two plates with ham and potato salad.

Before Jurnet had time to speak, the Hungarian put down the two plates and clasped the detective in a hug as painful as it was unexpected.

'Thank you! Thank you!'

Extricating himself with as little damage to the still unhealed portions of his flesh as he could manage, Jurnet said: 'I'm the one should be doing the thanking.'

'The Fire Brigade themselves say, without you, Steve wouldn't have had a chance.'

'All the same –'

The other raised a large, calloused hand.

'Not another word!' Eyes twinkling: 'Kindly note that as a bloody foreigner, unlike you, I do not hang my head with English modesty and murmur "it is nothing". You are grateful – good! To be in a policeman's good books can never be bad, eh? Who knows when it will come in useful?'

'You weren't in the Norfolk and Angleby, at least. Glad you got out without too much harm done.'

'Harm? Me? A smith is a salamander, didn't you know that? Fire has no power against him. Who can smoke an already kippered kipper? But now –' readdressing himself to the food – 'now is time to eat. Why is it funerals make you always hungry? Is it because they remind us to get on with it while there is still time?'

Jurnet said with calculated cruelty – the debt had been acknowledged, time to get on to the next thing: 'I don't suppose any of us will have all that much of an appetite when it comes to burying young Jessica.'

At that, the other moved away without a word; set the two plates of food down on a sideboard until he had found a small table to place at the side of Jeno Matyas's chair. Having spread a napkin over his friend's knees, he retrieved one of the plates, set knife and fork upon either side; and only when he had seen the crippled man set to did he return to the detective's side, there to receive the second blow which Jurnet had ready and waiting.

'I'm sure it's already occurred to you that if you'd only told Steve right at the start about his possible relationship to Jessica, the boy wouldn't be just out of intensive care at the Norfolk and Angleby, and that poor girl could still be alive.'

The Hungarian spoke softly.

'You do me an injustice, Inspector. I knew nothing.'

'Oh? Miss Appleyard says, that time I found you messing about with the Appleyard papers, what you were really trying to do was remove any letters you could find relating to the affair with Mrs Chalgrove.'

'There is nothing Elena does not know. At the Coryton party I saw, for the first time, that here was a man and a woman in love, no longer children playing a game. And I thought – yes, before Mr Shelden was even dead, I thought – I must get hold of the love letters, if there were any, that had passed between Laz and Jessica's mother. Those two must not be hurt. Not because they were brother and sister – of that, I swear, I knew nothing. To me, Mrs Chalgrove was just another of Laz's women that came and went like the leaves on the trees. One less among so many to be written in Mr Shelden's book would, so it seemed to me, make no difference to the biography. But it could make Steve unhappy to know.'

'This at the same time you were planning to make Steve very unhappy indeed by letting him learn all those other home truths about his hero father.'

'Different altogether!' The Hungarian shook his head energetically. 'The girl – that was something real, precious. A jewel to be safeguarded. The other, the destruction of a myth.'

Jurnet said slowly: 'It's a good story, Mr Szanto. It holds together, sounds good.'

'But you don't believe.' Statement, not question. 'What did I tell you? What it is to be in a policeman's good books!' Ferenc Szanto burst into gargantuan laughter, and clapped the detective on the shoulder. Jeno Matyas looked up smiling, warmed by his friend's good spirits. The other funeral guests, chomping with dedication, frowned over their loaded plates. There was a time and a place for everything.

Jurnet opened the door to Percy Toller's study to find somebody there before him, sitting at the little desk: a raw-boned young woman with a face of engaging ugliness. At the detective's entrance she looked up smiling, and shut an open desk drawer without embarrassment.

'Not there,' she announced. 'Pity. Mrs Toller said she'd have been sure to come upon it, but I couldn't resist taking a look all the same.' Then: 'I'm Pam Grant, Mr Toller's OU tutor, just in case you thought I was after the family jewels.'

Jurnet grinned, liking what he saw.

'And I'm Detective-Inspector Ben Jurnet, just in case you were. What *were* you looking for, if I may ask?'

'Percy's last essay. He was going to bring it to me the night he –' She broke off, and began again after a moment's sombre reflection. 'Not to me personally, that is. For forwarding to Bletchley, untouched by human hands. Finished essays go to OU headquarters for marking. I don't see them till they come back, and then I can go over them with students.'

'We reckoned it must have been swept away in the flood waters. Something about the English novel, wasn't it?'

'That's right. "From *Pamela* to *Sense and Sensibility* – the Emergence of the English Novel, 1740–1810". Were you a friend of his? Did he let you see it?'

'Yes to the first question: no to the second. He mentioned what he was doing. Couldn't get over his own surprise it was him actually doing it.'

'It wasn't a joke, you know,' the young woman insisted earnestly. 'He was marvellous – a true original, with a wonderfully fresh way of looking at things, but with a quick, analytic brain any academic might have envied. I'm sure I learned a lot more from Mr Toller than he ever learned from me.' Miss Grant got up from the chair and looked round the little room with a smile. 'Not quite what I expected, I must say. You should have heard him going on about his study – and his books. Gorgeous leather bindings, first editions . . . he must have got it mixed up in his mind with the Library at Bullen Hall. Ah, well.' Turning back to the detective: 'Did Mrs Toller tell you she's going to join the Open University herself, in Percy's memory? Isn't that marvellous?'

'Give her something to take her mind off things, apart from anything else.'

'Just what I thought. She'll do well, too. When you've had as many students through your hands as I have, you get to know what to expect. Not in Percy's class, of course, but a sticker. Once she's made up her mind to get her degree, she'll soldier on till she gets it, come hell or high water. With Percy, now –' fondly – 'that was the one question mark. Had he the patience, the concentration, to stay the course? He'd make those great intuitive leaps forward, not always making sure beforehand there was a net to land in –'

Remembering all those high-flying burglaries which had ended with good old Percy not only finding no net to break his fall, but a copper waiting with open arms to catch him, Jurnet concurred gravely: 'I know exactly what you mean.'

Mollie kissed him when he took his leave, and thanked him for coming.

Jurnet said: 'That's a grand idea of yours – to do an Open University course yourself.'

'Cracked, really.' Lips quivering a little: 'I wouldn't want you to think, Mr Jurnet, even in the bad old days – even times he was inside – I wouldn't rather have been Mrs Percy Toller than the highest lady in the land.'

'You *were* the highest lady in the land.'

'You've always been very kind, Mr Jurnet. Percy always said it was almost worth while being a villain to have the honour of making your acquaintance.'

'Did he say that? Best compliment anyone ever paid me.'

'Don't think he didn't mean it. What he said was, that you were a very parfit gentil knight – like in Chaucer, the Canterbury Tales. Did he ever tell you how I got him on to learning bits out of the Dictionary of Quotations, one every day? I've decided to carry on with that, too, myself. It helps to make Percy seem – not quite so far away. You just open the book anywhere, and sometimes it's a whole poem, sometimes just a snippet, doesn't even seem to make sense.' Like a child asking to be asked: 'Would you like to hear what I learnt for today?'

'Tell me.'

'John Donne,' Mollie Toller began. '1571 to 1631.' Then:

> '"Love, all alike, no season knows, nor clime,
> Nor hours, days, months, which are the rags of time."'

Jurnet said: 'I like it.'

Seasons, thought Jurnet, were different in town from what they were in the country. Out there at Bullensthorpe, autumn was coming in like a carnival: flames flaring along the stubbles, the ploughed fields shameless in their naked promise. As the detective drove into the forecourt of his block of flats, the melancholy of summer's end seeped out of the cracked concrete to envelop him. It settled dankly on the car, the rubbish bags

215

awaiting collection, the thin black cat watching him from the shadows.

He still did not know who had killed Chad Shelden.

He climbed the stairs heavily, feeling that he ought to know; feeling that someone, somewhere, had told him all that needed telling, if only he had had the mother wit to take note of it. It was simply not possible for a halfway intelligent person to know people as he had come to know that lot out at Bullen Hall, and overlook that one little foible – that one of them was a murderer.

A supper of baked beans put him into a better frame of mind: willing to admit that, whatever the season, Angleby, for him, would always hold delights denied to those condemned to live out in the sticks. Perhaps that was the thing about cities. They had no seasons, like love.

'Love, all alike, no season knows, nor clime,
Nor hours, days, months, which are the rags of time.'

He spoke the words aloud, pleased to have them come pat. Good on you, John Donne, whoever you were, whenever you were.

In an inexplicable burst of optimism he spent the evening cleaning the flat, not even depressed that, at the end of his labours, it did not look noticeably different from when he had begun. He went to bed and, drowsily, between waking and sleeping, made up his mind to get a Dictionary of Quotations himself, and follow the Tollers' example. A quotation a day keeps the doctor away. Who knows? – he might even join the Open University. You too can learn to write essays with titles like 'From *Pamela* to *Sense and Sensibility*: the Emergence of the English Novel, 1740–1810'. It'd be worth it if only to see the Superintendent's face the day he signed his name with B.A. after it.

Poor old Percy! All that work down the drain. Gone to the bottom of the river. The submergence of the English novel.

Suddenly Jurnet was sitting up in bed, wide awake. The square of window in the opposite wall was still filled in with that dingy dark which, in the city, passes for night. Yet light had dawned, nevertheless, and for a blissful moment the detective allowed himself to bathe in its refulgence. In that lovely illumination, no shadows, everything became clear. Doubts fell away, the pieces fell into place: the puzzle complete.

For a moment, head against the pillows, Jurnet contemplated this happy state of affairs. Then he leaned over and switched on the bedside lamp, discovering to his surprise, since he had no recollection of having slept, that it was nearly two o'clock.

Which, still, was as nothing to his astonishment that he now had two murders on his hands.

33

Without sounding peevish or even put out, the Superintendent had observed: 'I still can't see why it can't wait until morning.'

Smoothing away the condensation on the windscreen with the flat of his hand, Jurnet wished – as he had wished then, in the Hospital call box, waking up his superior officer in the middle of the night – that he could have thought of an explanation convincing enough to satisfy the possessor of that voice tinged with ironic amusement.

At the Hospital, at least, it hadn't gone too badly; the security man turning out to be an ex-PC of the old school who had known the Inspector when he was still wet behind the ears, and the senior administrator an insomniac who had sounded positively grateful to be presented with a task to occupy the dragging hours. Even the night sister, adamant that nothing, nobody, was to disturb her sleeping patient, had softened under the influence of that dark, Mediterranean charm which the detective – an observing inner self the while twisting a wry lip at the bugger's taking ways – knew how to turn on when the situation called for it.

That Elena Appleyard, rather than the guardian dragon Maudie, had answered the phone at Bullen Hall, was better luck than he had had any right to hope for. Turning the car into the empty driveway, Jurnet saw the light on in the east wing, a small hole in the night. He brought the car to a halt: opened the door to find Elena Appleyard waiting for him.

She held no torch, seemed to know her way in the dark, like a cat. When the detective took out his own torch and shone it in her face, she barely flinched. With her hair spread out on her shoulders, the soft, flowing lines of her white silk dressing gown and filmy shawl, she could have been a fairy tale princess who had slipped out of the castle to an assignation with her prince. Blink and look again, and you saw a goddess old as creation, and as knowing.

She said, without introduction: 'I've done everything you asked. I've turned off the alarms and I've unlocked the door into the Appleyard Room. Here are the keys you wanted. Is that the lot?'

Taking the keys she held out to him: 'Thanks very much. Again, I'm sorry about waking you up.'

'As I've already had occasion to tell you, I'm a poor sleeper.'

She half-turned away, as if she had better things to do with the rest of the night. 'Do you need me any further?'

'My colleagues will be along presently. You'll need to turn the alarms back on after us.'

'I shan't bother.' She frowned briefly. 'Have you spoken to Steve?' Jurnet nodded. 'Then you'll know it really doesn't matter any longer what happens to Bullen Hall.'

'That's for you to say.'

'I do say. Goodnight, Inspector.'

'Just a minute.' Jurnet put out a hand to detain her. The slender arm beneath the billowing silk felt strong and unyielding. 'Don't you think, maybe, you ought to come along? I don't want to be held responsible if something goes missing.'

'That,' she said evenly, 'is a chance you'll have to take.'

Miss Appleyard had left a single light on in the Appleyard Room. It was enough for Jurnet. More than. With compressed lips he hurried on to the Library where George Bullen, sardonic over the mantelpiece, had this much, at least, to be said for him: that he had been dead four hundred years and more. Whatever he and that hot-pants sister of his had or had not got up to, it wasn't a matter for Angleby CID.

Jurnet's business at Bullen took him less time than he had expected, even though, after the initial exultation at finding what he had been looking for, he had proceeded – he who was normally so quick in his ways – with an odd deliberation, laying out the evidence on a table close to the window, and bringing a table lamp from its accustomed alcove to illuminate it. There had been a moment when the detective had stiffened, fancying he heard a step outside, the snap of a breaking twig: only to resume his work with a slight nod of satisfaction, or understanding.

Well before the Superintendent and Sergeant Ellers were due he was back at the car, eyes straining into the night, which was blacker than ever, the sky blanketed with cloud. Miss Appleyard had switched off her light and the darkness was complete. For all his excitement, a familiar melancholy depressed the detective's spirits. Death was a lonely thing, only life lonelier. Why did he always, on the trail of a killer and closing the distance between them minute by minute, feel himself the hunted rather than the hunter?

The beam of headlights swinging round in a wide arc from the road was immensely cheering. In another moment, Jack Ellers, in the driving seat, braked to a halt alongside, and informed Jurnet through the window: 'Jeep turned left into the road just as we were passing the Bullensthorpe turn-off. That OK?'

'What I was hoping for. Saves us the trouble of lighting the fuse.'

From within the car, the Superintendent, informal in an anorak of couture scruffiness, leaned across to say: 'You lead on, Ben. We'll follow. Everything's laid on, just as you ordered, even unto the wellies.'

'The wellies? I never —' Jurnet stopped short, rendered speechless by admiration and loathing in equal measure.

'Logistics,' the Superintendent proclaimed, settling himself comfortably in his seat. 'That's the name of the game. No detail too large, none too small. That's what I like to see.' He inclined his head towards his subordinate in benign approval. 'On the wet side, marshes!'

They came to the coast from among the bracken-choked hills that tumbled down to the wetland, giving the coast road a wide berth and creeping into the car park of Hoope bird sanctuary with lights out and only the voice of a PC alongside murmuring which way to go. The night was as black as ever, but no longer impenetrable. Sound and smell had taken over from sight.

From below rose the unique tang of the marsh, brackish and ancient, yet full of an astringent freshness to cleanse the lungs and send the blood coursing through the veins with renewed vigour. In a small wind which seemed to be blowing simultaneously from all directions, the reed panicles whispered ceaselessly against a clatter of elderly leaves. Somewhere close at hand, water gurgled on and on, as if making a small joke go a long way; whilst in the distance, sounding now near, now far, the sea broke on a shingly shore and retreated, hissing, for another try.

Using his torch circumspectly, Jurnet counted ten men in all awaiting instructions, seven of them in uniform, the other three in well-worn levis and anoraks; all of them local lads with wind-chapped faces, and voices that curved up and over towards the end of every sentence like the combers homing to the beach. They listened to Journet's briefing respectfully, and melted away into the darkness almost before he had finished speaking.

The three from Angleby followed; at first gingerly, distrustful of a world as it might have been at the beginning of Creation – land, sky and water not yet quite separated; then with increasing confidence, filled with a sense of the airy spaces that surrounded them: an enlargement of consciousness which did not save the Superintendent from walking into a dyke from which he emerged wet to the thighs, but with spirits unquenched.

Not much longer now.

Jurnet, head down, intent on the narrow path between the reeds, suddenly became aware – of what, he could not say, except that there was something. How, back in the Coachyard, had the bookbinder described that mysterious prefiguring of dawn? *Something left over from an earlier stage of man's development – perhaps even earlier than that. An apprehension of life beginning.*

And ending.

Behind him, the Superintendent took hold of Jurnet's shoulders, twisted them gently, so that he was forced to raise his eyes from their preoccupation with where he put his feet. At first, nothing seemed changed, except that the wind had strengthened and now blew unremittingly from the sea. Then the detective realised that the darkness, without dissipating itself in any discernible way, had split in two laterally; the lower part dense and anchored, as against the continued nothingness above.

Out of this nothingness, someone, something, essayed a tentative '*coo-ee!*' which, even whilst the three, startled, peered upward in the attempt to discover its source, dissolved itself into a bubbling trill which lost itself in the reeds' rustling.

'Curlew,' the Superintendent pronounced, with that calm assumption of knowledge which always made Jurnet want to poke him one in the kisser. 'Unless it was a whimbrel' – an admission of possible error which should have put all to rights, except what the hell was a whimbrel, anyway, when it was at home?

Sergeant Ellers, in a voice whose tone encapsulated what the little Welshman thought of marshes in general and Hoope in particular, demanded: 'What's that big lump sticking up?'

'That must be the barrow,' replied Jurnet, who, in the hours of waiting, had had time to study a map.

'Don't talk daft! Over there!'

'Not a *wheel*barrow,' the Superintendent put in. *There he was, sod him, at it again!* 'A long barrow. A grave. Some Bronze Age chieftain, I suppose, who wanted to be buried on the cliff, in sight of the sea.'

'Ruddy cemetery,' snorted the Welshman, not sounding at all surprised.

However the phrase went, Jurnet thought, turning away from the chubby, aggrieved face, and happy in the realisation that he could actually see it, dawn did not break. It crept up on you insidiously, before you had a chance to say no. Here I am, another day, and sucks to you.

Day seeped over the marsh and revealed, beyond the reeds and the shallow pools that reflected the sky, a high pebble ridge between cliffs which shut out the sea. Not much of a barrier, it seemed to Jurnet, against the breakers banging away on the further side. That old chap in the barrow, or the followers who had borne him to his last resting-place, must have known the way the tides went, to keep him stowed high and dry and out of harm's way, how many hundreds of years was it? Couldn't hardly have been expected to take into account that one day some nosy parkers, in the name of archaeology or whatever, would be along to cart the old bones to a glass case in Angleby Museum, far from the sight of the sea and the sound of the curlews calling, to say nothing of the whimbrels.

For a bird sanctuary, thought Jurnet, the place seemed a bit short on birds. A few gulls appeared over the ridge, planing inland on the wind: otherwise nothing. Such signs of life as were visible in the lightening day were of another kind. Rising doubled-up out of the marsh like some strange creatures out of the primeval ooze came the local fuzz. Up the steep side of the ridge they stumbled, dislodging little streams of pebbles as they went. They were a good third of the way up when the Superintendent gave a shout and pointed.

From the seaward side, a head and shoulders had appeared, the head comical in a knitted cap topped with an outsize pompom. The next moment, a slender figure was running along the narrow spine of the ridge, as spare and economical as a figure on a Greek vase. By the time the Superintendent had got his binoculars to his eyes, a second figure, broader than the first and hatless, had come into view following after.

'Good God!'

The second figure was brandishing a whip, short in the handle but long in the greedy tongue that snaked through the air seeking its quarry. The wind, the waves, the reeds were too noisy: yet the watchers fancied they heard its vicious *crack!* as it cut through the sky. The front runner, far ahead, looked back over his shoulder and waved a hand, whether in derision or defiance it was impossible to say.

Jurnet, too, began to run, splashing through bog and reedbed, daring the quaking ooze not to support him. Behind him, he could hear his companions, but his attention was all for the two figures silhouetted against the dawn sky. He had the impression, though no sound reached him, that the one in the rear was shouting.

All at once the second runner stumbled, and went down on his knees. The runner in the knitted cap turned, darted back; and with a sudden, quicksilver movement possessed himself of the whip. For a moment he raised it aloft, as if in triumph, and

222

the detectives held their breath, waiting for the wicked leather to fall upon the prostrate enemy. But no blow was struck, and in another instant the runner was on his way again. The other man, disarmed, struggled slowly to his feet, and stood shaking his head from side to side, like a bear or a large dog.

When he had again put a considerable distance between himself and his pursuer, the man in the knitted cap stopped once more. Head tilted back until it seemed that the absurd headgear must fall off, he whirled the whip about him, describing wide arabesques in the air. Like the ringmaster at the circus – the comparison came into Jurnet's mind – about to introduce a new act.

And suddenly there was exactly that. Jurnet caught his breath in incredulous wonder. In that instant, and as if conjured out of the newborn day, the air was full of birds, swirling up from the shoreline, their high, excited cries vibrating over the marsh. Rippling now dark, now light, they wheeled and banked, dipped and circled; seeming, to the viewers below, almost to touch the whip encouraging their performance. Then, like a perfectly trained corps de ballet, one movement melting seamlessly into the next, the birds flowed into an arrowhead pointing westward, and made their exit down the sky as mysteriously as they had come.

The leading figure turned and began running once more. The other followed. The climbers were nearing the top of the ridge.

'The cliff!' Jurnet shouted over his shoulder, ignoring the fact that a long, cigar-shaped lagoon lay between him and his objective. 'We can head them off!'

He plunged boldly into the lagoon's fringes, only to feel his wellies filling with water colder than any he could remember. A pair of affronted whooper swans that rose protesting from under his feet almost sent him headlong.

Profiting by their colleague's discomfiture, the Superintendent and the Sergeant contrived to find a safer way; waiting and saying nothing with exquisite courtesy as the Inspector struggled up beside them and emptied out his reeking boots.

The cliff, while not all that precipitous, was coated with some kind of mossy growth slippery as glass. By the time the three police officers reached its top, even the Superintendent had lost some of his famous cool. The view from the top, of the young sun shrugging off its cloud cover, the sea bisected by a causeway of palest gold, should have been compensation enough for all their effort. But it was not.

The two men had vanished.

Sergeant Ellers exclaimed: 'It's just not possible!'

A little below them, and to their left, the locals were by now spread out along the ridge looking flummoxed. Jurnet fished out the gadget he so hated to use that he usually forgot to carry it with him; got on to the little party's leader, and gave a brief order. Then he set off again, at the double.

'The barrow!'

The top of the cliff, rabbit-cropped, was little less slippery than its side; but, their goal in sight, the three covered the ground sure-footedly. They circled the mound of the ancient artefact, ripping their clothing on the barbed wire which enclosed it, and ignoring the warnings of danger of everything from natural subsidence to unexploded mines; and found, on the seaward side, that most of the covering of earth and vegetation had fallen away, exposing the vandalised burial chamber and the large grey stones, some of them still standing, which once had supported its roof.

All this Jurnet at once took in and did not see, his conscious attention absorbed by what was happening under his feet. On the floor of the chamber, the whip beside him like a discarded serpent, Jeno Matyas lay silent and unresisting among the rabbit droppings while Ferenc Szanto squeezed the life out of him.

'Vermin!' the blacksmith shouted. 'Judas!' The enormous hands tightened. 'To steal from those who have received us in hospitality! To kill in this land which has given us life, and work, and human dignity –!'

It took the combined strength of the three of them to pull the man off the still, recumbent figure. Not until Ellers sank his teeth into one of the hands did he finally let go of the thin neck on which the imprints of his great thumbs showed like the pug marks of some large animal. Only the timely arrival of four of the locals, to whom they thankfully delegated the task of subduing the maddened bull who went by the

224

name of Szanto, enabled the three detectives to return their attention to the target of his frenzy and the object of all their seeking.

The man's powers of recuperation were amazing. Even as Jurnet bent over him he nodded as if in greeting, his head propped against the sandy wall of the chamber, but shrinking away from the ministering hands as if he preferred not to be touched. Already his face was returning to its normal pallor, the eyes that a minute earlier had been staring out of his head deep-set and contemplating the world with their customary air of humorous expectancy.

The expectancy deepened to a passionate joy as suddenly, once again, the air above the barrow was full of birds that swished across the sky like the twirlings of a matador's cape, before streaming away westward in their turn, another arrow fleeing the rising sun.

When the birds had gone, Jeno Matyas said, his voice hoarse but contented: 'They'll be going across to the Lincolnshire coast to feed. They'll be back when the tide changes.' He swallowed with some difficulty, and then repeated: 'When the tide changes –' as if the words, for him, held some special significance.

It was all Jurnet could do to quell an irritation with which, from long experience, he was only too familiar. Why the bloody hell did murderers so seldom look the part?

The detective got out the gadget again, and transmitted a request for an ambulance and stretchermen. Listening, the smile on the Hungarian's face widened. He began to laugh, a harsh jangle that seemed both to surprise and hurt him, for he put a hand up to his throat and held it there. Nevertheless, he persevered with the unsettling noise until Jurnet, between gritted teeth, felt impelled to demand: 'Going to let us into the joke?'

'Do I really have to spell it out?' The Hungarian looked down at his legs, what there was to be seen of them. From a little below the thigh to a little above the ankle, and covering both limbs, lay one of the great stones that had once held up the chamber roof. A single foot which protruded from it stuck out at an angle which made it hard to accept that it was actually attached to a leg, the stone itself so flat as to make it quite implausible that human limbs were concealed beneath. The trousers from thigh to groin were dark with blood.

Jeno Matyas said: 'Thank you so much for laying on a lift. As you know, I am not really able to walk.'

34

'In this country, it seems, it is not enough to say to the officers of the law, "Yes, I am a thief. Yes, I am a murderer. I confess!" I still have to be badgered to explain how and why I am a thief, how and why I killed Chad Shelden and Percy Toller. Such morbid curiosity! Is it, perhaps, because you think I may be a lunatic in addition – one who does not understand what he is confessing to? Or that to suggest cutting short the solemn rituals of the public trial is a kind of blasphemy?

'Or is it because you yourselves harbour guilty consciences which require to be exorcised with appropriate ceremony before you can bring yourselves to cage me up like a wild animal, out of sight of the sea and the birds flying?

'How refreshing your English justice is! How touching in its innocence! Your tongues are hanging out to hear my story, yet still you provide me, gratis, with a lawyer whose prime function appears to be to impress upon me that it's no part of my business to do the prosecution's work for them. Stay mum, and let the police bring forward their evidence, such as it is. And what can that be, I ask myself? Some old books that have been tampered with, a pair of cuff links; an essay for which the Open University is still waiting? Is there more? I hardly think so, for I have been very careful.

'There I go again, making dangerous admissions! The lawyer, I fear, will be sadly disappointed in me. He takes me, I think, for an intelligent man. Nevertheless, I retract nothing. I am sorry for what I have done: I am not ashamed of it. It was, shall we say, a regretable necessity.

'If it does not sound too absurd to put it so, there was nothing personal in my murder of Mr Shelden. Five months before ever he came to Bullen Hall I knew I should be obliged to kill him.

Miss Appleyard came into my workshop one morning with a Book of Hours that needed a page repairing – a lovely thing, of the highest quality. She told me, in the way of conversation, that she knew I would be interested to hear that she had arranged for Mr Chad Shelden, the well-known writer of biographies, to take over as curator of Bullen Hall when Francis retired in five months' time.

'Oh, I was interested!

'It was Ferenc Szanto, as you may or may not know, who first brought me to Bullensthorpe. What a stroke of luck it seemed, to fall in by chance with one of the great men of the 1956 rising! But when I saw the Bullen Library, I saw the finger of destiny.

'Let me explain. I was an exile because, one day in Hungary, a bomb had gone off under a car in which a Soviet general was travelling. I had to get out of the country fast: but that did not mean I gave up the fight to free my homeland from under the heel of the Russian jackboot – only that I was forced by circumstances to change my *modus operandi*. Resolve and dedication, however deeply committed, are of themselves useless against an enemy armed to the teeth. We too had to have arms. And arms cost money.

'In the dining room at Bullen, over the fireplace, there is a Rembrandt which, turned into cash, could equip a small army – but how, assuming one could remove it successfully, to dispose of a painting known the world over? Ransom, perhaps? But ransom means that one must be prepared, in the last resort, if the deal falls through, to destroy the evidence – and I admit frankly that, given the choice, I would rather murder a man than a Rembrandt. There will be other men: a Rembrandt is irreplaceable.

'The books, on the other hand, were a different matter. I soon discovered that not only did Bullen possess a collection of antiquarian books of superb quality and worth, but one that nobody ever so much as looked at. So long as they were there, on their shelves, no blank spaces, all was well. Who would ever miss one, or two, or three, or four?

'The trustees were delighted with Ferenc's discovery of me. Old books – this much at least they knew – need looking after, and I was a skilled bookbinder and restorer. A workshop was provided in the Coachyard, the keys to the cases were turned over to me with a trustfulness that was almost embarrassing, and I was in business. For one small Caxton alone, the first English-French vocabulary ever printed, my contact in London obtained £63,000. Not bad, eh? And so it went on. It hardly seemed like theft, so little was anybody deprived. Making up convincing dummies to replace the originals I had abstracted became an enjoyable hobby; one at which I became very proficient. So long as nobody actually took one of my replacements down from the shelf – and nobody ever did – I had nothing to worry about.

'It was too good to last, and the day Miss Appleyard came in with her Book of Hours time began to run again, against me. Francis Coryton was an ignoramus, but Chad Shelden was a serious historian. It was unthinkable that, given such a library on the premises, he would not find occasion to use it.

'So, he had to die.

'The first stage of Mr Shelden's dying was that I became a cripple. Who would suspect a cripple of murder? First I limped, then I shuffled, then I found it impossible to get along without sticks. Ferenc, poor foolish fellow, was dreadfully upset at my increasing infirmity. I hardly need to tell you, after what he tried to do to me, down there by the sea, that he had no idea what was going on. Hero of the rising he may have been, today he is an ageing buffoon who is so besotted with being an Englishman that he keeps his certificate of naturalisation framed on the wall, and all but crosses himself every time he passes it by, as if it were a holy icon. Besides, to him, Bullen and all it contains is Steve's patrimony. He would never knowingly allow me to steal any of Steve's books, even if it was only an old copy of *Playboy*.

'Ferenc insisted I should see a doctor, and ask him for a letter to the specialists in the Norfolk and Angleby. Making a great thing about not making an unnecessary fuss, I complied: – that is to say, I had him drop me off at the doctor's surgery, and leave me at the Hospital entrance. When he came by later, to pick me up, I did not, of course, mention that, on both occasions, I had not got beyond the vestibule. Tears came into his eyes when I reported that the doctors had said there was nothing they could do for me.

'The secret of a successful pretence is that the pretender must himself believe in it. I not only acted the invalid, I thought myself into invalidism. I thought myself into pallor and sunken cheeks. Even at the coast, on the marsh and the shore, where there were only the birds to check whether I was lame or leaped like a hart, I moved along painfully on my sticks. Only in the back room behind the printing press, where, late at night and hour after hour, I rode the exercise bicycle I had bought so that my muscles would not waste away and render me incapable of the task I had set myself, did I temporarily become again Jeno Matyas, the whole man.

'For all that I speak of him now so disparagingly, let me make it clear that I have, in the past, been fond of the man, Ferenc Szanto; and – as I have already made clear to you – I shall give you no help whatever should you wish to proceed against him for attempting to murder me. For that I bear him no ill will whatever. What is murder, after all – even one's own – but an insignificant acceleration of the inevitable? However, let me also make it clear that I am no longer fond of him. There was I, on Hoope beach, calm and contented, waiting for the dawn and the birds, and he comes storming along, wielding the whip which, ironically, I made for him. He had been recalling nostalgically the days at Kasnovar when he and Laz Appleyard, as boys, had ridden on the huge hay waggons, driven by the waggoners with their great whips: and so I made just such a whip, and gave it to him for Christmas.

'A strange return for a gift to have a maniac thrashing at your legs and screaming, "Run, damn you! Run!"

'Naturally, I answered him: "Ferenc, what is this? You know I can't run." And it was true. I couldn't. I had thought myself back into being a cripple. The pretence had become real again.

'He did not, would not, listen. "Run, you bastard! Run!" he shouted, the whip whistling through the air and striking my calves, my ankles. I tried to crawl away from him, crying out, "Have you gone mad?"

'After that, he said nothing more. But the whip! The whip spoke for him – my God, how it spoke! – and at last, to my shame, I could stand the pain no longer. The pretence dissolved. I sprang to my feet and ran.

'And so I think, perhaps, when I say that I am no longer fond of Ferenc Szanto – when I say that I hate him more than I thought it possible to hate anybody except a Red or an Avo – it is really myself I hate for my own weakness: – a man ready to give his life for his cause, so I prided myself, who, faced with the test, could not even stand a whipping.

'But that was all in the future. In the meantime, making plans for the death of a man I had not even been introduced to, was rather like making a coffin without knowing the measurements of its prospective occupant. Of two things only was I certain – that my victim would be moving into the curator's flat in the west wing; and that I must kill him without hanging about: for what more natural than that a writer, so soon as he had unpacked his toothbrush and his pyjamas, should be attracted to the Library as iron filings to a magnet?

'I knew – we all knew – about the state of the Bullen Hall roof. Every now and again we would find a stone that had fallen from the balustrade, and Mr Benby, the estate surveyor, would warn us yet again, if ever we went up there, to stay away from the edge for God's sake, unless we wanted a nasty accident.

'An accident! That was the answer to my problem. All I had to do was strike Mr Shelden unconscious, carry him up to the roof by the stair from the minstrels' gallery, and drop him over the end directly overlooking the moat, into which he would fall and conveniently drown, if, by chance, the fall itself were not enough to finish him off. What more natural than that the newly arrived curator should explore his new domain, including the roof above his quarters, and, forgetting all warnings in his eagerness to see all that was to be seen, lean against a parapet which gave way under his weight? That's life, we would all say, shaking our heads sorrowfully when we heard the news: not to say death.

'As soon as I heard that the Corytons were planning a party to coincide with Mr Shelden's arrival, I decided that the deed must be done that very night, after the guests had gone. I knew that the Corytons often slept out on the roof on hot summer nights, and I hoped they would recommend the habit to their successor. It would save me a lot of trouble to find him already up there, ready and waiting.

'Well before the great day I managed to get hold of the key to the roof long enough to have a duplicate made, and the original returned with no one the wiser. It was not only a question of needing the roof for the actual act. Shelden would obviously have been expected to lock and bolt his front door once the partygoers had departed, and, if the "accident" was to be credible, those locks and bolts must be found in place in the morning. To go through the main part of the house was out of the question. I had no knowledge of the alarm system, and no means of learning without attracting attention to myself. I had both to come and go from my rendezvous with Mr Shelden via the roof.

'There are several skylights and stairs to the Bullen Hall roof in different parts of the building, but, apart from the stair from the minstrels' gallery, none of them is used to any extent. What's more, most of them, so far as I was able to make an inspection, are so stuck up with paint or rust as to be useless for my purpose. I would be bound to leave traces which, if noticed, would inevitably prejudice a verdict of accidental death.

'It therefore took a little while to figure out a way of accomplishing my goal; but I found it at last – that same little turret where Francis came upon his precious letters. One side of it fills in a corner of the North Courtyard: the other, as you've doubtless noticed, projects out from the west front. I asked Francis for the key quite openly – said I wanted to make sure there were no books stored there – and, again, I was able to get a copy made before I returned it. The importance of the turret is that there is a narrow window at the top, just wide enough for a thin man to squeeze out of – you will be able to verify this for yourselves – from which it is only a short jump to the nearest area of flat roof. Once there, of course, any part of the Bullen roof is equally accessible, all of it covered with a wonderful kind of marl which, in dry weather at any rate, shows not even the shadow of a footprint.

'I do not, however, recommend that you attempt literally to follow in my footsteps. The distance from turret window to rooftop is short, but not as short as all that, especially from a standing start on a narrow, sloping window ledge. I practised it many times in the small hours, and more than once found myself hanging by my fingernails from a ledge that threatened to give way at any moment. But there, all life is a gamble, and I felt supremely confident that all would come right on the night.

231

'As indeed it did, give or take the odd unforeseen hitch which, I have come to believe, is so much part and parcel of all such enterprises as not to be, except at the conscious level, unforeseen at all. Inspector Jurnet will confirm that the party was a great success. For me, the main interest was in meeting Mr Shelden face to face for the first time. Although the man himself was a disappointment – a shallow person, I thought, and tainted with ambition – the sight of him in the flesh challenged and excited me. Waiting for the party to end, I found it hard to play the cripple. I felt stretched, larger than life – though not too large, I hoped, to go through that turret window!

'I wouldn't, by the way, want the Inspector to think that I misled him completely when, later, I told him what I had seen during the early hours of that fateful morning. I did indeed settle my gear in my car, since I intended to leave for Hoope as soon as I had finished my business with Mr Shelden: and I did indeed, as I told him, see, coming from the direction of the west wing, the figure of a weeping woman who could well have been Anne Boleyn bewailing her fate. Except – and this last small detail I must confess I omitted when recounting the story – that suddenly, when it had almost passed from my astonished view, this same mournful apparition raised one of its arms, whipped off its head of luxuriant dark hair, and ejaculated, in the unmistakable tones of Master Mike Botley, the single word, "Shit!"

'I gave the young fellow a few minutes; started up the car and parked it at the bottom of the drive, out of sight of the house: then set out for my turret. I unlocked the door, ran up the spiral stair with mounting elation; swung myself out of the window and across the intervening space with an easy abandon that made me want to shout with laughter. As you can imagine, I restrained myself, moving swiftly and silently in my dark track suit like a hunting cat, and only slowing down when I came to the chimney stack which all but cuts off the view of that peninsula of roof above the curator's flat. There, I edged round the chimneys and, to my delight, saw Chad Shelden standing at the balustrade with his back to me.

'True, it was the south-facing wall instead of the one giving directly on to the moat: but there, one can't have everything.

I've been trained in unarmed combat, and Mr Shelden would never have known what hit him had I not stumbled over a corner of the mattress which I hadn't noticed spread out on the marl. Even so, he had no more than a fraction of a second to turn and stare in astonishment before I was on him with a lightning movement that up-ended and tossed him over the parapet. Anyone hearing the sound he made as he fell would have taken it for a wood owl calling its mate.

'I heard him thud on the grass below, and, looking over the edge could see his ankles gleaming with a surprising whiteness. The feet were not moving: but the man had seen me, and I had to make sure he was dead. I stayed on the roof only long enough to push out a couple of stones from the west-facing parapet, then went down the stairs into the flat.

'The door was unlocked, and I did not need to use my key after all. The Long Chamber smelled stale after the party. I wore rubber gloves but, even so, was careful to touch nothing. Except that when I came into the hall, I saw that the bedroom light was on, and, when I peeped inside, there on the dressing table was Mr Shelden's wallet as well as a handsome-looking pair of gold and sapphire cuff links. There were three fifty-pound notes in the wallet, and I took two of them, fearing that a complete absence of paper money might excite suspicion. I also helped myself to the cuff links, all grist to the mill, and continued on my way downstairs, to tuck their owner into that bed where he would sleep sound and safe, the moat.

'There are, as you know, windows in the downstairs hall on either side of the front door. I had just reached up to pull back the upper bolt when some protective fate nudged me to glance out of one of them. I drew back my hand just in time.

'Outside, bending over Shelden where he lay sprawled on the grass, was Miss Appleyard, dressed in a handsome housecoat, with a shawl over her shoulders. As I watched, she reached for an arm and felt for a pulse, quite as if she were a professional. Then she listened for a heartbeat. In another moment she straightened up, quite composedly – but then, I imagine, it would take more than death to frighten Miss Appleyard – wrapped her shawl more closely about her, turned and walked away, I could only imagine to call the police.

'I gave her time to turn the corner of the house, then quickly undid the bolts, opened the door, and hurried outside to see if Shelden were still alive. He was, but deeply unconscious, his breathing shallow and irregular.

'He didn't look as if he could last long. Still, I couldn't take the chance that there might be some brief recovery of consciousness during which he might name me as his attacker. Notwithstanding that the intervention of Miss Appleyard now meant it would be known that the man had not fallen straight off the roof into the moat, I dragged him down to the water just the same, as being the easiest way of finishing him off without inflicting some injury which one of your clever forensic surgeons might diagnose as being man-made. Miss Appleyard would be bound to say that she had found the man alive. All to the good! It was surely conceivable that he had come round after her departure, tried to crawl to get help, and, in his agony, not knowing what he was doing, had ended up in the moat. When later, after all my careful attention to detail, the police nevertheless declared that Chad Shelden had been murdered, I was amazed. How could you possibly know? – until you released the information that Shelden had been paralysed by the fall, and so could not possibly have dragged himself over the grass, not so much as an inch. Then, too late, I told myself off for the fool I am, not to have thought of such a possibility.

'There were still things I had to do. I had to go back indoors so that the door could be bolted on the inside; which meant making my way upstairs, and over the roof again, back to my turret, and so down to the ground. I made the jump back from roof to turret with as little thought for the danger as when I had done it in the reverse direction. Despite Miss Appleyard's unexpected appearance, I remained unalterably convinced that it was my night.

'And so it was: my night and my day. I came out of the turret door, locked it, and ran with all speed along the west front, past the spot where I had dumped Shelden in the moat, round to the front of the house, and so to my car. No police had arrived. I started up the car as quietly as I could, and didn't switch on the lights until I was well along the road. No police passed me on their way to Bullen, no vehicle of any kind, all the way to the coast.

'When I got to Hoope, I parked the car, and hobbled on my

two sticks down to the beach. I was a cripple again. I could no longer remember when I hadn't been a cripple. When, settled cosily in my hide, I saw, just as the sun was coming up, a Dusky Warbler, a bird all the way from the Himalayas which has only been recorded at Hoope three times before, my happiness was complete.

'As for Percy Toller, his death was the real accident, a quite fortuitous concatenation of circumstances which, to my regret, left me with no alternative but to kill him. He was an uneducated man, but a true lover of books – not only their contents, but the look of them, their feel, their mystery. He often came into the Coachyard to watch me at work, or to repeat to me his quotation of the day. Did you know he used to learn a fresh one every day out of the Oxford Book of Quotations?

'He told me, shyly, that he had enrolled in the Open University, and, when I didn't laugh at his aspirations, was emboldened, I think, to let me know how much he wished the Bullen Hall books were available for private reading. The thought of studying the set texts in first editions or in handsome library bindings seemed quite to intoxicate him. Ironical, was it not, that this ignorant little fellow, totally lacking in educational advantages, was the one person at Bullen interested in the books?

'I think he had hopes that I, with full access to the collection, would offer to get him a few books on the side, but of course I was always the soul of rectitude and never took the hint, however broad. Once he told me – possibly in jest, possibly not: you will know the truth of it – that in his younger days he had been a burglar, and only the influence of his wife, Mollie, kept him from a relapse into his old bad ways, and from taking by stealth some of the books he longed most to read.

'The afternoon of his death, just after closing time, he came into the workshop in a very agitated condition; and when I saw what he had brought with him I was almost equally agitated, although this, I flatter myself, I managed to conceal. He began by telling me that Mollie was away, that he had been finishing an essay for the Open University to do with Jane Austen; and what with one thing and another, Mollie's restraining influence being absent, he had taken the opportunity to break into one of the bookcases and forcibly "borrow" a first edition of *Sense and Sensibility*.

'That was the book he held in his hand – or would have been, if that particular edition of Jane Austen's masterpiece hadn't been sold some six months previously to a collector in the United States.

'He was no fool, was Percy; and he was in a blazing fury. Had he discovered that I was the murderer of Chad Shelden I don't think he would have been half as angry.

'"How could you do it?" he shouted, shoving the dummy book under my nose. "How the bleeding hell could you go and do a thing like that?"

'I managed to calm him down eventually. I spoke to him about the Soviet oppression of my country and, in the end, had him almost in tears with my stories of children starving in the streets, and Cossacks galloping about the countryside ravishing virgins and then disembowelling them. I rather fancy the burglar story may have been true, because, otherwise, I think he would never have come to me for an explanation, but gone straight to the police. As it was, he finally promised to say nothing, so long as thenceforward I left the books alone. In his opinion, not even starving children nor ravished virgins justified the rape of one first edition of Jane Austen.

'We shook hands on it, and off he went, leaving the telltale dummy safely on my worktable. He left in something of a hurry, our conversation having taken up time he hadn't budgeted for. I gathered he was going home to snatch something to eat, and then he would be cycling into Angleby for an Open University tutorial, at which he intended to hand in his completed essay. Mollie, it appeared, was not due back in Bullensthorpe until later in the evening.

'After he left, I sat for a little while. I liked Percy Toller. I also knew there wasn't a hope that, sooner or later, he wouldn't give Mollie a full account of what I'd been up to.

'I shut up shop, perceiving there was no way out. Ferenc had borrowed my car to go and see the Marx Brothers. I took up my sticks and slowly made my way to the forge.

'The jeep was parked in its usual place in a kind of open lean-to with a roof of corrugated iron. Ferenc, Steve Appleyard and I all had keys to this vehicle. Before the mysterious ailment attacked my legs I used to take it out quite a bit; but the clutch had a kick like a mule – quite beyond the control of a crippled man!

'This, however, was an emergency. I hoisted myself into the driving seat, placed the sticks on the floor by my side, and drove off through the wood to the Hundred Field, taking the path that Steve had been taking daily during the harvest. No one was going to notice an extra set of tyre tracks.

'When I got to the field, I parked the jeep on the headland, and, first pulling on my rubber gloves, made my way, parallel with the road, to the corner of the field which adjoined the bridge over the river. The Bullen estate, I soon found out the hard way, looks after its hedges. I had brought one of my sticks along with me, but even with its help to force back the worst of the quickthorn, getting through that hedge was no joke. I couldn't have left the field by the gate and reached the bridge by walking along the road in case any of the Bullensthorpe people drove by and recognised me.

'A bit battered, I crossed the bridge, and immediately concealed myself in that opening on the further side which the village children use to get down to the river. Through the sparse sprinkling of bushes that dotted the slope it was perfectly possible to keep watch on the road from Bullensthorpe without being seen oneself. It was very peaceful – a pair of collared doves calling in the woods, otherwise everything enveloped in that dense quiet which often seems to fall out of the sky with the dusk.

'Fortunately for me, Percy Toller came along while there was still sufficient light for me to be sure it was him.

'"Percy!" I said, in a jolly way, grasping my stick and stepping out into the road. "Hello there!"

'"Mr Matyas!" he exclaimed, and got off his bike to speak to me.

'He had no time to say more. I hit him hard on the left temple with the crook of my stick which is made from some wood as hard as stone, and he fell without a sound. The bicycle toppling over in the road made more noise than he did.

'I dragged him on to the verge, wheeled the bicycle down to the water and left it there, one handlebar sticking well up into the air. Thank goodness it was getting dark! I hadn't expected the water level to be so low. Then I put Percy in the river, face down. It was a gentle death.

'There was one of those flat, modern cases on the carrier, and before I put that in the river I took a look inside. I found a mac, some pencils and a note pad, which I left, and a large manila envelope addressed to the Open University. It contained the famous essay. When I turned it over I saw that Percy had printed his name and address on the back, together with the essay's title: "From *Pamela* to *Sense and Sensibility*: The Emergence of the English Novel, 1740–1810". Seeing the title I thought I'd better take that with me, just to be on the safe side, far-fetched though it seemed that anyone would make the connection. That was an error of judgment, wasn't it? If I'd left it in the river I doubt if anybody would have thought twice about it.

'Having retrieved it, it was even more of an error not to destroy it. I kept the essay at first because I was genuinely interested to see what Percy had written; and when I had read it, I was so enchanted with his fresh, exuberant approach to literature that I didn't like to get rid of it. I even had thoughts of printing a little book from it when all the hue and cry had died down – a small gesture of personal homage – bound in tooled leather the way Percy would have loved it.

'Foolish sentimentality! The bomb that blew up the car with the Soviet general also killed two little girls who happened to be wheeling their dolls' prams along the pavement at the moment the car passed by. My job was to detonate the bomb by remote control from a shed less than a hundred yards away. I could see the street, I could see the children coming along, and then I saw the Russian car. Should I have let it pass unharmed for the sake of the lives of those two children? If your answer to that question is yes, you will never change the fate of nations. I pushed down the plunger and detonated the bomb.

'After that, killing Percy Toller was, as you English say, a piece of cake.'

35

The Superintendent said: 'That administrator at the Norfolk and Angleby – he belongs to my golf club. He wanted to know if we always operate like that, waking people up in the middle of the night.'

Jurnet looked surprised.

'I thought he seemed quite pleased; once, that is, he understood I wasn't asking him to divulge confidential information about a patient – quite the contrary. He told me he was usually up till all hours.'

'Oh, he wasn't complaining. Merely curious. Naturally, I told him we did it all the time.'

'He was very helpful. So was the computer bloke, once he got his eyelids propped up. Ada's what he called her – the computer. All the while he was plugging in and switching on he kept murmuring endearments, like it was a bird he wanted to have it off with.'

'Every man's fantasy,' the Superintendent observed wryly. 'A woman you can programme always to come up with the right answer.'

'She did that time all right, even if it was, in a manner of speaking, no answer at all. Nobody by the name of Jeno Matyas ever was a patient at the Norfolk and Angleby. The bloke checked it twice over, just to be sure. The second time, Ada practically spat at him for doubting her word. The only real obstacle I came up against was the night sister when I asked could I have a word with young Steve.'

'Whereupon you turned on that Latin charm, and she became as putty in your hands.'

Jurnet reddened slightly, the Superintendent's shot in the dark having landed precisely on target. It had been worth it, though. The boy had come awake, a damaged ghost under the dimmed light; but he had responded to being questioned with avidity, almost with a kind of pleasure that there were other things to remember than the death of Jessica Chalgrove.

Yes, as a matter of fact, he *had* noticed something different about the jeep when he went over to the forge to pick it up the morning he found Percy in the river. He had thought at first it must have sprung a second leak overnight, because there were two patches of oil instead of the single one he had got used to seeing on the concrete standing. But then he had realised it was the same old leak after all. All that had happened was that somebody – so far as he was concerned, it had to be Ferenc – had either moved the vehicle a few feet, or else taken it out and then reparked it in not quite its former position.

'An essay on Jane Austen, a computer print-out, and a patch of oil under a jeep,' the Superintendent enumerated. 'Sherlock Holmes couldn't have done better!'

Jurnet said simply: 'Don't know about that, sir. I know *I* should have, sooner. Trouble was, I'd been looking at Percy's death the wrong way. So long as it was accepted as an accident, it didn't seemed to matter, from the police point of view, that his famous essay had gone for a Burton. Swept away by the flood water just as you'd expect, and that was that. But taking a different perspective – saying to oneself, suppose there was something fishy about the whole business, after all – why then, the disappearance of that essay was something that had to be accounted for, like every other detail in a murder investigation. Percy, you could be sure, would never have left his precious homework naked to the elements when he could have packed it in his swanky briefcase to make sure it arrived at its destination fresh and clean. But there was only a notepad and some pencils in the case when we found it. Which – still thinking the worst for the sake of argument – could only mean that somebody had taken the essay out before throwing the case into the river.'

'Why should anyone want to do that?'

'That was the 64-dollar question. "From *Pamela* to *Sense and Sensibility*" – it had to be something to do with books. To do with the books in the Bullen Hall Library. It was then I began to put two and two together. I remembered what Mollie had said about Percy being mad to get his hands on them; and how there they were, row upon row, and nobody reading anything but the title on the spine.

'When is a book not a book? That was the thought that came into my mind – and since it was all to do with Jeno Matyas the bookbinder, the thought that came next was something Jack said about the fire: – how Matyas had taken a few steps to follow his pal into the burning house, and then fallen flat on his face. Supposing he'd forgotten the pretence in the stress of the moment, and only remembered just in time? In other words, when is a cripple not a cripple?'

'God knows what the DPP's going to make of it.' The Superintendent did not sound all that eager to play guessing games. He got up from his desk and stood glowering out of the window. 'And don't tell me Matyas has made a full confession. We still have to go into court on a solid basis of evidence.'

Sergeant Ellers took a calculated risk and spoke up.

'You've got to give the bugger a little credit, sir! After all, it's thanks to him we've traced the shop in Cromer where he got the keys cut. We've recovered Shelden's cuff links, and got Percy's essay. The lab's got so many bits and pieces of his jacket and slacks out of that hedge he went through, it's a wonder Percy didn't take to his heels at the sight of him. And that's to say nothing of him giving the game away at Hoope, prancing along the beach like a bargain basement Nureyev.'

'Exactly as the Inspector planned it, of course!' The Superintendent was not yet ready to abandon his ill humour. 'Getting Miss Appleyard to telephone the other Hungarian with some nonsense about intruders in the Library, and then making sure he got a sight of those fudged books –'

'It worked, sir, didn't it?' the little Welshman persisted. 'Ben knew if anyone could flush Matyas out, get him walking, it would be his pal Szanto –'

'Hold on!' Jurnet nevertheless smiled gratefully at his mate. 'Don't have me knowing all the answers. First go off, I thought the two of 'em were in it together. It certainly wasn't any part of my plan to have Szanto take along his horsewhip to make sure Matyas got on to his own two feet and no two ways about it.'

The Superintendent remarked sourly: 'It's no offence I know of to pretend you can't walk when you're perfectly able to. So far as I'm aware, Matyas was neither soliciting alms, claiming disability allowance, nor making bogus demands upon the National Health Service.'

'He is now,' Jurnet pointed out sombrely. 'Not bogus. The latest is that one leg may have to come off.'

241

'My heart bleeds,' said the Superintendent. He came back to his desk and picked up the copy of Jeno Matyas's confession, turning the pages to the closing sentences, about the little girls and their dolls' prams, which he read, slowly and with a close attention, as if reading them for the first time. Then he raised his head from the typescript and said in a quiet voice that conveyed more than invective: 'These people who talk about nations, the fate of nations, all mankind – they're the really depraved ones. There is no *all* mankind or anything else – only one and one and one, and one, and so on, ad infinitum.' He looked directly at Jurnet, and said, with a simplicity the detective longed to believe in: 'Well done, Ben!'

Jurnet offered, with a certain diffidence: 'There was one other small pointer, once its significance dawned on me. I'm still not sure Percy wasn't trying to pass me a message in code – telling me something without actually shopping a fellow-villain in so many words. His quotation for the day, that last time I saw him at the Hall, was just one line: "Rob me, but bind me not, and let me go." Bind me not,' Jurnet repeated, then, pronouncing the surname and the Christian name of the poet so that they rhymed: 'It's by a geezer named John Donne.'

The Superintendent corrected him kindly: 'You mean John Donne' – pronouncing it Dunn, the bastard.

But then, thought Jurnet, he would, wouldn't he, bless his heart.

If asked, Jurnet would have been hard put to it to produce a convincing reason for driving back yet again to Bullen Hall. Surely he had seen enough of the place to last a lifetime!

With the passing of summer's heat, the great lawn in front of the house was greener than ever. The world had rolled round a little since that broiling day when the detective had heard the peacock scream. Now the sun, so mellow on the old brick, gilding afresh the little pennons atop the turrets, packed beneath its benign exterior a spiteful undercurrent of chill. The trees had a slatternly look, the rookeries exposed by the thinning leaves.

Nothing stayed the same, Jurnet reflected, accepted: things changed even as you looked at them. All the same, he felt a need to fix the place in his memory, set it in jelly like one of Rosie Ellers' celebrated moulds in aspic, every slice of cucumber in its appointed place.

The Coachyard was moderately crowded. Considering the time of year, the shops were doing good business. Anna March, in the middle of selling a pair of earrings to a hard-faced woman in her sixties, suddenly looked up, saw the detective watching her, and turned back to her customer. Her expression, which signalled the end of the relationship – the relationship with Danny, that is – upset Jurnet less than the sight of the merchandise she was flogging. Did the woman have to sell that raddled old bag earrings which were the exact replicas of the ones she had made for Miriam?

A brisk young woman had taken over Mike Botley's basket business. The shutters were fastened over the bookbinder's place, but a few doors away a new shop had opened, an art gallery, full of Broadland landscapes. Outside the shop, a couple in their mid-forties were supervising the efforts of a young man – their son, Jurnet guessed – to attach a red-and-white striped awning to some hooks high up on the fascia. The father held the ladder firm, his wife smiled upward, a little anxious whenever the ladder teetered on the cobbles. The three formed a pleasant, self-contained unit among the moving throng, at ease in each other's company.

The young man, who was scarcely more than a boy, was amazingly handsome – golden tan, a cap of shining chestnut hair, a neat body that moved with little of the unsureness of youth. In this day and age, Jurnet was quite certain, it was inconceivable that a boy could reach that boy's age and be unaware of his natural advantages, and of the power they gave him. So that the detective was not all that surprised to see Charles Winter, still wearing his grubby yellow sweater, leaning over the stable door of his workshop, watching the boy: nor to read, in the way the boy tilted his head and moved his shoulders, that he was well aware of the other's scrutiny, and of all that it implied.

A voice said: 'Alan and Mary Loring.' The detective turned to find Mrs Coryton at his side, bright-eyed and indomitable in a tweed suit subtly tailored to combine high fashion with just a soupçon of dowdiness. Her face was completely healed. 'Their

243

son's called Christopher. They ought to do well. They've got some very nice stuff.'

'Windmills and yachts,' Jurnet commented disparagingly. 'You'd think that was all Norfolk was made of.'

'Oh come! Even you wouldn't want sugar beet or a natural gas terminal on your living room wall!' Changing tone as she observed the detective's gaze unshiftingly intent on the silent communication between Charles Winter and the boy on the ladder: 'I'd hoped I'd convinced you that all forms of love are equally precious.'

'Oh ah.' Then: 'Last week we had a bloke up in court for having sex with a five-year-old kid.'

'You know what I mean! So long as it does no hurt.'

Jurnet said: 'All love hurts.'

Again the woman insisted: 'You know what I mean! Really! You're like Procrustes with his bed – you construct a model of the world the way you'd like it to be, and then snip off all the bits that don't fit.' Demonstrating that she, too, could be cruel, she ended: 'Is your girl back from Greece yet?'

'Not yet.'

'She will, soon. The season's over. The weather over there will be breaking up any day now.'

'Very flattering.'

Not one to sustain spite, Mrs Coryton said with a sad smile: 'Haven't you learnt yet, Inspector, to be thankful for what you can get?'

'Not yet,' Jurnet said again; and, because his nature was less forgiving than hers, added: 'I saw Mr Coryton in the Norfolk and Angleby. I thought he was looking very chipper.'

'Yes,' she agreed bleakly. 'Very.'

At the forge, the jeep was gone, the fire was out. Jurnet was not sorry to find Ferenc Szanto away from home. What was he expected to say to the blacksmith? Apologise for having suspected him wrongly? The bugger was lucky not to find himself on a charge of attempted murder himself.

He came out of the yard, crossed the rutted track which led to the back entrance, and entered the belt of trees on the further side. Beyond lay the field that, as on that first day at Bullen, divided him from the river. It was still full of sheep, their young fleeces grown a little shop-soiled. A few of them stared at him in a mindless manner as he followed the chain-link fence to the gate beside the hedgerow oak where Jessica Chalgrove had hanged herself.

The gate was padlocked and he climbed it doggedly, concentrating on keeping his jacket and slacks clear of the new strand of barbed wire along the top. Safely over, he did not look back; crossed the field with an uncaring directness that scattered the baaing ninnies to left and right: climbed a second gate, and dropped down to a strip of grass patterned with yellowing leaves that had fallen from the willows along the river bank.

The little stream, replenished after the summer drought, slid down its invisible gradient with the calm deliberation common to all Norfolk rivers. Were it not for some leaves travelling unhurriedly with the current, it would not have been immediately obvious which way lay the sea.

The detective turned upstream. Past the willows, the grass gave way to rushes and cabbage thistles, the withered umbels of hemlock and wild angelica. Burrs and feathered seeds attached themselves to Jurnet's clothes: morsels of stalk found their way into his shoes. Intent upon every step, it came as a surprise, when at last he raised his head, to discover that he had rounded a bend of the river. The mill loomed ahead of him.

It came as even more of a surprise to find Elena Appleyard sitting on a fallen tree trunk, looking out at the river.

She wore a dress of fine grey woollen, long-sleeved and effacing, and she sat so still and quiet that, for a moment, until she turned her head, and her body with it, and regarded him, neither welcoming nor forbidding, Jurnet thought he must be imagining her. Easy to accept ghosts in that setting: — the mill on the opposite bank, a shell of black brick, pierced with door- and window-holes out of which poked bushes and saplings and clumps of rosebay willowherb; the partly collapsed sluice gate, a length of metal tubing that had once done service as handrail for the catwalk along its top, trailing rustily in the water. Where the river, its path still narrowed by the obstruction, pushed through the dam opening with uncharacteristic noise, the jagged remains of a centre board hung crazily above the water.

Appleyard of Hungary's guillotine.

Elena Appleyard said: 'Surely not still looking for clues, Inspector?'

Feeling unaccountably embarrassed by the encounter, Jurnet replied: 'Just that I never had a chance to come down here to the mill before.' As the woman made no comment, he floundered on: 'From the look of it, it won't be here much longer.'

'Do you think so?' she said then. 'It looked exactly the same when Laz and I were children. Those stone steps – do you see them? We used to climb all the way up to the top floor. The stairs inside are still there, just as they used to be; and still quite safe, so long as you know where to put your feet.'

Jurnet stared.

'You don't mean to say you still go inside there?'

'Frequently.' She smiled for the first time. 'Everyone needs some private place, don't you think? The mill is mine. Though how much longer –.' Miss Appleyard turned her face away from a contemplation of the mill towards the detective. 'You've visited Steve in hospital. Did he tell you what he intends to do once he's well again? He says he's going to Australia, he and Ferenc. He says he's never coming back to Bullen, not even to say goodbye.'

Jurnet began awkwardly: 'He did say something –. About going to a place that has no history –'

'Can you understand it?'

'Frankly, yes: given what's happened –'

'But an Appleyard!'

Her calm assumption that Appleyards were not as other mortals made Jurnet bite his lips to suppress a grin. But then, how right she was.

Aloud, he said: 'I'm sure you understand that Bullen Hall could hold memories Steve can't bear to –'

Elena Appleyard cut him short.

'Memories! Don't you suppose that I too have memories, Inspector, when I come here, to the mill?'

'You're made of sterner stuff than he is.'

She considered this for a moment, head a little to one side. Then agreed: 'Yes, that's true.' She stood up, a little stiffly, as always, raised an arm with a lovely grace, and pointed. 'Do you see that window on the second floor? There, to the left of the grating?' And when she was satisfied that the detective had pinpointed the spot: 'That's the one room which still has a proper floor. They used to store the sacks of grain there, so I suppose it had to be specially strong.' She looked at Jurnet brightly. 'That's where Laz used to take Carla Chalgrove.'

Jurnet, not knowing the right response to this piece of information, mumbled something unintelligible.

'Do you know?' – with a trill of amusement – 'she said it was too uncomfortable, making love on the bare boards. She made poor old Laz bring a mattress down from the house. How ineffably bourgeois, don't you think? That's how I first found out what was going on. And that –' Miss Appleyard continued, in a tone which, for her, was almost chatty – 'is how I came to kill him.'

Her words took Jurnet's breath away, as no doubt she had intended they should. Before he had time to regain it she went on, as if in answer to a question he had put to her: 'Oh – because he loved her. I can't think why. She was no different from all those other brainless women he went to bed with. But Laz thought she was. And I couldn't have that.'

Jurnet said, tense and still unwilling to believe: 'But I understood she died when Jessica was born. By the time your brother met with his accident, she'd been dead for years.'

'His accident! How charmingly circumspect you policemen are! While she lived, I never realised the true nature of their relationship. And when I did –! Laz died the day he told me that what he had felt for Carla he had never felt for any other woman. Including me.'

'You were brother and sister!'

Elena Appleyard looked at the detective with something like disappointment.

'And I'd fancied you were a man to understand something at least of the nature of love!' Her voice, for the first time in their acquaintance, became dark and intense. 'How can you hope to discover the boundaries of love except by going beyond the boundaries?'

'I suppose I'm a bit of a bourgeois myself.' Jurnet pulled his thoughts together. 'Do you want to tell me what happened?'

She nodded shyly. An unexpected blush made her look suddenly young and unsure of herself. 'I've always wanted to talk to someone. Justify myself, even boast a little. When I arranged for Mr Shelden to do the biography I had, just for a moment, a crazy idea of adding an epilogue to explain what had really happened. But of course that would have been quite impracticable.'

'Not much more practicable to let on to a police officer.'

'What can you do about it, Inspector Jurnet? What evidence do you have, other than my word? If you do try to do anything, I shall throw up my hands in amazement, and say the man must be out of his mind.'

Defeated, Jurnet attempted nothing more. Raising her arm to point again, the woman went on: 'We had made love that day in that same room, on the bare boards. A splinter from the floor stuck in my shoulder blade, but he never knew, until we'd finished. Even then, he couldn't understand how I could be glad about the splinter, glad of the blood; that it was a sacrament, a symbolic act. He dragged the old mattress out of a corner, and said we should have used that. It was mouldy with damp, and mice had made a nest in it; and when he saw that, he suddenly began to cry. Real tears! That was when he told me that Carla was the only woman he had really loved. That stupid tart!' Miss Appleyard looked at Jurnet wide-eyed, inviting the detective to share her astonishment.

'As always, after we had made love at the mill, Laz went for a swim, diving straight from one of the windows into the water above the dam. It was deeper in those days. With the sluice gate shut you could build up quite a head of water. The centre board rested on little projections at either side – that was when you wanted to let the water through. Otherwise, you could let it right down to the river bed. There was a kind of long-handled fork which you hooked into a slot at the top, and with that, you could raise it or lower it as much as you liked.' She leaned over the water, frowning. 'I threw it in afterwards – the fork thing. If it hasn't disintegrated, it ought to be down there, somewhere.'

'You didn't go swimming, too?'

'Not that day. I didn't want to wash the blood away, not for a little.' A small smile of reminiscence played about her lips. 'We used to open the sluice just before we were ready to go in – yank up the centre board as high as it would go, so that all the pent-up water could come plunging through, and we could plunge with it. Glorious! I remember, that afternoon, I stood on the catwalk naked, with the sun warm on my body. I couldn't believe that any woman could be more desirable than I was at that moment, even though I was no longer young. And then I took the fork and raised the centre board. Only, instead of propping it in the notches, as usual, I held it well above the water, balanced on the fork, and waited for Laz to come through. I had to get the timing exactly right or I might have maimed him instead of killing him, and I needed to have him dead.'

Jurnet said, between gritted teeth: 'You damn near took his head off.'

'It seemed a good way for an Appleyard to die.'

After a moment Jurnet demanded: 'You're sure this isn't some fantasy you've dreamed up over the years?'

Elena Appleyard looked at him calmly.

'A fantasy's a device for accommodating truths we're otherwise afraid to acknowledge. I'm proud to acknowledge what I've done. I'm glad to have had the opportunity to talk about it.'

Jurnet took a deep breath and moved a little away. He could not bear to stay near her.

'Well,' he said at last, 'I reckon you aren't the first, nor won't be the last, murderer to get away with it. Nor yet the first nor last who, once it was done, would've given anything in the world to undo it.'

For a moment longer she looked at him, her face contorted. Then, she put up her hands to cover it: veined, elderly hands covering the face of a moaning old woman. He left her there to do what she would, made his way back to the front of the house, got into his car, and drove home.

The phone was ringing as he came through the flat door. He lifted the receiver off the hook, and a great thankfulness flooded through his whole being as he heard Miriam's voice.

He hardly took in what she said to him. It was enough to know that she was in touch, that she was back in England. Something about being in London, at her mother's. Couldn't wait to see him. Something about, was he off duty tomorrow?

Jurnet forced himself to concentrate, slow the beating of his heart.

'Yes,' he answered, determined so to arrange it, even if he

had to resign from the Force to do so. 'I'm off all day. What would you like to do?'

'The weather's so lovely,' Miriam said. 'Why don't we take a run out to Bullen Hall?'